DEVILSEED

DEVILSEED

✤

FRANK YERBY

DOUBLEDAY & COMPANY, INC.
GARDEN CITY, NEW YORK

Library of Congress Cataloging in Publication Data

Yerby, Frank, 1916–
  Devilseed.

  I. Title.
PS3547.E65D4 1984   813'.54   83–45191

ISBN 0-385-19340-8

First printing

DEVILSEED

1

MIREILLE SAT IN THE DRESSING ROOM SHE SHARED WITH THE SIX other "pretty waiter girls" at the Dirty Spoon and stared at her reflection in the mirror. A macabre image, scarcely recognizable as her own, stared back at her, its eyes blue-ringed, sunk far back into its head, its lips cracked and swollen, while its sick, corpselike pallor contrasted with the fiery red of a chin and cheeks scraped raw by the wiry mustaches and whiskers of drunken and amorous clients, whom to call beasts would be to insult the entire animal kingdom.

With acute distaste, she gazed at the uniform that Big Jules Tinderman forced his "pretty waiter girls" to wear. The backless halter of that uniform was made of fishnet, dyed black to contrast with the whiteness of her skin, and deliberately chosen from a grade whose mesh was so open that the nipples of her breasts protruded nakedly through the webbing, since, of course, she, like all her fellow workers, wasn't allowed to wear anything under it at all. Her nipples had erected from the damp cold in that dressing room. They ached dully and were badly discolored—not merely blue, but a wine-dark purple from having been bitten so often, while their tautly swollen areolas were no longer the warm, brownish red normal in a brunette, but various shades of green, blue, and black.

Looking down, she could see the teeth marks on her inner thighs, since the bright red skirt she wore had its hemline one inch below her hips when she was standing up perfectly straight. If she bent forward even slightly, her lissome buttocks—mottled with bruises from the pinches, squeezes, slaps they always received as she passed among the tables—were immediately exposed, for Big Jules totally forbade his girls the time-wasting extravagance of wearing underwear. She was, of course, required to sport black net stockings, held up by huge and frilly garters, and high-heeled shoes that made walking with a whiskey-laden tray a tricky chore.

Small and dainty as her feet were, those shoes hurt them; but she hardly noticed that, since she ached in so many other places simultaneously, including areas so esoteric, so normally protected by the very contours of the human body, that the possibility one could be made to feel pain in them had never even occurred to her.

It was early yet. Her shift didn't have to begin work for almost another hour. She didn't know whether she was glad of that, or sorry. Waiting for what happened to her—and to all her co-workers—every night to begin could be as bad as enduring it. Or almost. So she occupied her mind with thinking about (insofar as they were endurable even in thought) all the things that had brought her to where she was at that dismal moment, the dressing room of a "pretty waiter girls" saloon in San Francisco's abominable Sydney Town, while simultaneously converting her into what she also was: a waitress in the peculiar type of establishment such enterprising businessmen as Big Jules Tinderman had set up for the entertainment and refreshment of prospectors returning from the goldfields. But she got no comfort out of the rather pleasant title she and her fellow workers were called by. The pitiful image in her mirror hurled the truth back into her face. A "pretty waiter girl" was nearly always a victim of the white slave trade and, by exact definition, a whore.

Her journey toward this man-made (though in part, she was honest enough to admit, self-inflicted) hell had started years before, and was a classic of its kind. It had had its stages and its stations: from Mademoiselle Nicole's School for Young Ladies in her native New Orleans, where she'd been the star pupil, to the Convent of Our Lady of Perpetual Help in which she'd been confined—since, in spite of its high-sounding name, the convent actually was a reformatory for female juvenile delinquents—on the proven charge of having committed mayhem upon the boy who first seriously made an attempt upon her maidenly honor. His offense had been compounded in Mireille's eyes by both their racial origins—he was a dirty pig of an American; she, a highborn French Creole. That she was an American too was an inconvenient historical fact she hadn't been, and still wasn't, prepared to accept. Whatever treaties Napoleon Buonaparte and Thomas Jefferson had signed, however many millions had changed hands for her beloved Louisiana, couldn't change her soul. And her soul was French. So was her mind. And every drop of blood in her veins, although she'd never seen her ancestral native land.

The rest of it had been an ever quickening downhill slide. Her attempt to avenge—physically and violently—the murder of her beloved father by her mother's lover. Her falling into the hands of one Howard Tellefair —as unconscionable a professional pimp, gambler, and white slaver as ever drew the breath of life—just when her need to flee what she conceived of as impending doom was most imperative. Her escape with him —by steamship from New Orleans to Aspinwall, Panama, across the Isthmus by train, boat, and muleback to Panama City, then northward by a Pacific Mail Line steamer to San Francisco, where dear Howard, a mediocrity even as a blackguard, had promptly lost not only all his money but even Mireille herself, when, desperately trying to recoup, he'd put her up as the final stake in a night-long poker game against Big Jules Tinderman.

Big Jules, of course, had at long last convinced her of the futility of rebellion or flight by beating her slowly and artistically into insensibility every time she'd tried it. She knew now how she'd leave the Dirty Spoon finally—the only way any of the girls ever did: feet first, in a narrow pine box without even an inscription on it.

Two of the girls from the afternoon shift came running into the dressing room and made a dash for the brimming slop jars in the corner that, since no one ever had time to empty them, made the whole place reek abominably. The girls were always in a hurry as they came off a shift, or business became slack enough to let them get away, because the amount of cold tea they drank—which the clients paid for as whiskey—made relief an imperative necessity.

As they perched precariously upon the porcelain chamber pots, one of them, a generously endowed blonde called Ruby, sang out to Mireille:

"See you're still here, Frenchie!"

"Yes," Mireille said, "but I 'ave not given up yet. I will think of a way . . ."

Paquita, the slim, dark Mexican girl, having finished what she was doing, got up, came over, and rested her still remarkably pretty face against Mireille's shoulder. Mireille didn't shrug her off, or push her away. Kindness, even from another woman, was too rare a luxury to be rejected now. She realized but did not resent the fact that Paquita was almost in love with her, because she knew why: Mireille, the Mexican girl had tearfully confessed, was the one white person she had known in her entire seventeen years of life who consistently treated her like a human being.

"Please, Miri," she murmured, "you weel please not to be foolish! I beg you not to! You're all I have . . ."

"Look at 'em, th' lovebirds!" Ruby hooted. "Tell me, how do you all go about it? A wee bit shy of the proper equipment, ain't you, sweeties?"

Mireille ignored her, largely because she was too tired to pursue a quarrel.

"Foolish?" she said to Paquita. "But to stay here is foolish, Paci. Here we'll end up as diseased wrecks! Or die at the hands of one of these ravenous brutes, who happens to be a little too drunk one night, or—"

"Out there," Paquita said sadly, "we would die at once, and very badly. Tell her what happened to the last girl who ran away, Ruby."

"Plenty," Ruby sighed. "Th' Sydney Ducks caught her. She was raped twenty-seven times in the first hour. After that, even them filthy swine lost count. We found her dead in th' morning. Face-down in a mudhole without a stitch left on her. And every place they could poke it into was full of their muck . . ."

"One does not escape," Paquita said soberly, "from an establishment in the middle of Sydney Town, *querida*. Not even Lola and Merchi have been able to do that . . ."

"All right," Mireille said, "stop talking over my head the way you two always do. Explain me a few things, will you? Starting with: Who are Lola and Merchi? Why do you call this cesspool of a district Sydney Town? And who are the Sydney Ducks?"

"Thugs, footpads, slingshot artists, pickpockets, pimps—swine," Ruby said. "Every kind of crook and bastard anybody ever heard of. Got the name because most of them come from Australia—escaped convicts from the British penal colony at a place called Sydney in New South Wales. And from Van Diemen's Land. Don't ask me where them places are—I'm only telling you what a toff from there told me. Not all of 'em escaped, of course; some of 'em's ticket-of-leave men, who can be halfway decent fellas. And th' rest are larrikins—that's what Aussies call roughnecks in general. Anyhow, just as soon as the news got back to Australia that gold had been found here in California, the bastards started arriving on every eastbound ship. Pure poison, most of 'em!"

"They are no worse than the Hounds were," Paquita said grimly. "Better, I think!"

"The Hounds?" Mireille said.

"New York thugs," Ruby explained. "Used to be members of such gangs as the Bowery Boys, the Dead Rabbits, or the Plug-Uglies—all of 'em from Five Points or the Bowery in New York City. Come out here with Colonel Stevenson to fight ag'in Mexico; but the war was over before they got here. So they was discharged in California, and started to make San Francisco over into the Bowery or Five Points. They were pure death on greasers, I can tell you that. And they didn't have no love for niggers and Chinks, neither. Seen a nigger brush up ag'in a Hound in front of the Shades Saloon on Kearny Street one night, plumb accidental-like, and them bastards sliced that poor jigaboo's ears clean off his head. . . ."

"But—why 'Hounds'?" Mireille said.

"That's what they call themselves," Paquita said, "which was to insult the real dogs. They hated my people worst of all. Last year, in July, they attacked our settlement around Telegraph Hill and shot and beat to death dozens of our men, raped all the younger women, and some not so young, and destroyed all our *chozas*, our shanties. They were so barbarous that the decent white people of San Francisco rose up against them and ran them out of town. They are why *I* am here, Miri dearest—my fiancé could not stomach the idea of taking as a bride a girl who had been raped thirteen times. . . ."

"*Bon Dieu!*" Mireille whispered. "And who are—what were those two names you said? Those Spanish names?"

"Lola and Merchi. Lola which is short for Delores and Merchi for Mercedes. They are friends of mine, although they have, I think, a certain contempt for me. You see, although they both work in Manuel Garcia's *Cabeza de Jabalí*, which means Boar's Head in English, sweet Mireille, they are both still virgins. No man, of all the hundreds who have tried, has been able to—violate them, or make use of them immorally."

"I don't believe that," Mireille said flatly; "Garcia's place is that awful fandango den down the street, isn't it? The one we pass on the way here?"

"*Sí, querida,*" Paquita said.

"Then they have been violated. There they would have no more chance to escape being—used—than we do here."

"Yet all the same, they have escaped it," Paquita said.

"How?" Mireille demanded.

"That is a secret. It would not be wise of me to tell you—or anyone—that . . . ," Paquita said gravely.

"Then *I* will!" Ruby hooted. "Them two li'l Mex bitches carry a dirk in each garter, and a slung shot on a cord around their necks—pushed down twixt their tits, which them Mex-type frilly fandango dresses they wear gives 'em plenty place to hide, considering how skinny they both are. And they're the friendliest pair of hot and wiggling li'l critters a poor dumb bastard of a miner ever saw. All over him, kissing him and squirming and panting and shoving their hands down the front of his pants to get him all worked up. Then they sells him on the idea of how much more fun *two* girls at the same time can be than just one. He goes for that, they draws the curtains around the booths just like we do here, and one of 'em starts to shuck off—very slowly. But long before she's down to bare hide, the other one's done cracked his head for him with the slung shot . . ."

"And if he insists upon taking only one?" Mireille said.

"Same deal. One of 'em waits outside till she hears the signal. Something like: 'Oh, no! Eet ees too beeeeg! It weel hurt me! Let me—' Say, Paci, how d'you Mex gals say 'toot on that ol' skin whistle' anyhow?"

"We do not!" Paquita said indignantly. "We have not such vices among us!"

"Horse business!" Ruby laughed. "That's the one Spik word I know. *They* do, your cute li'l murdering friends. It's their favorite trick: Just as soon as one of 'em's got half a yard of Yankee heifer-prod down her throat, the other one cracks him over the head or pushes fifteen inches of dirk through his guts."

"You mean they—*kill*—the men?" Mireille whispered.

"Not if it can be avoided," Paquita said; "only if the gringo is insufficiently unconscious for them to rob him properly do they use their knives. . . ."

"*Bon petit Jésus!*" Mireille said. "And they have not been arrested? Tried? Jailed?"

"Nobody gets arrested for killing people in San Francisco," Ruby said flatly. "There's been close to five hundred murders in this town since the Gold Rush started, and not one hanging. Of course, being greasers, them two li'l bitches could get themselves lynched if they was ever to get caught red-handed. But, for one thing, Garcia protects 'em all he can for a cut of their take. For another, nobody sees 'em do them horny bastards in, and when they're through whittling on a fella, the house bouncer drags th' corpse a good twenty feet away down the alley. In this burg, that's plenty far enough for th' Law to hand down, 'Met his death at the hands of persons unknown. . . .'"

"*Los Americanos,*" Paquita said quietly, "violated both the wife and the daughter of Don Manuel during the riots of July fifteenth, 1849. Naturally he does not burst into tears when a gringo is killed, dear Mireille. . . ."

"I can comprehend how they might have envy to kill one of those swine," Mireille said bitterly; "*I* often would like to. The Maniac, *par exemple* . . ."

"God, yes!" Ruby said. "But don't try it, baby. Big Jules would beat a girl to death who done something to a client. Not 'cause he's so all-fired law-abiding, but 'cause 'twould be bad for business. The filthy, unnatural pigs that come to this place know they can do anything what pops into their twisted-up minds and not risk a scratch on their little pinkies. . . . But if you really want to get away from here, Mireille honey, I can tell you *when* to do it. That is, if you've got anywhere to go."

"And when is that?" Mireille breathed.

"The next time there's a big fire. And there's gonna be one soon. . . ."

"And how do you know that, Ruby?" Paquita said.

"My gentleman acquaintance told me. Fellow I'm walking out with. Oh hell, I might as well tell the truth. He ain't no gentleman, and he's a helluva lot more than an acquaintance. He's my—solid man. And he's one of the Sydney Ducks."

"Then you're right," Paquita said grimly. "There will be a fire. Soon. An enormous one. Three quarters of the city will burn to ashes. . . ."

"But what makes you so sure?" Mireille said.

"Muy a menudo se lo hacen ellos," Paquita said; *"los Patos de Sydney—"*

"English, please?" Mireille sighed; "or French, if you know any."

"Unfortunately I don't. So English, then: I said they often do that, the Sydney Ducks. Set the town on fire. They have done so three times so far: on December twenty-fourth of last year and on May fourth and June fourteenth, this one. The first time, a whole city block containing fifty houses burned; the second, three blocks with three hundred houses destroyed; and the third, everything between Clay and California streets, from Kearny to the waterfront. In the excitement, those criminals rush out of their dens and loot the stores and houses. And Ruby is right, you could easily escape at such a time. Nobody would pay you any attention. But where would you *go?*"

"Don't know," Mireille said morosely, "but anywhere would be better than here, wouldn't it? Even the bottom of the Bay. . . ."

"Miri!" Paquita gasped. "You weel please not to say such things! You weel please not to even *theenk* them! Oh my darling, please! I love you! Without you what manner of life would I have?"

"D'accord," Mireille sighed; "I won't do anything to myself *this* week, Paci—but if I am still here by *next,* I simply will not promise you. . . ."

The following morning Mireille stumbled along on Paquita's arm, crying very slowly and terribly and hopelessly as the Mexican girl half-led, half-carried her through the noisome alleyways of Sydney Town. As they did every morning at this dismally early hour, they were going back to the boardinghouse that Big Jules Tinderman owned just behind Telegraph Hill on a lot between Greenwich and Filbert streets. Paquita, of course, should have returned to the rooming house the night before, since she was—for the moment, anyhow—on the afternoon shift. But she had stayed in the dressing room of the Dirty Spoon all night long, catching catnaps in a hard, uncomfortable chair whenever the fiendish and practically continuous uproar from the dance floor, and from the curtained booths all around it and on the balconies above, would let her. She did this almost every night, and for two reasons: she wanted to wait for Mireille, around whose serene beauty and quiet strength she instinctively sought, as the emotionally starving will, to rebuild the shattered wreckage of her life; and it was simply safer for her to wait until daylight and go home with her new friend when the Sydney Ducks were no longer "quacking in their pond" as the saying went in San Francisco.

And now she was glad she had waited. 'I can't leave her alone today,' she thought, 'not for an instant!' Then more slowly, what she almost didn't dare shape into words, even in her mind: 'Because if I do, she—she will kill herself, surely!'

At that moment they were approaching Manuel Garcia's fandango dancehall-saloon, the Boar's Head, and just before they reached it Lola and Merchi came out. They were not alone. A slim, golden boy walked between them, clutching both of them possessively by their elbows. He was, Paquita thought, absolutely the most beautiful male human being she had ever seen. Then she gave a little gasp of astonishment, because the beautiful boy was a gringo with dark blond hair and blue eyes, which was contrary to all Lola's and Merchi's principles, since the two of them had sworn eternal war on all Americanos, and to the death, at that.

"*¡Hola!*" Paquita said, a little breathlessly. Mireille didn't say anything. She went on crying.

"*¡Hola!*" Merchi said contemptuously.

"Who's the slut?" Lola asked, even more contemptuously.

"She's nobody's slut!" Paquita said angrily. She was getting distinctly tired of the airs these two gave themselves on the basis of a presumed virtue that was highly technical, anyhow—since they permitted everything except actual penetration—and that didn't extend beyond the narrowly sexual, murder and robbery being perfectly all right by their lights. "She's my friend."

"An American girl?" the boy said softly. "She has very white skin . . ." Slim as he was, his voice was wonderfully deep and rich. His Spanish, Paquita heard, was perfect; his accent, Mexican.

"*No,*" she answered him shortly, "*una francesa.*"

"What's the matter with her?" the boy said, his voice filled with genuine concern; "she seems sick."

"Not sick—" Paquita said bitterly, "—killed."

"Can I help her in some way? She seems bad off, for a fact," the boy said worriedly.

"No, you can't, Willy!" Lola snapped. "They're a couple of whores who've had a bad night, that's all. They're used to it, and it's none of your business. Come along!"

"It's a pity," the boy called Willy murmured. "She has the face of an angel. She's so little, pretty, sweet . . ."

"Willy!" Lola and Merchi chorused furiously. "Come on! Leave those beat-up sluts and let's go home!"

"Sure I can't do anything for her?" Willy persisted.

"No, nothing," Paquita said bitterly.

He turned to leave then, reluctantly, but before he had got two yards away, Mireille herself ended the matter in a way that was shockingly convincing.

"Paquita . . ." she whispered; "I'm afraid I—I can not go any—further. I feel—horrible. Weak—sick . . . and I—I *hurt* so!"

"I weel help you, my darleeng," Paquita wept. "Try to walk—"

"I—can't. I—*Oh, bon petit Jésus! Je me vais évanouir!*" Mireille got out, and immediately translated those words, which none of them understood, by her actions. Translated them perfectly, and changed the whole emotional climate of the moment. She who was usually so graceful physically collapsed like a sack of potatoes—went down in a dead faint, striking her face with an audible thud against the ground.

"*¡Dios!*" Willy said, and dashed back to where she lay. Bending, he swept her up into his arms. As he did so, her bare legs flashed free of her skirts—she hadn't wanted to wear those horrible black net whore's stockings home, and all her own were full of holes which sheer fatigue kept her from mending—and they all saw the long, thick streaks of blood that had dried and clotted on her thighs and calves.

"What the devil!" Willy whispered. "She's been raped, the poor little thing! And she was—chaste. She's still bleeding. . . ."

The temptation to lie was almost overwhelming, but facing those clear, utterly candid blue eyes of his, Paquita couldn't do it. Not even to perhaps ensure, by that desperate gamble, the future of her friend.

"No," she sighed, "she was not—virgin. This—has another cause. There was a man. A gringo. A huge brute more than two and a quarter yards tall. He's a vicious beast, that one. We call him the Maniac."

Staring at her, Willy whispered, "*¡Jesús!*"

"He is—always after the girls. But especially does he persecute her—the poor Mireille. You see how innocent she looks? How sweet? That inflames him. He comes into that abomination to end all abominations where we work, the Dirty Spoon, and tosses bags of gold dust—I'm sure he gets them by robbing the miners; no man alone could pan that much gold—down on the tables. The girls cannot refuse him, you know—not because they are so anxious for gold, but because Big Jules would beat a girl half to death who denied her body to a client for any reason whatsoever, and then pack her off to a crib in a cowyard, which is an existence even worse than that of being a 'pretty waiter girl' at the Dirty Spoon. . . ."

"It seems to me," Willy said judiciously, "that someone should kill Big Jules Tinderman. And this Maniacal One. Me, for instance. Please go on, *querida*. Let us say that this Maniac, the vicious one, has arrived. What happens after that?"

"He, the Maniac, has the vice of—cruelty. He is of those who find little pleasure in—the act of love, itself, alone. No. In order to—ejaculate —obtain his satisfaction—forgive me for saying it so clearly and crudely, but I am a poor, ignorant Mexican girl who knows no other words . . ."

"It's all right, my dear," Willy said gently. "Please go on."

"All right. This madman, this beast, while making love—ha! What an evil joke it is to call what he does 'making love'!—while tormenting a poor helpless girl with his own outsized enormousness—his father was evidently a stallion or a bull!—cannot obtain his twisted variety of pleasure unless he simultaneously pounds her with his fists, which are the size of hams, until she is black and blue, or bites her breasts or her throat until the blood runs down, or claws furrows along all her flesh with his filthy fingernails. That is, if he even molests himself to make love—bah! —to make use of her at all. He quite often doesn't. Instead, he diverts himself by performing various experiments upon her poor, tortured, naked body, as, for instance, attempting to shove various working implements up her—the handle of a pickax being his favorite. Or he may whip her with his belt—to make, he declares, her flesh more tender. With the buckle end of it free, naturally. The screams of a woman, he insists, are the sweetest music in all the world. . . ."

"And this poor little one?" Willy said. "What did he do to her?"

"I do not know. I was not there, and did not witness it. All manners and kinds of bestialities, surely. She refuses to say. She is—too ashamed. Willy—that's how you're called, isn't it?—would you—?"

"Yes, I am called Willy—that is, Guillermo. *Guillermo el Dulce*, Sweet William, all the girls say. And I will take her home, no matter what manners and kinds of objections these little witches my sisters may raise."

"Thy *sisters!*" Paquita gasped. "But you are white! An American with blond hair and blue eyes and—"

"And a pink pole like those of the Yankees," he said solemnly. "Nevertheless these little witches are my sisters, *Aztecas* though they are. We had the same mother, but different fathers. Mine was a gringo. And a Catholic. And a good man. Proof of which is that he married my ugly little Indian mother in the Church. Now, show me the way to your place. I will carry her there in my arms. She weighs nothing, the poor little thing. As we go, you must tell me about her—and about thee. How art thou called?"

"Paquita—that is, Francesca," Paquita said as they started off in the direction of Telegraph Hill, with Lola and Merchi trailing along behind them and burning holes through her back with their coal-black Aztec eyes; "because Paquita is only a diminutive, a sort of nickname, you know . . ."

"I do know," he chuckled. "Spanish is my mother tongue, *querida.*"

"*¿Pero hablas Inglés?*" Paquita said; then, switching into it, "You *do* speak English, don't you?"

"Yes. Why yes, of course. My father taught me. And because I adored him, I learned it very well in order to please him. I have tried to teach it to my sisters, but they have no ear for it, and besides they are consumed with hatred for all gringos."

"With much reason!" Paquita said.

"Yes. Gringos are—swine. That my father wasn't doesn't change their nature. He was the exception that proves the rule. But you speak English well. Why do you?"

"I was forced to learn it, the hard way. On my back," Paquita said bitterly. "But now I wish to speak to you in it in order to explain you a few things that are not for the ears of your so sweet sisters. Unfortunately, they understand it much better than they pretend to. . . ."

"What things?" Guillermo said.

"About—her," Paquita said, and nodded toward his inert burden.

"Ah! That interests me—much! How is she called?"

"Mireille. And, as I told you, she is not American, but French. And she is *not* a whore. Nor am I, for that matter. . . ."

"Then what are you doing in this district?" he said a little sadly, the doubt in his eyes very clear.

"Whoring," Paquita said flatly; "both of us. But we are not whores!"

Guillermo stared at her.

"You will explain it, this paradox?" he said.

"You are a Catholic. You know very well that the Church grants absolution for crimes, sins, that one is *forced* to do. And we were both forced into the bad life, Guillermo. I—my case is simple—my promised left me when he found out that the gringos had—violated me thirteen times during the riots of July last year. The *taberna* where I worked was destroyed. Its owner, murdered. All our *chozas* were torn down. Starving is a most unpleasant way to die. And, since I no longer had any virtue left to preserve . . ."

"Poor little one!" he murmured. "I, too, grant you absolution—for whatever my absolution is worth . . ."

"Would you marry me?" she asked him sharply. "You are Mexican, for all your gringo looks! And Mexicans do not take—*used* women as wives. Or, since it is clearly *she* who interests you: would you marry *her?*"

"I do not know," he said sadly. "The idea of taking a girl who is no longer *virgen* as a bride—is repugnant to me. I am a son of Old Mexico, just as you said. Whether that *repugnancia* could be overcome is a thing I am uncertain of. At the moment, I doubt it. So tell me about her, that I may think about it, anyhow. . . ."

"Her case is even simpler. Big Jules Tinderman saw her passing by on the arm of the man she was engaged to marry. And, as soon as he could arrange it after that, tricked that man into playing cards with him for very high stakes. When he had won his last penny off this fool, Big Jules proposed that he put Mireille up against all his losses—"

"And he did that?" Guillermo said; "His own fiancée?"

"He was a gringo. And all gringos are swine. Except your father, I suppose."

"Yes. Except my father, who was very nearly a saint. But did he—this swine of a gringo—tell the little Mireille what he had done?"

"Of course not! The first thing she knew, she was being dragged down the stairs by her hair, after having been beaten bloody for attempting to resist Big Jules. Abduction—then slavery in the Dirty Spoon. The white slave traffic in its purest form. *¡Dios!* Can't you see how innocent she is?"

"Yes. Innocent. Pure. Decent. And—terribly abused. This troubles me, Paquita. Perhaps in her case I could even forget the age-old customs of my people. But first let us attend to her. When we have put her to bed, I will go bring her a doctor. A good one. The physician who attends the members of our band—"

"But who are the members of your band?" Paquita asked him.

Solemnly he winked one of those eyes that were so startlingly blue in the Mexican copper of his face.

"I talk too much!" he said. "Do we still have far to go?"

"No. It's just beyond the second street we'll come to next," Paquita, *la casamentera*, the matchmaker, said.

But when Mireille came back from that limbo where the souls of people tortured past all bearing go, she flatly refused to allow Guillermo to bring a doctor to see her. For she considered the location and the nature of her hurts far too embarrassing. Which meant she retained both modesty and shame, so the possibility of her remaining a woman existed still. It would not be easy to reduce her to—a thing.

"You—attend me, Paci," she whispered. "If you will help me to wash myself—and to apply a soothing salve . . . Do we have enough money between us to buy some?"

"No," Paquita said sadly. "We will need tincture of laudanum and some olive oil to mix it with. The tincture will cost us one hundred dollars an ounce. *All* medicines cost one hundred dollars an ounce in San Francisco, whatever their nature."

"Then *I* will buy it," Guillermo said.

"No—" Mireille faltered; "no—I—I—cannot permit you to, Señor—"

"Kilpatrick," he laughed. "My father was an Irish gringo. Unfortunately, Comanches killed him one day on our *rancho* down south in Sonora. So my family names are Kilpatrick-Calvo. Very convenient. When I wish to be a gringo, I am William Kilpatrick. To turn Mexican, I merely don a poncho and a wide-brimmed sombrero and call myself Guillermo Calvo."

"And these—young ladies?" Mireille said.

"My sisters. My mother married again after my father's death. And produced these two *Azteca* witches. So their names are Guerra-Calvo. Also appropriate. *Guerra* means war, which they are always making, and *calvo* means baldheaded which I am going to snatch them if they do not learn to behave themselves. And now I go—to buy you your medicines, lovely *Mirla.*"

"No! I cannot allow—"

"How are you going to stop me, little bird? That is what your name means in Spanish. *Mirla*—a little blackbird. And in French?"

"The same, I think. But Señor Kilpatrick—"

"Guillermo, to you. *Guillermo el Dulce*—Sweet William. Which, in English, is a little pink flower that smells very sweet. I smell very sweet. At least when I wash—which is once a year. *¡Hasta luego,* lovely *Mirla!* I go!"

"Wait!" Lola said suddenly and, surprisingly enough, in English. "D'you 'ave enough mon-nay, Willy?"

"Yep. *Sí*. Sure thing. I am rolling in cash. Why do you ask, my little witch?"

"Because I weel let you 'ave some eef you need eet," Lola said.

"And I," Merchi added.

"No," Willy said shortly; "I really don't need it—and borrowing money from you two costs too much! Just stay here and help Paquita take care of her till I get back. *¡Hasta luego,* everybody!"

He went through the doorway, leaving Mireille lying there, staring at his sisters in purest astonishment. She had heard and understood all too much of the bitter exchange they had had with Paquita when first they'd met.

"You—you were willing to—to give him money to—buy *me* medicines?" she whispered.

"But yes. You are not—*gringa,* but *francesa,*" Lola said; "Which means you are a human being. Besides, our brother like you. He like you vairree much. We weesh 'eem to be 'appy . . ."

"Ees thair anytheeng else we can do for you, *Mirla querida?*" Merchi said.

"Nooohh . . ." Mireille faltered; then: "Yes! Oh, yes, there is! Señorita Merchi—or you, Señorita Lola—would one of you, or both—do me a very big favor?"

"How respectful! How polite!" They laughed. "Thees of 'señorita' ees not necessary, *querida Mirla.* We are frans, no? Call us by our names. What ees eet you weesh of us?"

"A knife," Mireille said quietly, "like the ones you've got in your garters. I—I need one like that."

"No!" Paquita shrilled. "For God's sake no! She's very depressed—very sad! She will kill herself! She'll commit suicide, surely!"

"No, Paci," Mireille said; "I shall not kill myself. I want it only to—discourage the Vicious One when he comes back again. As he will. You know that . . ."

"Our brother," Merchi said, "weel be in town all of thees month. And at the Boar's Head every night to serve Don Manuel as bodyguard, seence wan of the Sydney Ducks has sworn to keel heem. That ees why Don Manuel sent for Willy in the first place. So eef this vicious brute attempts to rip you apart again, send Paci for Willy. He weel feenish this peeg for you, *querida.*"

"But—but—Guillermo is—so small! So slender and—"

"Can shoot every spot out of the ten of diamonds held een a man's hand from twenty paces away," Lola said. "But—*mientras*—take this. As a geeft from me. You put the *vaina*—the sheath—in *tu liga*—your garter, thus. Thees peeg grabs you, you draw *el puñal* thus! And sweeng eet—slashing! Wherever eet touches, eet weel cut to the bone. Eeet ees vairree sharp. *Yo me afeito mis piernas con esa daga todas las noches . . .*"

"She says she shaves her legs with that stiletto every night," Paquita explained. "But Mirla, dear heart—you weel not—?"

"No. Me, no. Him, yes! With pleasure," Mireille said.

2

THE MAIN TROUBLE WITH A DEUS EX MACHINA IS THAT IT NEVER works, as Mireille almost immediately found out. For when the Sydney Ducks set San Francisco afire for the fourth time, on September 17, 1850, she was in no condition to take advantage of the resulting confusion to make her escape because she was hovering on the very brink that separates life from death.

The fire made very little difference to the denizens of Sydney Town themselves. For as usual, when the coves and Larrikins and other assorted miscreants set out upon one of their enthusiastic and generally successful attempts at arson, they carefully held back their squads of firebugs until they were absolutely sure the wind was blowing strongly from the east and north, thus ensuring that not even a cinder would be borne into Clark's Point or the streets adjacent to it, which meant the Sydney Towners—those of them who weren't participating in the wholesale looting of the burned-out districts the fire had been set to make possible in the first place—could come out of their vile-smelling warrens, stand in the cesspools, mudholes, and blind alleys that served them as streets, and enjoy the awesome spectacle of the destruction their colleagues had wrought, while remaining all the time as safe as though they were in church.

The visitors to Sydney Town—miners in from the goldfields and sailors on shore leave—didn't even bother to do that. A mere fire, even when it was fueled by five or six city blocks of houses and stores burning to the ground, simply didn't interest them enough to make them spend more than a few minutes gazing at it. They were in from long, lonely weeks in the goldfields or months at sea, so they much preferred their usual pursuits: gambling, drinking, and tumbling whores.

Among those visitors was, of course, Mireille's *bête noir*, known to the

girls as "the Maniac." He came staggering into the Dirty Spoon about
nine o'clock of that night of September seventeenth, took another long
pull on his jug of rotgut, and roared:

"Whar's thet prutty li'l Frenchie? By Gawd, I'm agonna tickle her
tonsils t'night—wit'out goin' pas' her teeth! By th' lonnnnnng route!
Gonna spit 'er on my pole jes' like a Christmas turkey! Cause damn effen
she ain't got th' cutest li'l hairy quim I ever stretched! Oh, thar you be,
honey! Now, jes' you lay back real nice, spread them snow-white thighs
o' yourn, 'n' tek a deep breath! Then—whooooosh! In it goes, hot 'n'
heavy, sugah!"

Mireille made a desperate dash for the door, thinking that if she could
get out into the streets she might be able to dart from house to house,
hiding momentarily in the shadows until she got to that blazing inferno,
and lose herself there among the burning buildings. Or throw herself
bodily into the flames. It was, she knew, a horrible way to die, but it
would be over very fast, while its alternative wouldn't. The Maniac, she
was dismally sure, meant to go right on splitting her practically in half, or
otherwise torturing her to the point of death, forever.

She didn't make it. She felt that huge hand clamp down on her shoulder. Effortlessly, he whirled her around to face him, wrapped his massive,
hairy arms around her waist, lifted her feather-light body high off the
floor, slammed her down across the nearest table, sprawled atop her,
bringing, before she'd got back the breath his immense weight had
knocked out of her, his two bear paws up and pinning both her wrists,
spread out wide above her head to the rough boards of that long trestle
table.

Mireille waited, sure that he was going to have to turn loose one of her
hands at least, in order to free his own to loosen his belt, unbutton his
fly, push down his pants. 'And when he does,' she thought with savage
joy, 'I've got him!'

But the Maniac either read her thought, or simply acted out of so
much experience in the art of rape that he checkmated her planned
move before she could even make it. Quickly he brought her wrists
together above her head, and held both of them to the table with one of
his hands, which, since he had the strength of a gorilla, made all her
efforts to wrench them free of his clasp, in order to reach and draw that
stiletto she had in her left stocking's garter, absolutely futile.

She felt him fumbling at his belt buckle, heard the rustle of his rough
work pants dropping, smelt the fetid stink of unwashed male.

The rising roars of laughter from the crowd beat against the ceiling.
For the Maniac, whose aberrations included exhibitionism, along with

every other heterosexual perversion then extant, plus a few he'd invented himself, never bothered to take his victims into one of the booths designed for that very purpose, and draw the curtains Big Jules had so thoughtfully provided, the way the other clients did—for part of his fun consisted in staging his circuses, performing his blunt-instrument vivisection upon outraged female flesh publicly, for the benefit of every amateur voyeur in the house. Which included, of course, one hundred percent of the Dirty Spoon's clientele.

She felt that elephantine rod of flesh prod against her, hot and hateful, errantly probing, seeking ingress, and screamed, her voice bone-saw shrill, reaching a pitch actually hurtful to human hearing: "No! Oh, no! Please, no!"

"Take it—sugar!" he crooned, and slammed forward like a moving mountain. The pain was unbelievable. Worse than ever. She sensed her consciousness leaving her, tiptoeing sweetly and softly away from—horror. But she fought with a courage that was almost leonine against that blessed relief, knowing that even a momentary surrender to nausea, disgust, weakness, pain, would finish her last chance to terminate this abomination forever by the only means now possible, which was to end the author of it. So she clung to consciousness, clarity, thought, endured that excruciatingly agonizing martyrization of her small, slight body, until the boar-grunting, bear-snorting, dog-panting, stallion-whistling beating about her ears slowed, died down, commingled, transmuted into one long, shuddering, sobbing gasp that was the audible manifestation of his strength-destroying explosion into spasm, pulsation, jet and scald, tactually perceptible to her even through her awful agony—and waited for the chance she knew he'd have to give her now.

It came. He turned her slim hands loose, laid his sweaty face alongside her own death-white one, and mumbled, crooning the words, meaning them:

"I loves yuh, baby!"

Mireille's left hand crept slowly down her own half-butchered form until it reached the stocking top. Her fingers—fluttering like moth wings from sheer nerves, exhaustion, anguish—perceived the sudden hardness of the stiletto's hilt, closed around it. She moved her face away from his, stared at that bestial countenance, seeing the slobbering, opened mouth gulping air, and, estimating the distance, judging it with uncanny accuracy, drew that stiletto free of its sheath tucked into her garter, lifted it slowly, stealthily upward until she had it high enough to make missing an impossibility. Then, with a thrill of pleasure that was close to orgasmic, she rammed it up one flaring nostril, slashed forward and outward, so that the whole right side of his nose opened into a pair of obscene lips, and his breath gurgled and whistled through the cascade of his blood.

He screamed like all the fiends in hell. Reeled back, out of, and away from her, tried to turn, but his own rough, stiff blue denim work trousers, still down around his ankles, tripped him so that he fell like an axed-through sequoia tree, splintering into firewood the nearest table with the impact of his immense weight.

Mireille straightened up, dropped like a cat to the floor, hurled herself upon him, that blade glittering blue in the lamplight as she lifted it, held it high, her eyes alight with pure feline ferocity, seeking the right, perfect, fatal spot to plunge it into and thereby end this one, at least, of all her nightmares, forever.

An instant too long. Another grimy, horny paw closed over her wrist, twisted cruelly. The stiletto clattered to the floor. The bewhiskered old miner known as Teetotaler Bill because he never drank—which was why his reaction time had been so damnably fast—jerked her to her feet, bent close to her ear and hissed into it:

"Couldn't let you do thet, baby, for all th' bastid had it coming. Cost you too mickle much trouble! Now scat, will ya? Run fer it whilst you's got th' chanct!"

Then Mireille's luck ran out on her. Big Jules Tinderman, who seldom bothered even to visit the Dirty Spoon, occupied as he was by half a dozen other enterprises he owned outside of Sydney Town, around Nob Hill and beyond, including one of the flossiest brothels on Portsmouth Square, chose that very moment to walk through the door, just as she was dashing out of it.

He caught Mireille by the shoulder and slammed her down into a chair, growling at her; "Don't move, bitch-kitty!" Then, seeing the awed and silent crowd standing around something on the floor, he bulldozed his massive way through it and stood there looking down at the Maniac.

"Who done it?" he grunted.

"Th' li'l Frenchie!" a chorus of voices supplied. "He—rough-plugged 'er—ag'in. 'Pears like he's got a powerful yen for that there li'l black-maned filly, and—"

"Two of you boys go over there and hold her. See that she don't sneak off. Ned, go git me Langley outa th' kitchen," Big Jules said.

He lit a long black cigar and stood there, his big red face wreathed in smoke. Glancing toward the door, he saw that two of the clients were holding Mireille as ordered. She wasn't even struggling. She sat there, white-faced, sunk in total apathy.

Langley came. He was the Dirty Spoon's chef. Rumor had it that a billy goat would refuse to eat his grub; and that the leftovers from the meals he cooked, thrown on the city dump, were poisoning all the buzzards.

"Heat me a couple of pokers, Lang," Big Jules said calmly. "Red hot. Gotta cauterize this here notched-snoot hawg, or else he'll bleed t'death. Can't have that, y'know. Give the place a bad name. . . ."

"What about—her? Th' li'l Frenchie?" one of them asked.

"Strip her. Hang her from th' transom by her wrists. I'm gonna tenderize her li'l ass proper. After I gets through changing her from th' mule-stubborn jenny-ass she is into a damn good imitation of a zebra, she's on th' house. For free. And if she's tough enough to make it through till tomorrow morning, I'll put her in a crib in my cowyard on Kearny Street. At two bits a tumble. Or a dime, maybe. For as long as she lasts," Big Jules Tinderman said.

And since Luck is the capricious goddess as changeable as she is mindless, Mireille's veered a full one hundred eighty degrees again. Ruby, the big beefy blonde, got to the dressing room where Paquita was waiting for Mireille, and dozing as usual, two minutes after the Maniac rattled all the windows with his shrill, unbelievably terrible scream as they clapped the irons to his bloody face and he passed out altogether. And it was perhaps a demonstration of the utter amorality of fate that the Draconian method of cauterization stopped the bleeding and saved his life, for a little while longer, anyhow.

La Cabeza de Jabalí, where Sweet William worked temporarily as chief bodyguard for Manuel Garcia, was exactly twenty yards up Pacific Street from the Dirty Spoon. The only real delay involved was getting Paquita waked up enough to understand what was going on. A party of prospectors, flushed with luck, had come in from the goldfields that afternoon, and Paquita's stunning dark beauty had caught their ribald fancy. As a result, the poor thing had made over a pound of gold dust— roughly two hundred forty dollars—flat on her aching back atop the hard boards of the benchlike tables inside the curtained booths, that afternoon. So it wasn't until Ruby had screamed into her ear:

"Paci, he's beating her bloody! He's going to kill her! Oh, for God's sake, wake up!" that her weary, blue-ringed, deep-sunk eyes fluttered open, flared into slow, dawning comprehension, then into horror.

Three minutes after that, she was back with Guillermo Kilpatrick.

The first thing Willy saw when he came through the doorway of the Dirty Spoon was poor Mireille hanging from the transom of the inner entrance between the foyer and the dance floor like a slaughtered she-goat. In that brief interval Big Jules had striped her slim, naked body from head to heel with whiplashes, most of which had broken her tender skin, brought blood. And, because she had refused to scream at all, or give vent to any sound more audible than a sharp, whistling intake of breath each time that mule skinner's whip bit into her flesh, her courage —or her stubbornness—got Big Jules wild, so that he went on beating her long after he would ordinarily have stopped.

So Guillermo stopped him. The young Mexican-American didn't even hesitate. First he pulled his kerchief up over his mouth and nose, with a deftness that betrayed long practice. That done, he slowly and carefully drew his old-fashioned Paterson Colt revolver, which caused Ned Clark, the Dirty Spoon's bartender and bouncer to snarl at him:

"Hey, you! Ain't no guns allowed in here! You gotta leave 'em with me until—"

That was as far as he got. Willy practically parted his hair for him with a shot that then went on to shatter the expensive plate-glass mirror above the bar. At the sound of that shot, but even more so at the noise of the crashing into fragments of a mirror that had cost him a full two thousand dollars to have brought around the Horn by clipper ship from the East Coast, Big Jules Tinderman stopped virtually flaying poor Mireille alive and whirled, roaring like an enraged bull.

Whereupon Willy shot him in the belly.

Big Jules dropped the whip. Clutched his middle with his two hands. Did a dance step that was surprisingly graceful for so big a man. Having made that one small concession to brutal shock and agonizing pain, he pulled his right hand away from his torn gut, thrust it beneath his frock coat, and came out with the derringer he had in an armpit holster there.

Willy's second bullet, slamming into the shoulder of his gun arm, made him drop the little pocket pistol unfired. Then, spreading his arms wide like a bear, Big Jules came roaring in.

Willy shot him in the belly again, from a distance of two yards away. He might as well have been shooting blanks for all the effect it had on Big Jules Tinderman. So, with the huge man practically on top of him, his massive arms spread wide to sweep Willy's slender form into what was sure to be a rib-cracking and ultimately fatal embrace, Willy lifted the Paterson Colt high and fired it, from six inches' distance, into the red maw of Big Jules's opened, bull-bellowing mouth. And, sidestepping as gracefully as a ballet dancer, he allowed the big man, impelled by his own momentum, to crash forward on his face.

The young Mexican-American stood there, staring down at Big Jules's corpse and shaking his head in wonder. After that he looked at the

Paterson, which, being like all Sam Colt's revolvers before the Walker a five-shot gun, was now completely empty. His lip curled in purest disgust under his kerchief.

"You damned old peashooter!" he muttered; "I've got to get me a new gun somewhere. . . ."

He thrust the nine-inch barrel of the big Paterson back into his belt and took his razor-edged bowie knife out of its scabbard in order to cut Mireille down. By that time, she was mercifully unconscious. At that moment, seeing what looked like to him a golden opportunity, one of the Dirty Spoon's clients sang out:

"Rush him, boys!"

Willy put the bowie knife back into its scabbard. He reached behind him and pulled, with no special haste, his little hideout gun out of a hip pocket carefully lined with oilskin so that the grease from the stubby, sawed-off little revolver wouldn't ruin his pants. It was a Paterson Colt too—but the baby, pocket model, and the ball it threw was only .28 caliber, instead of the big, belt-model Paterson .34. Therefore its muzzle velocity and shocking power were even more dismal than the bigger weapon's were, a fact of which Willy Kilpatrick was sadly aware.

So, sighing, he coolly and carefully shot the enthusiastic client in the belly, which ended the matter. The man sat down on the floor, clutching his perforated abdomen and moaning. The rest of the miners and sailors fell back, muttering:

"Look out! Li'l sumabitch's gotta nother gun!"

"Gentlemen," Willy said politely, "I'd advise you to sit down. Or better still, treat yourselves to free drinks on the house. Don't think the owner of this establishment is likely to object. . . ."

They all sat down, mumbling picturesque profanity under their breaths. Willy calmly turned his back to them and proceeded to cut Mireille down. He didn't consider the gesture to be too much of a gamble, because like everyone else in Sydney Town he was aware of the fact that ever since one of his "pretty waiter girls" had been accidentally killed in a shootout between a miner and a crooked gambler in the fall of forty-nine, Big Jules had strictly enforced the rule that the clients had to leave not only their firearms, but the awesome assortment of cutlery they also carried, with the bartender when they entered the place. Ned Clark and his assistant, Murray Tyler, searched every man who, their experienced eyes told them, was concealing an "Arkansas toothpick" or a hideout derringer on his person, even after he had surrendered his bulky and visible revolver.

So Guillermo assumed, accurately enough, that none of them would be either sufficiently a fool, or even, at that early hour of the night, drunk enough, to start a bare-handed rush in an effort to overpower, by sheer weight of numbers, a man armed with not only one, but two of Sam Colt's revolvers, for which they had a very healthy respect indeed.

"¡*Tengo que buscarla ropa!*" Paquita moaned.

"Don't speak Spanish!" Guillermo hissed; "When they start out after me, I want them to be looking for a gringo—understand? And don't worry about her clothes! There's no time! Here, take this and cut down one of the curtains around those booths. We can wrap her in that. . . ."

Paquita took the bowie knife and cut the curtain down. Between them they wrapped Mireille in it. Then Guillermo tossed her over one of his shoulders like a sack of flour, which, while it wasn't the gentlest method possible for carrying a girl as bruised, welted, striped all over as poor Mireille was, at least left his gun arm free for action. Turning back to face the Dirty Spoon's clients, he said cheerfully:

"Don't think I've got to tell you that following us would be mighty unhealthy, do I? Gentlemen, good night! Enjoy yourselves!"

Then, carrying his inert burden, and with Paquita scurrying along beside him, he disappeared into the night.

"You may cease to look behind you now, Willy," Paquita said; "they will not come after us."

Willy stared at her. "What makes you so sure?"

"I know them. They are swine, but they are also cowards. They will not dare. Besides, Big Jules has broken too many of their heads for them, or kicked them in their mangy seats. They have insufficient love for him to want to avenge him."

"But—the other fellow?" Willy said.

"Even less. They probably don't even know him. On any given night most of the clients will be strangers to one another. Besides, if they were going to pursue us, they would have done so long before now. We have been—lucky. In two ways."

"Two?" Willy said.

"Yes. That they did not chase after us, and this of the fire."

"What has the fire to do with our luck, *linda* Paquita?" Willy said.

"Do you think you could walk through Sydney Town with a naked girl in your arms without having to fight off at least twenty of them were it not for the fire? But since they are all watching it in order to steal from the burning buildings everything light enough for them to carry away, you do not have the necessity of shooting your way through a mob of Sydney Ducks, engaged in trying to kill you in order to take poor Mireille

—and perhaps even me—away from you. Whereupon we should both be dead—of abuse—by morning. . . ."

"*If* they got you two away from me, which would take some doing," Willy said grimly. "Can you see her face? I can't, carrying her this way. And I dare not change her position, just in case we encounter another gringo swine with a craving to receive a bullet through his guts. If you can see her angel's face tell me: how is she supporting this voyage through hell?"

"Yes, I can see her. She is still profoundly unconscious—which is perhaps just as well, or else she would be suffering horribly," Paquita said. "Where are you going to take her, Willy?"

"To Señora Gonzales' inn in Stockton Street," Willy said, "which is in the heart of Little Chile, as the gringos call our quarter. And since it, our quarter is just behind this one, the wind keeps the fire out of it, too. Besides, it has practically burned itself out, our magnificent fire, hasn't it? I will rent a room for the two of you at the Gonzales *posada* for a month."

"But, Willy—that will cost you a hundred and fifty dollars! More, perhaps, with the meals . . ."

"Yes, that much surely," Willy sighed; "the prices in San Francisco are outrageous, aren't they? But I cannot take her—or thee—to the lodging of my sisters. They would raise a cry to heaven if I did. I know, I know! They haven't any right to, for surely they define that which they call their virtue much too narrowly. Still, what this poor abused child needs is both rest and care, which thou, I am sure, will provide her. For I cannot call just any doctor, Paci. I have to call our special quack, and he, unfortunately, is not in San Francisco, but in the Sierras, curing a friend of mine who has been badly wounded. . . ."

"But if he is a quack, I don't see what you want with him," Paquita said, logically enough.

"Because he *isn't*," Willy said. "We only call him 'quack' as a joke, because we love him so. Enrique Sepúlvera Varón is the best doctor and surgeon in California. You see, his family were very rich before the gringos came, so he was educated abroad—first in Spain, and afterward in both France and, what is more important, Germany. The Germans, you know, lovely Paquita, are the most advanced nation on earth when it comes to medicine."

"It seems to me that you and your friends could hardly afford the services of such a one."

"He gives it voluntarily. The same old story, my dear. Somebody started the rumor that gold had been found on the Sepúlvera estate, so the gringos invaded it, killed his aged father, chased his mother away. Fortunately he had no sisters for them to rape, but his mother died of a broken heart. So now, although he is a native Californian of purest Spanish blood, with no Indian in him at all, he defends the cause of us poor Mexicans. But as I said, he is out of town at the moment, and I dare not call anyone else. If I bring in a Mexican doctor, he will surely wonder aloud to his wife what a gringa whose snow-white skin has been striped all over with whiplashes is doing in a Mexican Roadhouse. And the news will be all over the quarter by morning. On the other hand, if I should seek out a Yankee quack—which I could by changing my clothes and speaking English through my nose, and ungrammatically—we risk starting a riot worse than that of last July. I can hear him now: 'By Gawd, boys; them greaser bastids have kidnapped a *white* woman!' "

"True," Paquita sighed, "but Willy darleeng, where are you going to get so much money?"

"I have it," Willy said.

"Would it be too—daring of me to ask you how you became so rich? You do not prospect for gold. And I know Don Manuel. The salary he pays you to act as his bodyguard is surely a pittance. Yet you have already spent several hundred dollars on a girl you hardly know. And you are planning to spend even more on her, and on me, who are—however much you accept our . . . excuse for being so—a couple of whores. Is it that you plan to make her—or me—your mistress?"

"Or both of you," Willy teased her solemnly. "You are both very beautiful, though in different ways. I could sleep in the middle, with her on my right and thee on my left. Then every night I'd toss a coin, heads or tails to see which of my ardent mistresses I should favor with my manly attentions next!"

"No. That, no," Paquita said.

"And why not, lovely Paquita?"

"Because," Paquita said, the choked-back tears drowning her voice, "Thou art such a one, dear Willy, as a woman could learn to love very truly. Thou'rt very handsome. And kind. And gentle. And—sweet. Yet thou'rt also brave as a lion. I could love thee. So could she. Perhaps we— the two of us—already do. Therefore, sharing thee would be—an impossibility. . . ."

"Then I am forced to choose between you?" Willy sighed. "That is— very hard. I ask counsel of thee then, beautiful! Which of thou two should I choose?"

"Neither of us," Paquita said sadly.

"*¡Ay Yai!* But this is harder still! Why not, my heart?"

"Because if you choose me, it would break her heart—and thereby mine, for she is, very truly, the sister of my soul. And if you choose her, it would shame her past all bearing, because, you see, dear Willy, she *wants* to be a good woman. Moral. Decent. A faithful wife. The mother of the sons of a man who not only loves, but also *respects* her. And since thou wouldst always remember what she has been—that also is an impossibility, no?"

Willy bowed his head, looked up again.

"Let us not speak of this anymore," he said harshly.

"All right. But that of the money—please. It will trouble me, unless I know you can afford it, truly."

"I can afford it. And, as proof of the fact that I trust thee, pretty Paquita, I will tell thee how I get it. From the gringos. At pistol point—as they descend from the mines."

"*¡Dios!*" Paquita said.

"I worked a claim near Sonora. Not the Sonora I am from in *Mejico;* but the new Sonora, here, that we have named in honor of the old one. We, my companions and I, found much gold there. But word of our find reached the gringos, so they jumped our claim in overwhelming numbers and drove us away, killing three of us in the process. . . ."

"You decided to become a bandit because of that?" Paquita said. "It is a thing that always happens. I was born here in Upper California, and yet now they say I am a foreigner . . ."

"I know. But I did not become a *pistolero* because of that. You see, I had—a wife—"

"Oh . . ." Paquita breathed. "But you seem much too young to—"

"Have wed? No. I am twenty-eight, which is ten years older than my sisters. It is their evil ways that make them seem so old. Actually, they are *niñas*—children. . . ."

"Thy—wife," Paquita whispered; "speak of her . . ."

"An angel from heaven," Willy said gravely, "whom I married in the Church. Chaste. Pure. Decent, moral, honorable, faithful. I left her in the cabin of a married couple much older than we, while I went to search for a new claim to work. And—she was very beautiful. Even—gravid, she was—"

"Pregnant?" Paquita got out; "and—the child?"

"Was never born. While I was in the Sierras, the gringos came. With many blows they drove away the older couple I had left my Sara with. Then they attempted to violate my poor Sara. There were only two of them, so she was able to fight them off with the pistol I had given her.

She wounded one of them, who died a full two weeks later. They came back, hundreds of them, shouting, 'Give her a fair trial, then hang her!' "

"Holy Mother!" Paquita said.

"A Yankee doctor and a decent man—gringos sometimes are, y'know —testified that my Sara was with child, and told them they could not hang her. They made him run the gauntlet, and beat him almost to death with staves. And, after that—they hanged my Sara. . . ."

"Oh, poor you!" Paquita sobbed.

"Yes—poor me," Willy whispered. "Now dost thou see why I cannot dishonor her memory by taking to wife a woman who is—in any way, for *any* reason!—less than she? The mother of my sons must be all *she* was—"

"Chaste. Pure. Moral. Virgin—untouched," Paquita murmured bitterly. "Yes. You are right, Willy. And because thou art, we—Mireille and I—cannot accept your money. *I* will pay for this. I made over two hundred dollars today for the sale—or the rental—of—of my putrid flesh. So spare us your charity, accompanied as it is by thy contempt. We—even such as she and I—have some pride left, y'know. . . ."

"Of course you have—and much reason for it," Willy said somberly. "I feel no contempt for her—or thee, Paci—but rather love—and pity. Put it this way: I would never scorn a crippled man; but then, neither would I enter him in a footrace. The—shame and sorrow that you both bear is—no fault of thine. But still less is it of my sons! And they would be burdened lifelong by it. Enough of this! I need my breath. Light as she is, she grows heavy over such a distance—"

"And—insupportably so, over—a lifetime, eh, Willy? I'm sorry! Forget I said that—"

"It is forgotten. It has no importance," Guillermo Kilpatrick said.

But it did. All the importance in this miserable world. He'd learn that soon enough. So, bearing that burden his heart, anyhow, would never be able to put down, Willy walked on toward the inn. . . .

3

"MIRI," PAQUITA SAID PLAINTIVELY, "YOU WILL PLEASE NOT TO fall in love with Willy. Promise me?"

Mireille stopped brushing her hair, stared at her own image and Paquita's in the mirror before her. She had to admit that Paci looked much better than she did. In the nearly three months they had been in Doña Marta Gonzales' inn, the Mexican-American, or, more correctly, Hispano-California girl had put on several decidedly becoming pounds and appeared rested, relaxed, and prettier than ever.

'While I,' Mireille thought morosely, 'have become a ghost—a phantom. A gust of wind would blow me away. In part it is because I cannot eat Mexican cooking, and she can; but more, it is because her heart is at ease, and mine—isn't. . . . It was kind of Doña Marta to give her the job of chambermaid and waitress here. Willy's influence, of course. But also—self-interest. That first week, when the inn was overrun with unexpected arrivals, and Paci pitched in voluntarily and helped out, Doña Marta, Señora Gonzales, *saw* how good she is at this kind of work, how quick, how willing. And how neat and clean! Unlike the other three slatterns who work here. What did it take, really, to recognize a treasure? On Doña Marta's part, the setting aside of some stern Catholic scruples, that's all. *Dieu*, what a talking to she gave poor Paci the day she hired her. "You are not, *hija mia*—to look sidewise at a man! You are not to smile. You are to answer only *'¡Sí, señor!'* or *'¡No, señor!'* as the case may be. You are not to accept invitations from any client—to dance, dine, or even take a walk—However gentlemanly they seem. Men, daughter mine, are not to be trusted." —As if either Paci or *I* needed to be told that!'

"Why do you not answer me, Miri?" Paquita said. "This which I have

said to you is very serious. It would be a mistake of the gravest for you to
—surrender to his good looks and his charm and—"

"Hurt *your* chances with him, Paci? You adore him, don't you? Admit
it!" Mireille said.

"Yes. I love him. But there is no way under heaven you could hurt my
chances with Willy, Miri darling, because I haven't any. He is scarcely
aware that I am alive. Therefore I am in no danger. While you *are*. In
grave danger, my dear one. The gravest kind of peril—"

Mireille went on staring at her friend's dark, lovely face in the mirror.

"I—don't understand you, Paci," she whispered.

"One day," Paquita said quietly, "I shall meet a man who does not
know my—past. A man who can be—mine, before God and in the sight
of men. And after I have taught him to love me as a man must love the
wife of his heart—the wife and mistress of his home, the mother of his
sons—with nobility, with respect, I shall *tell* him of my terrible past, risk
losing him altogether before attempting to live a lie, to deceive the man I
love for the rest of our lives together. It cannot be done, in any case, and
if it could, the strain of fearing that one day he would find out, that some
pig to whom I was forced to sell myself would reveal it to him, would be
enough to drive me stark raving mad."

"Paci, I still don't follow you," Mireille sighed.

"I know you don't. I'm saying that after what has happened to us,
dulce Mireille, there are only two paths that we can follow. The first is—
by miraculous luck to find men noble enough, broad-minded enough, to
make us their wives, or—to remain spinsters forever. We have been
reduced to garbage, dirt. And now we have started to climb back up out
of the mire—at least a little way. I will *not* fall back again. I will be a
man's good *wife*, or nothing. Wife, yes—kept woman, never!"

"Oh!" Mireille said. "Paci, you're saying that even though Willy
seems—fond of me . . . He *does*, doesn't he? Or am I imagining
things?"

"Worse than that. He is—in love with you. Desperately in love with
you. And that is what makes the whole thing so sad. Worse than sad—
tragic."

"You mean that no matter how much he loves me, he wouldn't—
wouldn't—?"

"Marry you? You put it badly, *querida*. Not wouldn't—*couldn't*. He is
a Mexican of the landowner class, for his father, Señor Kilpatrick, took
Mexican citizenship and acquired thousands of acres of land in Sonora.
Of course, like the sons of so many other great landowners in these
troubled times, Willy has lost his property and sunk in life. But he

remains in *all* ways—speech, bearing, comportment—an estate owner, a Hidalgo, a somebody, and by that very token a gentleman. Mexican gentlemen, my dearest one, do not marry whores. Not even poor, sweet, angelic-looking *ex*-whores. All right, Guillermo is half gringo—but by training, by instinct, he is *all* Mexican. He's suffering horribly because of you, already. As a foreigner, you cannot even imagine the degree of this suffering which you have caused him. Of course, if you fall into his arms, into his bed, he will take you, gladly. He is all man. And as his concubine, his mistress, his kept woman, you will be treated with great kindness, enormous tenderness, even a certain amoung of, say, circumspection, care . . ."

"In that case," Mireille said morosely, "why shouldn't I settle for that much? Since, as you say, I can't have more, what's wrong with taking what little I can get?"

"Because," Paquita whispered, tears drowning her voice, "one day he will make his way in this world. He is brilliant of mind, Miri; he has considerable force of character. Then he will marry, as he *has* to, a young lady of high birth, of a great family, straight out of a convent school—pure, chaste, untouched. And your children, *querida*, will not be allowed within twenty *miles* of *la casa grande*. They will be bastards, and wear your name, not his. His visits will become—infrequent. And one day, being a woman, when you can no longer resist the desire to complain of the hardness of your lot, and you forget yourself and your lowly position in the scheme of things so greatly as to speak the name of her who is his legal wife and mistress of his—respect, anyhow, for in such marriages love is seldom the primary consideration—he will roar at you, 'If you ever again dare to mention the name of my wife, I'll make you swallow it along with your teeth, whore!"

"Bon Dieu!" Mireille whispered. She sat there thinking about that, comparing and contrasting it with all the patterns of behavior, traits, modes of thought she had prudently and carefully observed in Guillermo Kilpatrick. And it didn't seem to coincide with her observations at all. 'He's not like that!' she thought hotly; 'he's not! He would never throw me over for something that wasn't my fault at all, and—'

Then she stopped, for the basic romanticism of her warm young heart had run hard up against the ice-cold realism that time and bitter experience were beginning to inflict upon her eminently logical, and respectably intelligent, mind.

What did she know about Guillermo Kilpatrick, really—as a person, as a man? The answer to that was—nothing, or very nearly. And one circumstance that had puzzled her at first, and by now was beginning to trouble her badly, came back to lend Paquita's contention dismal force: In the three months she had known him, despite all the many, very nearly unmistakable indications he had given her that he was much more than fond of her, he had never so much as tried to kiss her—even once.

'Perhaps he thinks I have—a disease. And I could have, by now,' she thought miserably. 'I—I'll have to ask Doctor Enrique about that—'

But she had to face a more immediate problem: What, if anything, to do about Willy Kilpatrick. About—herself.

"Paci," she said sadly, "he—Willy—is supposed to call for me today. In a rented buckboard—to take me and my luggage down to Dr. Sepúlvera's *rancho* south of San José, for the winter. It's warmer down there. Drier. Dr. Enrique thinks it would help this cough of mine to leave San Francisco and go to a place with a better climate. So he's invited me to his estate, *El Rancho Santa Clara* . . ."

"Didn't know Dr. Enrique Sepúlvera *had* a *rancho* anymore," Paquita said. "Willy told me that the gringos drove the Sepúlveras off it, and then wrecked it completely in their search for gold."

"True. But that was in 1848, the first year of the Gold Rush. They didn't find any gold, not even a speck of it. So they abandoned *El Rancho Santa Clara* soon enough. Don Enrique has reclaimed it, put about a hundred fifty acres of it into cultivation: potatoes, yams, vegetables, fruit, grape arbors. And he's making a fortune. You know what fresh fruit and vegetables cost on the market here in San Francisco, don't you?"

"Yes. An outrage. But *that*, dear Mireille, is not what you started to tell me in that oh-so-sweet and gentle little girl's voice of yours, is it?"

"No. And it's ask, not tell. Paci—should I go down there with Willy? I—I've had troubles enough. I just couldn't stand anymore. And I don't want to cause him any—"

"*Sí.* Yes. Go with him. But stay out of his arms. Send him away, as soon as you can. He will respect you, Miri, if you stand your ground firmly . . ."

"I know," Mireille said sadly.

"But you have no desire to stand your ground against Willy—even a little, not to mention firmly, eh, Miri?" Paquita said.

"I—I don't know. I like him. I like him an awful lot, Paci. But, strange as it may seem to you, I *don't* love him. Not yet. Maybe I could if I'd let myself. No—that's wrong, too. Maybe I could if love were—possible—for me anymore. But I don't think it is. After the Maniac and his gentle friends at the Dirty Spoon, I'm quite sure that if a man were to touch my fingertips—even accidentally—I'd throw up . . ."

"Poor little you, then!" Paquita said mockingly. "You'll get over that, *querida*. Time itself will cure those feelings. One night there will be a moon over half the sky, and the whippoorwills will be calling, and you—"

"Will play with myself," Mireille said bitterly, "or send for you—a girl like me—and say, 'Come, Paci, make love to me . . .' But another stinking beast and brute of a *man?* No. Oh, no!"

"I would not come to you," Paquita whispered—"not because I do not love you, but because I do. It would be—too easy to fall into such twisted ways with you, dear heart. But I want—I *mean* to rebuild my life. To become one day the wife of Mr. X—and with much honor! And you must, too—"

"With someone else, not—Guillermo," Mireille said bitterly.

"With someone else, not Willy," Paquita said. "Which is a pity. You and he would make a wonderful couple. Only, he knows what he knows about your past, and therefore it is not possible. So please to push him off. Who knows? Keep him dangling long enough, and perhaps even his ancient prejudices of a hidalgo may crumble. Besides, you cannot stay *here* any longer."

"And why not?" Mireille snapped. "As long as Willy is willing to pay for it, has the money, and asks nothing in return, I don't see—"

"You never see. You are almost as awkward as a gringa, love. For instance, you might start by asking Willy *where* he gets the money to pay for your meals and lodging. Oh, no! Don't ask me. I will not tell you that. But perhaps a better reason is that a slim, blond gringo was here this morning, asking after you. He said his name was How-ward Tel-lefair—"

"Bon petit Jésus!" Mireille said.

"I told him you were not here—that, in fact, I had never heard of you. He asked me if I were Paquita Villa Roque, and when I said, 'Yes,' he grinned at me and said, 'You're lying, baby! Go tell Mireille I want to see her . . .'"

"Ohhhh Lord!" Mireille said.

"So then, I played it cleverly. 'Mireille?' I said. 'Oh, you mean the little French girl we call Mirla! She is—no longer here. The doctors sent her to a drier climate'—we'd talked about this, remember, Miri? I got the idea from you—'Because, you see, sir, she has galloping consumption. Much do I fear she is going to die, coughing blood the way she does. So they—banished her to Santa Barbara—or even below that . . .'"

"Did he *believe* you?" Mireille said.

"Yes. I'm quite sure he did. You should have seen his face. It fell almost to his boot tops when I mentioned that business about your coughing blood. . . ."

"I might, one day soon," Mireille said darkly. "If I don't stop coughing soon, I just might. Dr. Enrique asks me that every time he sees me. 'Have you seen any blood on your handkerchief, dear Mireille?' he says; 'even a tiny drop?' "

"You should grab *him*," Paquita said; "at least you could talk French to each other. Lord, what a language! You snort half of it through your nose, and gargle the rest of it down your throat!"

"While Spanish sounds like gas on one's stomach!" Mireille teased her solemnly; *"RRRRRR Rooooom! Deeeee Os Meeeee Oh eee Tantoh Ownrahhhhhhh!"*

"All right, all right!" Paquita laughed; "all languages are strange to the ears of people who do not speak or understand them. But, just the same, it is perhaps better that you go away from here for a while."

"I don't see why. If you've convinced How-ward I have tuberculosis, he will leave me alone. He conceives of me—of all women—as merchandise, goods for sale. And since not even the most beastly of men want to —couch themselves with a woman whose lungs are rotting away, he—"

"Not him. He is—not much of a man, and therefore harmless. Your other great friend: the Maniac—"

"Oh, no!" Mireille breathed.

"He was hanging around—walking to and fro through this block half the morning. I do believe he *followed* the other one, your ex lover Howward, here. And little mother of my soul! What a monster! He was never excessively handsome, but after you so kindly and gently slit his pig's snout for him, and Big Jules improved upon even that by clapping redhot irons to that enormous slash—Jesus, Joseph and Mary, what a sight! Those red-hot irons have left him with a scar that would turn the stomach of a nanny goat. I'm sure that the girls refuse him in every whorehouse in San Francisco, now—"

"Except the Dirty Spoon," Mireille said bitterly.

"Even there," Paquita said, "now that Big Jules is no longer owner of it—or of anything, except the deepest pit in hell. But seriously, *querida*, anywhere would be safer for you than San Francisco, now. . . ."

"I agree," Mireille sighed; "when Willy arrives, I will go south with him. But do not preoccupy yourself, Paci love; I shall keep my sweaty little paws off him. Of that, you may rest assured. . . . So come along, dear girl, and help me pack my clothes. My old dresses are all too big for me now, but they will have to do—"

"Oh, you'll gain weight down there quickly enough," Paquita said; "just make sure you don't gain it all in front!"

"You look like a little saint and martyr," Willy said as the smart little rig he had rented whirled them around the southern end of the Bay. Before them to the east and south lay the long, limpid curve of California, stretching away to Mexico. To the west, there was only the bright, metallic disk of the ocean, folding over the world's vast rim to the islands of the sea, and beyond, over unimaginable vastnesses to the Orient—the Philippines, Japan, China.

"A what?" Mireille said absently.

"A saint," Willy said. *"Una beata*—I know not how to say that in English: something like 'a blessed one,' I think. But mostly like a poor, pale little martyr, languishing away of starvation in her cell, dying very slowly, offering up her life in atonement for the sins of this world . . ."

"Only I'm not a saint. Nor a blessed one," Mireille said gravely. "A martyr? Hmmmmmnnn—could be. Stretching the point an awful lot. But it is my own sins I am dying for, dear Willy. Or rather from the punishment they have brought down upon me. The cruelest chastisement, torture imaginable; the one most perfectly calculated to drive me mad, destroy me . . ."

Willy stared at her with troubled eyes.

"And what is this punishment, my dear?" he asked her.

She turned and faced him, let her own eyes become dark pools of purest misery, light-blazed, brimming, blind, reflecting in each night-black pupil a tiny image of his face.

"Your—contempt," she said bitterly. "I—disgust you, don't I? You—despise me."

He stared at her, and his eyes were very bleak.

"No," he sighed; "you're wrong, Mirla. On all counts, though I wish you weren't. The truth is—I love you. That God pardon me for it!"

She turned away from him, gazed out over the metallic blue and silver glitter of the ocean.

"Thank you," she said; "I'm very flattered. Touched. Overwhelmed by this great and passionate love you don't even want to feel for me. That you ask God to forgive you for!"

He looked away from her, out over the sea. Looked back again. Held her eyes with his blue and candid gaze.

"I'm sorry. I wish it could be different. Truly I do, little Mirla," he said.

"Well, it can't be, so let's not talk about it anymore. Besides, you're right: I don't deserve you. I am—all the dirty words you can think of, and some you don't even know. Fit only for one thing: to be pounded into a sweaty, stinking, drippy mess atop a mattress. Or on the floor; the ground. Tell me: Would it please you if I were to—offer myself to you as —your little mistress? Your—kept woman?"

"No," he said grimly; "it wouldn't please me."

"I mean—only until you wed. After that, *cher* Willy, I should, of course, set you free. . . ."

"Set me free, how?" he said.

"Don't know. Cut my throat on the church steps as you and your bride come down them from the altar, I suppose. Then she could dip one white rose from her wedding bouquet in my blood—and keep it for a souvenir . . ."

He stared at her.

"Do you often have these kinds of moods?" he said.

"Now—yes. Now, quite frequently. I—encourage them. Going mad takes—practice."

"Mireille, for the love of God!"

"No—for *your* love, Willy darling. Then you don't want me to climb into your bed with you tonight?"

"No, I don't."

"Then it will have to be the barnyard instead of the church steps. Will you lend me your razor?"

"God save me!" he said.

"I'm—sorry. Willy—I—I haven't a—a sickness. I'm quite sure I haven't. And I am—very expert. I have had, after all, much practice. I could make you—temporarily, anyhow—very happy."

"No," he said; "you couldn't. Somebody else could, maybe. But not you, Mirla. Never *you.*"

She searched his face, his eyes. Whispered, "Why not, Willy?"

"That's hard to explain. I'm not sure my English is up to it . . ."

"Then say it in Spanish. Paquita's been teaching me, y'know."

"Would you understand it? It's very complicated . . ."

"No, I wouldn't. Neither in English nor Spanish nor French, or any language whatsoever. I don't understand anything anymore, Willy, except that there's a hole in the middle of my breast where my heart used to be, and that my head doesn't work right, and that I hurt . . ."

"Poor little Mirla!" he murmured.

"I don't want your pity, lord and master Guillermo Kilpatrick-Calvo! I don't want anything from you. I've been trying to get you to make love

to me, haven't I? Ha! That's what *you* think! D'you know what would
happen if you kissed me?"

"No," he said sadly; "what, Mirla?"

"I'd vomit all over you. That's the only response I have to men now—
nausea."

"Then I won't try to kiss you," he said.

"All right. That's a relief. Oh, no, it isn't. You see, I *want* you to kiss
me. But please don't. I'd still throw up even though I want you to. And
I'd make you the worst mistress in all the world, lying there rigid and
revolted and sick to my guts, letting you use me and hating every second
of it. Hating you. Hating *me.*"

"I could never make use of *you,* Mirla."

She stared at him again and said sharply, "And why not?"

"That same, complicated reason. The one I don't think I can explain."

"Try!"

"All right," he sighed. "But it'll probably come out all wrong. Look, I
haven't been a saint. I've been to the whores like most fellows my age.
But I quit that a long time ago. It doesn't work for me. I'm not talking
about morality. It just doesn't work, that's all."

"Why not?"

"Rag dolls. Sacks of guts. No longer women—no longer human beings. Do you understand?"

"Of course. Like me."

"No. That's just the point. *Not* like you. Wait! I—I've never mentioned this before to you, but I've been married—"

"I know. Paci told me. And widowed. The dirty pig Yankees killed
your wife and, with her, your unborn child. So, ever since, you have been
searching for your perfect love. And what do you find? Me. A whore."

"*¡Santa Madre de los desamparados!*" he said.

"Holy Mother of the helpless?" she translated. "*Bien.* Good. Also like
me."

"Mirla," he said, "you are *not*—a bad girl. You were forced into that
life, and—"

"I was not!" she said mockingly. "I entered it voluntarily. I have
always been—what is that phrase that Paci always calls me? Oh, yes! *Una
chica muy cachonda.* A hot little girl. *Je m'avais couchée avec la moitié de
Nouvelle Orleans*—" She stopped, thought of a way to put that in English that would be as shocking as possible. "I'd taken off my pantalettes
for half New Orleans—gratis, free—before it occurred to me that I'd
better profit from the only talent I had, and—"

"Shut up!" he said angrily. *"Lo que eres es muy bruta. Una asna de verdad.* Quit insulting me, will you?"

"I insult *you?* When you call me—a stupid wench and a jenny ass? You see, I understand bad words in *any* language, Willy dear!"

"You are. Both. Lying to me like that. Insulting my intelligence, and my taste. I love you, Mirla. You're the second girl in all my life I've loved—"

"The first was—your wife?" she whispered.

"The first was my wife. And for the same reason. She was—a person, too."

"And I—am a person to you, Willy?" she said softly, slowly. "Not just —a sack of tripes? Not just—an apparatus of flesh—sufficiently warm, soft, wet for you to—push *yours* up into and—get your rocks off, as the miners say?"

"¡Jesús!" he said, his voice high, tight, vibrant with actual pain.

"I'm sorry. I'm a whore, so I talk like one. Besides, you ought to thank me. I'm trying to keep you from making a terrible mistake: confusing me with a human being . . ."

He whirled then, swiftly, almost savagely, caught her small face between his slim, strong hands. Bent and kissed her mouth. A long time. A very long time. Softly, slowly, gently. With aching tenderness. Cherishing it with his own.

When he drew back at last, she couldn't see his face for the downrush of her tears.

They didn't talk any more until they got to the main gate of the Rancho Santa Clara, and the ancient cowboy who had no other name than *Juan el Viejo,* "Old John," came hobbling out of the little guardhouse to open it for them. Then Willy turned and smiled at her.

"You didn't vomit," he said.

"I know," she whispered. "But—it would have been better if I had. . . ."

He didn't say anything, then. They responded to Old John's greetings, drove through the gateway and were rolling down the long, oak-shaded road that led to the barely visible *casa grande* at the far end of it before he took her up on that remark.

"Why would it have been better, little Mirla?" he asked.

She shrugged.

"What are you offering me, really, Guillermo," she said, "except— more sin, more shame?"

He stared at her, said, flatly, "I am offering you—nothing, Mireille.

No relation at all. I only said I love you, which, unfortunately, is true. I
didn't say I planned to do anything about that love. As a matter of fact—
and if the question interests you—I don't."

She smiled at him. It was, he thought, the single wickedest smile he
had ever seen on a human, female face. Not sensual. Not lewd. Just—
wicked. Perhaps even evil. The difference was vast.

"Thank you," she said.

"For what?" he answered harshly.

"For being—a gentleman. Though I may put the matter to the test—
tonight, after Don Enrique has gone to bed. Don't bolt your door, Willy.
. . ."

He studied her face, searched her eyes, then said, very quietly, "I
won't."

"That's not a *promise*, y'know. I may sleep like a log, all night long. I
mean to. I hope I do. But—if I don't—"

He went on studying that small, heart-shaped, truly angelical face that
was contradiction's very self.

"All right," he said.

"All right—to *what?*" she shot back at him.

"Either way. To whatever you decide to do. Or not to do. Agreed."

"Willy—" she whispered then in a hushed, choked, broken little
voice, "you couldn't—just *forget*—what I've been? Not—ever?"

The silence between them weighed tons. His sigh, breaking it, was a
ripple on dead, still waters. Then he defined, once and forever, the
central tragedy of both their lives.

"No. Not—ever," he said.

"Don Enrique," Mireille said to her host, "how old are you?"

Enrique Sepúlvera looked at her and wondered, for the thousandth
time, why he found her so—shocking. During his student years Dr.
Sepúlvera had been one of the gayest blades of the bohemia of Paris;
years of study and observation had brought him to the conviction that
nothing that human beings did, or could do, was really abnormal, and
that whether it was moral or immoral, wicked or saintly, was the concern
of theologians, philosophers, and, ultimately, the law, but never of a
scientist. "I observe; I do not judge!" was his watchword. Yet, despite the
fact that he was immensely fond of her, Mireille shocked him. 'Perhaps
because she looks like an angel, and *is* a devil,' he thought. '¡*Mierda!*
Another *moral* judgment! I must be getting old and soft in the
head . . .'

"Don't you want to answer me, dear Doctor?" Mireille said in her best 'sugar and spice and everything nice' sweet little girl's tone of voice.

"Of course, my dear," Enrique chuckled; "I don't mind at all. I'm too bloody close to fifty for comfort, but that's not to be helped. I'm forty-seven, to be exact. Why do you ask, little Mireille?"

"And you have no wife. Are you a widower? You're a Catholic, so you can't be divorced. Don't tell me you've never wed?"

Enrique looked from her face to Guillermo's.

'Women!' he thought. 'So this is why you've been speaking English all evening instead of your droll and delightful Louisiana French! For Willy's benefit. Poor boy, he seems well hooked! All right, I'll tug on the line too, in order to see exactly what you're angling for, you lovely little witch!' Aloud, he said:

"Well, child, after I'd finished my studies, late in my thirties, and had time to think about the matter, I soon perceived a strange social phenomenon: all the girls fled screaming from any room as soon as I entered it. Especially if they were pretty. And any maiden hardy enough to endure my presence without falling into fainting fits burst into gales of hysterical laughter the moment I popped the question. So I decided that I obviously wasn't husband and father material, and gave the whole thing up as a rum job. Why, my little Circe?"

"Circe?" Mireille said.

"A sorceress. Like—you, dear."

"You mean a witch, don't you, Enrique?" Willy said darkly.

"Well—to some extent, yes. But a charming one," Enrique Sepúlvera laughed. "Come now, Mireille; why are you pretending interest in my legal state?"

"I'm not pretending, Dr. Enrique. I think you're one of the handsomest men I've ever met. And the kindest. Would you marry *me?*"

Enrique smiled at her, threw a quick wink in Willy's direction, and said, "Don't know. Why don't you propose to me and find out?"

Mireille pushed her chair back and came around the table to where the doctor sat.

"Turn your chair around—please?" she said.

Smiling, Enrique turned his high-backed Castilian-style chair around. Mireille knelt at his feet and took his two hands in her own.

"Dearest Don Enrique," she said solemnly, "will you do me the high honor of becoming my lawfully wedded husband, and the father of the twenty children I hope to have?"

Enrique threw back his head and laughed aloud.

"Heaven forbid!" he said.

"Why not, dearest darling Don Enrique?" Mireille said dolefully. "I love you. I love you very dearly."

"Horse business!" Enrique chuckled. "Go ask Willy—whom you *do* love. And who loves you, or I miss my guess!"

"I did, already—more or less. He doesn't want me. Because, as you know only too well, dear Doctor, I have been—am—a whore."

'So that's the rub!' Enrique thought. He said, in a troubled tone of voice, "A pity. A very great pity. But I have to admit he has a point there, my dear . . ."

"Ohhhhh!" Mireille wailed theatrically, and jumped to her feet. "And me thinking you were broad-minded, Don Enrique!"

"I am. I'd marry you in a minute if you were nearer my age, which you aren't, and if you loved me, which you don't. And also because I'd be perfectly capable of beating hell out of you every time you needed it, which would be, I sadly fear, daily. But Willy is a romantic, an approach to life that should be prohibited by law. So—a marriage between the two of you probably wouldn't work. Look, my dear, in my medical practice I've seen a good many weddings between ex-demimondaines and scions of old families. Practically all of them ended badly. Certain experiences leave—scars. Invisible scars, of course, but—"

"Mine are visible," Mireille said quietly. "I look like a zebra. Or I would, if they were black. Instead, they're white—whiter than the rest of my skin. But they show. Because a man considered me—such a thing as he could strip naked before a crowd of other men, and—beat. With a bullwhip."

"I know. I treated those whiplashes of yours, remember?" Enrique sighed. "But even so, it's exactly the sort of experience I meant. For the scars it left in your tender flesh are far less important than the ones it burned into your psyche, Mireille. Living a lifetime with another person calls for patience, tact, comprehension, willingness to forgive and forget, that are very close to heroic, my dear. Look, I don't scorn you. If marriage were a thing that concerned but the two of you, I'd say, 'Go right ahead; you have my blessing!' But it also concerns, terribly, your offspring. D'you know what kind of mother a woman who has been taught to despise herself makes? Well, I can tell you in a line: the sort who fills up the reformatories, jails, and brothels with her children!"

"All right," Mireille said gravely. "Lend Willy a penny, Don Enrique . . ."

"A penny? Good lord, child—why?"

"To pay me for going to bed with him tonight. That's all I'm worth.

And I can't, for free. That would be—unprofessional, wouldn't it? Anyhow, I'm going to. You don't mind, do you?"

"Yes, I do mind. But not for any hypothetical question of morality. Rather because you seem to be contemplating this—act—for the wrong reasons, my child. Abed, a couple should make love, not vent their anger, disappointments, feelings of unworthiness, of guilt upon each other. . . ."

"Agreement's off," Willy said grimly; "I'm going to bolt my door!"

"I'll wake the whole house up, screaming outside it in the hall, if you do," Mireille said solemnly. "Or take an ax, and break it down, or—"

That was as far as she got. A slim young Mexican, sombrero cocked jauntily on one side of his head, boots and spurs on his feet, two Colt Dragoon revolvers in holsters slung from his belt, came pounding into the dining room, with fat Josefina, Don Enrique's cook and serving maid right behind him.

"Halt Three Fingers!" Josefina shrieked. "I told you they were eating and you—"

"It's all right, Josefina," Don Enrique said; "we have finished supper. Leave him alone. Well, Three Fingers, what can I do for you?"

The young Mexican pushed his sombrero back off his forehead, and Mireille saw why he was called *Tres Dedos*, "Three Fingers." On his right hand only the thumb, third and little fingers were left. Someone—with a machete, very likely—had severed the other two.

"For me, nothing, Don Enrique," Three Fingers said in Spanish; "But for the friend of this loveliest of ladies, much."

"*My* friend?" Mireille said. "Which friend of mine, Señor Three Fingers?"

"A girl called Paquita. Also very beautiful. Or she *was* . . ."

"Good God!" Mireille said.

"What happened to her, Manolo?" Willy said.

"A gringo has raped her," Three Fingers sighed. "A very big gringo, who is also mad. Doña Marta told us he is called *el Maniaco*. . . ."

"Oh, no!" Mireille wailed. "Not again!"

"*Oh, sí,*" Three Fingers said, "once more! It appears to be a custom of his, this of violating *chicas*. We had gone to the *posada* searching for thee, sweet William! Because Joaquin wishes that your worship should bring your good-for-nothings to join forces with us on a job. . . ."

"*¡Basta de bromas!*" Willy snapped. "Get to the point, Manolo!"

"The point has already been got by the loveliest girlfriend of your also too lovely little friend here. Or rather it has been shoved up her by this brute of a gringo. Along with breaking all her bones, or nearly. Doña

Marta asks that you come with all speed Señor Don Doctor Killer of the Healthy! Doña Marta is distraught. She fears the lovely Paquita will die. I think she is wrong. La Paquita seems to me to be in not much danger, though yes, in considerable pain. I, too, respectfully ask that you come along with me, Señor Doctor! I desire that you cure La Paci as soon as possible—that I may shove *mine* up her once she is well. With her consent, of course. And her cooperation, presumably ardent!"

"Animal!" Willy said.

"Willy!" Mireille said. "Go hitch up the horses to the buckboard! I've got to go back to San Francisco to take care of Paci. She'll need nursing, and—"

"No," Dr. Sepúlvera said sternly. "You must rest, Mireille, or else *you* will go into a decline. You're on the edge of a consumption now. When I can—when she is up to it—I will bring Paquita down here, too. She's that stunning little dark creature who's so devoted to you, isn't she? No arguments, now! I forbid you to leave here, Mireille! Willy, I leave you in charge of the *rancho.* Now I'll go get my bag . . ."

"And I'll go saddle a mount for you," Willy said. He turned to Three Fingers. "Have you eaten, Manolo?" he asked.

"No. And I have much desire to. Starting with this dainty little morsel of thine. Raw."

"She is tougher than she looks," Willy said; "also indigestible. Very. I'll tell Josefina to bring you some supper. Don't be afraid of him, Mirla; all his force escapes him through his mouth. . . ."

"Señor Three Fingers—" Mireille began, once Willy had left the room.

"Manolo to thee, loveliness. That's my name. Three-Fingered Jack is only a nickname which I was given for obvious reasons. But I call myself Manuel Garcia, the same as the owner of the Boar's Head, though we are, thank God, not even kin. Therefore, Manolo at your service, beautiful! Such a service, for instance, as violating thee a little, and very gently, before this idiot of a Willy comes back! What d'you say?"

"Why, yes, of course!" Mireille laughed, "but it will have to be some other night, Manolo dear. It won't take Willy more than ten minutes to saddle the doctor's horse, and being raped that quickly isn't any fun. I prefer to take my time, especially with a handsome man like you! Now tell me about Paci. She—she isn't dying, is she?"

"No. She has simply been beaten black and blue, and has her right arm broken. Also three ribs. We have this Maniac tied up in the wine cellar of Señora Gonzales' inn. Tonight, very late, when all the gringos are sleeping, we will take him out and drag him at the end of our lassos as we gallop up and down some very rocky mountain trails. When we have finished, he will be dead. But he will have died very slowly, and very badly. There will scarcely be enough meat left on his bones for the buzzards to eat . . .."

"No," Mireille said; "don't do that, Manolo."

"And why not, Loveliest Mirla? I have been told that it was thee who notched his snout for him. Is this true?"

"Yes. And for excellent reasons which also, doubtless, you have been told. No matter. I don't want you to kill him. Promise me you won't."

"Same question again: Why not, mistress of my heart?"

"Killing is too good for him," Mireille said in a slow, still tone of voice that made Three-Fingered Jack stare at her in sudden wonder, as many another man was to stare at her throughout her long life when he suddenly perceived her real quality: that she was made of frost and flint, and had a backbone of tempered steel. "And any way you do it, it's over too fast. So, don't kill him. *Cut* him."

"Cut him?" Three Fingers whispered. "You mean—?"

"Exactly what you think I do. Let him go through life like that. Unable to do *anything* to a woman. Remembering how it used to be, before, when he was still—a man. Or anyhow, a beast and a brute. Can you think of a worse punishment? A lifetime of—*nothing* before him. Melting into grease. His voice growing high and squeaky. Throwing away his razor because he doesn't need it anymore. And—no woman in his bed. Not *ever*. If anyone gave you the choice between *that*, Manolo, and death, which would you choose?"

"Death!" Manolo said. "Without even having to think about it, Mirla!"

"Exactly. So would he. Therefore, do not give him that choice. He has been—a bull, long enough. Convert him into—an ox. A steer. Will you do that for me, Manolo? And for—Paquita?"

"Yes," Three Fingers whispered. "Oh, yes. And with great pleasure, little Mirla!"

"Thank you," Mireille whispered, and going up on tiptoe, kissed Manolo Garcia, Three-Fingered Jack, slowly, lingeringly, on the mouth.

At three o'clock of the morning of that same night, Guillermo heard the knocking on his door. It wasn't loud enough to have awakened him if he had been asleep. But he wasn't asleep. He had been lying there on his narrow bed all night long, as rigid as a bone, waiting for that knocking to start.

But when it came, finally, he didn't get up and let her in. He lay there sweating, as cool as it was. And—suffering.

He thought: I can't, I won't. This is no good and will end badly if I do. Because you see, Mirla, I love you. Just like I loved Sara or maybe even more. And you've been the plaything toy of a thousand men, two thousand, five—who knows? All those stinking unwashed louse-infested gringo swine have forced your slender milk-white thighs apart, impaled you upon their billy-goat bull-beast stallion-*pollas* and humped and bucked and snorted, gnawing at your lips your throat your breasts until you'd drained all the heat out of them, all the fury, leaving them sprawled like dead necrophiliacs atop your mashed flat breath gone bruised, bleeding, profaned and trembling little corpse—

So I can't—take you—the way—the only way I want you which is as the wife of my bosom and the mother of my sons. I'd always remember. And go mad. And if any child of ours were a daughter—*¡Jesús!* I can't I can't I won't I—

And then he heard, faintly through the stout wooden door, the soft, utterly hopeless, throat-raking rasp and gasp and strangle of her crying.

He got up then, went to the door, opened it, let her in.

She came into the room. Stood there looking at him in the lamplight. She went on crying in a way that was very bad, gut-shredding, ugly, but that he couldn't turn away from, or close his eyes to, or otherwise halt, or lessen its impact upon his mind. The tears on her face weren't individual droplets but a solid, downwashing sheet, a flood. Her lips quivered like an idiot child's—helplessly, hopelessly—making a pale pink blur, moving, moving in the small, heart-shaped desolation of her face.

He stood there staring at her until he couldn't bear what was in her eyes anymore, couldn't support that much heartbreak, longing, anguished tenderness, all intermixed with such bleak, abysmal shame, so he stepped up to her, took her in his arms, bent and kissed her mouth.

Her hands came up and locked behind his head, her slender fingers, trembling and remote, working, working through his thick dark-blond hair. She tore her mouth away from his and buried her face in the hollow of his throat, grinding nose and opened lips, and wild, darting tongue tip scaldingly against his flesh, all over his adam's apple, his chin, as high up his cheeks as she could reach; crying, sobbing, crazy, wild, her hands become claws, dragging his face down to within the reach of her feral, devouring kisses, her whole body beneath her thin muslin nightgown transformed into an instrument of torture, lacerating him all along his length.

He stiffened his arms, pushed her away from him. Held her there.

She said, sobbing the word, "Please!"

He bent, swept one arm behind her knees, the other around her back just below her shoulder blades, lifted her off the floor, carried her to the bed, laid her down.

She caught his right hand, dragged it down, curving his fingers with her own two hands over and into the chaste neckband of her gown where it lay in a soft, ruffled curve, high around her slender throat. Then she was still, staring at him, her eyes tear-glazed, blind.

"Rip it off me," she said with terrible bitterness. "Treat me like the whore you think I am . . ."

His fingers opened, came away, leaving the gown intact. He stood there by the bed, looking at her. He didn't move. Nor breathe. Nor think.

Slowly, holding him with her eyes, she put down her hands and caught the lace-trimmed hem of the nightgown, raked it waist high, sat up in bed, clawed that modest garment upward in a twisting swirl of white over her head, hurled it to the floor. Lay back down again in the sooty smoke cloud of her endless mane of hair, her body whiter than white, than any possible similes, metaphors: milk, snow, moonglow, starlight, a cry. Except where it wasn't, where it tangled his breath with the shock of abrupt and startling contrasts: a pubic brush bristling high as a Mohican's scalp lock, crow-feather straight, blacker than sin at midnight, sable on snow, inkblots on a love letter, death and forever, jet, pitch, shame; the huge, wine-dark areolas, busy about their desire-triggered female witchery-bitchery of tumescence, slowly swallowing the already long since erected twin phalli of her nipples, as they puckered and pouted under the wonder and worship of his gaze.

She stretched out her slim white arms to him, said—what? He saw her lips trembling into the shape of syllables that were surely an invitation, a caress, but her tears drowned them out of intelligibility, so that what reached his ears was but the strangled rasping of a sob.

He wrought a momentary destruction of beauty, continuity, poetry, as he bent to the unaesthetic, awkward, all but comical necessity of pushing the knee-length white cotton drawers that were the only garment he had on, down his slim flanks until they dropped around his ankles. He hopped and skipped frantically out of them, which had the saving grace of making her smile. Then he leaped into bed beside her, tried to pull the coverlet up over them both.

He couldn't. Mireille was lying on top of it.

"No," she whispered, "please, no. I—*want* to see you. I want you to see me . . ."

"You—you're beautiful!" he breathed. Then his pale eyes congealed—froze. He put out his hand and let his fingertips trace one of the livid, dead-white scars of Big Jules's whiplashes. It curled around her rib cage, blazed pink-silver into her flesh, up, even the soft, conical mound of her left breast, almost to its wine-red taut swollen peak.

"I'm *glad* I killed him!" he grated.

"I'm not," she said gravely. "Somebody had to, I suppose. But—somebody else. Not—you. . . ."

"He—he hurt you! He—"

She loosed a curiously girlish little gurgle of laughter.

"All right," she said solemnly, "suppose you kiss it—and make it well."

He bent to that task with considerable enthusiasm.

She stroked the burnt-honey, sunlight-threaded, thick thatch of his hair.

"Mama's baby," she crooned with tender mockery; "mama's little, hungry, baby boy!"

He straightened up at once, glared at her. He had, of course, a sense of humor, but it was of the Hispano-American variety. Jokes turning upon his dignity or his manhood—chronological or sexual—simply had no place in it.

"I'm sorry," she said. "I was only teasing. Don't look at me so ferociously, please! Willy—"

"Yes, Mirla?"

"Let's not spoil tonight. It may be—the only one we'll ever have. Let's be—very careful with each other. Please."

"All right," he said. "But you needn't worry, little blackbird mine, I'm not the sort of brute you're accustomed to."

She bent her head. Held it bent a small aeon, a tiny age. He saw her tears drip off her pert, upturned nose tip, splash against her breasts.

"God save me!" he groaned. "Mirla, I'm sorry! I—"

"It's—all right," she said slowly, sadly. "You can't forget what I've—been. You—never will. I don't even expect you to. But I do ask you to remember—just one thing—"

"Which is?" he said contritely.

"That tonight it—my past—doesn't apply. You're—you. And I love you. Nothing in my life—no experience I've had—has prepared me for the way I feel about you. And d'you know what, Willy? I—I'm scared to death!"

"So am I," he said, meaning it.

She loosed a little purr of laughter, humid with choked-back tears.

"Good!" she said. "Willy, will you—let *me*—make love to *you?*"

He was anything but insensitive; he caught the emphasis, slight as it was, she had placed upon those words.

"Why?" he said.

"Don't know. Because I—*want* to. And to—change your mind about a couple of things . . . ."

"What things, little Mirla?"

"About—me. About—you. About—us. About—a man and a woman —together. About—love. *This* kind of love, especially. Men don't know *anything* about women."

"Nor women about men!"

"Granted," she said with another sad little silver tinkle of laughter, "if you'll grant me that there's much less to know. We're—far more complicated, my darling! For instance, if it had been left with you, we'd have *finished* making love by now."

"You're right," he sighed; "we're horny little bastards, aren't we?"

"While we women are—sensual. We want love—the act of love— making love—to last as long as possible. Or even longer than *im*possible! To go on and on and on—sweetly, slowly, softly—"

"*Softly* won't do much good if one is a man!" he quipped.

"Oh, you! Willy—lie back down. For the next hour—I hope!—you're *mine*. To do what I want with. Agreed?"

"Short of decapitation—or castration, anyhow," he said solemnly, "agreed!"

"Death by exhaustion is—much more interesting. And the wearing away of—protuberances—by erosion, say—is more pleasant than the knife. Now, shut up, will you? Let me—see . . . Let me see . . . ."

She knelt beside him on the bed. Her hair spilled down like a night cloud, shadowing his face.

"One more thing," she whispered, laughing, laughing. "Whatever I do to you—no matter how *awful*—you must promise me to keep perfect-ly still! All right?"

"All right," he groaned.

A few minutes later, a very few, he cried out in the voice of a man being slowly strangled:

"Mireille, stop it. I can't take any more!"

"We said—an hour. That was the agreement, Willy darling. You're a very bad sportsman. What's the matter, aren't you game?"

"You said you were going to make love to me—not *torture* me to death!"

"*This* is torture?" she purred, and went on with what she was doing, which was to flower-print his whole body with soft, warm, wet kisses, pressed open-mouthed against his flesh, a delicate, spiral tracery of tongue tip, then on and on and on, her fingers straying, straying, moth wings, white butterflies, vibrant upon his coppery skin.

"*¡Jesús, María y José!*" he all but wept.

"All right, all right; I'll—ease you," she murmured, and curtained his loins with the foaming midnight of her hair. He felt that hot, sweet wetness engulf him, and stretched out his hand to pull her away from there. But his very strength failed him, drowned, lost in waves of indescribably exquisite sensation: softness, warmth, moisture, slow-sliding ingurgitation, diabolically persistent and controlled, the halts calculated to an unmeasurable fraction of a second to prolong his agony, the auditory accompaniment woodwinds played underwater, sea-bottom deep; soup sounds, gently gurgling, muffled, unbelievably thrilling, sweet . . .

He felt two claws, one of fire, the other of ice, bite into the back part of his brain, ripping, tearing, dragging everything out of him: mind, spirit, will, identity itself, erupting lavalike, bursting, spurting, jetting, thickening the soup sounds, drowning them. He died. Flew up to heaven. Plunged down to hell. Came back to earth. To that narrow bed.

She smiled at him, her lips warm, milky, glistening.

"Feel better—now?" she said.

"No!" he groaned; "I feel like hell! Why on earth did you have to go and do—that?"

She shrugged. "I love you," she said quietly. "Therefore to me—all of you—is sweet. . . ."

By morning, he realized that he was both lost and damned, that he would be enslaved by this carnal witchcraft until he died. Despairingly he turned his eyes from her, gazed out of the window into the graying dawn.

"Look at me!" she said sharply.

He turned, stared upward into her small, tormented face. She sat fully impaled upon him, upright astride his loins, riding him slowly, slowly. About her little witch-queen's head swirled the Stygian midnight of her hair. Strands of it plastered filaments of darkness, wild-tangled, wet across her cheeks, trailing into her mouth between lips dark-bruised, blood-gorged, shockingly swollen, caught in convulsively bitten tufts by the locked and savagely grinding mist-pearls of her teeth. Through that Tartarean veil, her eyes gleamed dully, blue-ringed, bloodshot, deep-sunken, utterly weary. She looked like a martyr at the stake, three quarters dead of torture. Like the patron saint of all the whores on earth. Like

Hecate, primordial mother of all witches. Like Circe, the swine-maker. Like hell.

"I—can—now—again," she whispered hoarsely, pushing the words out on little pulsations, spurts of breath. "Come, I mean. For—the—last time, surely. Can you, too? With me?"

"I don't—know," he said, tiredly; "you have—used me up, Mireille. . . ."

"Try!" she said harshly. "I want to feel you—let go, start pumping—steam-scalding all my insides out . . ."

"Look, Mirla, I—"

"You *can*. I'll make you. Now put your hands up and clutch my breasts. When I say 'Now!'—squeeze them. *Hurt* them. Try to make them—burst—between your fingers—"

"God!" he said.

"I am going to do away with the two of us, Willy darling. By—exhaustion. The perfect ending to our love story, isn't it? Dying—of love itself. What other—finish—could be so sweet?"

"You're crazy, Mirla! Stark raving!"

"Yes, I am mad. Mad for the love of a man I cannot—keep. So now to see that—no other bitch-kitty gets her claws into him! This is our last goodbye, sweet Willy! You don't believe me? You'll see—you'll see!"

She stiffened her knees, rising, rising; slammed down again with terrible force, twisted her hips, her pelvis through an incredible thirty-degree alternation of arc, her head thrown back, her hair swirling, foaming, her whole body sweat-glistened, pounding, gyrating, grinding upon him with berserk ferocity, using up the last of her own strength—will—desire, so that when her mouth tore open finally, gulping air, her teeth glittering eerily in the morning light, the cry she gave—birdsong at dawning!—throbbing, trilling poignantly, unbearably sobbing-sweet—wasn't even loud.

"Now!" she wept, breathed, gasped, murmured, her voice a tropic tide, far off and faint, ebbing slowly out of time and mind as it beat in receding wavelets against his ear; "Now! *Oh Bon Petit Jésus!* Hear our funeral bells at midnight! How I love it love it love it! Love—you. . . ."

And collapsed like a lighted taper, melting, melting into every pore of him, all her fair flesh a-shudder, fighting for breath, for life amid the whirlpool, the black Lethean waters of that small, but by no means less dreadful, death.

He lay there stroking her wet, wild-tangled hair and listening to her crying. It was very nearly impossible to bear.

"Hush, Mirla," he crooned; "Don't cry, my love! I am here. And we—"

"Willy," she whispered, *"must* you leave me? Can't we just—stay together? I—don't ask anything of you but—once in a while—your presence. I'll wait—very humbly—in your blind alleys—the back streets of your life. No priest—no papers. Just—*you.* Whatever little of you I can have. Some hours—some days—or a week or two, when it's possible, stolen out of your life and granted to this—famished beggar, for as long as you're willing to let her live!"

He turned his head. Looked out the window. Said bleakly, slowly, fighting against his deepest convictions, against all the concepts of male honor he believed in, held dear:

"You were—forced into that life. Who am I to hold it against you? You'll have your papers—and your priest—Mirla. My name and my pledged word before God and man. When Enrique comes back, we'll arrange it. We'll ride into San José, and—"

She surged up like a wild thing, and almost broke his mouth, clung to him, crying, crying.

But actually, she knew better than that. Life just doesn't accommodate profound changes in a man's—or a woman's—character, insurmountable obstacles thrown down by pure—or impure!—love. Not *her* life, anyhow.

So even as she clung to him, weeping from what she told herself was joy, she was dimly conscious of the fact that at least half of her tears were born of—fear. She resisted that knowledge fiercely.

She shouldn't have.

Lacrimo ergo sum! (I weep, therefore I am!)

4

GUILLERMO KILPATRICK LOOKED AT MIREILLE. SHOOK HIS HEAD with the weary resignation of a saint grown accustomed to perpetual martyrdom.

"Our Father which art in Heaven! What's wrong *now*, Mirla?" he said.

"Nothing," Mireille said, and went on crying.

"People do not cry over nothing," he pointed out to her, trying to keep the exasperation out of his voice; "not the way you're crying, little blackbird. Come now, tell a fellow: What's wrong?"

"I told you it was—nothing," she said sullenly. "Oh, all right, all right! Since you insist upon prying into things that don't concern you: *J'ai tombée du toit . . .*"

"Whaaat?" he said.

"*J'ai tombée du toit*—I have fallen off the roof. Oh, *merde!* I mean it's the wrong time of the month. I have my period—the *curse,* dammit!"

"Oh—*that,*" he said. "Good! Now I'll get a little rest!"

She glared at him.

"Willy—" she said bitterly; "don't—sound—so *glad.*"

"Now, Mirla—" he said.

"I've told you and told you that you don't have to marry me. Not even if I were going to have the baby you haven't been obliging enough to give me. Especially since you so obviously don't want me as your wife. That has nothing to do with this."

"Mirla, you agreed to wait until Enrique comes back. You said yourself that you wanted Paquita to be your bridesmaid. So you know what the problem has been—"

"Yes. That poor Paci has internal injuries, as well as all those broken bones. That Doctor Enrique has had his hands full to merely keep her from dying. Willy, Old John told me that Three Fingers was here yesterday—another thing you didn't bother to mention, or rather have deliberately hidden from me—and that the two of you had a long, long conversation out on the south range. Did *Tres Dedos* come through San Francisco? He usually does, doesn't he?"

"Yes," Willy said shortly.

"Then he told you about Paci. He's awfully smitten with her, as you know very well. Willy! Don't tell me she—she's *worse!* Is that why you didn't tell me Manolo was here? Or even bring him up to the house? Or —or anything?"

"No; she's not worse. In fact, she's much better. She's going to get well. . . ."

"Oh, thank God!" Mireille said fervently.

"Amen," Willy said dryly.

Mireille peered at him.

"You don't seem very happy about it," she said.

"Oh, I am. Paci's a sweet child. She deserves all the best. I admit I'm —well—a little preoccupied, but not about *her.* If you must know, I'm kind of worried about—Enrique . . ."

"Doctor Sepúlvera? *Sacre Nom*, Willy—why?"

"According to Manolo, Enrique's—fallen in love with her, the damned old fool!"

"Oh!" Mireille said.

"Don't look at me like that! It has nothing to do with *us*—"

"Hasn't it?" Mireille said, very, very softly.

"No. Absolutely nothing. But Holy Mary, Mirla! Enrique is forty-seven years old! How old is Paci?"

"Eighteen," Mireille lied; "nineteen, maybe. Why?"

"That's too much difference. Nearly thirty years. When she's thirty, the age when women really begin to get some pleasure out of life—to enjoy being bedded, to tell the unvarnished truth about it!—he'll be sixty, or thereabouts . . ."

"I'm glad to know *that*," Mireille said.

"You're glad to know that Enrique's *asking* for the disastrous situation of being a graybeard with a young and delectable wife?"

"No. I'm glad to know that I'll enjoy it even more at thirty than I do now. If so, *you'll* be in a disastrous situation, love of my life. Such as having to use a wheelchair to get about in. That is, if you haven't skipped by then. Which is probably what you've got in mind. And exactly what you *ought* to do."

"I only have it in mind when you're being even more of a witch than usual. But, for curiosity's sake: Why d'you think it is what I ought to do?"

"Because you don't trust me. You think—rather *know*—that I'm—a whore. A real one. By—instinct. *Born* that way, I mean."

"*¡Mierda!*" Willy swore. "Mirla, I'm going to *hit* you in a minute!"

"Go ahead. It might make you feel better. And nothing could make me feel worse . . ."

"No thanks! Look, little bird, I haven't any doubts—reservations— about you. About us. Not anymore. If you were—had been—the kind of a *chica* who just drifts into the bad life because of her natural tendencies, and because she'd made such a mess out of her life that it was the only thing left for her to do, I wouldn't have fallen in love with you in the first place. But you were forced into that life. So I'm sure that, given any kind of a chance, you'll make a good and faithful wife, and—"

She stared at him. "You're mad. Crazy. What is that you say in Spanish? Oh, yes: *'¡Loco de remate!'* Crazy enough to be rekilled. Stark raving. Tell me something, lover mine. Haven't my—sweet and gentle— bedroom manners taught you, even yet, that you are wrong?"

"No. Just the opposite. Listen, Mirla, I told you that I haven't been— well—exactly a saint of chastity. So I know what the girls of the bad life are *really* like . . ."

"Not like *me?*" she said.

"Not at all. You are—a warm-natured girl, to put it mildly . . ."

"I am a maniac. Just like *el Maniaco* who almost killed poor Paci. Only I don't beat men to death. I just wear them out. Kill them by exhaustion. Which is more diverting. But you were saying that the girls for sale—or rather for hire—*aren't* like that? Paci isn't, that's for sure."

"No. Not at all. They're cold. A hot-natured girl couldn't stand that life. It would kill her . . ."

"Hmmmmmn—true. It almost did, me. Go on."

"Besides, they hate men. A good many of them are *tortilleras, marimachos, lesbianas* . . ."

"Also like me. I tried to seduce Paci. But she wasn't having any, thank you. A pity. That would have been—very interesting, don't you think?"

"Oh God!" he groaned. "Can't we have a sensible conversation, ever?"

"I doubt it. Let's see what we've got to: Since I'm hotter than a stove lid, and an unsuccessful lesbian, that makes me a *good* girl?"

"If either were true, which they aren't, they would still make you very far from the type of poor bedraggled slut who falls into that life. Your sins would be different. Grander. You'd probably be the kept mistress of a prime minister, or a prince—"

"I am," she said gravely; "of a prince, anyhow. The sweetest, best, handsomest, bravest in all the world. Right out of a fairy tale. And I'm going to love him till the day I die. Even after that. I'll either chant hosannas to his name in heaven—or scream it out from amid the fire and brimstone down in hell. . . ."

"Oh, Mirla!" he moaned, and kissed her.

"Willy," she whispered, "you're right. I *was* forced into that life. But how you define that word 'forced' might depend a great deal on your way of looking at things. If you ever found out that I wasn't all that forced— or maybe, from your point of view, not forced at all—what would you do? Leave me?"

"I don't know. Go crazy, likely. Or—die. Yes—surely die. Of a broken heart."

"Oh, Willy!" she wailed, and started crying again.

"There, there! Let's stop talking nonsense—and gloomy nonsense at that. Look, dearest, I have to go away. For about a week. Maybe a little longer . . ."

"Oh, no!" she said.

"I'm sorry, blackbird, but I have to. It's—a moral obligation. I owe it to the man who once saved my life."

"Then go. But first, tell me his name."

"Why?" Willy said.

"So I can bless him in my prayers every minute of the day and night. What does he call himself, *mon amour?*"

"Not Your Love, that's for sure. Though he probably would, if he ever saw you. Only Rosita would shoot him if he tried it. And she's just as good with a gun as he is. . . ."

"Rosita?" Mireille said.

"Rosita Felix. His wife."

"Then his name is Señor Felix?"

"No! No, of course not. Women in the Spanish-speaking countries don't lose their maiden names when they marry. They merely add *Señora de,* wife of, and their husband's name behind them. You'll be Mireille Duclos, *Señora de* Kilpatrick, soon now. . . ."

"I hope so. But you're stalling. Whom is she Rosita Felix 'of'?"

"I'd rather not tell you. Not his family names, anyhow. Oh no, not because I don't trust you—but if there ever were any kind of a slipup, say, it would be much better for you not to know. If the sherriff of this county came here asking questions, he'd see in a minute that you really haven't the first idea what this is all about and leave you in peace."

"Then he's some kind of a criminal, this friend of yours?" Mireille said.

"*I* am a criminal. I killed Big Jules, remember. And another man whose name I don't even know . . ."

"Over me. Exterminating vermin is an honorable profession. What's his name, Willy?"

"Joaquin. Settle for that, will you? I *won't* tell you any more."

"All right. I'll pray for Joaquin, then. God will know *which* Joaquin I mean. Willy, tell me something else: Does Paci—reciprocate? Don Enrique is—bald. Short. Not at all good-looking. And Paci is a romantic sort of a girl. That Don Enrique is rich might not matter all that much to her. So tell me, Willy darling, what does Paci think about having a middle-aged man like Don Enrique in love with her?"

"She seems delighted with the idea, according to Three Fingers. And quite honestly in love with Enrique, too. The whole thing got started when Enrique told her she was out of danger. So she asked him—with the requisite downcast eyes and bated breath, of course!—whether that meant he'd be leaving for the *rancho* soon—"

"And he said, 'Why yes, my dear, of course.' Whereupon she burst into tears and wailed, 'Ohhhhhh, Don Enrique! I'm going to miss you so!' "

"Lord!" Willy said. "Her exact words! You *are* a witch, Mirla! Or else you saw Manolo before or after I did, and he—"

"No. Nobody told me. No one had to. I just know women, that's all. We really aren't very original, are we? So Don Enrique, who has never been very successful as a lady-killer, was—quite flattered. Paquita is very lovely, Willy. And, unlike you, Don Enrique is broad-minded. He'll trust Paci not to warm his bed with somebody else the first night he's out of it. Speaking of which, you were clever, weren't you? You picked just the right time to leave me alone—when I can't do anything much to get even. Oh, well, I'll think of something. There's more than one way to skin a cat, y'know!"

"I'll adopt the one the late Big Jules tried on you. Maybe a few more stripes would improve that terrible disposition you've got. For, as Enrique used to say whenever the subject of marriage came up, 'Willy, my boy, as both a preventative and a cure, wife beating has much to recommend it!' Now pucker up and give me a kiss. I really must be off, blackbird. I've got an awfully long ride in front of me. . . ."

When he was safely out of sight on the road leading north toward San Francisco, Mireille immediately went in search of Don Enrique's cook, Josefina. The conversation she intended to have with Josefina presented grave difficulties, for, although fat Josefina was an incurable gossip who would readily and gladly tell her all she wanted to know, the fact remained that Josefina must necessarily deliver that information in Spanish, a language that Mireille was only just beginning to learn. But Mireille was sure that because both her native French and Josefina's Spanish sprang from Latin, she'd be able to understand Don Enrique's overstuffed cook readily enough.

She was wrong. What Mireille spoke was Louisiana patois, somewhat purified by her schooling; and what Josefina spoke was Mexican—that is, Spanish much corrupted by Aztec, Tarascan, Toltec, Mayan, and a number of other aboriginal tongues. Besides which, Spanish and French are about as far apart as it is possible for two Latin languages to get. So poor Mireille had quite a struggle of it.

Joaquin, she gathered, was a formidable uncle and a hero. (It wasn't until months later that she learned that "uncle" in racy folk Spanish was a slang expression for "type," "character," or "individual," so that *"a* formidable uncle" and *"my* formidable uncle" meant two different things, for while the first signified any picturesque ruffian who excited interest or admiration, the second indicated the imposing and respected brother of one's father or one's mother.) His name, she deduced from the flood of Mexican Spanish that Josefina poured into her defenseless ears, was Joaquin Carillo, although he had recently changed it to Joaquin Murieta; just as his wife, Rosita Felix, was no longer called that, but Antonia Molinera instead.

Now Mireille had lived in San Francisco's underworld long enough to learn that when people changed their names their reasons for doing so probably wouldn't stand public scrutiny. Besides, that name "Murieta" rang a bell in her memory. She had heard the miners in the Dirty Spoon frequently discuss one Joaquin Murieta, which discussion always consisted of bluesmoking the very air with unspeakably vile, and imaginatively inventive, profanity at the very mention of his name. She'd shut her ears to most of it, being still a well-brought-up Creole young lady in her heart of hearts, but one thing had stuck: after running up and down his family tree in hobnail boots, and accusing him of maintaining incestuous sexual relations with all his close female relatives, and even of committing sodomy upon his horse, the stream of almost unbelievably filthy invectives had always ended with the words, "murdering greaser bandit!"

So evidently here was a radical division of opinion. The man whom Josefina called *"¡Un tío formidable y un héroe!"* was, in the opinion of the gringos, "A horse and mother-gripping greaser bandit." So she asked Josefina that:

"¿Pero es un bandido?"

The way she pronounced that Spanish phrase made Josefina roar with laughter.

"The gringos call him that," the cook explained. "To us, *los Mejicanos*, he is a fighter for freedom, and one of the greatest heroes we've ever had. You see, lovely miss Mirla, he first started his private war against the Americans after they had jumped his claim in the goldfields, violated poor Rosita before his very eyes, beat him, Joaquin, bloody with horse-whips, and murdered his brother. So, naturally, Joaquin swore eternal vengeance against all gringos. By now he has killed every man who jumped his claim and abused Rosita. He has also killed every man who hanged his brother and cut his back to ribbons with whiplashes. . . ."

"I don't blame him. I know how *that* feels," Mireille whispered. "But why do you think he's a hero, Josefina?"

"Because he *is*," Josefina said firmly, "a very great hero, Señorita Mirla! Much of what he steals from the gringos he gives to the poor of our race. And since the gringos tax us as foreigners for the right to stake a claim—we who were here before them, for the most part—and then jump our claims when we find gold, rob our cattle, destroy our *ranchos* and rape any woman of our people who has less than eighty years and happens to be a little prettier than the hindquarters of a burro, we are mostly poor. Don Enrique escapes our fate because, having no Indian blood, his skin is whiter than that of most gringos. And *tu* Willy is not recognizable as a Mejicano once he puts on gringo clothes and speaks English."

"Josefina—tell me: What is the connection between Three Fingers-Manolo Garcia and Joaquin Murieta?"

"Tres Dedos" is Joaquin's lieutenant. His second-in-command," Josefina said.

"Then—then—" Mireille gasped, "Willy is—*also*—?"

"A member of Joaquin's band?" Josefina said. "No, Señorita Mirla, he is not. Willy has his own band—braver and better fighters, for the most part, than Joaquin's—always excepting Joaquin himself, who simply does not know what fear is. Sometimes, of course usually at Joaquin's request, the two bands join forces—"

"Oh God!" Mireille moaned. Josefina stared at her.

"In this you are right, señorita," she sighed. "It is—much too danger-

ous. That's one thing. Another is that Willy has not the true temperament of a bandit. He is much too kindhearted. In a fight, when his blood
is up, he can kill a man—"

"I know," Mireille whispered.

"But he has not this—sickness of cruelty that Joaquin has developed.
The other day, Joaquin raided a mining camp of Chinamen. He tied the
pigtails of all six of them together, and then cut their throats. He and
Willy quarreled over that. Willy swore at him, saying that such unnecessary killings and bootless cruelty are demeaning to our cause. It was,
Three Fingers told me, the second time they have disputed hotly over
this subject."

"And—the first?"

"When *Tres Dedos* showed him what they'd done to *el Maniaco,* in
vengeance for his *violación* of that poor little friend of yours—Paquita,
her name is, no? That sight made Willy sick. He lost his lunch . . ."

"What had they done to that awful brute, Josefina? What thing bad
enough to make Willy—vomit?"

"They had castrated him—very completely. They cut off of him not
only his seed sacks, but also his goad. And, to make sure the gringos got
the point, they kept that beast prisoner in a cabin in the Sierras and
nursed him most tenderly to make sure he would not die. Meanwhile,
what they had cut off him they buried in a snowbank. And once he was
well enough, they left him on Kearny Street, corner of Pacific, with his
hands tied behind him, and with that which had been formerly attached
to his belly, stuffed into his mouth as a gag. . . ."

"Bon petit Jésus!" Mireille said.

"It was perhaps excessive," Josefina said judiciously, "but, as I was
saying, dear Señorita Mirla, you are very right to fear for Willy, if he
continues robbing the gringos. They are too many, and too strong. One
day, all such as Joaquin and Guillermo will be killed. You must induce
Willy to leave it, this robbers' trade for which he is not fitted. Joaquin
was a horse trainer, a circus mountebank. But Guillermo was—*is—un
caballero, un hidalgo.* And however much justice it may have, this business of stealing back that which they originally stole from us, it will
surely end badly. You allow me to give you some advice?"

"Of course, Josefina! Any counsel of yours would be welcome."

"When you are wed, take Willy to live in San Francisco. And *not* in
Little Chile. As far away from it as you can get. Make him always to
speak English, always to dress as a gringo. To become wholly the *Yanqui*
he is half, anyhow . . ."

"And to be the swine that they are, as well?" Mireille said bitterly.

"Not all of them are. Don Enrique has many friends among *los Ameri-canos*—all men with studies—and these are, as the father of Guillermo was, admirable men. One of them, whom I have got to know well, because he visits Don Enrique frequently here at the *rancho*, Judge Alain Curtwright, is the kindest and best man of *any* race I know. 'Twould pay you and Willy to make his acquaintance—through Don Enrique, of course—for he could open many doors for the two of you, of that I am sure. . . . Poor man! His life is so very sad . . ."

"Why is it sad, Josefina?"

"Because of his wife. She is a very beautiful woman many years younger than he—only, unfortunately, she is—mad. . . ."

"Mad?" Mireille echoed.

"Yes, stark raving. They came out here by wagon train from the East. Of the thirty wagons that started out from Independence, Missouri, together, *five* reached California. And those five only because four of them were driven by the brothers of the wife of the judge, who were too cowardly, or too weak, to dispute his leadership. The rest? The heat, the cold, the weariness, hunger, the Indians . . . and last of all—thirst. The cholera. And in the Sierras, the wolves. Don Alain was both lucky and courageous. His wagon and the four wagons of his brothers-in-law got through—though *his* reached California bearing inside it a beautiful gibbering idiot, with her mind entirely gone. . . ."

"How sad life is!" Mireille murmured. "She is in an asylum, then?"

"No. We haven't any asylums for lunatics yet in California. Don Alain keeps her at home in a special room in which everything is padded so that she may not hurt herself, and attends her with great tenderness. Poor man! It would be much better for her to die. You see, he has this terrible longing to have—a son. But he is getting along in years, being nearly sixty. So if she will not be obliging enough to kill herself soon in one of her maniacal rages, it will be too late. . . ."

Mireille smiled at Josefina impishly.

"Why are you telling me all this about a man I have never met?" she asked. "Is it that you think I should meet this judge of yours—and steal him from his poor crazy wife?"

Josefina grinned back with equal, or even superior, mischief.

"You could do worse. In fact, you *are* doing worse. Willy, for exam-ple," she said.

5

MIREILLE SAT IN THE SLIPPER-SHAPED BATHTUB THAT DON Enrique had brought back from Paris years before anyone had ever dreamed that gold would be discovered in California. She lay back as far as she could in the warm, soapy, perfumed water and closed her eyes.

'Willy will be home tonight,' she mused sensuously. 'I'm sure of that —and I—am ready for him. I shall burn him alive! Hmmmmmn . . . I'd better make him take a bath first—he'll smell like a cross between a horse and a billygoat. And love is ever so much nicer when one is clean. The possibilities are vastly increased. . . . I wonder if I could get him to—to—'

She giggled girlishly at what even she had to admit was an exceedingly wicked thought.

'He'd be—shocked speechless! I enjoy that. That amuses me. It is very diverting—to shock him until he's red and spluttering! I am very perverse. So what? Long live perversity! For instance, just thinking about him already I have a great desire to do something stupid, to—touch myself—down there. To play with myself—and why not? If doing that really drove you crazy the way people claim, I'd have been in a lunatic asylum years ago! Besides, it's—nice. So—nice. Hmmmmmmnn . . . Where are you—ticklish little bud of mine, hidden away down there out of sight, beneath all—my fur? I am an animal! A beast . . . A vixen. A —cat. No—a goat—a wild nanny goat, the most shameless of all the beasts! Ah. Ah! *There* you are! Down there in—my swamps. Amid my— boiling springs. Ah. Now—again. Once more. Softly. Softly. I mustn't— make you—sore. Softly. Slowly. Hmmn. Hmmn. Hhhhhm- mmmmmmmmmmnnn—Oh, please! That doesn't arrive! Come on, will you—silly little thing? Please—oh, please! I beg of you! Why are you holding back? Tormenting me? Tormenting—me—tormenting—Ah.

Ah! There! There it is! Ah—Ah—Ahhhhhh! It is so good—so marvelous! Mmmnnnnn—*Zut!* How—perverted I am! I love—Willy. I love—
Paci. I love—*me!*'

And it was then, at that precise and delicious moment, that she heard
the creak of harness, the whir of wheels, and the clip-clopping of hooves
slowing to a halt just outside in the courtyard.

'I should go and greet him just as I am!' she thought merrily—'stark
naked—and so beautiful! He probably wouldn't even let me get back
inside the house before—*Mais non!* I have had such a nice bath and—
getting splinters and straw and sand all over—and into various parts of
me—is hardly an appealing idea, is it not so? Besides, it would certainly
be more prudent to make him take off his spurs!'

Then she stopped short. Her face fell into an almost comic expression
of woe.

'He didn't take the buckboard!' she realized, remembering. 'He rode a
horse. So—it is not Willy. Not—my—Willy. Paci! *Mais, bien sûr!* She
must be well enough to travel by now, so Don Enrique has brought her
here. He said he was going to. *Oh, bon Dieu!* I must hurry! Dry myself—
get into my clothes—'

She was right, of course. It was Paquita and Don Enrique. But she was
also wrong. For Guillermo Kilpatrick was with them.

She saw Manolo Garcia, Three-Fingered Jack, first. At the head of
that—stretcher. And behind it, another slim young fellow, far younger,
and absolutely as male-animal beautiful as Willy himself. It didn't occur
to her at the time that the second stretcher-bearer was Joaquin Murieta,
whose legend, in California, would never die. It is very likely that she
didn't even *see* that greatest, bravest, and, in some ways anyhow, most
admirable of all outlaws, by then. Her brown eyes had turned into sepia,
ocher, umber, topaz flame; and her opened mouth adjusted the draft
with murderous precision to burn away her brain.

She tried to say his name, or at least the diminutive, "Willy," but she
couldn't get it out. Her lips formed the shape of it, in speechless agony,
in a mute, cord-ripping, would-be moan that transcended sound. Her
reaction was—prehistoric. It dated back to tribal times: the fallen war-
rior's woman expressing her grief in the most awful way immediately
possible to her. Or perhaps even—Grecian. Straight out of the un-
equaled horrors of the Dionysian *tragoidia*. Euripides might have drawn
a scene for his *Medea* from it. She lifted both her hands turned inward,
dug four of her fingers, metamorphosed into claws, into her eyes, and
tried, very seriously, to tear them from her head.

"Mireille!" Paquita screamed; "oh, no!"

She didn't succeed, of course. The body has its defenses against even madness. Her nails ripped her eyelids—closed in instantaneous and involuntary reaction against her furious assault—almost to shreds, raked downward, bit into her cheeks, dragged furrows of skin, of the flesh beneath it, slowly toward her lips, followed by the swift-brimming rivulets of her blood. . . . It was, quite simply, the most terrible sight, the most awesome manifestation of pure grief, that any of them had ever seen.

"Goodbye, my love," she whispered then, her voice out-ranging the farthest limits of horror in its utter calm; "I'm going to join you—at once!"

The sound of it unlocked Enrique Sepúlvera's limbs from the paralysis pure shock had held them in. He leaped forward like a clumsy bear, caught her in his arms, almost crushing her slight form in the pressure of his terrified embrace.

"Mireille!" he roared. "You're mad! He isn't dead! Very gravely wounded, yes, but not yet dead."

"He—isn't—dead?" she whispered. "You—you're *sure?*"

"Of course I'm sure! My God, your face! Your face! You have all but ruined it, child! I knew you were a little crazy, but not so much! *¡Ay,* Mireille, Mireille, Mireille!"

"I didn't want to see another face," she said simply, softly, "not ever again—with him—gone. Nor look into any other eyes, until the day I—died. Doctor—will my sight come back? Willy is going to need me. And right now—I'm blind. I see only—the color—red. . . ."

"With your eyes full of blood, what the devil else d'you expect to see? My faith, but you picked an inopportune time, my child! Now, precisely *now,* you have to go and blind yourself—and ruin the beauty that ought to be a comfort to his eyes."

"I will get better. I *will.* He needs me. So I will."

"Magnificent demonstration of female logic!" The doctor snorted. "Come on, Joaquin, and you, *Tres Dedos*—let's get him up to bed. Your eyes will have to wait, Mireille, for I have no time. I only hope you haven't damaged them too badly. Paci dearest, *you* attend to her. I've got to dig half a ton of lead out of this shot-up hulk. Wash her eyes out with a mild borate solution. It's in the medicine cabinet . . ."

Paquita bowed her head.

"Sir—" she whispered, "someone—will have to—give it to me. I—I cannot—read. . . ."

"You *can't?* Oh, damn! Call Josefina, she'll find it for you. There,

there, dear heart! It's nothing to cry over! I'll have you reading soon enough. And in Latin and Greek, to boot! Now come on, boys—careful there! Don't jolt him too much . . ."

Three days later, the situation at *Rancho Santa Clara* had changed practically not at all.

"How is he, Doctor?" Mireille said.

"Don't know," Sepúlvera grunted, and went on with what he was doing, which was swabbing out her eyes with a little cotton wound around an ivory wand and dipped in some sort of liquid that burned like fire.

"Señor Doctor," Paquita breathed, "is she—going to be able to see?"

"Yes. No thanks to her, that's for sure. May have to wear eyeglasses, though . . ."

"Oh, no!" Mireille wailed. "Eyeglasses make one so ugly!"

"Wasn't that what you were trying to do?" the doctor said grimly—"make yourself look like the hindquarters of a zebra? If so, you've succeeded, *chérie!* So even if I *do* get poor Willy up from there, you think he's going to want to marry a girl whose face looks like she stuck it into a barrelful of angry tomcats, or tried to kiss a windmill in a hurricane?"

"*Docteur*," Mireille whispered, "he—he's not going to—to die—is he?"

The doctor sighed.

"The truth is, I don't know, Mireille," he said. "I had to bring him way down here, instead of operating up in San Francisco as I should have —and would have, if the situation had permitted it. But he was dressed in Mexican clothes, that extravagantly gaudy *charro* outfit and huge sombrero that he and the other self-appointed avengers of my people wear when they're about a little plain and fancy highway robbery. And he was delirious. Unfortunately, one is always delirious in one's mother tongue; and the risks of trying to explain to the owners of any of those stinking butcher shops they call hospitals up there, why they should bother to admit a shot-up greaser, or even identifying myself as a member of that downtrodden race were far too great. So, he lost too much blood. I could have done a transfusion—bled you, you silly lovesick wench, even whiter than you are, to give him the blood he needed; but if your blood and his didn't match, yours would poison him, and he'd die. And nobody knows why some people's bloods match perfectly and others' don't. Again, too big a risk . . ."

"Oh, *Dieu!*" Mireille moaned.

"Worse still, I had to open him up—with nothing to put him to sleep so he wouldn't feel the pain. Davy discovered nitrous oxide, 'laughing gas' in 1799; it was used in Hartford, Connecticut—in dentistry, anyhow —in 1844; von Liebig found out how to make chloroform in 1826; Crawford Long, in the benighted southern state of Georgia, used ether in surgery as far back as forty-two, though he waited till two years ago— 1849—to publish his generally successful results. But could I find or buy any of these miraculous sleep-producing pain-killers in the magnificent city of San Francisco, in gold-plated California? I could *not.* Though I have to admit that, under the circumstances, I didn't seriously try—"

"So—as you probably heard even in that inn in San José I sent you and Paquita to, to keep you, anyhow, from driving me out of my mind while I was trying to work—the poor boy had to scream his guts up until he lapsed into unconsciousness. He had three revolver balls in his body. One of them had perforated his small intestine, which, thank God, was empty! Any half-digested food, or fecal matter there, and he'd be dead by now. Another nicked the bottom lobe of his right lung—and caused him to bleed like hell. I cleaned that up. The third was in his left shoulder. That was unimportant. He may have a slightly lame arm for the rest of his life. That is, if he *has* any life. . . ."

"Doctor—Don Enrique—" Mireille said quietly, "is it permitted to bury two people in the same coffin? Or even if it isn't, could you arrange it? With my arms around his neck and—"

"Both of you stark naked, so you can thump your way to kingdom come?" Enrique chuckled. "Besides, who's supposed to kill you—me?"

"Would you be—so kind? I'd probably make a horrible mess of things. You could—open my veins, very neatly. Or give me something to take, or—"

"Or—*¡Mierdas!* Paci, lead her out of here! She's tempting me too much! Only my methods wouldn't be so gentle. Right now, I'd gladly beat her to death—and enjoy it!"

"*Sí, Señor Doctor,*" Paci said.

"And stripe your little seat as well, the next time you call me *Señor Doctor!* Call me love, heaven, lover, heart—but *not Señor Doctor!* Understand?"

"*¡Sí, Señor Doctor!*" Paquita got out, then: "Oh God! Forgive me, *Señor Doctor!* I didn't mean to say '*Señor Doctor*'! How awkward I am! How stupid! How—"

"Lovely, sweet, angelic," Enrique murmured, and bending forward, kissed her.

"I love you!" Paquita sobbed; "Ohhhhh, how I love you! You're so good! So gentle! So—"

"Foolish—like any other man in love," Enrique chuckled; "but damned if I don't believe you're worth it! Now take this little French witch upstairs and make her go to bed until tomorrow. If she tries to get up before breakfast time—except, of course, to make *aguas menores*— call Josefina to *sit* on her!"

" *'Aguas menores'?"* Mireille said blankly.

"Pipi," Paci said. "You have heard truly courteous Spanish, as spoken by a gentleman. Dearest! Good night, *Señor Doc*—I mean, my love!"

Six months later, the question was still the same, only this time it was Paquita who asked it. She and Mireille were having breakfast together in the master bedroom—a pleasantly lazy custom they indulged in whenever Dr. Sepúlvera was away from home, as he often was nowadays, attending his growing practice among the better class gringos of San Francisco.

"How is he, Mirla?" Paquita said, pushing back her chair from the table. She crossed her long, beautiful legs beneath her nightgown, which was of pure Chinese silk, with huge pagoda sleeves, and adorned with billowing oceans of creamy, lace-trimmed ruffles, as befitted her new and vastly—for the better!—changed status. Mireille's gown, made of muslin, was much simpler, but it was just as ample, as the moral concepts of those times demanded.

"Don't call me 'Mirla'!" she snapped; "it's not my name, and I—I hate it!"

"All right—Mireille. To repeat my question: How is Guillermo this morning?"

"¡*Vaya!* Look what fine manners we have now! How correct, how formal! How goes this wonderful married life of yours, *Doña Francesca Villa Roque, Señora de Doctor Don Enrique Sepúlvera Varón?* Did I get it all right, this time?"

"You did. And my married life—goes well. Or rather, so-so, to tell the truth about it. My darling husband is nobody's spring chicken, y'know," Paquita said a little ruefully.

Mireille flashed her a smile of pure, delighted wickedness.

"You mean he—he *can't?"*

"Oh, no! Don't be malicious! He *can* all right! And—divinely. Often —he often doesn't want to. Too often to suit *me*, anyhow. Strange as it seems, even to me, with *him*, I—I *like* it!"

"Good love! Don't tell me you're—missing—your nights at the Dirty Spoon?"

"No. Of course not! Are—you?"

"At times—yes," Mireille said morosely; "those dirty types down there—a few of the more decent ones—were almost—fun. . . ."

"Hmmnpf!" Paquita sniffed. "Which brings us back to the original question: How is Willy, Mireille? You don't mean to tell me that he— well—neglects you? How goes this sinful *un*married life of yours?"

"I mean he is still very weak and tired; so much so that I don't dare try to—to interest him—in making love, too frequently. We haven't—in— in over two months. The last time we tried, he got so sick afterward that I became frightened. So now—when he—attempts something, always halfheartedly, I make some excuse, or gently push him off. Poor boy, he's quite despondent. . . ."

"Why?" Paci said. "Because you—won't?"

"No, I think he's secretly glad of that. It's just that he had his heart set on becoming the owner of a great *rancho* again, one day. And your darling husband says he can't. Not ever, anymore. That he must seek a less strenuous occupation. He wants Willy to go to see Don Ernesto Martin, of E. Martin and Company, Merchants and Brokers, in San Francisco."

"But Willy doesn't know anything about commercial merchandising, or the brokerage business!"

"Or the law, for which they want him to read, as a part of his training. True. But they're willing to teach him. In fact, they told Don Enrique they'd be delighted to have him work for them, and have offered him quite a good salary to start with. We—could even get married on it, Paci . . ."

"But—" Paquita said slowly, "my life has taught me that people are capable of anything—except generosity, my dearest. And an offer like that is—generous, it seems to me."

"It seems to you, wrong," Mireille said. "They're not being generous and they know it. Willy would be worth a fortune to them, and they know that, too."

"You—you've lost me, I'm afraid, Mireille dearest—"

"It's because of where they're located, Paci sweetheart. On Washington Street, on the new filled-in land where part of the Bay used to be. In the heart of the gringo business district. So a nice clean-cut young, sup-posed-to-be executive out in their store and front office to greet the public—and to keep the Americans from even realizing that E. Martin and Company is not a *Yanqui* firm—would be a godsend, provided he were a gringo. But what gringo could they trust? So—Willy. Blond, blue-eyed—a trifle tanned, but no matter. Perfect English. More than perfect

Spanish. Lord, Paci, he'll save their *lives* commercially, as they realize very well!"

"Sounds wonderful. Is he going to try it?"

"With the patient resignation of a martyr going to the stake, knowing he has no other choice. He absolutely cannot ride wild mustangs or broncos anymore, or rope and brand cattle. In fact, Don Enrique is going to give us a surrey for our wedding present. And has told my poor forlorn lover exactly why. That almost broke Willy's heart. He did so love to ride. . . ."

"And now he can't? Not even—*¿Una pequeña yegua blanca como las nieves con una melena larga más negra que la noche?*" Paquita whispered, her voice as warm as a tropic tide.

" 'Not even—a little snow-white mare' " Mireille translated bitterly, " 'with a long mane, blacker than the night?' That's what your Spanish meant, wasn't it, Paci? And the answer is, no. Now he can't. Or rather, he shouldn't. I asked Don Enrique about that, quite frankly. I am simply not of the temperament of a nun. Or equipped to be a wife in name only. . . ."

"What did Enrique say?" Paquita asked her.

"That that's going to be all right. In another three or four months. And even then, we'll have to be—careful, until we're sure his damaged lung is not going to give way. Can you imagine *me* being careful? So now —I suffer. *Tant pis!* Willy is worth it. All the same I—stay so hard up— so hungry for love—that I'm glad a boy as handsome and as full of the devil as Three Fingers has decided to stay away. Though that was on your account, Paci, not mine!"

"I know. And I'm—glad, too. Damned men!"

"Paci—" Mireille said.

"Enrique has been away a week. And the week before that—he—well —he was tired and—"

"Paci—" Mireille said again.

"What, Dear?" Paquita said morosely.

"Let's—get—even with the bastards!" Mireille said.

Paquita turned and stared at her.

"Get even—how?" she said.

"Stand up, and I'll show you," Mireille said with a gamine's grin that made her small face the very portrait of enchanting diablerie.

Slowly, wonderingly, Paquita rose from her chair. Said, in a low and slumberous tone of voice that fell on Mireille's ear like a felt caress: "And how could a pair of females like us avenge ourselves against— men?"

"Like this!" Mireille laughed, and got up, too. Holding Paquita with her eyes, she pushed her nightgown off her shoulders, very, very slowly, let it slide down to her hips, gave it another little shove, and wiggled sinuously until it lay in a snowy heap about her ankles.

"Mireille, no!" Paquita gasped. "I—"

Mireille flattened whatever her dark, lovely friend had been about to say against her speaking mouth with her own half-playful, half-avid lips. She went on kissing Paquita open-mouthed, hotly, wetly, a long, long time, until she had the response she sought: Paquita kissed her back. They stood there wrapped in each other's arms, exchanging exploratory lingual invasion and ingurgitative reception, on the democratic basis of alternation, tentatively at first, then seriously, all tenderness gone, mouth grinding into mouth, arrogantly demanding, becoming feral.

Mireille drew back and smiled at her.

"Get out of that circus tent of yours, dear heart!" she said.

"Mireille—no! We can't! I won't—I—"

Mireille laughed freely, gaily. Caught the tail of Paquita's expensive silk gown, and with a sudden, brusque motion, yanked it over her head. Left it there, with Paci's face hidden in its folds.

Then she dropped to her knees before that abruptly revealed expanse of lissome, coppery, bifurcating flesh, wound her arms around Paquita's slim waist, and traced a mocking spiral all around her navel with a diabolically busy tongue tip, probed into it mischievously.

"I can't breathe!" Paquita gasped; "I—Oh. Oh, no! Not—down there! Not—Ah. Oh, God! Ah—God the Father up in heaven—forgive me this sin—this terrible sin—that is—¡Ay de mí!—so sweet—so sweet —so very sweet—¡Ay—yeeee! Do it to me! Slowly—slowly—Don't rush, my love—your mouth is like honey! Your tongue is a serpent of fire—¡Ay de mí! Have pity on this sinner, God! Poor me! Ay. Ay. Ay. I am damned! Ay. Ay. Ay. Ayyyyyyyyyyyeeeeee—"

"Come," Mireille said; "let's go to bed. It's my turn now. . . ."

"Mireille," Paquita said.

"Mireille, what?" Mireille said.

"With—the hands—the fingers—all right. It is—a small sin, which does not particularly matter. But—the other—no. It—awakes—a repugnance in me. I—I—cannot. It is—too grave. We cease to be women, doing that. Become—marimachos—real lesbians."

Mireille stared at her. Loosed a hoot of derisive laughter.

"Now, then!" she said mockingly. "Now, all of a sudden, the exquisite señora wife of the celebrated doctor has scruples! After she has enjoyed herself. Enjoyed, *merde!* After she has come like the midnight express! After telling me my mouth's like honey, my tongue's a fiery serpent. Who was it that said: 'Do me this! But slowly—slowly'? Paci darling, you're a coward. Don't just stand there—come on!"

"Have—you—no shame?" Paquita wept. "No sense of—sin?"

"I'm supposed to be ashamed of loving someone as beautiful as you are, dear heart? That makes no sense! Sin? Sin is what hurts people, not makes them gloriously happy. *Bon Dieu!* She wants to discuss morals, while I want to make love! *Will* you come on!"

Paquita bent her head. Looked up again, all her face awash with tears. *"¡Sí, querida!"* she said.

Paquita let her long, slender fingers trail over Mireille's face, tracing the pale, white-on-white scars her distinctly *locita*—less than, or not quite, crazy was the way dear Paci put it—little friend had dug into her own eyelids and cheeks with frenzied fingernails.

"The day I thought poor Willy was all dead, instead of only half," Mireille mused bitterly.

"Enrique was wrong," Paquita murmured; "it did not destroy your beauty. Enhanced it, really. . . ."

"Having a face that looks like somebody pushed it into a meat grinder in a butcher shop has made me more beautiful? Paci, you're crazy!"

"I know. We've just proved that," Paquita said.

"Oh, bon Dieu! You're not going to be remorseful, are you? I've never been remorseful about a single thing I've ever done in all my life. If I— enjoyed it, I keep it in my crazy head to remember—with pleasure. If I didn't, I forget it—completely."

"And it doesn't matter whether it was—good or—bad?" Paquita whispered.

"If I enjoyed it, it was good. If I didn't, it was bad," Mireille said with total conviction.

"And—*this*—was—good?" Paquita said sadly.

"This was—divine! Glorious! You're—sohhh beautiful, dear girl! Even —down there—you are. Soft-furred—like mink. And these two little copper mountains tipped with blood-roses! Hmmmmmn—I'm going to kiss them again—make them stand up and quiver—"

"Mireille, stop it! Don't you get started again! Please!"

"And why not, my dearest darling Paci? Are you going to tell me you didn't have a per-fect-ly wonderful time?"

"Oh, all right! All right! I did. And that's what I hate most of all. I want to be a *woman*, dear. A wife. If possible—a mother. Tell me, aren't you the least bit ashamed of having—cheated on—Willy?"

Mireille sat up in the bed like a jack-in-the-box and stared at Paquita in unfeigned astonishment.

"But I haven't!" she gasped. "I could cheat on him only with another *man*—and you're a *girl*, dear heart!"

"Am I? Today you've made me doubt it. So all the horrible—terrible —lovely things you did to me—and made me do to you—don't count?"

"Of course not, silly! Tell you what: s'pose you go to Don Enrique, with downcast eyes, and say, 'Dear husband mine, I have deceived you with another! And what is even worse, I am with child—*enceinte*— *embarazada*—pregnant. Dooooo forgive me, beloved husband mine, for this terrible sin, this offense against your honor! What's that? Who is the *father* of little Don No-Name, this bastard child I'm going to present you with? Don't ask me that! You—insist? Why, Mireille, of course!' "

"Oh, you!" Paquita laughed. "What a barbarity! What a beast you are! Yet in a way, I suppose you're right. As long as we don't turn completely away from men, I don't suppose *this* is all that important . . ."

"*Men* turned me away from men," Mireille said bitterly. "Even Willy, by getting himself shot up, and having—to neglect me. Paci, you say I'm not ugly? Even with this face of mine?"

"You—you're beautiful, Mireille. You always were. But now you're— exciting. Odd. Exotic. Your face looks like a tiger cat's, especially with those two stripes running down vertically, straight across your eyes. Now tell me the truth: How's your sight? When you pick up a book, you squint fearfully. And you put down whatever you start to read almost immediately . . ."

"I'm as blind as a bat! Oh, I see faraway things. Anything beyond a yard or two. But close up, everything blurs. I need spectacles. But don't tell Don Enrique that, or he'll make me wear 'em."

"You fool," Paquita sighed; "you sweet, tender, mysterious, passionate, gentle, wild, crazy little monster of a fool! The best person I've ever known. And the worst. At the same time. ¡Dios, Mireille, you invented contradiction!"

"I think I was meant to be twins, and something slipped," Mireille said solemnly. " 'Cause I'm at least two people. Though sometimes I'm a dozen. But all that dozen love you, Paci. Hmmmmmmmmmmmn—I'm rested now. I feel wonderful. So—an encore, dearest?"

"No! Josefina will be in here to clean up at any minute now. Which reminds me, we'd better put our nightgowns back on—"

"Let's don't. Let's shock her speechless! Like, say, letting her catch us in the act—with me on top, of course, so you can tell Don Enrique I raped you. I did, didn't I?"

"Very nearly. Mireille, *will* you behave?"

"Of course not. I never do. Hmmmmmmnn—you smell so nice! That's another thing about being half blind: all the other senses grow much keener. A boy once told me I smell like rich cream cheese down there. Let me—discover *your* special smell, my dearest. So I can—bottle it. Sell it to La Tour et Lefèvre Parfumeurs . . ."

"Dear God!" Paquita said.

"And—your taste. Hmmmmmmmmmmmmnnnnnnn—Hmmmmmmmm-mmnnnnnn—buttermilk. She-goat's milk. Curds and whey. Hmmmmmm-mmmmmmmmmnnnnnnnn—"

"*¡Ay!*" Paquita moaned; "Mireille, *por favor!* Please—"

"Señora—" Josefina began; then, "Sacred Virgin!"

Mireille straightened up; grinned at her like the perfect little imp from hell she was.

"It's all right, Josefina," she said with a delighted giggle; "I was only teaching the señora a few filthy tricks! Don't you know any? Let's compare notes! Come on in, will you?"

Josefina came into the bedroom, her moon-shaped countenance aflame.

"There's—*un caballero* to see *you, Señorita* Mireille," she got out; "*un gringo—un Americano.* Blond like Willy. Blonder, maybe. He says he is called How-ward Tellefair."

"Oh God!" Mireille groaned. "Not again! How on earth did he trace me here?"

"Quite easily," Paquita said sadly. "He went to Doña Marta's *posada* and talked to those slatterns there. Josefina, I—I've always treated you well, haven't I? Mira—Look, you have seen what you have seen—but we all have—our occasional weaknesses—commit indiscretions and— What I'm saying, my dear, is—*must* you break Don Enrique's heart by telling him—a thing—he doesn't need to know?"

Josefina drew herself up proudly. As the poorly educated always do, she spoke in the clichés derived from the cheap literature of her times. She was an ardent reader of *novelas por entregas,* those serialized half-peso romances so popular in the Spanish-speaking countries. So she knew just how to deliver her message:

"Señora, my lips are sealed!" she said. Then she turned to Mireille.

"Señorita," she said uncertainly; "about this gentleman? Shall I say that you are not here?"

Mireille smiled then, in a way that awoke, more profoundly than ever, the desire Paquita often had to strangle her. To break her absurd and wicked little neck.

"No, do not tell him that . . ." she murmured.

"Then what *shall* I tell him?" Josefina demanded.

"That I shall come down—immediately," Mireille—*La Perversa!*—said.

GUILLERMO KILPATRICK LAY THRE AND STARED AT THE CEILING. HE
knew where Mireille was, because she had told him:

"I'm going to have breakfast with Paci. You don't mind, d'you, love?"

And he had answered her, quietly, "No. Not at all. Go ahead, Mirla
. . ."

When it came to that, he didn't mind, really. He needed to be alone
to do some thinking, to sort out and put in order the tattered remnants
of his life. 'Maybe I should just give her up,' he thought gloomily. 'How
long is a girl with a temperament as—ardent—as hers is, going to put up
with my enforced neglect of her? Or with an old shot-up wreck like me?
Not very long, that's for sure!'

And, almost as if in answer to his thought, suddenly, startlingly, he
heard her talking just outside his window, her voice crisp, clear, almost
ringing.

"Come away from there, How-ward," she said.

"Why?" a pleasant tenor said.

When Mireille spoke again, she did so much more quietly, but, because of the natural, crystalline purity of her enunciation, though uttered
in a whisper, that phrase carried much too well.

"Because—my—fiancé is in that room. And there are a whole lot of
things I'd just as soon he didn't find out," she said worriedly.

"Such as?" the man called How-ward purred. "That you peddled your
dainty little *derrière* to all comers at the Dirty Spoon?"

"He knows that. He got me out of there. C'mon, How-ward!"

Willy leaped from his bed. Stood there, swaying dizzily, until his momentary fit of weakness passed. Shoved his bony feet, like all the rest of
him now almost skeletal, into his bedroom slippers. Put on his dressing
gown over his nightshirt. Got his baby Paterson Colt out of the chif-

forobe where he kept it hidden under his shirts in the second drawer, and, gun in hand, rushed out the door.

He didn't see them. Then he saw that the stable door on the other side of the walled courtyard surrounding *la casa grande* was open, but only a crack. Enough to let some light in, so that they—

"*¡Jesús!*" he whispered in almost prayerful anguish. He crossed the courtyard in five long strides. Put his left hand on the stable door to tear it open. Then he stopped.

'Wait!' he told himself in ice-cold, maniacal fury. 'Give them time to get *very* busy, and then—'

He opened the door a trifle wider. Saw them. They were still standing up, still fully clothed. Howard had Mireille in his arms. She was struggling against his embrace. But not very hard.

"You stop that, How-ward!" she said.

"Why? I know you, baby. You want it. Want me. And with all this nice, cozy hay handy—"

"No," Mireille said, miserably.

"Why not? You're as hungry as old hell, and it shows!"

"You're right," Mireille sighed; "I am. But that's only because my fiancé is—sick. No. He's been shot. And I'm perfectly willing to wait till he's well again. Besides, I wouldn't do it again with *you*, How-ward Tellefair, if you were the last man on earth!"

"And why not, may I ask?" Howard said mockingly. "You used to like the way I threw it to you, Mireille, sugar. 'Ooooooh, How-ward!' you used to scream; 'do it to me hard, darleeeng! Harder! Faster! More, lover-man; give me more!'"

"I was a fool. An inexperienced little fool," Mireille said bitterly. "You really aren't worth much of a damn in bed, y'know. Only I didn't realize that, then. . . ."

"And now you do? Thanks to this greaser bastard of a fiancé of yours?"

"Don't call him a greaser bastard!" Mireille flared. "But if you must know: yes, thanks to him! He's a *man;* while you—"

"Some man. Who'll take a thousand horny, louse-infested boar hogs' leavings. Who'd marry a filthy little slut like *you.* Look, baby, don't give old Uncle Howard an act. You're pissed off at me because somebody told you that I put you up as the stake in a wild poker game. That ain't so. That proposition came from Big Jules, not from me."

"But you accepted it!" Mireille said.

"Yes! But only because I thought I had him cold. I'd rung in a marked deck. And just before I started to deal th' cards, he sung out over his shoulder, 'Ned! Bring us a fresh deck, will you?' I couldn't object—he'd have gunned me down like a dog. So I had to depend on luck—and luck's a bitch, baby. A worse one than *you* are, though that takes some doing. . . ."

"How-ward, you stop insulting me!"

" 'Tain't possible. Your contention is that I sold your nice, sweet, unbusted little virgin tail into vile slavery, ain't it, Mireille? Thought you'd took me in with that river showboat melodrama about them eight or ten horny li'l bastids raping you in N'Orleans, didn't you? Well, sugar, while we were waiting for our steamship to arrive and waft us off down to Panama, I investigated. And I found out that you *peddled* your hairy little quim to them dear old friends of yours to get steamboat fare out of town, both because you'd run away from that reform school for wayward gals the juvenile court had put you in for a couple o' other fast ones you'd gone and pulled previous, and because you thought you'd killed your miserable old pus-gutted strumpet of a ma, and maybe even me. Got eighty-five dollars for the deal. So don't give me that maiden wronged gooseshit, will you? Go pack your things!"

"Go—pack—my—things?" Mireille whispered.

"Yep. Or would you druther that I dropped in on this here greaser bastard of high degree you're mixed up with now, and give him a book, chapter, and verse account of your interesting past history, sugar?"

"That will be unnecessary, Mr. Tellefair," Willy said with icy calm. "You already have. Accidentally, of course. I trust you have a revolver in one of your pockets? I have a certain squeamishness about gunning down an unarmed man."

"Willy!" Mireille moaned.

"You—you'd fight a duel—maybe even kill me," Howard quavered, "over this—this—"

"No," Willy said; "I don't fight over—cheap *putas*, Mr. Tellefair. But you have called the legitimacy of my birth into question. Insulted my mother's honor, and my race. Excuses enough, if I needed any. But I don't. I kill gringos because it amuses me. And to rid the world of vermin. You *are* armed, aren't you?"

"No," Howard lied; "never was a believer in th' wisdom of gun-toting, young fella. I ain't much of a shot, and packing a shooting iron is a prime method o' getting yourself killed, anyhow, so—"

"Then I'll borrow one for you," Willy said grimly; "have the goodness to wait, Señor Tellefair—"

He turned toward the door.

The exact second he did so, Mireille saw Howard's hand go snaking toward his left armpit. She didn't waste time and breath screaming out a warning. She simply threw herself upon Howard Tellefair, caught his right hand by the wrist as it drew the gambler's derringer from its shoulder holster, and hung onto it, despite all Howard's efforts to shake her loose. So Howard brought his left hand whistling around, and slapped her to the stable floor.

The first fraction of an instant that her falling body gave him a clear target by sharply reducing the risk of his hitting her instead of Howard, Guillermo Kilpatrick thumbed off a shot, which was the fastest way to do it. Granted the obvious fact that killing Howard Tellefair would have been a meritorious public service, he should have waited a little longer and taken better aim. As it was, the .28 caliber ball from the baby Paterson only plowed into the shoulder of Howard's gun arm, causing him to drop the derringer.

"Shoot him again, Willy!" Mireille cried; "kill him! Kill him dead!"

Guillermo looked at her, his eyes blue ice floes, reflecting immeasurable profundities of pure contempt.

"No. You will have need of your pimp, now," he said.

Riding beside Howard—who had his right arm in a sling, a circumstance he took advantage of by groaning theatrically the whole time—in the stagecoach up to San Francisco, Mireille's dark gaze was even more immeasurable, deeper still. She seemed to be gazing out upon immensities beyond both space and time.

"Oh lord, baby!" Howard groaned; "don't look like that! We—you and me—are going to be just fine. Course I'll be laid up awhile with this here damned arm. That is, if some sawbones don't have to take it off, after th' way them greaser rangehands dug into it with their bowie knives. . . ."

"The knives were clean," Mireille said quietly; "I saw to that. To leave the ball in a gunshot wound makes gangrene certain, Dr. Sepúlvera says. You'll be all right in a couple of weeks. That is, your arm will. *You* will never be all right, How-ward. . . ."

"Now, honey—"

"You—are a coward. In a man there is nothing uglier, nothing worse. Except being a pimp, maybe. Which doesn't matter either. You and I— are finished, How-ward. Get that through your head. In one way or another, we already are—"

"Mireille, for God's sake!"

"If you ever again approach me for any reason whatsoever, I shall kill you, How-ward. Or have it done. And I can. Either way. Believe me, I can."

"Mireille—" he moaned.

"So let's not talk anymore. Looking at you, listening to your voice, make me want to vomit. When we get to San Francisco, drop me off at Señora Gonzales' inn. I'll stay there tonight. Long enough to decide— what I'd better do. . . ."

"Now, baby—" Howard began.

"No. Not what you're thinking. I don't mean to—kill myself, Howard. From now on, I mean to—win."

"To win?" he echoed blankly. His shoulder was aching damnably, which was no wonder, he mused, stifling a groan, after the exquisite job of butchery the Mexican *vaqueros* had done on him with their knives, getting that ball out. And Mireille was right, he *had* behaved badly, screaming and crying like that before the cold, contemptuous blue eyes of the man who'd shot him. Funny, the young fellow didn't look like a Mex, or even sound like one until he talked Spanish. Then he did. Then he became totally Mexican, *more* than Mexican—a grandee of Spain, maybe. . . . 'But I'm wool-gathering,' Howard realized. 'Hurting like this don't make it easy to follow nobody's chain o' thought, not t'mention a way o' looking at things as mixed up and plain damned *female* as Mireille's is . . .'

"To—to win?" he muttered.

"Yes. So far, everything I've tried to do, I've ended up—beaten. I've scars all over my body, thanks in part to you, you filthy pimp. I've seen my own blood run down my back and puddle between my feet on the floor amid the sawdust and the tobacco-flavored spit—from a whipping worse than any poor damned nigger ever took. But the scars in my heart —are even uglier, How-ward. The ones on my soul. Remembering what my Willy's face did, the way his sweet—so sweet!—lips curled, the expression in his eyes, when he said, 'I don't fight over—a cheap whore . . . '"

"Lord, Mireille!"

"But he—he's going to come back to me, How-ward. I'm going to make him come back—crawling on his hands and knees. And when he does, I'll decide whether I'll take him for my man again—or put my slipper's sole into his face, flat across his nose and mouth, and kick him down the stairs. . . ."

She paused, then went on, slowly, quietly.

"Not only him. All this filthy burg you brought me to. The place where I was reduced to a 'pretty waiter girl' in a cheap concert saloon.

Which is only a polite way of saying a whore. Goods for sale—or, what's even worse, for *rent*—to two-legged animals who called themselves men so that they could use me—*me*, a person, a human being!—in order to temporarily appease the length of dangling gut they're all enslaved to. And for a pinch or two of gold dust, that's all. So I'm going to own this place one day, How-ward. San Francisco is going to be mine. Maybe I'll decide to burn it down, and shovel the ashes into the Bay. Maybe I'll let it live and grow, as long as it shows me the proper respect. But it's going to be mine. Just you wait!"

Howard Tellefair stared at her. When he spoke, his voice was humble somehow, awed.

"Don't know why; but damned if I don't believe you, Mireille baby!" he said.

Mireille sat upright in the straight-backed chair, with her slim, dainty feet together and stared at the large, florid blond woman on the other side of the desk she was facing. The woman was dressed in black silk, and her clothes had cost a fortune. Of course, they were out of style, but Mireille didn't know that. By the time any Paris-designed dress reached the Pacific Coast of North America, even by the few available mail steamships of the 1850s, it was always old-fashioned, even if it had left Paris as the last word.

"Your name?" the blond woman said.

Mireille shrugged. Her papa was dead. And her mother, Josette, had already sullied the name Duclos worse than she ever could. Besides, in the unthinkably unlikely event that she should ever go back to New Orleans, she had no reputation left in the city of her birth to defend, anyhow. She had been incarcerated in a convent correction school—a reformatory for wayward girls. And there were eight talkative louts who could swear—and surely by now had sworn—on the Holy Crucifix, or a stack of Protestant Bibles, that they had enjoyed her body for a price. An alias made no sense, required memory. She shrugged again.

"It's—Mireille Duclos," she said.

"French?" the woman said.

"Oui, Madame," Mireille said.

"From what part of France are you?" the woman asked her, in the perfect French of a native of that country.

"From no part of it," Mireille said wearily; "I have never seen my country. I am from Louisiana, Madame Emma . . ."

Madame Emma—French Em to all San Francisco—put out one of her thick, red, dockworker's hands, every finger ablaze with diamond rings, and groped in a lacquered box on the desk. Came out with a long, black, pencil-thin cigar. Struck a match, and waited until it spluttered and smoked and stunk for almost half a minute before bursting into feeble, wavering yellow flame, as the matches of the 1850s always did. Then she lit the cigar, blew twin tendrils of blue smoke through her broad nostrils.

"New Orleans?" she said.

"Yes, Madame Emma."

"You are—entirely white?" French Em asked her.

"Why!" Mireille gasped. "How dare you!"

"Come off of it, will you," French Em chuckled. "Ninety-seven percent of you Creole sluts are tarbrushed, and you know it. It's no skin off my nose. I've married off two dozen fillies that any fool could see were quadroons to some of the richest and most cultured men in San Francisco. Octoroons, I don't even worry about. But some of those girls were so close to *mulatas* that any day now I expect some old fool and his lawyer to rush in that door with a little nigger in their arms, demanding damages!"

"I am—white," Mireille said coldly, "and French. That is—I am American, Louisianan, but of French descent. Pure. I have no other blood."

"Less bad," French Em said. "Get up, will you?"

Mireille stood up.

"Walk to the door. Now—walk back again. Hmmmmmm—not bad. Not bad at all. Now, strip."

"Toute?" Mireille whispered. "I must take off—everything?"

"Everything. Stark mother-naked. Bare-assed. I'm not in this business to amuse myself, dearie, so I've got to *see* what I'm peddling. . . ."

Mireille shrugged. Stripped.

"Hmmmmm—" French Em said; "not bad—not bad at all. But those —scars. Fellow pay you to take that whipping?"

"Pay me?" Mireille got out.

"Some do. Get their rocks off that way, watching a poor bitch twist and scream. You run into all kinds of rare types in this business, *bébé.* All right. Who cut you to ribbons like that, and—why?"

"A—man," Mireille said. "The owner of—of a place I was in. I— objected to what one of the clients wanted me to do, so he—"

"You didn't want—'to French'—as these *salauds* out here call it. As if *we* invented that business of knob-polishing! *Merde!* I'll bet the English gentlemen invented it. In their public schools for boys. With each other,

since they just don't like women, anyhow. No matter. Listen, dearie: how
violent are your objections to that particular practice?"

Mireille shrugged.

"That—depends," she said.

"Depends on—what?" French Em said.

"The—man. That he is not—too repulsive. That he bathes—oftener
than once a month. Apart from that—it's better than procuring—abor-
tions, isn't it?"

"Good! Spoken like a true professional. All right, *bébé;* you've got a
place here. This is a first-class house. I treat my girls right. . . ."

"I know. I checked. That's why I came here."

"You don't say! Cool little number, aren't you? All right. Split is seventy-five percent of your take, yours; twenty-five, the house's; and that's
downright generous, you have to admit. Medical expenses, if any—your
own. I've a quack who looks the girls over at regular intervals. I run a
clean house, and my clients know it. That detail pays. Clothes—you buy
'em, but the selection's subject to my approval. I don't want any girls
looking like tarts. That's sure ruin."

"What are we supposed to look like, then?" Mireille asked her.

"Like nice young ladies of the upper class, straight out of finishing
school. In regard to which, you're to *stay* fully dressed until you go
upstairs with a client. No lolling about in your underwear—and certainly
not nude. No profane language. Discreet behavior. The perfect whore,
my child, acts like a vestal virgin, even after she's upstairs. Then she
allows herself to be seduced, most reluctantly. Only after she is in the
arms of her gallant does she thaw out. Not too abruptly. She finds herself, to her own evident astonishment, slowly being swept off her feet,
tempted beyond her poor, maidenly strength by his splendid masculinity,
his princely charm. Always works. The only thing stupider than a man is
a mule. And I doubt even that. If mules could talk, we'd probably find
out they're smarter. Tell me, you've got a pimp?"

"No. What I make, I mean to *keep*," Mireille said.

"Good! That's intelligent of you, *bébé!* By the way, you mean to use
your own name? Mireille Duclos, I think you said?"

"Yes, that's it—Mireille Duclos. I have no family, and I'm not wanted
by the police, Madame Emma. So I'll use my own name, thank you! Any
objections?"

"No. None at all. Come now, my child, I'll show you your room and
introduce you to the other girls," Madame Emma said.

7

"No," Doctor Enrique Sepúlvera said. "You have been lucky —again, Mireille. There is nothing. You may put your clothes back on, my dear. . . ."

"Why?" Mireille said sullenly. "Afraid I'll tempt you too much, Enrique?"

"You *do* tempt me too much," Enrique chuckled. "But the day—or the night—I can no longer resist that temptation, I'll come up to Kearny Street and pay you a little visit—at French Em's. . . ."

"Oh, *merde!*" Mireille said, and started to dress. She said plaintively, "You—you're sure I haven't caught anything awful, even yet?"

"You haven't caught anything. If you follow the precautions I outlined, taking those blue pills—their chief ingredient's mercury, so you mustn't overdose yourself, child; mercury's highly poisonous, you realize —a disinfectant douche, as quickly as possible after each—hmmmn— contact, extreme personal hygiene, a bath before and after work—you should be able to avoid a—well—disease of the unfortunate nature one usually catches in such places—for a considerable length of time. But the *only* sure way to escape ending up as a palsied, poxy wreck, darling, is to quit what you're doing. Altogether. Now."

"All right," Mireille said. "I—mean to. I'm going to. Enrique, you haven't any other patients waiting, have you?"

"No. You're the last. That's why I gave you this hour. I knew you'd want to talk."

"You were right. But could we go somewhere else? To a restaurant, maybe? I—I don't have to go back before midnight. I told Em I'd be out until then. I'm inviting *you.* You'll let me pay for your supper, won't you? Or are you afraid to be seen with me? Or—ashamed?"

"Neither," Enrique said cheerfully. "You dress both tastefully and discreetly, Mireille. And your manners would pass muster anywhere. Besides, Paqui—or, as you call her with that tricky accent of yours, Paci—knows you've become a patient of mine. She asks after you frequently—always with great fondness. Nothing would make her happier than to know you've got out of the bad life, child . . ."

"Told you I'm going to!" Mireille said angrily; "only—don't rush me, Enrique!"

"*I'm* not rushing you—time is. The law of averages. Here it is September 1854. And you've been an inmate of Em's parlor house since the fall of fifty-one—since shortly after the Vigilance Committee cleaned up San Francisco, or tried to. Funny—that was one of the greatest events in this city's history, and all it struck the vast majority of average citizens—including me!—as, was a couple of lynchings, and a lot of noise. Three years. All right, you still look like a schoolgirl, or an angel; but how long can you keep it up? Tell me: Have you had any—well—false alarms? I mean—"

"Have I got caught? Yes. Twice. But I don't have to *do* anything, Doctor. I—miscarry. Before three months. I know that, because I didn't *try* to do anything. I—hid—my condition from Em so she wouldn't call that murdering quack she keeps on her payroll to—snatch unwanted bundles from heaven. I—I *wanted* my babies. Whoever the hell their fathers were. . . ."

"Mireille, you're crazy!" Enrique groaned.

"I know. What of it? Come on. Where shall we go?"

"How about La Fonda Mexicana between Montgomery and Sansone?"

"Oh no!" Mireille wailed. "All those chili peppers and such will put me to bed for a week! Or give me the trots. What d'you say to Dalton's? It's in the same area, and the food is—edible, anyhow. The atmosphere is nice. Cozy. Quiet. We can talk there without shouting at the top of our lungs. . . ."

"All right. Anywhere you say, my dear. Tell me something, Mireille: How old are you? Twenty-two? Twenty-three?"

"Oh, Lord!" Mireille said.

"Sorry!" Enrique said. "So I'm giving you a couple of years too many?"

"More than a couple. I am exactly nineteen years old, Enrique. And you can check that with Paci. She knows how old I was when we first met. You mean I look—"

"Anywhere between twenty-three and twenty-seven. Yes. So, that life *is* getting to you, Mireille. Get out of it, child. I beg that of you—on behalf of all of us who love you!"

"Including—Willy?" Mireille said, very quietly.

"Including Willy," Enrique said.

"By the way—how is he?" Mireille said, with elaborate casualness.

"Very well. His lung has finally healed up altogether. And he has adapted almost completely to life as a gringo. I'd swear he even *thinks* in English now. Ernesto Martin has made him a full partner. Once Willy resigned himself to the business world, he took to it like a duck to water. Says he finds it exciting, that matching wits with canny negotiators is almost as much fun as rounding up cattle. He's even brought new blood into the business. A merger is in the offing: soon it will be Martin, Kilpatrick and Kinnan—the papers are already being drawn up. Well, here we are. . . ."

They entered the Dalton House, were conducted to a table, sat down. Enrique ordered for them both: steak, salad, red wine, and, for dessert, apple pie.

"Who is—this Kinley?" Mireille asked. "You say Willy brought him into the business?"

"Kinnan, not Kinley. Sean Kinnan—a young Irishman, highly educated, charming. Son of a well-off family who emigrated to Australia a few years ago; didn't like it, started home again, stopped off here en route—most sailing ships from Australia to England do, y'know—found the Gold Rush in full cry, and decided to stay, largely because business opportunities were so good. Went into banking and real estate. Made good from the outset, being rather superior people themselves. Anyhow, it seems young Sean heard somebody call Willy by his family name, Kilpatrick, in a tavern one day, and struck up a conversation with him on the basis of their both being Irishmen."

"Strange. That's true, isn't it? At least by half," Mireille murmured.

"It is. Anyhow, they quickly became fast friends. But Willy brought Sean into the business in self-defense. And, even at that, accidentally. You see, Ernesto had been parading his eldest daughter Marimar—María del Mar, to be strict about it—before Willy. But he wasn't having any, thank you!"

"Thank God!" Mireille said.

Enrique looked at her.

"Child," he said sadly; "don't go on—entertaining hopes. That can never be. Not now. Believe me, it can't."

"I know," Mireille said morosely. "Go on, will you, please!"

"It seems that young Kinnan was admiring with great fervor the beauty of a girl of the type of my Paquita, so Willy, to test him, drawled, 'Would you *marry* a little sunburnt greaser wench like that one?' "

"And?" Mireille said.

" 'In a minute!' Sean shot back at him, and added, 'I say, old boy, the prejudices of you Yanks are a bit hard to take at times! I think that Mexican girls are absolutely stunning!' "

"So then Willy took him to the Martins' and introduced him to María del Mar, and he fell for her—?"

"Like a ton of the best!" Enrique chuckled. "The wedding's scheduled for the first Sunday in October—that is, next month—at the Catholic church on Vallejo Street, just below the bull ring. No problems, not even religious. Kinnan is Irish, and hence automatically Catholic. The business is booming. And after the engagement was announced, the all-gringo Merchants and Traders Club voted to invite Ernesto Martin to become a member. Nobody blackballed him, not even the Americans who have businesses in the same block, and hence knew he's Mexican. So Ernesto's walking on air. Sean's father, Ross Kinnan, called on the Martins and was delighted with his daughter-in-law-to-be. Gave her a hearty kiss and told her to call him 'Papa'! 'Twas he who suggested the merger. So everybody's happy, even Willy . . ."

"What's he so happy about?" Mireille snapped. "If I know anything about people, it's a wonder he didn't maneuver himself out of a job!"

Again Enrique looked at her.

"Mireille, how any one as smart as you are ever managed to make such a mess out of her life, I'll never understand." He sighed. "You're right. By pushing dear little Marimar—who's a lovely child, and would have made him an excellent wife—off on Sean Kinnan, he did narrow his own opportunities considerably. In fact, I strongly advised Willy to marry her."

"But he doesn't want her. He wants *me*," Mireille said with quiet stubbornness. "And just as soon as I can figure out how to get out of this filthy business, I'm going to—"

"Mireille—no. You can't. It's—too late," Enrique said.

"Why—too late?" Mireille said.

"That wedding. It's going to be a double wedding," Enrique said. "Willy's going to marry Molly Kinnan, Sean's younger sister. I don't know whether you've ever met any Irish lassies, but some of them are— exquisite. Molly is. Hair like a sunset; eyes like the sea. Complexion like a rosebud on a misty morning with the dew still on it. Sean took Willy home to dinner the night after Willy had presented him to—and with! —Marimar. That night Willy met the whole Kinnan family, including

Molly, who apparently didn't impress him too much, for again he hung back—still dreaming of you, I suppose. But our Willy is quite a boy, as you know. It seems that little Miss Kinnan was impressed with him; very much so. In fact, before the supper was over she was on the border of apoplexy! And since her dearest darling didn't bother to call again, that state of temporary insanity we call love got steadily worse, until it reached such a fevered pitch that her brother felt compelled to take the matter in hand. He called on Willy and put it to him squarely: 'I say, Old Boy, what d'you think of my baby sister? She's completely *gone* over you, y'know. So if you've someone else in mind, you'd better let me know. I'll have to start force-feeding her like a Christmas goose ruddy soon now, or she's going to disappear! She's given up eating altogether, Mother tells me. And when I'm at home, I need an oceangoing steam packet to navigate through the floods and floods of tears!' So Willy rushed right over and did right by the little Molly, thereby ensuring his happiness and his future at one fell stroke, my dear. To acquire one's self an heiress and a stunning blonde in one delectable little bundle is quite a coup, it seems to me. . . ."

Mireille sat there. She didn't move. Or speak. Or breathe. She only sat there. And distilled diamonds. Poured them down her cheeks.

"I'm—sorry, Mireille, but you had to be told," Enrique said.

"Don't be. Are—Lola and Merchi going to be invited to the wedding?"

"Can't be. They've disappeared. Willy thinks they're—dead. So do I, for that matter."

"Dead?" Mireille whispered.

"Yes. You know the Sydney Ducks set the town on fire two more times after the conflagration of September 1850 that made it possible for Willy to get you and Paqui through Sydney Town and all the way over to Marta Gonzales' inn without having to stage a gun battle, as he surely would have had to do if the Ducks hadn't been so busy about their looting. You were out at my ranch when both of them happened. The first was on May third and fourth, 1851, and the greatest, or worst, of the six major fires San Francisco has suffered so far. Twenty-two blocks burned, over two thousand buildings—among them, by a freakish gust of wind that drove the flames across Pacific Street *toward* Sydney Town for once, both the Dirty Spoon and Garcia's Boar's Head—"

"And Merchi and Lola—got burned up, you think? I didn't like them very much, for all that they were Willy's sisters; but just the same . . ."

"No. Not then. But on June twenty-second ten more blocks burned, as well as parts of six more. Between Clay and Broadway as far west as

Stockton, and even Powell. Lola and Merchi disappeared during that
one. . . ."

"But what were they doing in that part of town?" Mireille demanded.
"Little Chile doesn't extend south of Broadway; and generally speaking,
people who look as Mexican—no, *Indian*—as Lola and Merchi did stay
out of the American districts, especially when they're *women*. So?"

"Ah! That's the question. I suspect that having lost their incomes
when the Boar's Head burned, they decided to do a little sneak thievery
among the gringos, and chose the night to do it very badly indeed. The
bodies of the people who died in both the 1851 holocausts were usually
unrecognizable. When a corpse has been charred into a charcoal
mummy, even its sex becomes difficult or impossible to determine, you
know. I'm quite sure we've seen the last of those two poor little bitches.
So is Willy. He stopped his search for them all of two years ago. . . ."

"He must be—relieved," Mireille said quietly. "They were a pair of
disgraces, those two. And they were much too dark-complexioned to
have done him any good with his new in-laws, weren't they?"

"He *is* relieved. And for exactly the reasons you said," Enrique said.
"Yet he loved them, and wanted to give them Christian burial. But
finding any trace of them, or of their bodies—has proved impossible.
Mireille, may *I* ask you a favor?"

"Such as?" Mireille said tartly.

"That you refrain from appearing at Willy's wedding—and arming a
scandal. Give the poor boy a chance, will you?"

She peered at him. Flashed him a grin that was wickedness' self.

"Mind reader!" she said.

"Mireille, please!"

"Ah, but I am *not* pleased, dear Doctor! He threw me over. Called me
a cheap whore. Sent me away with How-ward Tellefair because—"

"Not because Tellefair, who is one of the most despicable pimps extant, lost you to Big Jules in a poker game, my dear. Willy knew that. So
it must have been because Tellefair—or someone—supplied him with
some new and startling information about your past. I don't know what
that information was. I don't want to know it. I only want to retain what
fondness—and what respect—for you I can. Besides, the only pertinent
question about the whole murky business is this, Mireille: Was whatever
Tellefair told Willy—true?"

Mireille bowed her head.

"Yes," she said bitterly. "And it wasn't even *all* the truth. How-ward
doesn't know the whole story of my life. Shall we turn this booth into a

confessional box, so that I can give you a day-by-day recounting of my sins? I warn you it'll take hours!"

"No, thank you!" Enrique said.

"Well, I will tell you *one*. An item that How-ward doesn't even know. Nor Willy. Nor—anybody—except—Paci. I'm—a lesbian. A *marimacho*. Paci knows that because she's my lover. I—I turned her!"

Enrique threw back his head and laughed aloud.

"If you did, *I* turned her back around again, my dear," he chuckled; "and one hundred eighty degrees at that. She's seven months pregnant, right now. . . ."

"Ohhhhhhh, Enrique!" Mireille gasped. "How wonderful! I'm so happy I could cry! *Merde!* I *am* crying, aren't I? Oh, dear, dear Paci! Dear—*you!* Can I give you a kiss? To take home to Paci, anyhow?"

"Of course, child," Enrique said.

She kissed him. Then she said sadly:

"No. Don't take it home. Go—wash it off. Right now. A dose of the clap or the pox would be a hell of a gift for an unborn kid, wouldn't it? And anyhow, what makes you so damn sure you're the father?"

"I'm not sure," Enrique said with a complacent grin, "but I assure you I haven't the slightest intention to investigate the matter at all, not to mention thoroughly, Mireille. 'Where ignorance is bliss, 'tis folly to be wise!' And at my age, looking a gift horse in the mouth is not only foolish, it's insane!"

He smiled at her peacefully, happily. But what he saw in her face sobered him.

"Mireille, you—you won't spoil Guillermo's wedding?" he said. "Promise me?"

"I promise. I won't spoil Willy's wedding. I'll only make it coincide with—my funeral. That won't spoil it, will it?"

He thought, 'That doesn't worry me. You aren't like that, little Mirla. You won't kill yourself! You are—much too brave!'

He said, "Come, I'll take you home now . . . ."

And she, "No. Home is a whorehouse, Doctor! I'll go alone."

That same night, Mireille saw Judge Alain Curtwright come into the parlor of French Em's; and it came to her, all at once and very completely, what to do. Judge Curtwright, the same man whom Enrique's cook, Josefina, had told her about in great detail some months before she ever had occasion to meet him, was a remarkably well-preserved, even handsome, gentleman of some sixty-one or sixty-two years. His behavior puzzled French Em's riding fillies completely. That is, unlike any other client of Em's establishment, he played no favorites—going upstairs, on his infrequent visits "To this house of love and beauty!" as he, with gentle mockery, called it, with each of the girls in turn, no matter how old or ill-favored any particular one of them might be.

And now, suddenly, Mireille realized why. 'He's afraid,' she reasoned. 'Scared that one of us might stop being—a piece of tail. Lying there— wiggling. Warm. Soft. Wet. Better than Widow Thumb and Her Four Skinny Daughters, but not much. Change what he's doing, getting a little relief from a rock-hard cock and a pair of aching balls, into an act— no, an exchange—that means something, because the creature he's doing it to—with!—has become a human being. A person. Not a pair of tits, more or less—nice. A round, soft behind. Two thighs to lock around his pumping arse. A hot and hairy slit to be rammed into, used. No. A person. With a *face* on her. That can be recognized, identified. Maybe even—a mind. Who *is* somebody. Who can't be disregarded as—a hired cunt. Because she's more than that, much more. So he'd have to feel something for her. Even—love, maybe. And he couldn't bear that. That *would* be cheating, wouldn't it? On his poor mad helpless wife . . . So —bless you, Josefina! You've given me the key to this gilded cage. A one- way ticket out—with no return! So now, to take advantage. Believe me, dear, kind old man!—in comparison to the slimy scum who come here— it will be no sacrifice. I'll wager you were as beautiful a wild sweet male thing at twenty-six or seven as my—dear God!—lost Willy is now . . .'

She raised those enormous dark eyes of hers—and smashed the paral- lel, ruler-straight, twin, light-locked beams of her gaze like very nearly physical battering rams into his face. Held him there with a look so fixed, unblinking, unwavering, intent, that his—awed and astonished!—mind shaped the thought, 'Jesus! The flesh is going to drop off my bones in another second or two . . .' But then that sun-glare-through-topaz feral intensity abruptly softened, and he saw that what couldn't be—the ut- terly impossible—actually in that moment *was*, against all his experience, all he knew of life: the swooning tenderness swimming in those Stygian pupils, drowning the double-imaged reflection of his face.

He crossed to her at once. Said, "Why are you looking at me so strangely, child?"

She whispered, her voice a murmur of light-filled, crystalline waters:

"Because I—I love you, sir. Wait! I know. That sounds like a lie—and what's worse, a whore's lie. And it—isn't. Come. Go upstairs with me. Not to—make love. No! Not to go through that filthy, stupid farce of making love. That charade that doesn't fool anybody—neither the men who come to this meat market, nor us—the not quite living flesh on sale.

Or for rent, temporarily anyhow. Instead to—talk. To allow me to explain to you—what you mean to me, what I *feel* . . ."

He stared at her. Said, sadly, "Mireille, daughter—I'm an old, old man; and you're the most beautiful girl in this house. So don't tell me that—"

"I love you? All right, I won't—if you don't want me to. But—do me a favor, will you, sir? Come upstairs with me. For an hour. Half. Twenty minutes. But during that time, talk to me. Treat me like—as though I still were!—a human being. After that I—I'll do anything you want. No matter how disgusting—vile. You name it—and it's yours. But I'll still be grateful to you, sir—for having given me back—*me*, even for that little while. Myself. Who I am. Or, at least, who I was—before—"

"Before—what, child?" he asked.

"I became—garbage. Dirt. Goods for sale. Shoddy goods at that. Will you do me—that favor, sir?"

He peered at her, his wise old blue eyes filled with wonder, and with doubt.

"Of course," he said crisply; and, turning, walked over to the desk.

"Em," he said, "I'd like to have a private chat with little Mireille—upstairs. Couple of things I—we—need to clear up, old dear!"

Mireille saw, with blissful satisfaction, how the two or three girls whose turn with Judge Curtwright normally came before hers were glaring at her. The Judge was a great favorite among the inmates at Em's. He was very generous, unfailingly gentle—even polite and considerate—with them all. Which, in San Francisco in 1854, wasn't the usual behavior of a whorehouse client. Naturally the poor creatures were almost fond of him, sought pathetically to please him. And failed at it, they being what they were; and he who, and also what, he was.

"Well, Mireille—?" he said, once they were in that sickeningly ornate bedroom.

She put her hands on his shoulders, went up on tiptoe, and kissed his mouth, her lips on his trembling, trembling, anguished, tender, almost prayerful, lighter than a breath, a sigh. Stood back, staring at him. Let the great tears glaze her eyes, brim upon her sooty lashes, pour—topaz and silver!—down her cheeks.

"My God!" he said.

"Please," she murmured, her voice tear-drowned, choking; "may I say —'I love you'? Just this once. But I *need* to tell you that. There's a— compression—an oppression—all around my heart from trying to hold it back. From trying to hide—repress—the way I feel about you, I mean . . ."

"Now, Mireille—" he said.

"Why can't a young girl love an older man? You—my darling old Creaky Bones—have done it so well! Got old, I mean. You—you're so beautiful! Rubbed down and polished, with all your rough edges—and splinters—worn off. Talk to me! I—I love your voice. It's so kind. So genuinely kind. You're—so good to us. That's why—I took a chance. I don't think it would be impossible to convince you that I am—a girl. A real, live girl—who thinks, and feels, and who could even—love—if anybody would let her . . ."

"You've done that already, child. Convinced me, I mean. But what I don't understand is why you picked *me* for this—well—experiment of yours. Mind telling me that?"

"Because you're you. Because you're old. I can't stand young men. I think I must be—incestuous by nature . . ."

"Good Lord!" he said.

"I am. I must be. I adored my father, and spent my whole life fighting pitched battles—no, screeching cat fights!—with Mother, until I grew up enough to realize that I was just plain jealous because Papa belonged to her, and I couldn't have him for all my own. And I wanted to. Oh, how I wanted to! I honestly don't know what would have happened, if— after I was thirteen years old, say—Papa had ever picked me up, and carried me off to bed . . ."

"Dear Jesus!" Judge Curtwright said.

"Only—he died—was killed, when I was about that age. So look at it this way: Would it be—almost normal—for little girls who adored their papas to be—attracted toward older men when they grew up? What are little boys to little girls, anyhow, sir? Noisy, rough, smelly, cruel little beasts who pinch us and punch us, and pull our hair and break our dolls and make us cry. While Papa is—almost a god. Who takes us in his arms, tickles us, and tosses us, squealing with delight, up to the ceiling. Brings us candy when he comes home from work. Spoils us rotten—that, yes!—but how we *love* being spoiled!"

Alain Curtwright gazed at her intently with his shrewd old eyes, studied her, really.

"Child," he said, "you're kind of crazy, aren't you? But there's method in your madness, I think. What are you getting at? What do you want from me?"

She came up very close to him.

"I—want you to take me out of here. Put me—in a little house, on a quiet street," she said slowly, simply. "*Not* a big, expensive house. A little, economical one that I can run without servants. I don't want jewels. I don't want furs. I don't want a carriage. I don't want fine silk dresses. I only want one thing, really—"

"And that is?" he said.

"To be—*yours*," she said quietly. "To—belong to you."

"Mireille, child," he said, "that's awfully hard to believe."

"Then—don't believe it. Just try it. Give me a chance."

"Mireille, I—I can't. I have—"

"A wife. I knew that. And also that—she's mad. So you can never divorce her. I suspect that, being a man of honor, you don't even want to. Oh, this is so hard! You haven't a—home. Under those circumstances, all you have is a house that's a combination jail and—lunatic asylum. I want to make a home for you. To be—not your mistress, but your wife. In every way but the one I can't be, which is legally. I don't want to be a rich man's toy. A doll in a fancy, overdecorated dollhouse, filled with velvet cushions and potted plants! I want the chance to make you fall in love with me. To learn to—respect me. To let me be the good, decent girl I should have been—but wasn't allowed to be . . ."

"Child, with your beauty and your charm you could still, even yet, meet some young, unmarried man, and become a wife in every sense!" Judge Curtwright said.

"No. That's not true—as a man as wise as you are ought to know. I've had too much of a past to have any future, that way. I—I tried it once. Getting married, I mean. Our planned wedding didn't even come off. He got to brooding over—all the men who'd had me, enjoyed my body—and left me. Even if I could go somewhere else, a place where I'm not known, the risk would still be too great. Just let one fellow, out of all the —thousands—who've come upstairs with me for—a ten-dollar tumble— show up in the place I ran off to, hid myself in, and my new life would be wrecked. And the only thing you can guarantee about a marriage to a man who'd known me while I was the star for a night in Emma's house of ill fame is that the first time he got mad at me he'd call me 'filthy whore'! Or that he'd go crazy wondering whom I was warming his side of the bed with, the minute he was out of the house. Or if—our children— were really *his*. With you, my dearest, darling Judge, I wouldn't have any of those problems . . ."

"I don't see why not! I can be as jealous as the next man, I assure you!" he said, only half in jest.

"Because you're—intelligent. Wise. After you'd tested the matter for a month or two, and found that you could come home at any hour of the day or night, and find me there, patiently waiting—No, breathlessly listening!—for the sound of your footsteps on the stairs, you'd learn to believe me. Believe *in* me. After you'd seen how glad—how awfully, awfully glad I'll always be to see you; after you'd learned the difference between given love, and faked passion—badly, stupidly faked at that. After you'd discovered your lightest whim was my law; your idlest desire, my ten commandments, your happiness, my very life—Oh, dear little Jesus! How can I make you see it—believe—"

She bent her head and cried; angrily, noisily, sobbing like a child.

He put his arms around her, drew her to him.

"Mireille," he said wearily, "don't try quite so hard . . ."

"You see!" she stormed, "you still don't believe me!"

"No," he chuckled, "I don't. And not being a fool, I probably never will. Which doesn't matter. You'll have your little house, on that quiet street—as soon as I can arrange it. . . ."

She stared at him with tear-blazed eyes.

"But—" she moaned, "since you don't believe me, I don't see—"

"It's worth it," he said gravely. "I've played by the rules all my life— and what has it got me? Nothing. An empty house, with a madwoman howling in it. So now—to gamble on you, as my good and oh, so wise friend Enrique Sepúlvera gambled on your little playmate Paquita—"

"You—you knew that? He—he—told you? What else did he tell you about me? Ohhhhh Lord! What else, Judge—Alain? What—else?"

"Nothing else, my dear. I didn't ask him. I didn't—and don't—want to know. Enrique's a gentleman. He doesn't talk about women, and certainly doesn't volunteer information about them. And since he se- renely believes that a man has a right to his private follies, he'd very likely approve of—this little arrangement of ours. He's always contended that a man's entitled to be any kind of a jackass he wants to be, except a blind one; so he'd say—knowing that the one thing I am not is blind— go ahead, my friend! Enjoy this gift from the Furies and the Fates, whatever little time you can . . ."

"It won't be a little time," Mireille swore fervently. "It's going to be —years and years! All the rest of your life. All the rest of mine!"

Judge Alain Curtwright shook his head with weary, patient resigna- tion.

"Dear child—please!" he said.

8

"MA'AM," JASMINE SAID, "CAN I HAVE A WORD WITH YOU, PLEASE?"

Mireille looked at her maid. That Jasmine was from New Orleans was certain. She spoke patois rapidly, fluently, and without accent, but with certain turns of phrase, pronunciations, idiomatic expressions much more current among black Creoles than among white ones. Which meant the girl was very likely a quadroon, or even an octoroon. But it was her speech alone—and this only in French, not in English—that betrayed her origins; physically, considering the fact that she had reddish blond hair and blue-green eyes, she appeared more nearly a bona fide member of the white race than Mireille herself. Her name, Jasmine La Fleur, was, of course, preposterous. Nobody, Mireille was sure, had ever been named Jasmine the Flower in all of human history. It followed, then, that the name was an alias, and, in consequence, the fair Jasmine very likely a fugitive from some Basin or Royal street parlor house.

That deduction, surely an accurate one, bothered Mireille not at all. In fact, it amused her, appealed to her sense of the ironic. She knew perfectly well that ninety-seven percent of the so-called French "Cyprians" as the newspapers in San Francisco politely labeled harlots, came not from France but from Louisiana; and that ninety of that ninety-seven percent were either quadroons or *mulatas* fair enough to get by— to pass, as the absolutely idiotic saying went, for white.

'Hell of a lot of this burg's future leading lights are going to have an ol' Black mammy, or a liver-lipped, crepey-haired Uncle Tom hid away amid the branches of their family trees,' she thought gleefully, 'considering how fast the johns out here are marrying all th' riding fillies and turning 'em into ladies!'

"And what d'you want a word with me about, Jasmine?" she said.

"Has some fast-talking Mac skipped out of town and left you with a package?"

"Oh, no, ma'am!" Jasmine gasped. "I'm a good girl, me!"

"I'll bet," Mireille said sardonically; "specially flat on your back, with your nightgown rolled up under your chin. Come on, out with it, child: What's on your mind?"

"Business proposition, ma'am," Jasmine said. "Those water lots you own down on the Bay twixt Clay and Sacramento streets. Would you like to sell 'em?"

Mireille stared at her maid.

"Well, I'll be damned!" she swore. "And who, may I ask, told you I own waterfront property, saucy girl?"

"Oh, ma'am," Jasmine said, "I don't mean to be forward or anything. It's just that a friend of mine wants to buy 'em. And since she's the—person who brought me out here from N'Orleans—paid my steamboat fare and all, I was sort of 'bliged to favor her by asking . . ."

"Who's this friend of yours, Jasmine?" Mireille asked.

"Madame Pleasant, ma'am. Mary Ellen Pleasant. She—she's just about the richest woman in San Francisco. . . ."

"Hmmmmm—I've heard about *her*," Mireille said. "Colored woman, isn't she?"

"Don't know that, ma'am. She sure don't *look* colored if she is . . ."

"*You* don't and you are," Mireille said dryly.

"Yes'm. I'm a free Woman of Color. My mama was a quadroon, and my papa was a German from Law's German Coast. Tha's how come I got this here hair and these eyes. But soon as I've got enough money saved, I'm gonna quit being colored so fast it'll make your head swim. Move down to th' south part o' town pass Market Street and marry myself a white man. You gonna tell me that I can't?"

"No. You can, all right. In fact, you ought to. I approve. I'll be your matron of honor and give you away. And throw in a dowry on top of that, child. For anybody who looks like you to have to put up with what niggers have to is purely a sin and a shame. All right, tell me this: How did Mary Ellen Pleasant find out I owned those water lots?"

"Don't know that, ma'am. She's got ways of finding out whatever she wants to know. Maybe some of th' horny menfolks what go to French Em's told her—"

"Jasmine!" Mireille said.

"Sorry, ma'am! Didn't mean no disrespect. I was in a parlor house, too, till Madame Pleasant bought me out of it. Tell you something you don't know: She *owns* French Em's. Always did. Madame Em wasn't never doing nothing else but fronting for her. She owns three first-class boardinghouses—exclusive supper clubs, really, serving th' best damn food in town. A saloon on Sansome Street, a livery stable, three laundries, and more waterfront property than you can shake a stick at. And a lot of them places in what th' newspapers call the Barbary Cast nowadays. Used to be Pacific Street, Clark's Point, and Sydney Town, didn't it?"

"Yes," Mireille said. "But if Madame Pleasant knows so much, she ought to know that those lots were a gift from my—protector, Judge Curtwright, who would be offended if I sold them . . ."

"*Two* of 'em are," Jasmine said quietly; "the other *eight* you bought with th' money you made your own self, and I reckon we both can just kindly forget *how*. Wait, ma'am! Madame Pleasant told me to tell you that, if you raised 'zactly the objection you *did* raise. She needs that property *bad*, ma'am—"

"Why? Has somebody told her that the earth fill from the new streets being cut through the hills back of town with steam shovels has already brought six of my lots above the waterline, and that the rest will be dry land before 1855 comes in?"

"Yes'm. And she figgered on you knowing that, too. Them lots are gonna make you a rich woman. Told me to tell you she's willing to pay you every penny of what your property's worth. She ain't out to cheat you, ma'am. She's even willing to cut you in on the take of a couple o' th' businesses she's planning to start in th' buildings she's agonna build on that there land, if she can 'suade you t' sell. . . ."

"Hmmmmn," Mireille said. "But, Jasmine, I haven't any especial need for money. My—friend—the Judge is very generous with me. Besides, those lots are going to go on increasing in value with the years. Smarter to keep them as an investment, it appears to me. You realize the Judge—is not exactly a young man. Of course I'm sure he means to do all right by me when he dies, but—"

"But *can* he? Tha's th' question, ain't—isn't—it, ma'am? His crazy wife has got four brothers here in town. Come out in that there same wagon train with th' Judge and his missus. And since they ain't right bright, none of 'em, they ain't never managed to earn or save a dime. So they're waiting for that nice, sweet ol' man to die—them, too—so they kin git their greedy paws on whatever money he leaves their poor loony sister. And if he leaves too much to you, Madame Pleasant says, they're sure to contest th' will on behalf o' their sister, and under th' circumstances they'll win their case. Tha's what you mean, ain't it?"

"Exactly. And since 'Mammy' Pleasant knows so damn much about my affairs, she ought to also know that those lots are the best insurance for the future I have!"

"She do—does—know that. But she's got an idea tha's way better, ma'am. Best security you could ever get your hands on. She told me to ask you mighty kindly to call on her. She lives at 920 Washington Street, y'know. Says she's got a proposition to offer you that you just can't turn down, 'cause even if it ain't got nothing to do with cash money this very minute, it'll fix things up so you'll be damn nigh rich as she is in the future, by making mighty damn sure that every red copper the Judge has got will go to you in a way not nobody can take it away from you when he passes on. And on top of that, she says what she's got in mind will make you happy as a jaybird right now. . . ."

Mireille stared at Jasmine.

"Now I am intrigued," she said. "All right, I will call on her. Next Sunday night. The Judge never visits me on weekends because he feels duty-bound to stay home those days with his wife. You may tell her that when you see her. . . ."

"Yes'm. And ma'am, one more thing: Please don't call her 'Mammy' Pleasant when you go to see her. That really gets her wild. You see, when she first come out here, back in April of fifty-two, some newspaperman who wasn't even there wrote an article for his paper 'bout her. . . ."

"So?" Mireille said.

"He got it mostly right. Only Mr. Charlie Case and Mr. Charlie Heiser—yes'm, they was *both* named Charlie—wasn't on that dock on purpose to meet her 'cause somebody had done wrote 'em she was coming. That newspaper fella made that up, I reckon. They was there because they always goes down to Long Wharf every day to tend to their own export, import business. And when they seen her they was puzzled. Her's a little darker than you and me, but not much. She's been passing all her life, and is down on th' N'Orleans census rolls as white, as well as on the register in the Ursulines' convent school she was sent to as a child. The truth was they couldn't figger out what she was, and they was betting she was Eyetalian or Greek or some other o' them dark-complexion foreigners. So they come right out and asked her, and she told 'em she was colored. She's an octoroon th' same as me, ma'am. She was born on a plantation near Augusta, Georgia. Her papa was a white man, and her mama was a quadroon from Haiti. So Mr. Case and Mr. Heiser asked her if she could cook, and when she said she could, they offered her the job as cook and manager of their boardinghouse. Paid her five hundred dollars a month, with no washing—not even dishwashing—agreed to from the outset. . . ."

"Jasmine, what's the point of all this? I've heard a great deal about Mammy Pleasant, but—"

"That. That 'Mammy' business. That fool reporter wrote a piece saying she was coal-black, weighed two hundred pounds, and was a famous cook from N'Orleans. Now you know as well as I do, ma'am, that neither back home, nor not nowhere in th' South do folks call a Black woman 'Mammy' till she's sixty years old or thereabouts. And they don't never call a light, bright, damn nigh white woman like me or Mary Ellen 'Mammy' even if she's got to be a hundred. 'Sides, Madame Pleasant ain't but thirty-eight years old right now, and she look ten years younger than that. Another thing, she's been living as a white woman her whole damn life and running niggers to freedom on the Underground Railroad. That's how come she had to leave; them Southerners was breathing down th' back of her neck too hard. She's slim and real pretty, and menfolks go wild over her to this day. And since she ain't Black, and is sure Lord younger than anybody's ol' Black mammy ever is, that there 'Mammy' business gets her wild."

"I can see how it would," Mireille said.

"She ain't even rightly Southern. Born South, right enough. But 'sides from one year in N'Orleans, furtherest South she ever lived was Charles Town, West Virginia. She talks just like a Yankee, cause she's done lived in Missouri, Boston, Massachusetts, and Cincinnati, Ohio, and a heap more places I don't even recall. She don't speak French, cause what the Ursulines taught her when she was ten years old, she's done forgot. So you'll have to talk English to her. Only don't call her 'Mammy,' please! She's just about th' best friend you could ever look for when it comes to helping a body out, but, good baby Jesus! don't make an enemy out of her! People what does that, ups and disappears. Couple o' fellas what got her riled was found floating in th' Bay. And nobody could pin what happened to them on her, not nobody!"

Mireille stared at Jasmine. Then she said, very quietly, "You might inform your off-colored friend that I don't scare very easily, child. And that people who cross me live to regret it. That is, when they live at all. Now, get out of here, will you? I've things to do. . . ."

But that Sunday night, all the same, Mireille called on the famous, or infamous, "Mammy" Pleasant. To the clatter of the brass knocker on the front door of the house at 920 Washington Street, an imposing figure answered, a tall, powerful man, blacker than Cain's original sin of fratricide.

"Who're you?" Mireille demanded.

"William, ma'am. William Willmore. I'm Madame Pleasant's handyman. You want to see Madame? If you'll tell me your name, I'll go see if she's at liberty to see you," the Black man said quietly.

"Well, I'll be damned!" Mireille said.

William Willmore loosed a midnight bass chuckle that fell on Mireille's ear like a felt—and rather contemptuous—caress.

"Reckon you are, miss," he said. "Most folks be, nowadays. What did you say your name was?"

"I didn't," Mireille said dryly; "But since California's in the Union as a free state by majority vote, let's not stand on ceremony. My name's Duclos. Mademoiselle Mireille Duclos. And I rather think Madame Pleasant's expecting me. . . ."

"She is, mamzelle, now that you've done gone and told me your name. Said I was to show you into her sitting room th' minute you got here. Right this way, mamzelle. . . ."

He opened the massive oaken doors to the sitting room. Its furnishings were opulent; the taste with which they had been selected, as was usual in those middle years of Victoria's reign, horrendous.

"Can I brink you a li'l drink while you're waiting?" Willmore said. "Some sherry? port? A light wine, maybe?"

"No, nothing, thank you," Mireille said shortly. She thought, 'This is no place to pickle my brains in alcohol just like they did poor Joaquin Murieta's head. Ugh! What a sight! His head, and Three Finger's hand. Wonder what on earth made me go to see *that?* Of course, I didn't really know Joaquin. Only saw him that one time when he and Manolo brought Willy into *la casa grande* on a stretcher. But I knew *Tres Dedos* and liked him. I liked him very much. I guess that was why seeing his hacked-off hand—the one with only three fingers on it, naturally—in that bottle of spirits affected me so much. That head, now—was it really Joaquin's? Didn't look too much like him, as I remember him, but . . .' she paused; then went on with her thought, 'but I'm glad Willy is out of it for good. Playing Robin Hood may be noble, but you always end up like that—with your head or your hand in a glass jar full of whiskey, in a museum of horrors, corner of Halleck and Sansome streets. . . .'

"*Ma'moiselle* Duclos, I am delighted to welcome you to my home," that pleasant alto voice said, in perfect, accentless French.

Mireille whirled.

Mary Ellen Pleasant had, she decided at once, one of the most patrician and commanding faces she had ever seen. The face of a great lady. A very great lady. Of—a queen. An empress. She didn't remember which empress Mary Ellen Plaisance—to spell her name right for once!

—reminded her of. Later in life, when she'd acquired the leisure, and resigned herself to wearing the glasses she needed for reading, she decided that Madame Pleasant was the very image of Valeria Messalina, the third wife of the Emperor Claudius, as far as her austere, aristocratic beauty was concerned—and probably topped even that wickedest woman of antiquity when it came to sheer evil.

"I was told that you didn't speak French, *madame,*" she said.

"I don't!" Mary Ellen Pleasant laughed. "I've been practicing that one phrase ever since your Jasmine—sweet child, isn't she?—told me you'd agreed to call. But sit down, won't you, my dear? William has told me you've declined a glass, but how would a cup of tea suit you? Accompanied by some little cakes? *Petits fours* you call them, don't you?"

"That would be—lovely," Mireille said.

Mary Ellen pulled the bell cord. William appeared like a djinn summoned up from the abode of the damned. His mistress gave the orders, waved him imperiously away.

"Look, Mademoiselle Duclos," she began at once, "I need that property of yours between Clay and Sacramento—especially now that it's soon going to be something more than sea bottom. I realize that your selling me *all* of it presents difficulties. I know Judge Curtwright. He would take it amiss if you so callously disposed of the gift he made to you in order to ensure your future. And who could blame him? So, don't sell it all to me. Keep the two lots he gave you. Sell me the other eight you bought yourself."

"Mind telling me how you knew that, madame?" Mireille said.

"Not at all. A friend of mine works in the office of Martin, Kilpatrick, Kinnan. In the real estate department. You bought your waterlogged lots through them—out of loyalty to dear Guillermo. Charming lad. Very handsome, indeed! I approve of your taste, my dear. . . ."

"Good Lord!" Mireille said.

"Incidentally, just as I placed Jasmine in your—establishment—Mademoiselle Duclos, I also placed Julie in the Kilpatricks' home. Molly—Mrs. Kilpatrick—fairly dotes on her. As does Señora Marimar Martin *de* Kinnan upon the little Aurore I placed with *them.* So if there is anything you need to know—"

"Dear little Jesus!" Mireille whispered. "Do you operate an employment agency for quadroon tarts or a nest of spies, madame?"

"A little of both." Mary Ellen Pleasant laughed. "Information is—power, dear child. A good many of the girls I've placed are pure white, though; and even more, pure Black. Color is nonsense, Mademoiselle Duclos. Intelligence and will are all. Don't you agree? I enjoyed the story of how you—hooked the Judge. Sheer force of character, that—Ah, here's our tea. . . ."

"Suppose I don't want to sell?" Mireille said as she sipped that fragrant oriental brew.

"You do," Mary Ellen said serenely. "You may not know it yet, but you do. Everyone always discovers she wants to sell when the offer's high enough. . . ."

"And yours is?" Mireille said quietly.

"You may name your price. That's not important. The good Judge keeps you in extravagant luxury, so the money side of the question is not likely to interest you too much at the moment. So here's my proposition: fifty thousand dollars for your eight lots, plus William Kilpatrick, or rather—since it's his Latin aspect that excites you, isn't it, dear?—Señor Don Guillermo Kilpatrick-Calvo, back—permanently—in your arms. . . ."

"The sweet blue eyes of Jesus!" Mireille breathed.

"Were they blue? I doubt it. I suspect his eyes were brown or black, and that he looked rather like Solomon Levy, that ratty little Jew who runs the Cheap John clothing store on Pacific Street between Montgomery and Sansome. Don't tell me you're religious? A devout Catholic? That you once were doesn't surprise me; but that your faith survived a stay in the Dirty Spoon and French Em's does."

"No—it didn't. What God let happen to me doesn't incline my heart toward piety. But why do you call that flossy bagnio French Em's? It's yours, isn't it?"

"Yes, it's mine. Who told you that?"

"I have my sources of information, too, Madame Pleasant. And I don't reveal them. I don't want them converted into fish bait in Yerba Buena Cove."

"Good for you! You have spunk, don't you? I like that. Come now, what d'you say to my proposition?"

"Sounds—enchanting. But what becomes of—dear Molly, and the Judge? Especially the Judge. I'm rather fond of him, you know . . ."

"Nothing will happen to either of them. You—are very intelligent, Mireille. That you have the real and actual possession of dear Willy ought to incline your heart to sufficient generosity to enable you to lend him back to his wife and his children once in a while, it seems to me. And as for the Judge, with the devoted help of young Kilpatrick you ought to be able to grant that dear, kind old man his heart's desire. . . ."

"His—heart's—desire?" Mireille got out.

"Why, yes. A son. You know how dreadfully he wants one, don't you?"

"Good Lord!" Mireille said. "You—you're incredible!"

"On the contrary, I'm very *credible*. Which is why I am very nearly a millionaire. And so will you be, my dear, if you allow me to guide you."

"I'd allow anyone to guide me who'd give me my Willy back, even the devil himself," Mireille said; then she paused and added dryly, "or the queen of the witches. . . ."

Mary Ellen Pleasant laughed merrily at that.

"Which I *am*," she said with amusement bubbling through her voice. "The Black people of San Francisco firmly believe I'm a mamaloi, a voodoo queen—a belief I encourage since it gives me considerable control over them. But to return to the subject under discussion: What do you say, my dear?"

Mireille thought about that.

"All right," she said at last. "Fifty thousand dollars is fair enough price for some lots that were on the bottom of the Bay up till now. Some of 'em still are, y'know. But I guess at the rate that part's being filled in, they'll all be high and dry before Christmas time. Only there's another point I'd like to bring up. Before I sign anything, Madame Pleasant, I want to be certain that you can deliver what you've promised: to send or give—Willy Kilpatrick back to me, that is."

"Then you'll never sign," Madame Pleasant said flatly, "because I can't guarantee that. You see, it doesn't depend upon me, Mademoiselle Duclos, but rather upon you."

"But you said—"

"I know. And I repeat it: Fifty thousand dollars for your lots and William—or rather, Guillermo—Kilpatrick back, permanently, in your arms. That last is, of course, a gamble. All relations between men and women are. Without exception, child. But I wish I were as sure that all my other ventures are going to prosper as I am that that one is. . . ."

"What makes you so sure?" Mireille said in a sullen, suspicious tone of voice.

"In the Kilpatrick manse," Madame Pleasant said, "there are, dear little Julie informs me, frequent quarrels. And you, child, are always the subject of them. And their cause. That visit you paid to the church on their wedding day—I must say you handled it well. In fact, your performance was masterly."

"Don't see why. I didn't do anything at all," Mireille said.

"Just that. You simply sat in a back pew, on the aisle, and wept. Silently. With immense dignity. You didn't scream, make a fuss, try to interrupt the ceremony. You sat there—and cried. But you did it—so well! Head up and proud, a flood of tears inundating your lovely face. You are—you must know—very beautiful, my dear. Within minutes everyone—especially all the men!—in all the pews around you was aware of your presence, and that the degree of heartbreak that you exhibited simply couldn't be faked."

"It wasn't," Mireille said.

"I know. My informant—a man—told me he was seized with an almost overwhelming desire to shoot Willy Kilpatrick for having made you suffer so."

"I'm glad he didn't," Mireille said.

"So am I. A corpse is only useful to—worms. And Don Guillermo is going to be of great utility to both of us, my dear! Anyway, when the organist played the recessional and the newly united pair came back down the aisle, they saw you sitting there—still crying. Young Mr. Kilpatrick, I'm told, turned as white as a sheet, had all he could do to keep his feet; and she—"

"Hissed like all the snakes Saint Patrick is supposed to have chased out of her native Ireland, 'Wil-ly Kilpatrick! Who *is* this girl?' "

"Exactly. And that marriage was finished, then and there. Doomed. You had dressed with great simplicity and care. Your clothes were tasteful. Nothing about you proclaimed the—unfortunate profession into which you had fallen—and which, now, you've used His Honor, the Judge to escape from—"

"Go on," Mireille said.

" 'But,' said my informant, 'she had a thousand Etnas erupting behind her eyes! Her very gaze was a lava flow. Jesus, Mary Ellen! She baked him alive! I could see the flesh melt, drip off him, his very bones start to go!' Poetic, what?"

"No," Mireille said flatly. "True. Less than true. That's the way I feel about Willy."

"Which is why you'll get him back. You—you've enslaved him for life, my dear. How could a sweet, simple Irish lass compete with you? Abed, her performance—if it can be called that—serves for procreation, but not to cool the sort of desires you've awakened in him. He's been seared by that Etna, burnt alive by that lava flow, so that no tepid—or even cool —Hibernian springs can ease him. One more quotation—from Julie, this time: 'Goddammit, Molly!' the master yelled; 'you *freeze* me to death!' "

"Have you got those papers ready?" Mireille said. "I'll sign them, if you have."

"There's no hurry. Let me tell you how to go about rehooking dear Willy first. 'Twouldn't do to spoil things, y'know. . . ."

"So that plan, or any other that seems feasible to you, will surely work. Your reconquest of William Kilpatrick presents small difficulties to my mind, or none at all. The only problem I foresee lies in one or both of you becoming too greedy for the exclusive possession of the other, or of each other. Let him keep his wife, his family; do not allow him to separate you from Alain Curtwright."

"Why?" Mireille said.

"Apart from the fact that Judge Curtwright is a much better man than young Mister—or Señor—Kilpatrick is, a spartan diet of love and affection between you and your lover will preserve that love and affection, my dear! Marriage—or any form of constant cohabitation—is the sure death of romance, believe me. On another, more practical plane, the fact that Kilpatrick and the Judge are of the same physical type— blue eyes, fair hair—makes a complementary combination of the two relationships wonderfully apt. You must try to get pregnant by your young lover as soon as you can."

"I—don't think I can," Mireille said sadly. "I—miscarry, Madame Pleasant. Spontaneously. I've never gone much beyond three months. . . ."

"The next time you find yourself with child, come to me and I'll see that you don't lose it."

"But suppose I don't? Suppose I can't? It's been a long time now, since—"

"In which case, when I tell you to, and not before, you must inform the Judge you are with child, and ask him to send you East to spare you the moral suffering of having to display your condition as an unwed mother before all the world in a city where too many people know you. Once in Boston, in a house I own there, you will, after seven months have elapsed, have a photograph made. In a standing profile position, with just the right number and size of pillows beneath your dress. On it you will write: 'My own dearest, it is so hard to wait! All my love, Mireille.' "

"You," Mireille said with unfeigned admiration, "are the smartest operator I ever met!"

"So will you be, if you follow my counsels," Mary Ellen Pleasant said. "Upon your return—of which you will not have advised the Judge beforehand—I'll have your and His Honor's newborn son waiting for you, the right size, shape, coloring, weight—"

"But how?" Mireille gasped.

"I'll buy you a baby, my dear. From some little dilly from a poor but honest family who can't stand the disgrace. Or the offspring of some whore who couldn't bring herself to have an abortion. You'd be surprised how many of the dear girls won't. They're sentimental creatures, y'know, or else pimps like your friend Howard Tellefair couldn't exist. I must say you handled getting rid of him very well."

"That was no problem. He's an arrant coward."

"Most pimps are. And secret pederasts, at heart. Men who love women suffer from jealousy, and hence can't be Macks. Now tell me one more thing: Does the Judge have a blemish, a natural discoloration—a birthmark, anywhere on his body? Not a scar, mind you. Scars are worthless. . . ."

Mireille thought about that.

"No—I don't think so . . ." she began; then her eyes widened, flashed with sudden memory. "Yes! Come to think of it, he does! He has a little wine-colored mark behind his left ear. It looks like—a star. But it's not all there. I mean it would be an almost perfect five-pointed star except that it doesn't have the top point, or the right-hand one. I happened to see it one day when I was standing behind his chair after lunch and nibbling on his ears. I'd told him they were all I wanted for desert!"

"Mireille, child, you're a perfect marvel! Did you mention it to him, remark that you'd seen it at the time?"

"No. And I doubt he even knows it's there. He'd have to use two mirrors to see it, y'know—one held behind his head, and the other in front of him. Madame Pleasant, you don't mean to tell me that you're not only going to find me a baby who looks like Judge Curtwright, but who has—"

"An identical birthmark? Yes. Both. Matters that are child's play for an expert, my dear. The Judge, while a handsome man, is hardly a rare physical type, you realize. The ruddy blond blue-eyed Nordic man is a dime a dozen in this country. And the art of tattooing has been practiced since ancient times. You'll have to make me a drawing of that defective star, of course. As accurate a one as possible. By the way, don't call the Judge's attention to his birthmark. The emotional impact will be all the greater when you spring it on him the first time he doubts his darling son is his. As he will. Judge Curtwright is anything but a fool. The fact that he does have a birthmark is a great relief. I assure you that particular trick always works. It's one of the oldest ones in the business."

Mireille stared at Madame Pleasant, shook her head in wonder.

"But, to continue," Madame Pleasant said, "once we've got him thor-

oughly convinced that he has indeed been capable of a first-class performance even at his advanced age, you demand that he divorce his mad
wife and marry you. By next year, he can. She will have been mad all of
ten years, plenty long enough for an annulment or a divorce to be
granted him on the grounds of incurable insanity."

"And if he—refuses?"

"I don't think he will. But if he does, ask that he adopt his illegitimate
son legally, and settle a large sum of money on the child, and on you as
its mother. Now—or rather at that very moment. No court would set
aside such a provision. And as a *fait accompli* it has every advantage over
a will that's sure to be contested. Either way—married to him or endowed *de facto* by him—you're safe. You've got his fortune. And you've
got Willy Kilpatrick on the side. Neat, isn't it?"

"It is—except for one thing, Mary Ellen. May I call you that? We're
going to be friends, aren't we?"

"As long as you don't take it as your right as a member of the superior
race," Mary Ellen said bitterly, "and realize that I'm damned well going
to call you Mireille in return!"

"Of course. I'm not superior to you. You're much smarter than I am.
And though people say you're awfully wicked, nobody's ever accused you
of having been—a whore. And I have been. And am a kept woman. An
old man's darling. To quote you, color is nonsense. Besides, you're white.
White enough, anyhow. D'you know that when I went to Em's, she
thought I wasn't? Asked me if I were an octoroon . . ."

"Em's a fool. I knew better the moment I saw you. You've got that
bone-deep arrogance that nobody who knows she isn't really, or rather,
entirely white ever acquires. That's one place I'd like to get rid of, that
Kearny Street bagnio. Too many people know I own it . . ."

"Sell it to me," Mireille said without batting an eye. "I'll give you two
of my lots for it, and take cash for the rest."

"Four," Mary Ellen Pleasant said.

"All right. Four, then. But nobody must know I own it. Agreed?"

"Agreed. But you started to say something before, and went off on a
tangent. What was it, Mireille?"

"Just—this business of—well, arranging my future with the Judge.
What's in it for you, Mary Ellen? I've never heard of anyone's accusing
you of altruism!"

"I am neither a sentimentalist nor a fool. All right. D'you think you
could influence his decision in several Mexican land grant title disputes
I'm interested in?"

"No. You know better than that. He's so honorable it hurts. It would only make him suspicious of me if I were even to try it. And it appears to me that we ought to try to avoid that."

"You're right. We should. Well then, say twenty-five thousand dollars —in the case that I have to provide the baby. If you come up with your own little package of illicit joy—fifteen for my counsel, guidance, and technical help in seeing that you damned well do come to full term. Fair enough?"

Mireille thought about those two alternatives as well.

"Yes. It's very fair. Do we put it in writing?" she said.

"No. Too dangerous. A handshake and your pledged word will do. You're very smart, Mireille. Too smart to try to cheat. We'll go far together!"

"Yes—we will," Mireille said, and put out her hand to Mary Ellen Pleasant, who had not one mammy-like characteristic to her name: neither warmth, nor sentimentality, nor even—love.

But when the older woman took it, Mireille did a strange thing: she leaned forward suddenly, and kissed Madame Pleasant's cheek.

"I like you," she breathed. "You're all I've always wanted to be—and failed. Mistress of yourself. And of—the world. . . ."

Mary Ellen stared at her with cool amusement.

"Don't worry, child; you'll get there too," she said.

9

MIREILLE'S IMPOSING MAHOGANY-AND-ROSEWOOD-PANELED LANDAU swept eastward down Clay Street toward Portsmouth Square, drawn at a spanking trot behind her pair of night-black, imported Australian horses. Perched high on the driver's seat before her, the Swithers brothers, James and John, her coachman and her footman, sat, clad in livery every bit as imposing as the landau, their faces, under their tall silk hats, blacker than the hides of her splendid five-gaited pair, set in frowns of stern self-importance.

"Mammy" Pleasant had sent the two Blacks to Mireille with a note suggesting that she hire them, which Mireille had been pleased to do, even knowing that Mary Ellen Pleasant had surely placed them in her employ to spy on her. Now, staring at their sturdy backs straining against the frock coats of their livery, she had the wickedly delighted feeling that she had "turned" them both: that they now were, if not wholly on her side, at least double agents. For, by awarding them a treatment involving so much kindness, real consideration, even, at times, an easy, affectionate familiarity that no Black menservants in the 1850s could dream of receiving from a young, stunningly beautiful white woman, she got as much information about Mary Ellen Pleasant's weird, devious, and plain evil doings out of them as they carried back to the house on Washington Street about hers.

As she rolled along, with the rear calash top folded back and the breeze stirring her raven hair under her smart little bonnet, all the men on the sidewalks took off their hats and waved them in her direction. More than one of them grandly bowed. The women—what few there were—glared, and ostentatiously turned their backs. Mireille smiled with quiet satisfaction at that sight. Ever since the fabulous Lola Montez, mistress of the immortal pianist-composer Franz Liszt, mistress of the ex-

king Ludwig of Bavaria, mistress of—the list was endless!—whose Spider
Dance drove men of the cloth, not to mention mere miners and businessmen, out of their minds, had left San Francisco that preceding fall to
settle—permanently, she swore—in the pleasant little California mountain town of Grass Valley, Mireille had inherited, by default, Lola's
crown as the most celebrated demimondaine in the city. But she was
gaining something else, too, she was aware, that pleased her even more.
Gradually she was winning the grudging respect of the town's sober,
decent citizens. Her flight from a place in the lineup at French Em's to
Judge Alain Curtwright's arms had been a long step up, especially after
the fact—attested to by the rueful confessions of failure on the part of
the hordes of "dead game sports" who had desperately tried to get her
not to be—that she was absolutely faithful to the Judge became established beyond the faintest doubt. Nowadays, when he took her out to
dine, or to the theater, or for a drive in the landau he had given her—all
of which he did with ever increasing frequency and pride—the adoring,
worshipful attentions she showered upon him were so manifest, and
manifold, that one disgruntled citizen was moved to growl:

"Either that li'l fool Frenchie is in love with that old fart, or she's th'
best damn actress ever to hit Californy!"

Her smart new rig, the envy of every respectable woman in the city,
drew up before the doors of Kinnan & Kinnan, Bankers. With a bass-
voiced "Whoa!" James Swithers pulled up the team. Before they had
even stopped dancing, his brother John leaped to the ground and held up
his black hand—chastely gloved in soft gray calfskin—to his mistress,
helping her showily to descend from the landau.

"John, bring that canvas bag in for me, will you?" Mireille said.

"Why, sho, ma'am! Be happy to!" The footman beamed.

Mireille swept into the bank, with her footman following her. As she
did so, Ted Hodges, the head teller, clutched the little uniformed bank
messenger boy by the shoulder and hissed, "Go get who I told you to,
Timmy boy! Hurry now! Make tracks!"

The messenger boy scurried away. Once outside the bank, he broke
into a dead run, heading diagonally across the Square toward the Washington Street side.

"Good morning, Mr. Hodges," Mireille said brightly.

"Morning, Mamzelle Duclos! May I say you're a treat for the eyes, as
usual?" Ted Hodges said.

"Thank you," Mireille purred; then, turning to her footman, she said,
"Put it up here, John. Mr. Hodges will open the grating for us. He knows
we don't ride with Murieta's band any longer!"

"Well now, ma'am—I mean mamzelle," Ted Hodges laughed, as he opened the grating and took that surprisingly heavy sack from Swithers' hand, "I ain't rightly all that sure of that, considering the amount o' cash you've been bringing in lately. . . ."

He lifted the sack, turned it upside down, let a shower of greenbacks, nuggets, bags of gold dust, twenty-dollar gold pieces, and silver dollars pour out of it. His eyes opened very wide.

"Lord God, Mamzelle Duclos!" he breathed. "I wish you'd tell me your secret! I just don't know how you do it!"

"On the contrary, Ted," Mireille said solemnly, "I suspect you know *exactly* how I do it. But my secret, if any, wouldn't do you very much good, because you were born with the wrong variety of equipment to carry it out. . . ."

The teller threw back his head and roared. That sally, Mireille knew, like all the saucy, witty remarks she was becoming famous for, would be all over town by night.

'What won't be all over town—not ever, I hope!' she thought, 'is where the money comes from. The wages of sin. This week's take at French Em's, minus salaries and expenses. Including the Maniac's quite handsome salary. The ex-Maniac's now. Ray Coles's. Strange to find that he has a name, even a relatively civilized one, at this late date! It was—*so* kind of me to hire him as bodyguard and bouncer at Em's. Or—was it? Wasn't it, maybe—perverse, twisted—like everything I do? Who knows? All this lovely, lovely money! The earnings from the brothel I *own*. That Em runs for me. That I've got dear How-ward recruiting for, bringing me in ever fresh and flowery—talent—from all over the East. He's good at that, God knows—though I suspect he dislikes having to break them in. In that regard, he'd probably prefer recruiting little *boys*. Speaking of which—hmmmmmn—some of the new girls are—nice. They tempt me to—but no. I must keep that side of my nature in check. Oh, Lord! I never see Paci anymore. And I want to. Oh, how I want to! But if I were to, I—we—would—'

Then, looking up, she saw Guillermo Kilpatrick coming through the door.

His face was strained. He seemed to be fighting for breath. Two fiery red spots glowed in his cheeks. He had grown a mustache that was even blonder than his hair. And in the frock coat and striped trousers of a young executive, with his foulard-type cravat tucked up under his high wing collar, all the lithe, puma-cat Latin aspect of him that had so enchanted her had vanished. He looked like a gringo. Two hundred percent American. Even his skin, probably because his work kept him forever indoors, had paled to a shade much more nearly appropriate to his generally Nordic appearance than its former almost coppery hue had been.

'Why,' she thought bitterly, 'he looks like an—Irishman. Like—Molly's husband. . . . I'm not sure I even *like* him anymore.'

He came up to her. Grated, harshly:

"Mireille, I've got to see you. To talk to you. So—name the time and place, will you?"

She smiled at him. At that soft, speculative curl of her wine-dark lips, his face got redder still.

"Why not here and now, Willy darling?" she said.

"No!" he got out. "My father-in-law runs this bank—which is why you chose it, isn't it? So I can't—"

"What's the matter, my dear little henpecked boy? Hmmmmm—you do have on trousers, don't you? But you only wear them *here*, don't you? At home you take 'em off and give them back to their rightful owner—right, Willy dearest?"

"Mirla!" he thundered, quite beside himself.

"Mirla? Ah—that's better. That's much better. Tell you what: I have my landau outside. Why don't we go for a little spin in it, dear little husband of Molly Kinnan? By the way, how is she? And your lovely children?"

"*¡Jesús!*" Willy whispered. And that he said it in Spanish, pronouncing it "*¡Hay-zoos!*" proved how upset he was. Except when talking to the senior partner of the firm, Don Ernesto Martin, he carefully refrained from ever speaking Spanish at all.

"Well?" Mireille purred.

"Mireille, you know damned well that I can't ride through the middle of town with you in that showy rig of yours without arming—" he was immediately aware that his phrasing was Spanish, so he emended it "—causing—the scandal of the century, so—"

"So—*d'accord,* my charmingly uxorious ex-lover, ex-*Mejicano*, perhaps even ex-*man.*" She went up on tiptoe and whispered, her lips brushing scaldingly, his ear, "I've a nice little cottage out on Fremont Street, almost to Harrison. Y'know, in the new district beyond Market Street. I bought it for that. To meet all my—hundreds of lovers in sin without, as you've said, arming the scandal of the century. . . ."

As usual, what her French accent did to Spanish made him want to smile, even as angry as he was. He resisted that temptation.

"When?" he said.

"Let's see—it is Friday, isn't it? Tonight, then? About ten, say?"

He stared at her a long, slow time, as though he were trying to memorize her face. Then he said:

"All right." And marched out of there like a windup toy, a clockwork doll, half of whose cogwheels were broken.

In the dining room of that cozy little cottage Mireille had bought only a month ago, and whose very existence Judge Curtwright was blissfully unaware of, Willy sat across the table and stared at her.

Mireille was sure she had never seen so much pure, undiluted misery before in a pair of human eyes.

"You're not eating," she said accusingly. "I went to a great deal of trouble to prepare this supper, Willy dear. In fact, I cooked it with my own two hands."

"I know. And it's delicious. Absolutely perfect. You're a Cordon Bleu chef, Mireille—"

"Which you can only prove by eating some of it," she said.

"I—I can't. It's not the food; it's you, Mirla. You take away my appetite. Or—ruin it . . ."

She pushed back her chair, stood up. The diamonds at her throat and in the lobes of her ears flashed crystalline fire. But they were less bright than the terrible lightning in her eyes.

"Then go home!" she stormed. "Since I disgust you so, go home! Go back to your lace-curtain Irish biddy, and your brats!"

He sighed.

"You don't disgust me, Mirla," he said sadly. "I wish you did. My life would be so much simpler if that were so. Don't you know what a relief it would be for me to be able to despise you? But I can't. As God is my judge, I simply can't . . ."

She groped behind her with one bejeweled hand, found the chair, drew it forward again, sank slowly down into it. That rich silk dress, of the kind of shimmering blue only seen in portraits by Sir Joshua Reynolds, enveloped her almost startling pallor in a misty cerulean glow that was wonderfully becoming. The candlelight from the table pooled amber, topaz, flickering yellow silver in her eyes. Her hair, blacker than before light was and the footstep of God had yet troubled the waters, blended with the shadows the tapers' soft gleam cast against the walls and the ceiling behind her, foaming midnight, endless, moving, moving—

"Willy—" she said.

"I love you," he said. "A species of folly which has neither excuse nor palliative. I'm sick with love for you, Mirla. I am dying of it. You see how thin I am? That's your fault, too. You're the cause of it. . . ."

"Willy—" she moaned. Or mourned. Or both.

"The night—someone told me—that you were on the receiving line at Em's I—threw up. Not just once. All night long. By morning what was coming up was—blood. Enrique says I had—have—a gastric ulcer. It's better now, of course. . . ."

"Dear little Jesus!" she wept.

"Why did you do that, Mirla? Please tell me why?"

She shrugged.

"You sent me away," she said simply. "I—wanted to die, too, Willy. And since I knew—from experience—that I cannot kill myself, I'm just not brave enough—I figured that would kill me soon enough. Wallowing —in filth. Existing in a state of nausea. Hating, despising, loathing myself that much. Being—without *you*, would. Only I'm tougher than I thought I was. And a born bitch like me can accustom herself to anything, I suppose. It wasn't even—too bad. A great deal better than the Dirty Spoon, at any rate . . ."

"Only there was one difference," he said quietly. "You were sold— forced—into the Dirty Spoon. You walked into Em's on your own two dainty feet."

"I was *thrown* into Em's. Like so much offal, *basura*, garbage. By seeing this mouth, whose lightest touch could make my bones turn water —scalding water, vaporize, become live steam!—twist into the coldest, cruelest expression of contempt I've ever seen. By hearing this voice, whose every word tangled my breath up into knots of ice and brine and fire inside my throat, say, 'I don't fight over cheap *putas*—' "

"Oh God!" he said.

"You're right. That's all I am. A cheap whore. The cheapest of all whores. For you—gratis. D'you want me?"

"Like that—on that level—no. But now, you've come up in the world, haven't you? An old man's darling. The best-kept fancy woman in all California. Explain me that one, *querida* Mirla. . . ."

"It hasn't any explanation, really. Especially not—money. I could have found a richer, younger, handsomer man, y'know! An—escape from the other? Perhaps. That I admired—admire—the Judge wholeheartedly? That, yes—that, also. That I love him more than a little—with a strange, crazy, quasi-incestuous love? He is very like my father was, and that binds me to him. My mother always swore that the way I loved my father wouldn't bear too close examination. She was very likely right. I was thirteen or fourteen when he was murdered, so I—"

"Murdered?" Willy said.

"By my mother's lover. In her bedroom, where he'd caught them *in flagrante*. What chance did I ever have of being decent, Willy? What chance at all? I'm—devilseed, the product of all kinds of twisted lusts, with crazy passions howling through my blood—and any children that I have will carry the taint I'll pass along to them right down till the end of time. . . ."

"That's nonsense!" Willy said.

"Is it? Prove it's nonsense, Willy darling! I—challenge you to! I throw you down my gauntlet!"

"But how could I prove such a thing, dear little Mirla? Little blackbird who caws and shrieks and chatters forever through the bloody shreds of that which once I called—my heart?"

She got up then, and came around the table. Bent and kissed his mouth.

"Give me—a baby, Willy. Your son. A—little you. That's all I need. And all I'll ever want," she said.

"*¡Dios!*" he said.

"Please . . ." she whispered, the sound of that word angel-tongued, silvery, softly ringing, endlessly sweet.

"Mirla—" he said, "I have—a wife. A good, sweet girl in whom I find no slightest fault—"

"Except one. Except the greatest fault of all as far as you're concerned."

"Which is?" he said bleakly.

"That she isn't—*me.*"

He stared at her until he couldn't see her anymore, so blindscalded were his eyes.

"True," he said brokenly. "And who will deliver me from this—slavery? From the body of this—death?"

She straightened up. Put out her hand to him.

"Nobody. Certainly not—I," she said. "Now—come!"

10

❧

"You know, Mireille," Judge Alain Curtwright said solemnly, "I think I'd better—set you free. Let you go find yourself a younger man . . ."

Mireille turned away from the mirror of her vanity, before which she sat, busily engaged in her invariable morning ritual of giving one hundred forceful brushstrokes to her long, luxuriant hair. She was clad only in a peignoir that seemed to Alain Curtwright's delighted old eyes to be made of morning mists. Like that, she was something to be seen. She saw his gaze kindle, and realized that he had been teasing her, joking.

But she also realized that a possibility, so strong as to approach an actual probability, existed that this was one of those truths spoken in jest. In the three months since she had renewed her love affair with Willy Kilpatrick, she had given her ancient lover, whom she thought of always with authentic affection as "my darling old Creaky Bones!" a hard row to hoe, having made at least as many demands upon his failing manly powers as she had upon the presumably more vigorous ones of her much younger lover.

She stared at the Judge now, seeing the biceps in his upper arms grown slack and crepey, the bones of his rib cage clearly visible beneath his shrunken chest, the mat of hair on his flaccid pectorals silvery, his throat stringy . . . She couldn't see, of course, facing him, what she called her life insurance—the little, defective-star-shaped birthmark behind his left ear.

'Why *do* I bother the poor old darling so much?' she thought. 'Name of God—why?' Then she reasoned slowly: 'Because I—love him. I do. He is so—genuinely good. So—noble. Therefore neither his age nor the way he looks matters. Besides, he's not ugly, even yet. Quite the contrary: he's a beautiful old man. Mellowed like good wine by the years.

Having the patina of a statue falling into ruin, but that one can see was from the hand of—a Phidias, a Michelangelo—'

"Lord!" the Judge laughed, taking his right hand from beneath the pillow and making the playfully comic gesture of covering up his eyes. "Leave some flesh on my bones, will you, child? When you blaze away at me like that with those eyes of yours, you broil me alive!"

"You—you *meant* that, didn't you, Alain?" she said quietly, but with that gut-crippling intensity it seemed to him she could put effortlessly into her voice whenever she wanted to. "That business about—setting me free, I mean?"

He thought, 'A man who's never known a primitive, savage little she-creature like this one simply hasn't lived!'

"And if I did?" he said quizzically.

Without answering him, she got up from her vanity's chair and went over to the washstand. He lay there looking at her, his bemused gaze caressing the long, singing curves of her back, covered almost to the bend of her knees by the sooty midnight of her hair.

Then she turned, faced him. Since that peignoir concealed absolutely nothing, and only added a certain romantic aura to the stunning impact of her nakedness, making it less animal, more—it took him brief seconds to find the exact descriptive word—goddesslike, he didn't see at first what she had in her hand.

When he did, all his breath left him, leaving him without even enough lung-, throat-, mouth-entrapped air to force pure horror into sound.

She had the ivory handle of his straight razor clasped convulsively in her right fist. That homely tool, become a deadly weapon, was opened, its blade glinting bluely in the light. Slowly, holding him with those Medea eyes of hers, she raised it to her own throat. Pressed that fine-honed edge into her milky, snowy flesh. He saw the little scarlet rivulets well up around it.

"Mireille!" he screamed.

"Say that—again, Alain. That—you don't want me," she said.

"Mireille, baby-girl, child—" he moaned.

"I love you," she said very simply. "Without you—I don't even want to live. So if you're tired of me—plan to leave me, put me out—say it. And I'll—trouble you—and the world—no longer. Well, maybe a little, for another day. Or—my body will. A pauper's funeral in unhallowed ground really isn't that much trouble, is it? And it only costs thirty-five dollars, according to the *Alta Californian* . . ."

"Mireille, put that razor down!" he croaked. "Oh, God, baby, please!"

"Are you—tired of me, Alain?" she whispered, her huge eyes, which combined the antithesis of utter darkness with noonday sunlight, busy about their utterly maiming alchemy of distilling crystalline silver, jewels —topaz and diamonds!—and spilling them down her cheeks. "If you are, say so, and—" She pressed that blade in, deeper. Those rivulets thickened, beaded, rolled obscenely down her slender, swanlike throat.

"Child," he said calmly, quietly, finding at last the right tone to take, "I couldn't live without you. If anything happened to you, I wouldn't need a razor. This tired old ticker of mine would—just stop. Or burst. I wouldn't survive you for one whole hour. That's very sure—"

The razor came away from her throat, clattered to the floor. She came flying to the bed, hurled herself upon him, kissing his forehead, the tip of his aristocratic, high-beaked nose, his ears, his eyes, his cheeks, his throat —last of all his mouth, lingering upon it worshipfully.

"Make love to me, Alain!" she moaned. "Right now! Pound me to pieces, please!"

"Child, stop it!" he said sharply. "Let me patch up that nasty cut. You're bleeding all over the sheets . . ."

"That's all I ever do," she said sullenly; "*bleed*. Every blessed month, I —"

He stared at her. Said, "Go get me a little cotton to place against this for it to clot on. Go on, now, child. You went in a little too deep for comfort. That razor is sharp, y'know . . ."

Mireille got up, went to the washstand. Came back with some loose cotton. Handed it to him. He patted it against that long, shallow slash, effectively stopping the flow of her blood.

She smiled at him tenderly.

"Your hands are so—sweet!" she murmured, and hurled herself upon him again.

"Mireille," he said, "tell me something—"

"Don't want to talk! I want to—" She said the—in those days unspeakable, even unthinkable—four-letter medieval word.

"Mireille!" he thundered, like Olympian Jove.

She laughed merrily.

"Well, what d'*you* call it, my darling old Creaky Bones?" she said.

"Not—that," he said gently. "With you, child—not ever that. Say— the rites of spring. Renewal. Rejuvenation. Or, very simply—love . . ."

She stared at him. Very slowly her eyes filled up, brimmed, spilled.

"I'm—sorry, Alain," she whispered. "I'm an awful slut, aren't I? A whore . . ."

"No," he said solemnly; "you're none of those . . ."

"Then what am I?"

"A witch," he said; "an angel. You alternate—though sometimes you're both at the same time. Like now, for instance . . ."

"Alain—pleeeeease make love to me! I want it. I need it. Need—want —you—"

"Child, the spirit's always willing; but at my age, the flesh is often weak. . . ."

"Don't worry your sweet little old silvery head about that!" she hooted. "*I'll* take care of the flesh. Mighty good care, you may rest assured!"

"Mireille, no. Wait. There's time. We have all day long, y'know. Tell me something, first: Is this onslaught of wonderfully well-faked nymphomania—damned if you don't almost convince *me* at times—due to your having reached the age or the stage that your—well, maternal instincts are making themselves felt? In other words, is it that you want—a child?"

"Not *a* child. *Your* child, Alain," she whispered.

He stared at her with doubting eyes. Then his doubts sank down, diminished, died. All his years of experience as a trial judge brought, at that stunning, astounding moment, the irresistible force, his doubts, with smashing impact up against the immovable object, his sudden, unshakable conviction that she was telling the simple truth.

He was right. The only place he momentarily erred was in placing that qualifying modifier before the noun "truth." For, as he should have known, Mireille's truths were never simple. In fact, they were maddeningly complicated, as was everything about her. When she'd said, "Not *a* child. *Your* child, Alain," she hadn't lied at all. Each of the three times now, she had bent over her washbasin as she rinsed from her nightgown or her pantalettes the bloodstains of a menstruation she had convinced herself wasn't going to occur, and hence hadn't even taken the usual precautions to contain, the fear had grown in her that Guillermo's health, noticeably deteriorated by that bullet through his lung, had become too delicate to permit him to father a child any longer. But then she remembered that he had got no less than three on his Molly—'that Irish cow!' she stormed. 'Naturally! She just lies there placidly, like a cow!—so how can he miss? While I—burn him—and his seed—alive. Oh good Lord, why not? I want—a child. I need—a tiny sweet baby who —" And it was then that she'd thought it for the first time:

'Alain himself? Why not? He's old, but he's in perfect health. A son of his would be beautiful too. And nobler, better than Willy's, who can be, has been, a swine! So Alain's—sixty-four? Sixty-five? So what! That's not too old. Look at Old John out at Dr. Sepúlvera's *rancho*. He's eighty. And his youngest is not even ten years old!'

So she hadn't been lying, just telling an incomplete truth. The whole truth would have been difficult to phrase, since it went something like this:

'If I can't have a son by the man I love more than life, I'll settle for one by you, my ancient darling, whom I love only a little less. Not just—a child. Not just anybody's child. Willy's—or yours. His, first; yours, as second choice. Or—Good God!—one by each of you! Now wouldn't that be perfectly lovely!'

Which may be offered in evidence that when her closest friends, people who knew her as well, and loved her as much as Paquita and Enrique Sepúlvera did, swore that Mireille Duclos was as mad as a hatter, they weren't all that wide of the mark.

"Mireille, baby-girl," Alain Curtwright said sadly, "I fear I'm much too old to sire an offspring . . ."

Whereupon Mireille immediately repeated the argument she'd recently thought up in reference to the performance of Old John, caretaker of the Santa Clara Ranch, as far as the art, or—in his case surely—the miracle of procreation was concerned.

"Yes," the Judge chuckled; "I know Old John. And I strongly suspect that the last two of his three wives have put supplementary workers on the job. Maybe that's what you ought to do, child . . ."

"No. Never. He's got to be *yours*. Who else could guarantee that he'll be—intelligent, wise, grave, prudent, good, gentle, sweet? I—I want to preserve you, Alain! Make a perfect replica! Beautiful like you. Noble like you. Kind. Knightly. One of the good God's own elite. I—love you. Oh, how I love you! And when I realize that I can *never* convince you of that simple fact, I fall into the most profound despair!"

He drew her to him, and his tired old eyes were wet.

"You *have* convinced me, child," he sighed; "*now* you have. And I—thank God—for the marvelous gift—the unsought, undeserved manna from heaven—of you . . ."

"Alain," she murmured slumberously; "you can now, can't you?"

"Don't know. I doubt it. Look, child—you're miracle enough for one lifetime. Don't ask for two. That an old broken stick like me could ever become the father of a child of yours is too much to ask—even of the infinite mercy of the Almighty . . ."

"Yet, I do ask it. And—what is it you Americans say? *Ah oui!* 'God helps them who help themselves!' So—let me see, let me see. Oh poor little dead soldier! Let's see if I cannot resurrect him . . ."

"Mireille, no!" he said.

"One mustn't be such a prude, Alain," she murmured. "That doesn't arrange anything . . . Hmmmmmn . . . Hmmmmmmmmmn . . . Hmmmmmmmmmmnnnnnnnnn . . . There we are! Look how he stands to attention now!"

"Mireille—" he whispered, and bent to kiss her breasts.

"That's sweet. That's—so—sweet. And when *he* does it—this tiny one we're going to make now—it will be sweeter still. Alain—"

"Yes, baby-girl?"

"Don't—fondle me. I don't need it. I am ready. Touch me—down there. See how hot and wet I am? Now! There we are! Now—be very still—"

He nuzzled her throat, inhaled the rich perfume of her hair.

"Still," she whispered, "very still. The little soldier must not fire—his musket ahead of time. Now—move. Slowly. Slowly. Again—be still . . . Be—very—still . . ."

"At your orders, general!" he said.

"No. Not a general. A marshal. Commander in chief! Once more a little—Softly. Slowly. Slowly. Slowly. Like that—like that—so sweetly—Slowly. Wait. Wait. Now, move. Move. Move. Move! Soldier, *present arms!* Shoot! Shoot! Shoot! *Ah!* Ahhhhhhhh! There it is! Bull's-eye! How —wonderful! *Ah*, I die! I die! I'm *dead!*"

"You're the liveliest little corpse I ever saw, if you are," he said fondly.

"Alain, be still! We mustn't move! Not either of us."

"And why not, child?" he said.

"All. I want it all. Every drop. To make sure. To make very sure. Alain, d'you think we *did?*"

"Lord, child! How can anyone be sure of *that?*"

"I'm sure," she giggled. "You're—a papa, Alain! Or you will be, in nine months. What are we going to call him?"

"Mireille," he said solemnly.

"Oh, no! If it's a *girl*, I—I'll strangle her!"

"And if it's a boy, I'll throw him in the Bay!"

"Alain, you—you want a *girl?* A daughter?"

"Yes, child. Your image. Exactly like you."

"Ohhhhh Alain!" she sobbed, and kissed him. "Then it'll have to be twins. One for each of us. A boy for me. A girl for you. But we *need* a boy, darling. I'll put lawbooks in his cradle so he'll grow up to be a great attorney-at-law, a judge—like you. So—stern. So—just. So—fair. Oh, Alain, I *do* love you so!"

"And I love you, baby-girl," he whispered, and drew her closer to him, so that she would not see his tears.

The next night was Willy's turn; and it was, frankly, disappointing. Willy was tired, listless. What was worse, he and Molly had quarreled, violently. Dear Molly, who was nobody's fool, suspected that the all-night poker games Willy claimed he was indulging in with the firm's clients in the interest of commercial goodwill were anything but poker, and most certainly not cricket!

"Her!" Molly shrieked; "that little dark-haired witch who sat in the back pew at our wedding and cried and cried and cried! That's the one, isn't it?"

"Oh, hell, Molly; don't be unnecessarily tiresome," Willy said.

So it didn't work. Not at all. Mireille had to play single-finger variations on the basic theme to get a little relief after he had gone back home.

But this time, on the twenty-eighth day of her ovulation cycle, nothing happened. Absolutely nothing at all. Mireille, who was anything but a temperate soul, immediately soared up to the seventh heaven of perfect bliss, and continued to walk on air, or rather to skip from cloud to cloud, for all of a week.

Then she fell off, not merely the roof, in the classic French phrase she always used to describe that sorry nuisance the Almighty inflicted upon women, in punishment, perhaps, for the sins of Mother Eve, but from one of those clouds, which was a great deal higher, with the result that the shock—of disappointment, disillusion, deception, heartbreak, pain—was infinitely greater. In fact, it threatened her hold upon a sanity occasionally dubious anyhow.

She woke up to cramps, to some slight bleeding, and at once began to cry and scream with rage. If she had been born with a sense of moderation, or had possessed a single gram of sweet reason anywhere in her lovely but passionate head, she might have noticed that the occasion was markedly different from any such she had ever experienced before. In the first place, as Jasmine remarked to herself as she changed the sheets on her mistress' bed, "This don't look right. Not at all; it seems—queer." The truth was that the bloodstains, if they could even be called that, on Mireille's sheets were the palest of pink instead of the usual thick, dark red; and that scant menstrual flow stopped completely after two days, the second of which probably shouldn't have been counted at all, so greatly had those freakish menses diminished by then, instead of the five, and often six, of copious bleeding she had had to endure every month since she had reached puberty at thirteen years of age.

But Mireille, from the practice of lighter-than-air aeronautics—without, of course, a *Montgolfier* hot-air balloon—plunged into the deepest, most submarine, or subterranean, depths of despair. She had lost—Willy's baby. Or maybe Alain's. But, anyhow—*hers.* To drown her sorrows, she polished off a large glass of absinthe, and sent Jasmine to tell James and John Swithers to bring her landau around to the front door.

Now anyone who has ever downed even a dram or two of it can bear witness to the disastrous effects that absinthe has upon the normal workings of the human brain; and when that brain has been clouded by absolutely bottomless grief, that said disaster can go slipping and sliding down into a catastrophe of the first order of magnitude is self-evident. And in Mireille's case, it did.

Which the always malicious workings of ribald fate compounded even further. As Mireille rode aimlessly through the streets of San Francisco, brooding over her sorrows, bemoaning her absolutely abominable fate, she passed in front of the barnlike structure housing Volunteer Fire Engine Company Number Six. The firemen were all out in the street, whooping and hollering at the top of their lungs, and spraying each other lustily with the streams of water from three hand- and foot-pumped fire engines, glistening with brass and bearing plaques labeling them *Mechanical, Union,* and *Franklin.* Even as depressed as she was, the sight of this healthy, happy skylarking immediately lifted Mireille's spirits. So she ordered James to stop the landau, and sent John to inquire what all the hilarity was about.

"They sez hit's their anniversary," John came back and explained. "They's been organized as Engine Company Number Six since this heah same day las' year. So they's havin' a beer bust 'n' celebrating. And they wants to know effen they kin send a bucket o' suds up to th' pretty lady?"

"Tell them—no thanks! I can't abide beer," Mireille said. "But that I wish them happy anniversary. They really are—a fine-looking bunch of fellows, aren't they?"

"Yes'm. They's Baltimore men, and Philadelphians. Knowed each other and wuz frens fo' they come out heah. Firemen hafta be big and strong and healthy, too—considering how hard and dangerous they work is. . . ."

"Yes, that's true, isn't it? Drive on, James!" Mireille said. She waved her parasol at them as she passed. At which the firemen set up a lusty cheer.

Then the devil, aided by the most diabolical of his brews, absinthe,

sent a sublimely wicked thought stealing through dear, sweet little
Mireille's head:

'Fine-looking men. Handsome. Big and strong. Not—old and worn
out. Not shot-up wrecks. Hmmmn. Hmmmn. Hmmmmmmmm-
mmmmmnnnnnn . . ."

"Home, James!" Mireille said.

That night the members of Fire Engine Company Number Six received an invitation, beautifully penned in the most exquisite Spencerian
script, from Madame Em. The gist of that invitation was that since
today, as she had been informed by a mutual friend, was the anniversary
of the foundation of their illustrious company, those members of it who
were not confined to their posts by night duty on this happy date were
cordially invited to visit the Kearny Street establishment, where free
drinks would be served them, and what other—favors—they might desire, also granted them—gratis. After midnight, the house would be entirely theirs. . . .

Thereafter, for the rest of their lives, the members of Fire Engine
Company Number Six spoke in awed tones about their celebration at
Em's to those poor, miserable unfortunates who had drawn the night
shift on that red-letter date and could not, therefore, participate in it.

"Lord God!" they whispered; "that there li'l black-haired one—th'
tiny dame who said she wuz from Paris, France—the one who wore that
mask with spangles sewed onto it—"

"Spangles, hell! Them there was diamonds! And 'twarn't no mask.
More like a hood, so's a fella never could make out what her face looked
like a-tall . . ."

"Who gives two hoots up a hollow stump about her *face*, for Gawd's
sake? With that pear-shaped li'l arse she had hanging onto her, and that
pair o' tits, and a quim like a steam-suction pump, why—"

"She scalded me alive, tha's for sure! First she took Tim upstairs, and
five minutes later he come down ag'in walkin' on his *knees*. The blighter
couldn't even stand up no more and—"

"After that—Joe. Same deal. Laigs doublin' under him like a pair o'
busted fire hoses! Then—"

"George. No! George and Bill—"

"At the same time?"

"You bet your ask-me-no-questions-and-I'll-tell-you-no-lies at th' same
time! Then Matt, Hank, and Phil—"

"Holy smoke! You don't mean to tell me that li'l Frenchie shot herself
a triple!"

"You heard what I said, didn't you? Or ain't you washed yore ears this year?"

"Hell, that just ain't possible!"

"Your mama sent you to school, didn't she? You can count, can't you? So now, you tell me: How many doors has th' firehouse got?"

"Wal now, there's th' front door, and th' back door—and that li'l one-man side door. Counting that one, that makes—three. Lord God! You don't mean—"

"If, 'stid o' th' *side* door, you was to say th' *cellar* door, you've got th' idee, ol' buddy! And Matt and Hank and Phil is ruint fer life. Cain't lift a toothpick no more, not t'mention a hook 'n' ladder. I tell yuh, pal o' mine, we had ourselves a ball!"

But one month after the night that somebody—female gender!—had wrecked the morale and the morals of Engine Company Number Six forever, Mireille stared at the heavy black cross mark she had just penciled through that day's date, October 22, 1855, on her wall calendar—a gift from Martin, Kilpatrick & Kinnan, real estate brokers—with total horror.

"Thirty days," she whispered; "and nothing. Absolutely nothing at all. Not—a drop. Nor the palest, faintest stain. So now, I *am.* I've got to be. And I don't know *who*—or which, or—oh, *bon Dieu!* I just don't know!"

She bent her head and wept, noisily, stormily. A long time. A very long time. But when she'd got by that, another thing hit her. She clutched her slender middle and went flying toward her commode. Tearing its mahogany doors open, she dragged the porcelain chamber pot out of it, just before it would have been too late. She knelt there before that homely utensil—so necessary in a day when bathrooms were practically nonexistent, and most houses had a cunning little temple to the goddess Cloaca out back, with a half-moon carved into its door—and vomited into it for a full ten minutes. After that, still reeling, she called for the landau and ordered James to drive her to Dr. Sepúlvera's office.

Enrique growled at her, "How the hell would I know, this soon? Come back in a month or two, *bébé.* Tell you what though: since you honestly seem to *want* this little bastard, stay off your feet, dammit! Lie down all you can. The less jolting you subject your little belly to, the less likelihood there is that you'll miscarry."

Mireille took his advice. She went to bed. But she lay there and went out of her mind, day and night, until it came to her what to do.

She sent Jasmine over to Mammy Pleasant's establishment to ask the wickedest woman in all San Francisco's history to call on her.

"Have you told him?" Mary Ellen Pleasant said.

"Yes, Mary Ellen," Mireille said.

"And you are pregnant, really?"

"I sure am! I can't keep *water* on my stomach till past noon, and I skipped altogether this month, and—"

"We'll wait another month to make sure. If you have your menses then, or you miscarry spontaneously, you must carefully conceal that fact from the Judge, so we can ship you East and come up with a nice, convincing-looking little bastard, purchased on the market. But I hope you *are* in the family way, and don't lose the package this time, even though it's going to cost me money. . . ."

"Why?" Mireille said. "I mean why do you hope that? When you start getting generous, I start getting worried, Mary Ellen!"

"You shouldn't. I've always been willing to sacrifice exorbitant profits to perfect security, child. Letting the Judge witness a real pregnancy, go through all the thrills and worries and tender anticipations of prospective fatherhood, will melt him like a piece of butter left out in the sun. By the way, have you given him reason to believe he could be the father? Recent reason, child?"

"Of course! And he could even *be*. He's a healthy old man, Mary Ellen. Healthier than Willy is, by a long shot. The only trouble is—"

She explained the circumstances of that doubtful, could-have-been, and then again, maybe-not menstruation of the month before. By then, Enrique had told her that this often occurs in first pregnancies, and that it rarely indicates the loss of the fetus. "Even in an early miscarriage, the bleeding is always heavy," he had said.

'I hope he's right,' Mireille thought now, miserably, as she finished her tale of woe to Madame Pleasant. 'Oh, God, *how* I hope he's right—All that damned champagne! I woke up, hearing a noise like one of those new steam 'paddies' they use to cut streets through the hills, and there Ray Coles, the Maniac, was, down on his knees beside the bed, with his ugly, scarred-up face rammed all the way up between my—ughhh! Anyhow, I don't have to worry about *him*. I can take him off the list of possibles, that's for sure . . .'

"Hmmmm," Mary Ellen said; "then you'd better give the Judge another reason to believe he's going to be a proud pappy. A more recent one!"

"I can't! He won't. He treats me like I were made of cut glass and—and besides, that would cause me to lose my baby, Mary Ellen. And I want him, dammit! Whoever his father is!"

"Don't you *know?*" Mary Ellen asked her.

"No," Mireille said sullenly. "It could be—Willy. It could even be the Judge himself, just like I said. Or—"

"Any of two dozen other friends and gentle acquaintances, eh, Mireille, child? You enjoy life, don't you? No matter. The danger is slight, anyhow. Only one month's difference, the trouble being that the month's in the wrong direction. A seven- or eight-month delivery is easily explainable; a ten-month gestation isn't. So you'd better get rid of Enrique Sepúlvera. Right now. We'll have Joe Gammon, my quack, in. Joe will come up with a story about complications that the Judge will believe. That miserable crook of a sawbones is the best liar I ever met. Even convinces *me* at times. But getting Dr. Sepúlvera out of the picture is up to you, dear."

"Won't be hard. Enrique—disapproves of me. And—Paquita even more so, now that she's become a married woman and a mother."

Mary Ellen laughed merrily at that.

"Always happens!" she chuckled. "There's nobody more respectable than an ex-whore."

"Mary Ellen . . ." Mireille breathed.

"Yes, Mireille?"

"Buy me that extra baby, anyhow! A boy. A little blond boy baby with blue eyes. And, of course, that birthmark I drew for you. I told Alain— the Judge—that I might have twins. So, if mine's a girl, or if it's born dead, we'll still have an insurance policy. I'll pay you that twenty-five thousand instead of just fifteen. I won't quibble over the money. What I want more than anything in this world is the Judge's name on a marriage certificate. . . ."

Mary Ellen smiled, very slowly.

"So the same disease that has infected your ex co-worker at the Dirty Spoon, the now great lady Mrs. Dr. Sepúlvera, has also attacked you, eh, child? The craving for respectability. Your children mustn't ever know their mama was—a whore. Good! I approve. People without ambition are useless—to themselves, and to me. You'll get your extra little bastard: Joe Gammon will bring it into your bedroom in the special bag he uses for such purposes—with plenty of air holes in it!—when he comes to deliver your own. And d'you know what? You're going to achieve your ambition of becoming a great lady, too—achieve it, I'd say, to a far greater degree than your friend Paquita has."

"I doubt it," Mireille said morosely; "there're far too many people with excellent memories in San Francisco. . . ."

"Doesn't matter. It would, anywhere else; but here it doesn't count, Mireille, and for a very simple reason—"

"Which is?" Mireille said.

"San Francisco's too hard to get to for its population to reach anything like the normal proportion between the sexes any time soon. They'll never be able to bring enough women out here by wagon train. And around the Horn by clipper or steamship to the Isthmus, train across the neck, then steamship again up the whole coast of Central America and Mexico to here aren't much better. California will only be flooded with Yankee ladies with frozen posteriors, who can and will look down on whores, when the transcontinental railroad is finished."

"But they're building it right now, aren't they?"

"No. They're piddling around, making plans, surveys and the like, and haven't yet laid a yard of track west of the Missouri. And what's more, that railroad may never get built. . . ."

"I don't see why not," Mireille said.

"The slavery question. This country is going to blow apart, go up in smoke. And if the Southerners win—as they probably will, being much better fighters—they won't have the slightest interest in favoring a state like California who threw the pro-slavery element out, and has freed every nigger who has been brought across her frontiers."

"You may be right," Mireille sighed, "but I still don't see what good it does me."

"An immense amount. When men have no prissy, parasol-flaunting frozen-tails to marry, they take what's available. In San Francisco, that means they have the choice of a life of single blessedness or putting on double harness, legally, with whores. Human nature being what it is, no choice at all, my dear! Remember how many girls you've lost from Em's in the last few months?"

"Lord, yes! Half a dozen. If it weren't for dear How-ward, I'd have to go out of business!"

"So, in this burg, there're going to be so many skeletons rattling around in the closets of the oldest and best families—not to mention, considering how many of the little darlings actually are New Orleans quadroons, the number of distinguished colored gentlemen who're going to grace the ancestral woodpiles, that nobody's going to be able to point the finger of scorn at anybody else. Have you heard the miners' song?"

"No. But what's a song got to do with—"

"Listen!" Mary Ellen Pleasant said, and throwing back her head, sang in her husky, alto voice:

"The miners came in forty-nine,
The whores in fifty-one;
And when they got together,
They made the native son!"

"Neat!" Mireille said; "and true, too, isn't it? Oh, Lord, how I do hope I'll be lucky this time!"

"You will. I have no doubt of it. Now, before I go, is there anything else I can do for you, Mireille, dear?"

"No. Yes! You can find me a husband for Jasmine."

"Done. What kind of a husband would you prefer for that sweet, stupid child?"

"A Norwegian. A Swede. Somebody from one of the Scandinavian countries. You see, he's got to be fair enough so that there'll be no danger that their babies will be—"

"Black. That danger's slight. Jasmine could marry a *mulato* and she still wouldn't have a black child. That's an old wives' tale that bigots circulate to discourage race mixing. But if you prefer a towhead, I'll get you one for her. . . ."

She bent over and kissed Mireille fondly.

"You should have been my daughter," she chuckled, "for in many ways, we're exactly alike. Or we will be, when your steam-heated little tail cools off enough to let your head take over. . . ."

"Has yours?" Mireille shot back at her.

"No. I still—have my moments. But that's life, I guess. Be seeing you, child," Mary Ellen Pleasant said.

11

MIREILLE PUT THAT EVENING'S EDITION OF THE SAN FRANCISCO *Bulletin* down on the bed before her, and folded her arms despairingly across her abdomen. Naturally enough, by the date printed just below the *Bulletin*'s banner, May 20, 1856, said abdomen was perfectly enormous.

"Oh, Lord! That's all I need!" she said.

"Don't know why you take on so over it, ma'am," Jasmine sniffed. "You didn't even know editor King, so's how come you's a-grieving over him?"

"Jasmine, I swear you haven't any brains at all!" Mireille said. "I couldn't care less if all the newspapermen in San Francisco were to shoot each other, and sometimes I wish they would! But don't you see, child, that this is going to remind everybody of the Cora-Richardson case, because that was what started the fight between Jim Casey and James King of William in the first place?"

"That sure is a funny name," Jasmine observed.

"It's not editor King's name. He tacked that 'of William'—meaning 'son of William King'—onto his name because when he was working back East in Washington, D.C., he kept running into other men named 'James King.' It's an awfully common name, y'know. So when he ran into James King number thirteen, he changed his name legally to James King, son of William. I s'pose he got tired of writing all that out, so of late he's signed his editorials in the *Bulletin* 'J. King of William.'"

"Well, he ain't—isn't—gonna sign nothing anymore, tha's for sure," Jasmine said. "Took him a helluva long time to cash in his chips, him, didn't it? That there other newspaper fella, Casey, shot him all of a week ago . . ."

"Yes. On the fourteenth. Oh, good Lord! I've never had any luck!"

"Now, Missy Mireille, ma'am, there you's wrong," Jasmine said.

"You's one o' th' luckiest li'l girls I ever did see. You's got just about the richest man in town keeping you, and the bestest-lookin' fella in th' whole blame state in love with you, and here you goes moaning low 'bout you don't have no luck!"

"I don't. Look at it: I didn't know either James Casey or James King of William. I *have* seen Charles Cora and Arabella Ryan, and General Richardson and his wife, because the Judge and I happened to be in the American Theatre the night that awful business started. Last November the fifteenth. We went to see the Ravels in that play of theirs: *Nicodemus, or The Unfortunate Fisherman.* But I don't remember a blessed thing about that play . . ."

"Why not, sugar—I mean ma'am?" Jasmine said.

"Because the fight between Cora and General Richardson upset me too much. No, that's not true. Not the fight—the reason for it. Gave me an excellent idea of what *I* can expect in the future, as more and more decent women come into San Francisco."

"Honey, you's decent enough. You don't hardly cheat on th' Judge none atall. And just with one real good-looking fella, at that. Old as th' Judge is, he can't 'spect no better than that . . ."

"Jasmine, you're hopeless. That night I saw what's going to happen to me. General Richardson called the theater manager and practically ordered him to eject Arabella Ryan on the score that it was an insult to decent women like his wife to have to sit in a box next to a whorehouse madame like Arabella Ryan . . ."

"Done heard about her," Jasmine snorted; "runs that flossy parlor house on Pike Street, don't she? Charges more money than anybody else, even French Em. Her babes is younger and prettier and ain't nothing they can't or won't do. Heard tell one of 'em let a fella do it to her whilst she was standing on her head!"

"Jasmine, you shut up, will you?" Mireille cried.

"I'm sorry, hon—ma'am. Lord, you is—are—upset, ain't you? 'Tain't nothing to cry over, sugar . . ."

"Oh, yes it is! I thought that people would just forget—what I've been, what I was forced into—and now look! That fool tinhorn gambler goes and kills the general—oh, no, not that night; it was two or three days later, Jas—because the general called Arabella the whore she is. And Cora's trial drags on and on all winter, with Casey's newspaper defending him and King's *Bulletin* thundering away that he ought to be hanged. So then King and Casey start slinging ink—and mud—at each other. Then last week—and Cora's gangster friends put him up to it—

Casey goes and shoots King. So now the Vigilance Committee is organizing all over again, and the whole town is up in arms, and I am ruined!"

"Sugar, you's—you've—done lost me. I just don't see what all that there is got to do with you none a'tall, ma'am . . ."

"Look, Jasmine, you and Olaf Svenson are going to get married next month. How would you like for somebody to call everybody's attention, by writing about it in all the newspapers, to the fact that a good many of the girls from New Orleans who've married fine, upstanding white men here in San Francisco are really quadroon ex-whores from Royal and Basin street parlor houses?"

"I wouldn't like that a good goddamn, me," Jasmine said.

"And *I* don't like editorials roaring and foaming at the mouth about whorehouse madams who flaunt themselves in public and get good men killed!" Mireille stormed.

"But you ain't no whorehouse madam. Or is you? John Swithers says you's—you've—got an awful lot o' money coming in every week from somewheres, ma'am. You ain't went and sunk the cash Madame Pleasant paid you for them water lots in th' tail-peddling business, is you, sugar?"

"D'you think I'd tell you if I had?" Mireille snapped. "Don't be an idiot, Jasmine. Every horny fool in town and his hard-up brother know I was on the receiving line at Em's. And with the twins on the way, I thought I could get the Judge to divorce his raving maniac of a wife and marry me—"

"How come you's so sure you're gonna have twins, ma'am? Course that there is a mighty fine belly somebody's done hung onto you for a fact, but—"

"Not *somebody*. The Judge. Get that through your stupid head, Jasmine!"

"Well now, sugar—I mean ma'am; the Judge, he mighty old, him. While young Mr. Kilpatrick is—"

"Sick. Believe me, it's—they're—the Judge's. I know."

"All right. Far be it from me to argue th' point," Jasmine said cheerfully. "But, c'mon, tell me something, ma'am: how come you knows how many chillun you've got in there?"

"Doctor Gammon listened with his stethoscope. Heard two heartbeats, Jasmine. . . ."

"And what is they, boys or girls? Or one o' each?"

"Oh Lord, nobody can tell that, Jasmine! All I'm praying is that at least one of the two will have blue eyes and light hair . . ."

"Don't see how you could miss, there. Mr. Kilpatrick's real blond, him, for all that he had a Mexican mama. And the Judge must of been, too, when his hair had some other color to it 'sides white. So I don't see—"

"They might both take after me," Mireille said sadly; "and if they do, there'll be no way I can convince the Judge that—"

"He they pappy. Mighty hard for a man sixty-five years old to believe. Costs him to get it up, don't it?"

"Jasmine, it's a shame we're not back in Louisiana where I could have you whipped!"

"That I don't believe, me!" Jasmine hooted. "Us just like sisters, you and me, ma'am. Tell me something: You scairt you ain't got th' Judge softened up enough for him to slip that ol' weddin' band on your pinky and make a respectable lady outa you?"

"I know I haven't," Mireille said morosely. "Oh, he believes the twins are his, all right. It's just that he took his oath on the Bible never to divorce his crazy wife while she lives. He's going to adopt the twins legally, which makes them legitimate to all extents and purposes, and settle over two hundred thousand dollars on me outright, but—"

"But, sweet baby Jesus! What you bitchin' over, sugar? You's got it all!"

"Except the main thing, the thing I need more than anything else in this world," Mireille whispered.

"What's that?" Jasmine demanded.

"That M-R-S up front, and behind it, his name . . ."

"You'll get that, too, you plays your cards right," Jasmine said with calm conviction. "Now tell me something else: What time you 'spect them young'uns of yourn to get here?"

"Oh, in about a month from now," Mireille said.

But she was wrong. Exactly two days later, in the early morning of May 22, 1856, she went into labor. She was in labor all day until well after the mobs had come back from the monumental funeral of James King of William, the murdered editor of the *Evening Bulletin,* and the Vigilance Committee had hanged both Charles Cora and James Casey from a pair of beams thrust out of the front windows of their headquarters at 105½ Sacramento Street. During the last, more terrible part of her struggle to bring her child—or children—into this world, she was cheered by the news that Father Maginnis, who had been the first English-speaking Catholic priest to serve a parish in San Francisco, had married Charles Cora and Arabella Ryan one hour before the Vigilantes converted him into a corpse and her into a widow. 'Which gives me,' Mireille thought, 'still another weapon to use against the Judge . . .'

Half an hour after Cora and Casey had departed this life, Dr. Joseph
Gammon put a tiny, red, wrinkled, remarkably simian-looking creature—
for its tiny head was covered all over with thick black hair—into her
arms. She had no breath left to talk, and had bitten her own tongue
almost through in an effort to stifle her own cries, but she got that all-
important question out:

"What—is—it?"

"A girl," Joe Gammon said.

"Ohhhhhhhh Lord!" Mireille wailed.

"But this'un ain't!" Joe chuckled, and put that other, much heavier
burden into the crook of her other arm. Even though he too had been
born only recently—no more than a few hours ago or, at worst, a day, so
accurately had Mary Ellen Pleasant timed matters—that male child was
already as beautiful as it was possible for a newborn to be. The wisps of
curls on his well-shaped cranium were white blond, almost silvery.

"His eyes?" Mireille whispered.

"Blue, natch. For that matter, so are hern, which is gonna help matters a heap." Dr. Gammon leaned close. "Don't bring up that birthmark
business for about a week," he husked. "His poor li'l ear is swollen. Got a
mite o' pus back there. But once it heals up, it oughta pass muster. It
don't have to be perfect, y'know . . ."

"Thank you," Mireille murmured. "Now—tell the Judge to come in
here, won't you—Doctor?"

"Sure thing, honey. But one more item: You gonna nurse 'em, or you
want Mary Ellen to send you a wet nurse? They'll spoil th' hell outa
them lovely tits o'yourn, y'know . . ."

"Tell—her—to send me a wet nurse," Mireille croaked; "I still
haven't—got—th'—Judge, and—"

"All right, Mireille baby. You're being smart—as usual. I'll send ol'
dangling daddy in, now. Give him a good show, will you?"

The show was perfect.

Mireille lay there looking up at the Judge, her blue-bruised, bitten,
blood-crusted lips curved into a smile so sweet, so madonna-like, that it
would have melted a heart cast in armor steel.

"The—daughter—you—wanted, Alain," she got out on little whispery
spurts of breath. "And—my image of—you. . . . Tell me, are you—
happy?"

And Judge Alain Curtwright, man of measure, of perfect calm, of iron
self-control, dropped to his knees beside that bed, buried his face in the
covers, and wept like a child.

Half an hour after that, Jasmine La Fleur stole into the back of St.

Mary's Church on the corner of Grant Avenue and California Street in what had not yet become Chinatown. She looked around her until she located the slim, blond young man who was kneeling before a statue of the Holy Virgin above a side altar. He was lighting votive candle after candle, and crossing himself at a rate that made his arms seem to be powered by one of the new steam engines the Municipal Department of Streets was currently using to cut San Francisco's steep grades down into inclines gentle enough not to kill all the horses, while from his lips poured an endless stream of fervent prayers.

"Suh—" Jasmine murmured.

The young man whirled.

"Her says I was to tell you she's all right, her. And that it's—twins, suh. Boy and girl. Th' boy—he your spitt'n' image, suh. She didn't tell me t' tell you that. But I seen him, me, and I thought you'd like to know . . ."

"Oh, thank you, Jasmine! Thank you! And thank *you*, Holy Mother!" William Kilpatrick said.

"Why does he keep rubbing his little fist behind his ear like that, Mireille?" Judge Alain Curtwright said.

"Well, he had a kind of growth back there, darling," Mireille sighed. "And since it was—discolored—and sort of ugly, I had Dr. Gammon take it off. Fact is, *he* suggested doing that. Said it was better to remove it now, while it and our little angel are both tiny. Later on, he was afraid it might start to grow, and form those purplish, warty kind of bumps you see on some people's faces. It's healing up now, so it itches, that's all . . ."

"Hmmmmmn—let me see it," the Judge said.

Mireille held the baby out to him. With trembling hands, he took the already sturdy child from her.

"He's plenty solid, isn't he?" He laughed. "I keep expecting him to break when I touch him, but he looks like he's built to last. Come here, little fellow, let your old pappy have a look . . ."

He laid the child face down across his knees, and looked behind its left ear.

"Hmmmn—" he said. "It's *still* discolored, Mireille. Looks like some sort of a birthmark to me. And Joe Gammon appears to have punctured it, rather than cut it off."

"Didn't have to cut much," Mireille said calmly; "it was loose. Just hanging by a little piece of skin. You mean to say it's discolored under that? Under the place where it was? Oh, dear!"

"It's not bad, baby-girl. Looks like a little star, or a part of one anyhow. How's about little Number Two? *She* doesn't have any blemishes, does she?"

"Alain—I don't want to call her 'Mireille.' Please, darling; I *really* don't want to . . ."

"Why not? It's a lovely name," the Judge said.

"It's—bad luck. I want her to have a much better life than I've had. I —I wanted her, wanted both of my—our—children, to grow up in a normal household. Where their—father—lived with them. Came home every night. And where nobody would ddddare call them little bbbbas-tards!"

"Now, Mireille!" he groaned.

"All right! All right! I won't argue the point anymore. You jjjjust dddon't want me, and that's all. Not really. Nnnnot always, and for kkkeeps. I should have finished cutting my throat that time! I really should have!"

"Mireille, I can't put poor Susan by. I simply can't. If she were in her right mind, it wouldn't seem so—so callous. Besides, I've already ac-knowledged these little beauties as mine, given them my name, made them my heirs—which is probably presumptuous of me, a piece of ar-rantly vain folly on the part of an old duffer my age, but—"

"Alain!" she gasped.

"There, there, baby-girl! I'm only teasing! My sense of humor is sort of left-handed at times! I didn't mean—"

"No," she whispered, "you're not teasing. You meant that. You doubt that these children—that I went through hell to give you—are yours. But you—will take good care of them, won't you, dearest? Rear them to be decent, and cultured—and—smart—and good? And—even bring them—once in a while—to—to put some flowers—on my grave?"

"Mireille!" he got out.

"Yes, I'm going to kill myself, Alain. You—you've taken away my last reason—to live. Tonight. Tomorrow. One day when you're not—can't be —here. There's no way for you to stop me, y'know. Short of locking *me* up in another padded cell . . ."

"Mireille," he said brokenly, "forgive me. Please forgive me. I don't know what made me say that. I—"

"Alain," she whispered, "bring me my hand mirror, will you?"

"Your—your mirror? Of course, I—I'll be happy to!"

"I'm—not—crazy, Alain. This is not one of those sudden alternations of mood that mad people have. I just want to—show you something. No, don't bring me the mirror. Go sit down before my vanity and adjust the mirror on it so you can see your face."

"Looking at *my* phiz gives me scant pleasure, child," he said sadly.

"Don't know why not. You've—a beautiful face, Alain. From the hand of a Phidias, it has always seemed to me. Please do as I ask. Sit down before the big mirror on my vanity, and—hold my little looking glass behind your head, so that between the two of them you can see the back part of your left ear. Take your time. Do it—carefully. There's—no hurry, now . . ."

Wonderingly, he did so. But the adjustment was awkward. It took him some considerable time. When he'd got it right at last, his face turned as white as a sheet. It took him several seconds to find enough breath to whisper:

"My God!"

"I saw it—that time I was nibbling on your ears for dessert," she said with the saddest little laugh he had ever heard. "Probably means nothing. His—*my* baby's—'cause *I* can't deny him, can I?—*wasn't* exactly the same. Or at least not until Dr. Gammon cut the fleshy, warty part off . . ."

"But—but—in the same place! And—and a little star with broken points and—Oh, Mireille! Mireille!"

"Now, put the mirror down. Go over to the cradle and bring me—little Claire. That's what I'm going to call her, no matter what you say, you—you old doubting Thomas, you! Careful, now—don't drop her! There, there sweetie pie, don't cry, don't cry—*ta 'tite maman* loves you, anyhow, even though *ton papa* has disowned you . . ."

She held that tiny mite in her lap. Then, with infinite care, she pushed one of the infant's minuscule eyelids back with her thumb and forefinger.

"Look, Alain," she whispered. "*Your* eyes. Yours, all over again. The same shade of blue. Even though her hair is as black as mine. You will—be good to her, won't you? To your *own* daughter, now that she won't, can't—have—her mama anymore?"

"Mireille, for the love of God!"

"No. I—had to prove it to you. And that was—is—too demeaning. You've—always doubted me. You always will. Under those circumstances, Alain, I have neither the right, nor the desire—to live . . ."

"Not even to bring them up? Not even knowing they'd be—orphans, and at the mercy of my wife's pretty unscrupulous brothers—one hour, or less, after you committed so monumental a piece of criminal folly?" he said slowly.

"Ohhhhhhhhh Alain!" she wailed.

"I love you, child. My problem was that I've never believed that I—

deserved you. But let's forget our differences, shall we? Mireille, promise me you—won't? Not for my sake, but—for theirs?"

She held him with those matchless eyes of hers. Said, brokenly, "Give me your hand, Alain . . ."

He held out his hand to her. She took it, turned it palm upward, and pressed her lips against it. They burned it, scalded it, seared it to the nerve, the bone.

"For *your* sake, Alain," she said quietly. "For the sake of the man I love, worship, and adore. Alain—that money you're going to settle on me—"

"That I have settled on you," he said.

"Take it back. Give it—to an orphan home. To the Church. To your wife's brothers. Throw it in the Bay! Instead—marry me. Without a cent. Give me—your name. The high honor of being your wife. In God's sight. Before the eyes of men. I—I'll scrub floors! Pick rags! Beg! But then I can be proud, don't you understand? Proud! I can ttttake my cccchildren tttto cccchurch! Wwwwalk in the street with them! And—and with you. With mmmmmy hhhhhusband! *Oh, bon Dieu!* Can't you understand?"

He stared at her.

"All right, Mireille," he said quietly; "it'll take a little while, but I'll—arrange it . . ."

But he wasn't given that little while. Fate took a hand in the matter. Or one of the Furies.

The one named Mary Ellen Pleasant, very likely.

When they brought him into Enrique Sepúlvera's house on the corner of Clay and Hyde streets—for the Sepúlveras lived in San Francisco now, of which fact and the reasons for it Mireille, by Enrique's direct request to his old friend the Judge, had not been informed—Alain Curtwright had seventy-five percent of his body covered with second- and third-degree burns. In June 1856 a person who had even one quarter of his skin area so burned was doomed, and both Dr. Sepúlvera and Judge Curtwright knew it.

"How long have I got, Enrique?" Alain Curtwright said.

Enrique bowed his head.

"Too long, Alain," he said.

"How long—is—too long?" the Judge whispered.

"A week—ten days. God knows. Until—the infection sets in—irreversibly. As it will. I could keep a burn as small as the palm of your hand reasonably clean; but burns like these, no. You're losing—leaking—all your vital fluids through your skin. All I can do is try to keep you as comfortable as possible. Which means opium. In huge doses. And—toward the end, it won't work anymore. Of course, by then you'll be 'delirious—and, I hope, unconscious. ¡Virgen Santísima, Alain! How'd it happen? Your people say your house burned to the ground. Tell me—"

"No. First send for—Mireille. And—Father Maginnis. You can explain—the matter—to Paquita, later. I'll ask—Mireille—to stay away from here—after I'm gone. To visit you—no more . . ."

"To hell with that damned female nonsense!" Enrique snapped. "You *couldn't* marry Mireille, so Paquita has no right to—"

Alain Curtwright, with infinite weariness, smiled. For some reason or another, his face was only slightly burned.

"Nobody has any right to anything in this world, my friend," he whispered; "not even to his—next breath . . . Enrique, promise me to —to look after Mireille—all you can—She's going to—need—your help. Tonight she's going to—get her dearest wish: I'm going to—do right by —Our Little Nell!" He stopped, gave a deep, sardonic chuckle.

"But—Susan?" Enrique said.

"Dead. I tried—did my damnedest—to save her. My body is proof of —that, isn't it?"

"God, yes!" Enrique said. "Alain—how'd the fire start? Did Susan get her hands on matches? A kerosene lamp? Oh, no! Forget it. You shouldn't talk. Try to rest, now."

"No. I—want—to talk. Need—someone to bear witness. Call your nurse—back in here. You're—my friend. If there are legal troubles—you'll—Mireille will—need at least two witnesses—"

"Mireille will need—?"

"Witnesses to—her—innocence—of the charge—of murdering Susan —causing my own death. That fire—was set. I caught the—arsonist—at work. A Black man. A—Negro. Unfortunately, I—lost my head—and shot him—dead. So now—we'll never know who sent him. Or even—who he was. His body—burned past all possible—recognition in the fire. I don't know—many Blacks. This one was—a stranger to me. . . ."

"But why, Alain? Why? Who had motives to—"

"Burn me out? Kill—Susan? Before a court of law—the number one —suspect will be—Mireille. It—can be proved, of course, that her—economic reasons are—not so strong as people are going to think—they are. Enrique, call your nurse! This is important! And send for—that priest—for—Mireille . . ."

"All right," Enrique said. Then, "Mrs. Donaldson, will you come back in here a moment, please?"

When Mireille walked through that door and saw Judge Curtwright lying there with his eyes closed, his fine-chiseled old face blue-gray, still, she didn't utter a single sound, not even the syllables of his name. She took one step into the sickroom, another. Then she stopped. Loosened all over. Collapsed. Went down like a sack emptied of its contents. Like a body bereft of life.

It wasn't graceful. It wasn't pretty. And, above all, it wasn't faked.

She fell flat on her face, a thing the past mistresses of the histrionic swoon, so frequently employed as a defensive or an offensive tactic by female warriors in the lesser skirmishes of the war between the sexes in that epoch, could never bring themselves to do. The impact of flesh thudding against wood was distinctly audible. She came close to breaking, or at least disjointing, her pert, upturned little nose. Her teeth tore the inside of her mouth all to hell. When Enrique and Mrs. Donaldson turned her over, the blood poured out of it in streams.

By then Paquita, who had been informed by Josefina that the Sepúlveras' manservant, José, had been sent to fetch both Padre Maginnis and Mireille, was there. She took one look at Mireille's snowy face, at that scarlet stream inundating her chin and upper throat, and started to scream.

Upon the bed, the supposed corpse opened its eyes. Gave a low, rasping chuckle that was mockery's—and gallantry's, considering the amount of pain he was in—very self.

"Women!" Judge Alain Curtwright said.

"Father," Alain Curtwright croaked, "I am—not of your faith. Nor of —any other. Call me—a freethinker . . . which—doesn't matter. I shall—soon be arguing—religious questions with—his satanic majesty— down in hell."

"Oh, I doubt that, Judge," Father Maginnis said. "God knows his elect, his own, no matter how much bloody nonsense they spout. What is it that you wish of me, my son?"

"That you—marry me and Mademoiselle Duclos. Now. Tonight. I became—a widower—a couple of hours ago."

"Alain!" Mireille gasped.

"Shut up—baby-girl. *Padre*—if I have to join your church to do that— why then, join it I will—God's given me—reason to doubt—my doubts —tonight . . ."

Father Maginnis' red Irish face split into an enormous grin.

"Doctor!" he roared. "Clear all these people out of here! I've got to hear the Confession of this newborn son of God!"

Mireille's Confession was short and to the point; but it was wonderfully all-inclusive.

"*Mon Père,*" she said in her crystalline soprano voice, "I accuse myself of having broken—repeatedly—all ten of the ten commandments. Of having committed every venial sin there is, and all of the mortal ones. I further confess to having invented a few more of each that the Holy Fathers of the Church never even thought of, because they just didn't have the kind of minds I have. Only the Devil does, I guess. And if the matter were put to the test, I'm sure I'd beat him when it comes to sinfulness . . ."

Father Maginnis fought hard against the smile tugging at the corners of his mouth.

"Do you sincerely repent of 'em, daughter, and promise not to do 'em anymore?" he asked.

"I do," Mireille whispered.

"Then, as penitence, say ten Pater Nosters and twenty Ave Marias. No! Not now—there's no time. I absolve you of your sins, daughter. You can do your penitence later. Right now I've got to lift you out of concubinage and your children out of bastardy by marrying you to this charcoal-broiled hulk while he's still got breath in him!"

"Mirla—" Paquita sobbed, "can I give you a kiss? Please!"

"Hmmnpf!" Mireille sniffed. "No. You may *not* kiss me, Señora Doña High and Mighty! You—you've been living in town a year, and I just found it out tonight. You ignored me. You looked down on me. All right, I was living in sin, sort of, but—"

"Mireille," Enrique growled, "I promised Alain I'd take care of you. And since he's going to die—"

"Ohhhhhhhh Enrique!" Mireille wailed.

"I'm sorry, child, but he is. And since he's going to die, I consider that promise a sacred trust. It includes warming your dainty little fundament when you start in to be unnecessarily outrageous. As now. Go on, kiss Paqui. The two of you make up. I agree, she's behaved outrageously too. Paqui, apologize to Mireille, here and now. She's right. You have treated her badly. You never had any right to adopt the posture of moral superiority, y'know!"

"Mirla!" Paquita wept; "I beg your pardon on my knees! I've been very, very bad to you. Tell me that you forgive me! Say it, please!"

"Hmmnpf! Oh, all right; I forgive you. No, I don't. Don't have to. Never was angry with you in the first place. Just—heartbroken. I love you, idiot! Now, kiss me! And talk English, will you? I've no head for Spanish t'night . . ."

"Your children! Oh, Mirla, I'm just dying to see them!"

"And I yours. But I won't make you wake 'em tonight. Come to visit me tomorrow, and bring your kids along. Or rather, today. It's after midnight, isn't it? Tell me, why did you and Enrique decide to leave the *rancho?* I loved that place. I just can't imagine giving it up—"

"We didn't," Enrique said. "Not voluntarily. We were more or less thrown off it. You've heard of the squatters, haven't you? They come out here, occupy every decent piece of land, and start in to farm it, now that gold mining has proved the tremendous bust it always was. You try to put them off your place, and they go for their guns on the grounds that they're native-born Americans 'And you, you greasy Spik-speaking fur-riner, ain't got no right to no gol-durned land in this here country o' ourn, nohows!' Of course, if you can prove a Spanish or a Mexican land grant to a direct ancestor, the courts will uphold your claims against the squatters, because confirmation of such claims was one of the chief provi-sions of the treaty of Guadalupe Hidalgo that ended the Mexican War—"

"And you can, can't you?" Mireille said.

"Of course. Your friend Willy Kilpatrick swears mine is rock-solid. He's become an expert in land grant cases because nobody can dispute his command of Spanish or English, so he handles all such disputes for the firm. He's been reading for the law ever since fifty-two, and last month he was admitted to the bar."

"Fat lot of good that's going to do me," Mireille said, morosely, "even if I do get to be a widow, which the Good God forbid! That little lace-curtain shamrock plucker's got him. And this awful religion of ours. I give up. Except making him cheat on dear Molly once in a while, there's nothing I can do—"

"I'm glad you realize that," Enrique said. "But there is, now."

"Such as—what?" Mireille said.

"Give up the cheating. Live—decently, child. Set your own children a good example."

"Oh," Mireille said. "All right! All right! I will. From now on, I'm going to be a perfect angel. Enrique, if your land grant is so good, why didn't you just run those grubby, bewhiskered beggars off the ranch?"

"And have every cent I own end up in the pockets of the lawyers? That's what always happens. Proving a royal, or even a Mexican, land grant costs too much. You get ruined doing it. Besides, my practice here in San Francisco had already become much more profitable than the *rancho* even before that tribe of locusts showed up. That battle wasn't worth the trouble, considering, additionally, that once you've got your eviction order from the courts, who's going to enforce it? All the sheriffs are gringos now. And they stall around for months, doing nothing. Or openly take the part of the squatters."

"Enrique—about Alain. Can't you save him? I love him. I do. Truly."

"Yes, you love him. So much that you adorn his poor, tired old forehead with every conceivable size, shape, and convolution of antlers, and make him believe Willy Kilpatrick's bastard brats are his!"

"Why, Enrique!" she gasped.

"Well, didn't you?"

"No. All right—all right, I tried. Didn't work. I'm too much for poor Willy. What with his stomach ulcers, and his shot-up lung, and—"

"Didn't affect his performance with Molly," Enrique said.

"Maybe she put a couple of other workers on the job," Mireille snapped. "Enrique—my children are Alain's. Believe me."

"Mireille, anybody who believes you is a cretin. And I'm not a cretin."

"All right. Come see my kids tomorrow. Then tell me they're not Alain's!"

"Can't. I've got to watch over poor old Alain every minute. Incidentally, you can't go home either. He can't be moved, y'know. Have you got a good nurse for the babies?"

"Yes—" Mireille whispered.

"I'll send Josefina for your clothes and whatever else you need. And give you a room here. Into which you are not to invite Paqui. She neglects me too much now. Don't want you turning her again. In a word, you two dear little *tortilleras* leave each other alone. Understand?"

Mireille and Paquita looked at each other. Then, by mutual accord, they burst into gales of silvery laughter.

"Shut up!" Enrique growled; "Alain might hear you! You don't want him to think you're *celebrating* his passing, d'you?"

Immediately, instantly, on the spur of that same moment, Mireille's eyes filled up with tears.

"No. That's the last thing I'd ever celebrate. Oh, Enrique—save him! Save him, please!" she said.

12

⚜

BUT TO SAVE JUDGE ALAIN CURTWRIGHT PROVED IMPOSSIBLE. IN fact, it had been so from the very moment that that gallant old man had persisted in his efforts to save his mad wife, for it had been in breaking through, with her in his arms, the wall of towering flame roaring up the stairway, that he sustained the additional burns which cost him his life.

That Susan Sutton Curtwright was surely already dead of asphyxia by then—the padding covering the walls, ceiling, and floor of her bedroom cell had smoldered slowly, filling it up with dense clouds of smoke long before the first flickering, incandescent tongues appeared—was another aspect of the matter that Doctor Enrique Sepúlvera stopped considering at all, in defense of his own sanity, already reeling under the impact of all the fatal ironies involved. Nor could he, whose intellectual rejection of the Roman Catholic faith he was born to didn't extend as deep as the basic, emotional fibers of his being, bring himself to contemplate the obvious fact that he had on his hands a case in which any other course whatsoever except the immediate application of euthanasia was not only a gross immorality, but a cruelty of a magnitude difficult indeed to justify.

In Enrique's defense, be it said that he didn't reject the idea of putting Alain Curtwright out of his almost unbelievable misery, because that simple idea never even occurred to him. He was too busy doing what he could for a man who had fully three quarters of the surface of his skin converted into a mass of blisters, raw holes, and seared flesh, all of which dripped lymph, blood, and pus every moment of the day and night.

So the good doctor busied himself with inventing a sort of scaffolding, with heavily padded crossbars under his patient's head, buttocks, knees, and heels, which raised the Judge's body above the surface of the bed and effectively prevented nearly ninety percent of his back from touching anything at all, because whatever it touched, it stuck to. To achieve the same result as far as the Judge's chest, abdomen, and upper thighs almost to his knees were concerned, Enrique made a tent of the covers, propping them up with slender poles so that they couldn't touch poor Alain anywhere, either.

That was all he could do. The medical science of that day, and for close to a hundred years after it, existed in a state of abject helplessness when it came to saving the victims of burns as massive, deep, and extensive as Alain Curtwright's were.

The rest was up to Mireille. She nursed her dying husband with a tenderness that brought tears to Enrique's eyes. Quite often, she had to be removed from the sickroom bodily, after she had collapsed from sheer exhaustion. Paquita and Josefina took turns in watching over and caring for the Judge, of course; but Mireille insisted upon staying at his side until she was quite literally on the point of dropping before she would consent to letting either of them, or Mrs. Donaldson, take over.

So, by the very law of averages, it was quite normal that she was alone with him the night he died. She sat in the chair a little distance from his bed, where it was at least possible to endure the awful stench of a body that was rotting away while its owner still maintained an appalling degree of both life and consciousness. She was fighting to keep her sleep-drugged eyes open when suddenly, clearly, she heard his voice:

"Come—here—baby-girl—" he said.

She exploded up from that chair, flew to his side.

"I—can't—bear—it, anymore—child," he whispered. "I'm going—to have—to—scream. Wake the—whole household—up—the neighborhood—and I—don't—want—to . . ."

"Alain, please!" she moaned.

"I've—always—tried—to live—well—my dear. So—let me—die—well, too . . . Take—the pillow—you were—resting—your—sweet head—against—Hold it over—against—my—face. Two minutes—three—Weak as I am—that's all—it'll take . . ."

"No! Alain, no!" she said.

"Don't—you—love—me?" he got out. "You—Ayeee—God!—said you did—"

"I love you. You *know* I do. Only—don't ask me—to do—*this!* Please, Alain! Oh, God, Alain, please!"

"I don't ask. I—order—command you—to. Obey—me—sweet—angel-witchchild—of mine. In—proof of—the love—you bear—me. Out—of—respect for—the good life—the—impossibly—incredibly—good life

—we had—together. Mireille, I—I'm going to scream! I'm going to—
For God's love, child! For mine!"

She whirled, got that pillow. Pressed it with two wildly shaking hands
against his worn, tired, suffering, beautiful old face. Kept it there while
her own throat corded, knotted, jerking convulsively against the cries she
was holding in by main force, and the tears, which were the physical
manifestation of a despair almost unimaginably pure, burst, exploded—
live steam, lava, utterly corrosive vitriol—from her totally blindscalded
eyes.

When it was over, she bent and kissed his mouth, already growing
cold, turned and walked away, but no farther than the doorway. Stood
there a moment, not thinking really, just feeling, letting tidal waves of
grief, remorse, utter self-loathing, wash over her.

"I—lied to you," she whispered, "tricked you, betrayed you—cheated
on you. With—Willy. With the whole damned fire department, very
nearly. And now—I've—murdered you—Killed you dead—"

She turned, went back to that still figure on the bed.

"But I—loved you. That's the truth, Alain. You *know* it is. More than
anybody else—I've ever known. . . ."

Then, with sudden, decisive impulse, she bent, picked up the chair.
Marched to the doorway with it. Went to work at what she now had to
do, all her motions quick, forceful, sure. She unwound from her waist the
silken cord of the dressing gown Paquita had lent her. Made a loop in
that cord, tied with a slipknot. Put that loop around her neck. Climbed
up on the chair. Wound the other end of the cord around a corner of the
transom over the door, where one side of the hinged fanlight that could
be tilted open in summer to admit more air into the room gave her space
enough to pass it through. Straightened up. Whispered, "Goodbye, my
love—"

And without any hesitation at all, jumped off that chair.

Hanging, even when done by an expert, is an agonizingly slow way to
die. And Mireille wasn't an expert. She had no idea how to go about
tying the massive "hangman's knot" that breaks the victim's neck, and
makes death on the gallows both relatively swift—though, actually, slow
enough even so!—and totally irreversible. What was more, her material
was faulty: she hadn't a thick rope of hemp to use, but only a slender
silken cord.

Which stretched, even under her slight weight. Her toe tips touched
the floor and drummed a convulsive tattoo against it. Enrique and Paquita, whose bedroom was next to the one they had put poor Alain in,

heard that impromptu *danse macabre* and got there in time to cut her down just as her face was turning a lovely shade of blue.

Enrique made all the windows vibrate as he roared at her in three languages, while Paqui tenderly bathed her badly bruised throat, dripping her own tears down to mingle with the flood already inundating Mireille's face. Absolutely beside himself, Enrique had all he could do to repress his almost overwhelming desire to complete her suicide attempt for her, by strangling with his bare hands this absurd, tender, wild, fey little creature whom, despite all he knew about her, he could not help but love, so he caught her by the shoulders and shook her until her teeth rattled.

"And your children?" he bellowed. "What? Answer me, you impossible little idiot! What of *them?*"

Mireille's eyes opened very wide.

"Ohhhhhhhh Lord! I—I'd completely forgot them!" she wailed.

Yerba Buena Cemetery was at the extreme southern end of the city at the junction of McAllister Street and part of what afterward was going to be cut down and leveled off into Union Square, but which at the moment was a high sand hill, shifting its slopes under the driving winds. It was just about the dreariest site for a cemetery that the City Fathers could have found, being covered with shrubs that grew only knee high, and having a solitary manzanita bush with a blood-red stalk to lend the only relieving note of color to the general drabness of the area.

Yet, far as it was from the little house on the corner of Leavenworth and Bay streets that her departed lover, become, *in extremis,* her husband, had built for her, Mireille drove to the cemetery every day for the first two weeks after he had been buried there, to put fresh flowers on the Judge's grave. Even after that, she didn't stop making her daily pilgrimage to the tomb of the man whose name she now—with complete legality—bore, and whose respectable fortune she was soon to inherit; say, rather, she was stopped from doing so.

That day, the wild, windswept slope with the weathered angularity of wooden crosses, the bleak, terminal flatness of granite tombstones, and here and there, rarely, a small mausoleum of marble rising from amid the rounded clumps of sagebrush into the low, swirling mists blowing in from the ocean, seemed to her more desolate than ever. She knelt by Alain Curtwright's grave, whispering:

"I'm going to try to be good, Alain; but don't expect too much of me, will you? Most of the time I'm going to slip off the straight and narrow, sure as hell, being me. So I ask you to forgive me in advance, 'cause I'm going to go on trying and failing, and trying all over again, until one day I'll get there. Be good, I mean. For—always. Make you proud of me. And—of your little Claire. She's *yours.* She's got to be. She was born at just the right time to be, because that time I thought I'd lost her I really hadn't—and—and what I did with Willy about that time, too, didn't— count. It was—no good at all so it didn't—couldn't—*count!* Ohhhhh Lord! How *awful* I am! What a shameless slattern! What a species of a secondhand tart at bargain rates! What a cow!"

Her knees gave way beneath her. She leaned forward until she was lying face down across Alain's grave, ruining her black dress in the damp reddish sand, kissing the earth with fevered lips and crying, crying—

Then she felt that hand on her shoulder and whirled. Her eyes were so tear-blinded that she thought that the face peering worriedly down into hers was Willy's. In fact, she was just about to say his name, scream at him: "Go away and leave me in peace, will you?" when she saw it wasn't Willy. For one thing, he was clean-shaven instead of sporting a mustache like the thick blond one Willy had grown; for another, he struck her as being considerably less handsome, while obviously a good bit taller. And, of course, of the same generally Nordic type, the fair and ruddy northern European male who had always especially appealed to her—the attraction of opposites, she supposed. But on the spur of that same moment she guessed that this tall, thin, youngish man, with his almost comically solemn face, must surely be, by temperament, much milder, blander, less high-strung than Willy was or the Judge had been—and in consequence would be far, far easier for her to manage.

That the idea of managing him—this total stranger!—had come to her so readily shocked her to her heart's core. 'I'll never see him again!' she told herself furiously; 'and what's more, I don't even want to!'

Which, she realized even then, was a lie at least half the size of Saint Mary's Church.

"Please, ma'am," he said in a pleasant baritone voice, whose tone of concern was real, "are you—all right? Is there anything I can do?"

"No, nothing," she whispered. Then, "Thank you—for asking, any-how . . ."

Seeing she was trying to get up, he put out a hand to her, helped her to her feet, drew out his handkerchief, and tried, unsuccessfully, to brush the sand off the front of her dress with it.

"No, don't bother," she said; "I'll change as soon as I get home. I've a carriage waiting. May I—offer you a ride into town?"

"No, thank you," he said politely. "So happens I have my own rig, though it's nothing so fancy as a carriage." He nodded toward the grave. "A—relative? Your father? A brother?"

"My—husband," she said flatly, "and the father—of my two children . . ."

"Good Lord!" he said. "I'd given you about seventeen, no more!"

"Thank you. That's—very flattering. I'm—considerably older than that. Well, under the circumstances, I guess introductions are in order: I'm Mireille Duclos Curtwright. I—lost my husband—two weeks ago. His death was—accidental. A fire . . ."

He turned, stared at the tombstone.

" 'Judge Alain Curtwright,' " he read. "My heartfelt condolences, Mrs. Curtwright. My name's MacFarland. Andrew MacFarland. Seems to me I did read something about that fire in *The Alta Californian* or the *Evening Bulletin*, but—forgive me the bald truth—since the people involved weren't acquaintances of mine, I didn't pay much attention to the details. . . ."

She thought, 'Thank God!'

She said, "There was absolutely no reason for you to, Mr. MacFarland, so your apology is unnecessary. But enough of—*my* sorrows. May I ask what you are doing in the cemetery? Visiting the grave of a relative, I suppose?"

His rugged, a trifle too elongated face fell at once into an expression of lugubrious piety.

"My errand was identical with yours, Mrs. Curtwright. I came, as I do once every week, to put some flowers on my late wife's grave," he said.

Mireille reached out, caught his arm, gave it a tender little squeeze.

"I—I'm sorry," she whispered; "I'm—very sorry. It's—awful to—to lose someone you loved that much, isn't it? How long—has she been gone?"

"Close to a year. Longer than we were married. She—died—giving birth to—our daughter . . ."

"And—the child?"

"Went with her," Andrew MacFarland said, and dashed away a tear.

"How—dreadful!" Mireille breathed. "Andrew—Mr. MacFarland— call on me, Friday evening, say. I'll let you hold *my* baby girl on your knee. Which might be some consolation to you. Or—perhaps not. Perhaps it would make you feel worse . . ."

"No, I'm sure it wouldn't make me feel worse. I love children more than ever, now. Thanks for your offer; it's very kind indeed of you to make it. And I *will* call. Come, let me walk you to the gates. But first, tell me your address . . ."

"Oh, I'm easy enough to find. Corner of Bay and Leavenworth. It will be—pleasant—to have someone to talk to—again. Very well, let's go . . ."

But when they got to the gates of Yerba Buena Cemetery, they found the city marshal waiting there.

"Mamzelle Duclos?" he growled. "Got a warrant for your arrest. On th' charge o' murderin' Jedge Al-lain Curtwright and his pore loony wife. I warn you enthing you say may be used ag'in you. And I hope you'll come along quiet and not make no fuss . . ."

"Good God, man!" Andrew MacFarland burst out.

"No, Andrew!" Mireille said sharply; then, "Very well, marshal, I'll come along with you, very quietly. But first, may I ask a favor of you?"

"Like what, li'l missy?" the city marshal said suspiciously.

"Only that you ride with me in my landau, and let one of my colored menservants drive your buckboard into town. Since I'm confident I shall be able to clear myself of these ridiculous charges with the greatest of ease, I'd just as soon not proclaim to half San Francisco that I'm under arrest. And favor number two: I should like to go home first, before you take me to jail. I need to change my clothes, for one thing. For another, I am the mother of two infants less than a month old. I appeal to you, as a gentleman, to allow me to make some provisions for their care in case this—nonsense—drags on too long—"

"Wal, now," the marshal said uncertainly, "you ain't planning to pull th' wool over my eyes, are you? Like makin' a break for it, say?"

"That would be very foolish, marshal. And I'm not foolish. Andrew— Mr. MacFarland—"

"Andrew to you, Mrs. Curtwright—please!"

"Mrs. Curtwright, ha!" the marshal snorted.

Mireille whirled; faced him.

"I feel absolutely no compulsion to prove to you my right to my married name," she snapped, "but allow me two words with this gentleman, will you please?"

She turned back to young MacFarland.

"Andrew," she said crisply, "will you go to the offices of Martin, Kilpatrick & Kinnan on Washington Street and ask to speak to young Mr. William Kilpatrick? He's a friend of mine, and a lawyer. Tell him what's happened. Ask him to see what he can do . . ."

"I'll be happy to, Mrs. Curtwright. And, if you'll permit me to, I'd like to offer you the services of Ryker, Rogers, and Eiselberg. They're my father's attorneys, and will be glad to take your case if I ask 'em to."

"Thank you, Andrew. That's very kind of you. And the more legal talent, the better, I suppose—especially since poor dear Willy hasn't been practicing law very long, so I'm sure he could use some help. Very well, I accept your offer. Well, marshal, shall we go?"

At that time, the San Francisco jail was on Broadway. Therefore, considering the fact that Mireille's little house was a great deal farther from the cemetery than that, not to mention the additional one that she devoted her own sweet time to changing her clothes, and even more than that to softening the marshal up, in order to get some useful information out of him—which she accomplished with the greatest of ease by having Jasmine bring the twins downstairs and show them to that stern upholder of the law, Willy Kilpatrick got to the jail long before she did.

"Wal now, ma'am," the marshal said sadly, as they rode toward the hoosegow in the landau with John Swithers trailing behind them in the official buckboard, "I hafta admit I shore do hope you kin prove yore innercence. Be a shame to lock th' mama o' two sich pretty young'uns up fer a long, long stretch . . ."

"Oh, I'll be able to, marshal! You may rest assured of that!" Mireille said.

"Good God, Mirla!" Willy got out. "What have you done *now?*"

"There's my lawyer," Mireille sighed, "just bursting with confidence as to his client's perfect innocence. Oh, Willy, go home! I'll get somebody else. Somebody who believes in me a little bit, anyhow—"

"Then you'll lose your case. Anybody who believes in you, Mirla darling, is *non compos mentis,* and would be hauled away to the booby hatch before the case could get started. What fast one have you pulled off now? Used an Arkansas toothpick on somebody like you did on the Maniac, and whittled a little too close to bone?"

"No. I am, *cher* Willy, love of my life, charged with having sent a big black buck nigger to set the house of my late husband, Judge Curtwright, on fire. With what sad results you know, if you've read the papers. What you may not know is that, before he died, the Judge married me in order to legitimize the twin children he was most definitely the father of, and to make sure my right to the inheritance he left me could not be questioned. An indication, my very dear one, of how much he, one of the two victims of my alleged evil mechanisms, thought the current charges against me are worth."

"An indication of to what an extent a man—even a wise old party like the Judge—can be a love-besotted fool. Him, the father? Ha! Your Jasmine told me those kids—are my image!"

"Now aren't we modest!" Mireille purred. "Willy darling, the Judge's
—well—equipment was in working order *all* the time. You see, he'd
stayed out of fandango dens in his youth. So no dear little dilly of a
greaser with a rose in her teeth and a stiletto in her garter ever—clapped
up his waterworks, shall we say? Old as he was, he never—disappointed
me. Can you say the same, my darling?"

"I can say that hanging is probably too good for you, you little witch!
Tell you what: You sign over the custody of the kids to me, and I'll cook
up a plea that won't get you more than twenty years."

"And have your Molly hang 'em up by their thumbs and beat 'em
bloody every night before she tucks 'em in to sleep in the woodbin
behind the kitchen stove? No thank you, Mr. William Kilpatrick—ex-
Mexican, ex-human being! I'll get myself another lawyer who won't try
to get me hanged, which is what you'd like to do, wouldn't you, you
damned gringo, you?"

"Mrs. Curtwright?" a new, deep male voice said.

"Yes?" Mireille breathed.

"I am Otto Eiselberg. Young Mr. MacFarland sent me," the heavy-
set, immensely stately, enormously Teutonic figure said.

"Oh, thank goodness!" Mireille said. "Now, maybe I'll be able to get
something sensible done for a change! Go home, Willy!"

"No, please, no," Otto Eiselberg said; "I should very much like for
attorney Kilpatrick to stay. He could be of immense help to me in this
case."

"I don't see how," Mireille snapped; "he thinks I did it!"

"Do you, young sir? That's odd," the big Teuton said.

"Don't you?" Willy shot back at him.

Otto Eiselberg smiled.

"In my native Austria," he said placidly, "I've had a great deal of
experience with cases of this sort. And I must say that Mrs. Curtwright is
just about the person least likely to commit cold-blooded, premeditated
murder I've ever encountered in all my years of the practice of law.
. . . ."

"What about hot-blooded, screeching wildcat murder?" Willy demanded. "Like clawing out somebody's lights and his liver, on sudden
impulse? *Mine*, for instance?"

"Hmmmn. Under certain circumstances, yes. Such as having a deadly
weapon too readily at hand. But I doubt even that. I suspect that if she
ever caught you, young attorney Kilpatrick, in the arms of a—rival—
she'd stage a face-scratching, hair-pulling contest that would be a perfect
wonder to behold. But from all I've been able to ascertain about her so

far, she just isn't—cruel enough to kill anybody. That's not really the problem. If this were a civilized country, we'd have nothing to worry about. I'd simply point out to the magistrate who's going to have to rule on whether this case goes to trial or not, the absolute lack of any evidence whatsoever connecting Mrs. Curtwright with the Negro who committed the actual arson, and have the case dismissed out of hand . . ."

"But since this is a country of cowboys, Indians, *micks* and *greasers*," Mireille purred.

"Mireille, I'm going to *hit* you in a minute!" Willy howled.

"How would you go about it, attorney Eiselberg?" she finished imperturbably.

"Don't know, at the moment. That depends upon the degree and kind of provable evidence you can give me," attorney Eiselberg said.

At that time, the second Vigilance Committee was still marching up and down, chasing crooks out of town, staging meetings at Fort Gunnybags, and bluesmoking the air with thunderous oratory. So nobody paid much attention to the preliminary hearing before the magistrate's court to determine whether or not the charges against Mireille Curtwright *née* Duclos were well founded enough to warrant her being held over to be tried for murder at the next session of the criminal courts. The magistrate's court was practically free of spectators, except, of course, for a couple of police reporters looking for pay dirt for their abominably filthy yellow journals.

But in the third row sat a tall, fair-complexioned young man whose somewhat elongated face gave him the expression of a slightly baffled horse. A thoroughbred, of course, but one a trifle ashamed of himself at the moment for having knocked down the top bar of the watercourse jump, or merely placed or showed instead of having come in first.

Seeing him sitting there, Mireille had all she could do to hold back her tears.

'My next step up,' she moaned, 'and these greedy beggars have already ruined it for me. Whether lawyer Eiselberg—with some slight assistance from my darling Willy!—gets this unholy mess thrown out of court or not, I'm already lost! The MacFarlands, Willy says, are among the very richest families in town. Didn't come out here to scratch among the rocks like most of the grubby types who've immigrated to California. Brought their money with them when they came—as an outpost of a clan of Eastern business people. Established a branch office here with dear Andrew's papa heading it, and Andy as junior partner. And now, just wait until the Suttons' lawyer gets through describing how many calluses I've got on my poor little behind from going right back on it whenever anybody waved a picayune under my nose ever since I was twelve years old! Just wait!'

Her analysis of the situation was perfect. Of course, attorneys Eiselberg and Kilpatrick won her case hands down. They could hardly have lost, because there was not one shred of evidence connecting her with the Black who had actually committed the act of arson and its consequential, subsequential murders.

After he finally succeeded in cutting off a dilated diatribe on the part of the Suttons' attorney on the subject of Mireille's past and her practically nonexistent morals, by getting the magistrate to rule that her relations with other men were immaterial and irrelevant, Otto Eiselberg demolished the case of the brothers of the late Susan Sutton Curtwright with the greatest of ease, by pointing out that the Judge had settled a fortune on Mireille several weeks before he died, that he had adopted his children by her, legitimized them, given them his name, and changed his will in their favor at a time that he had no inkling of the cruel fate awaiting him.

More, on banker Ross Kinnan's testimony, he proved that Mireille had already been sufficiently well off even before the Judge's handsome gift to her not to have been forced into murder by pecuniary pressures, which was the only motive his distinguished opponent had attributed to her—without, evidently, having done his homework!—for having allegedly planned, plotted, and set in motion so vile an act. On those twin bases—that Mireille had had no discernible motives for committing the murders, and that no evidence whatsoever had been produced linking her to the "crazy Negro" who had burned down the Judge's house, Otto Eiselberg got the ruling magistrate to dismiss the case as unfounded.

Only, in doing so, in one aspect he went too far, and broke his young colleague's heart. To the Suttons' attorney's sneering gibe—which he could and should have ignored—that Mireille had put a host of dear old friends on the job of producing a pair of offsprings to melt the heart—not to mention the addled head!—of a man clearly in his dotage, Otto rang in Judge Curtwright's barber, and Dr. Sepúlvera, both of whom testified to having seen the broken-star-shaped birthmark behind the Judge's left ear on numerous occasions, and Dr. Joseph Gammon, his nurse, and all the household servants in Mireille's recently legitimized love nest, to testify that baby Stanford Curtwright had an identical birthmark in exactly the same position. He expostulated at length upon how remote the chances that the son of any other man would have so distinctive a mark were, while poor Willy's face got whiter and whiter and sicker and sicker, while his hand crept to his middle to caress the Napoleonic spot beneath which his supposedly healed ulcer was starting in to give him hell. Mireille felt so sorry for him, wounded almost to death in his male pride, that she almost cried.

Then she saw Andrew MacFarland marching out of the courtroom like a soldier, and she did cry. Bitterly.

She had reason to. Her future was ruined. Truncated. Stopped dead. Rendered hopeless.

Or, anyhow, so she thought.

13

WHEN MARY ELLEN PLEASANT OPENED THE SATCHEL MIREILLE HAD brought and saw that it was packed with greenbacks, she smiled.

"You're smart, Mireille. You're *very* smart," she said.

Mireille shrugged.

"I thought you'd prefer cash. Drafts can be traced," she said.

"You thought right. How much did you bring?"

"What we agreed to: twenty-five thousand."

"A fleabite to the rich widow," Mary Ellen said.

"You didn't expect a bonus, did you? You shouldn't have done that, Mary Ellen!"

"I shouldn't have done what, Mireille dear?"

"Sent that nigger to set the Judge's house afire. I know, I know! You didn't expect the Judge to be at home that night. Ordinarily he would have been with me. Only she—Susan—had been sick for the past few days, so he stayed home. Tell me: Did you try poison first?"

Mary Ellen Pleasant laughed merrily.

"Dear child!" she chuckled. "Dear *clever* child! Go on, tell me some more about my terrible crimes!"

"You had no intention to kill the Judge, because then there was no way for you to get any profit out of his death. Only that stupid nigger of yours spoiled things for you, didn't he? Or maybe you spoiled them yourself, by ordering one of your quadroon ex-*poules* turned housemaid-spy for you because you've promised to convert them into rich white ladies—"

"I deliver," Madame Pleasant said dryly.

"I know you do. In too many ways. That's why I decided not to risk making an enemy of you."

"To repeat, you're very, very smart, Mireille. Go on with this detective yarn, black series, of yours. You were saying?"

"That if you had one of your high yellow bitches slip some rat poison in Susan's soup, you crossed your own self up, because that mistake, if you made it, caused the Judge to be there, and to get caught in the fire. You didn't want to kill him. You wanted him to stay alive and marry me—"

"Of course! I've always had a tender spot in my heart for you, Mireille dear!"

"*Merde!* You haven't got a heart, not to mention having a tender spot any damn place in your body for anybody, Mary Ellen. If the Judge hadn't been there, and poor Susan had died all alone as you planned it, so later on her made-to-order widower could have married me, you'd have blackmailed me for the rest of my life by threatening to prove to the Judge just how little Stan got that birthmark behind his tiny pink ear. But now I'm free of you, thank goodness!"

"Until I get something else on you," Madame Pleasant said.

"Such as? Not only did you almost get me hanged because your nigger was a clumsy fool, but you've ruined my chances with—"

"Young Andy MacFarland. Scion of a family of Scottish 'bonnet lairds' who emigrated to these United States about a hundred years ago, and by their canny ways and tightfistedness became authentic millionaires. But now you're slandering me, dear. I did nothing of the kind. You never had a chance with Andy. Good Lord, Mireille! Maybe you could have prevented his finding out that you twitched your little bare bottom between the tables at the Dirty Spoon and was—had—for a pinch of gold dust atop them, right out in the open with a crowd of bearded, filthy, lice-infested miners enjoying the spectacle and cheering you and your momentary partner on. That was a long time ago, as time is measured in San Francisco, and the Dirty Spoon has since burned down . . . ."

"Go on!" Mireille said bitterly.

"But you were on the receiving line at Em's three years. Shall I give you the arithmetic of that, my dear?"

"Do," Mireille said.

"Subtract sixty nights for the five days each month you were—incapacitated—by your menses. You did subtract them, didn't you? Some don't."

"Yes. I subtracted 'em all right. I get sick as hell."

"All right. Still leaves three hundred nights a year. Which multiplied by an average of twenty-five tumbles a night means seventy-five hundred men, annually. In three years over twenty-two thousand horny bastards have been in there, dear child . . ."

"No. You're wrong. I had—lots of—repeaters. Men—liked—me. Who I am. Not just—"

"Your hairy little quim. A distinction of world-shaking importance! Or perhaps they were—enchanted by some of the—well—more delicate of your black arts. You had the reputation of being the best little—"

"Don't say it!" Mireille moaned. "Oh, Mary Ellen, don't say it, please!"

"Curious. The words offend you, while the act—the practice itself— didn't. And doesn't, to judge by the look of sleepy contentment on Willy Kilpatrick's face. No matter. You'll grant me my figures are correct?"

"No. 'Cause there weren't anything like that many. Em wasn't stupid. I made an agreement with her on the basis that I'd be more valuable in the long run if I didn't get worn out—and ruined. I—took vacations. Long ones. And she—allowed me—to refuse, and—"

"So there weren't twenty-five lustful louts pounding you to pieces every night. Say there were—ten. Five. Or even—which you know better than, my sweet!—two. To a family of dour Scottish Protestants like the MacFarlands, what difference would that make? Even if you'd never darkened Em's door, as the saying goes, who in San Francisco doesn't know you were Alain Curtwright's kept fancy article? That you gave birth to his bastard brats out of wedlock? That he subsequently remedied that sad state of affairs by marrying you, redounds to his credit, not to yours."

"Mary Ellen, you—you hate me, don't you? It wasn't my fault I was born white, or that you're a mean, twisted-up, hateful yellow nigger!"

Mary Ellen Pleasant stared at her.

"You've—the proper instincts, haven't you, child? You go for the jugular—or the gut," she said quietly. "Good! You'll get to the top. And I'm going to help you. To become Mrs. Andrew MacFarland, and the richest ex-whore in San Francisco's history."

"Why? I mean, why should you? What's in it for you?"

"At the moment, nothing. And there may never be. But there are other rewards than money in this world, Mireille. *Au fond,* I am an artist. So far, I've never found—material—sufficiently fine-grained, solid, sure —to create a masterpiece out of. You could be that. My masterpiece. You've got brains enough. Looks? Of course! And to spare. Your general culture is spotty; but that's easy to correct. Your major weakness is your temperament, which negates your very real intelligence, because your frantic desire to keep your lower end perpetually packed tight with pumping man-meat, to the blissful satisfaction of your rather depraved instincts, forever hangs a 'Vacant' sign between your ears. . . ."

"Ohhhhh Jesus!" Mireille said.

"So now, dear Andy. Mireille, if there is one sure thing in this world, it is that puritans are nearly always people of powerful passions. They become puritans in the first place because they're frightened to death at the prospect of what might happen to them—and to the world!—if they ever really turned loose—let go—"

"Go on," Mireille said.

"You'll never get Andrew MacFarland by playing the *beata*, the saint. Or even the maiden wronged, forced against her sweet, innocent will into that terrible, terrible life—which is the tactic that you've already thought of, haven't you?"

"Yes, I have. What's wrong with it? In a way, it's true, and—"

"And *merde*. What has the truth to do with anything in this life? Or justice, piety, goodness, chastity? Only three things count. They alone guarantee success."

"What are they, Mary Ellen?" Mireille asked.

"Will. Intelligence. Ruthlessness."

"You've got—an ugly way of thinking, Mary Ellen! But I suppose you're right. . . ."

"I know I am. Have you ever passed through Dupont Street where all those Chinese live? Or parts of Sacramento Street, as well?"

"Yes. Both. Why?"

"Ever poked your pert little turned-up nose into an opium-smoking den?"

"Yes. But I've a finicky stomach. The stench drove me right out again. Even so I was dizzy for almost an hour. . . ."

"All right. D'you know why those poor yellow devils—and not a few white ones, now!—smoke that horrible stuff?"

"No. Why do they?"

"Because they can't help it. It's habit-forming. They've become what medical science calls 'opium addicts' . . ."

"All right. I follow you so far, straight down this side street you've turned off into. And since I know you never waste your breath, get to the point, Mary Ellen! What have those dens of vice got to do with me?"

"You're a den of vice, child. William Kilpatrick is addicted to you. The two of you fight like tigers, I'm told, because quarreling with you is his way of blinding himself to the fact that he cannot give you up. And Alain Curtwright—wise, tolerant, measured, even cynical as he was— couldn't either. He was utterly besotted as far as you were concerned."

"So?" Mireille said.

"So don't try to play the wronged innocent for Andy! He won't be-lieve it. Slow-witted as I'm told he is, he remains, nevertheless, nobody's fool. In fact, no one does. Innocents seldom get wronged for the very simple reason that the only way a woman can stay innocent past a certain age is to be utterly unattractive, utterly dull, or utterly frozen, and some-times all three. Or—a lesbian. But then she still loses her girlish laughter, to some square-built, mannish female with shoulders like a hod carrier's and a voice like a yearling steer's."

"You're wrong. *I'm* a lesbian—a part-time one, anyhow, and I'm not built like that . . ."

"What you are is crazy, child. So you've played stinky-pinky with other naughty little girls? Or even swapped ends, male-mary lesbian style upon occasion? Bah! Who hasn't? You'd tumble a hat rack if nothing else were available. Listen to me. Your role with Andy must be that of the terribly advanced female who has consciously decided to live her own life. If you go to bed with a man, it is very simply because you like going to bed with men, and are somewhat—if only momentarily—fond of the man in question. As for your operating procedure, it shouldn't be that of vulgar brazenness, for such behavior would offend him too grievously, put him off; but rather of roguish impishness. An attack on male privi-lege. 'But, An-drew darling, why should you men have all the fun? I love making love!' "

"He'll be shocked speechless," Mireille said.

"And while he is, demonstrate to him the difference between a tepid *pas de deux* with other women, and engaging in that wild, sweet, tender game with *you* . . ."

"With the accent on the 'wild,' eh, Mary Ellen?"

"Exactly. The difference between mounting a livery stable nag for a Sunday morning amble down a bridle path, and trying to stay atop a bronco mare. The vast disparity betwixt attempting to get some of a response out of a pretty porcelain doll like your Willy's Molly, and trying to break free—while there's life, and breath, and sanity still in him!—of the tentacles of a female octopus. But you've got the idea, haven't you?"

"Yes. And you're right. That's just the way to go about it. Not to mention that it'll be a lot more fun than your usual dirty tricks. But, Mary Ellen, how'll I get him to visit me? I never see him anymore, y'know . . ."

"Go driving next Sunday. Not in that landau of yours with James and John Swithers along. Rent a smart and spanking little road cart. Drive it yourself. You can drive, can't you?"

"Yes. I got James to teach me. Didn't want your two Black spies along every time I went somewhere I shouldn't have, Mary Ellen! And Burrows' Livery Stable has the fanciest pair of high-stepping black trotters you ever saw. Nat Burrows gives me a discount when he rents 'em to me, because he says I'm such good advertisement for his services. People always ask me where I got those beautiful creatures from, and when I tell them, they go flocking to Burrows' to rent their horses . . ."

She paused, stared at Madame Pleasant.

"But why—next Sunday, Mary Ellen?" she said.

"He goes for drives on Sunday with the dear little creature he's currently sparking. She's nothing much. His parents selected her. In fact, they chose his first wife. He hasn't much initiative, poor boy! This one is even duller. But despite that, you'd better hurry. He's not a patron of the parlor houses, I'm told—and any dish looks appetizing when one is hungry . . ."

Mireille considered that. Then, very slowly, she smiled.

"I'll do that, Mary Ellen," she said.

All the old saws about what any given procedure can be easier than— eating apple pie, falling off a log, kissing a pretty girl—applied. Mireille already knew—because she had asked Otto Eiselberg, the day young Andrew had stalked out of the magistrate's court, his long face the very picture of equine dismay—where the MacFarlands lived. So it sufficed to station James and John Swithers by turns outside their imposing mansion of yellow sandstone on the corner of Minna and First streets, in the new Pleasant Valley residential district overlooking, but some few hundred yards inland from, the southern end of Yerba Buena Cove, to determine at what hours that sober, dutiful, and obedient young man sallied forth to call upon his new fiancée, found for him, as his previous one had been, by his much more enterprising father.

Once her Black spies, trained to an almost professional level by Madame Pleasant, had determined that Andrew *always* took Miss Jennifer Bainswaithe buggy riding on Sunday afternoons at four o'clock, that he *always* drove over exactly the same route with her, and that he probably *always* said the same—carefully rehearsed—phrases of endearment to her, at which she *always* blushed the same measured shade of peony pink —to wreck poor Andy's somewhat less than sorry scheme of things entire, and reshape it closer to her own merry, mocking, mischievous, not to mention ribald, heart's desire was child's play for a female freebooter, buccaneer, and enchanting little witch like Mireille.

She simply blocked their path with her pair of high-stepping, prancing trotters, melted Andrew MacFarland down into—well, not mutton suet; say rather saddle grease, with the dead-level, parallel, twin topaz beams of her imperious gaze, and said with icy hauteur:

"An-drew, you get down from there. Leave that dismal frump for a moment, will you? Come here!"

Now poor Andy had been obeying orders all his life—from his nursemaid, his mother, his schoolmasters, his father, even the family servants, all of whom bossed and bullied him around the way their actual inferiors always do those sweet-souled, gentle people who haven't one drop of hot rebellion in their blood. Andrew MacFarland was far from stupid, as his career, after Mireille took over what proved to be the rewarding and even pleasant task of managing him, was to demonstrate. His quite respectable brain, given time to ruminate over all the pros and cons of a question and reach measured and considered decisions, worked very well indeed. The real trouble was that his cerebrum achieved the eminently satisfactory results it did, not by brilliant flashes of intuitive insight, but by carefully fitting his ideas together until he got to conclusions whose logic was always sound. Which would have been perfectly all right except that, unfortunately for him, it arrived at those conclusions with ponderous slowness.

So it didn't occur to him to do what he should have done, which was not merely to disobey Mireille Duclos Curtwright, but to order her, as discourteously as possible—for politeness wouldn't have worked at all— to remove her disgraceful little permanent offense against public morals of a self the blankety-blank infernal regions out of his path, and leave him and his fiancée at peace, now, henceforth, and forevermore.

Instead, with a stunned expression on his handsomely equine face with its El Greco-like distortions along the vertical planes, and displaying that aspect of mournful piety so characteristic of the Hellenic-Iberian master's subjects, he climbed down from his buckboard, leaving, without a backward glance or even a muttered apology, the absolutely flabbergasted Miss Bainswaithe sitting there, and walked over to Mireille's smart little rig—which, incidentally, being her own capricious self, she had bought, along with those splendid night-black horses, not merely rented.

"Come closer, Andrew darling," Mireille said.

Andrew, not quite yet her darling, came closer.

"*Much* closer!" Mireille purred. "I want to whisper something in your ear . . ."

Again that serious and sober young man obeyed. Now obedience is always a dubious virtue, because the outcome of slavishly practicing it depends too much upon the personality of the person being obeyed, and the nature of the orders being given. As both Willy Kilpatrick and Enrique Sepúlvera could have told him, doing what Mireille Duclos told a man to do was usually a one-way ticket—and on a nonstop express train at that—to disaster.

Then Mireille leaned down out of her new and extravagantly expensive little road cart, and kissed Andrew MacFarland full upon the mouth.

Descriptions of intimate physical actions between the sexes always falsify them. Say then only that, for the first time in his life, poor Andy found himself being kissed by a totally expert and absolutely shameless woman, who had no scruples whatsoever against converting what should have been, and usually is, a gentle expression of affection, tenderness, love, into an overt sexual aggression whose resemblance to sheer rape was far closer than he had hithertofore believed possible.

Mireille had herself the time of her twenty-two years of life, and for a reason that any woman will readily understand. From the outset, she disregarded the romantic convention of slowly letting her lids droop shut; nor did she choose the alternative of gazing tenderly up at Andy from beneath downswept, sooty lashes. Instead, out of the corners of her eyes she kept the mingled bituminous nightsmoke-and-topaz luminosity of her gaze fixed upon Jennifer Bainswaithe's dumbfounded face as she destroyed that poor, gentle and therefore helpless creature, by annihilating the last and only hope she'd ever had.

When she had finished tying Andrew MacFarland's toes into a variety of intricate sailor's knots inside his shoes, and forced him—in acute embarrassment—to center his fashionable soft felt hat, with wide brim and low flat crown, which, of course, he'd automatically taken off as he approached her little road cart, over his pelvic region to hide the obvious physical manifestation of the effect that diabolically wicked kiss had had on him, Mireille turned him loose.

"Call on me tonight, dear boy," she said, quite calmly. "Now, go back to the frump. Take her home. And, by the way, I'd suggest you try tumbling her when you get her there. To give yourself some basis for comparison. So you'll have some idea what the difference is . . ."

"Well, I never!" Jennifer Bainswaithe gasped.

"That's obvious, darling," Mireille purred. "Who would—with *you?* *Au 'voir, An-drew, cheri! Jusqu'a cette nuit!*"

She opened the door herself to let him in. Jasmine was no longer with her, being, by then, already embarked upon her lifelong career of presenting Olaf Svenson with an ever increasing brood of the most perfect little blond, blue-eyed Swedes anyone ever saw. Only the day before had Mireille got around to replacing her, with the Swithers brothers' sister, Blossom. Both John and James had been sent to fetch her, with orders not to come back until tomorrow. Which, of course, was preparation for this visit. And excellent strategy.

"Mrs. Curtwright—" Andrew groaned, "you mind telling me why on earth you—"

That was as far as he got. Mireille went up on tiptoe, caught him by his large, red, not exactly inappropriately hairy ears, dragged his face down to within reaching distance, and repeated that afternoon's performance. With variations. And—improvements.

When she'd got through converting his knees into India rubber, his brains into boiling mush, and his blood into live steam, she stepped back and smiled at him.

"Come in, An-drew darleeeng," she said.

Andrew MacFarland sat up in bed and stared out into the swirling mists of morning. His blue-green eyes were clouded with aching doubts, but in their depths something glowed; and that something was very close to awe, to wonder.

"D'you know, An-drew darling," Mireille said, "you look just like a horse. A sort of—sheepish horse, who's thoroughly ashamed of himself . . ."

"I am," he said sadly.

"*Bon Dieu*, Andy—why?"

He turned and stared at her. Then, very quickly, he turned away. She was lying atop the covers, and she hadn't a stitch on. He was afraid of the effect that sight might—*would*—have on him. Again.

"Aren't *you?*" he said.

"No. Of course not, silly boy! No, silly *horse*. What d'you call a red-haired horse, Andy?"

"A bay. No, that's not right. A bay is a reddish colored horse, but his mane and tail are black. Say—a chestnut. Or a sorrel. Depending on whether you mean dark red or light red."

"Then you're a sorrel. A *sorry* sorrel! A silly, sorry sorrel who's ashamed of having had a perfectly lovely time. They told me you Scotchmen were like that. That you *hate* enjoying yourselves. That's why you invented whiskey. You have to get drunk before you can turn loose and act—like human beings . . ."

"You mean—like animals, don't you?" he said morosely.

"That was—animal? *Alors, vive l'animalité!*" she hooted.

Now he did turn and look at her. And enjoyed the sight. But he held himself in check. For one thing, he was tired enough to be able to, by then.

"Mireille," 'he said with aching wonder, "you—you're not ashamed? Not at all?"

"No. Not at all. Not in the slightest. Why should I be?"

"You—I—we've sinned. We—we've had—carnal knowledge of each other, without being married . . ."

"Long live sin! And carnal knowledge! Especially carnal knowledge, 'cause it's the nicest kind of sin there is. Don't you agree?"

"Mireille, I just don't understand you!"

"Don't try. It's impossible. *I* don't understand me, so how d'you expect to? Besides, you're wasting time. I want you to make love to me some more. All the rest of today. And all night tonight. And all day tomorrow. And all night tomorrow night. And—and maybe I'll let you get up sometime next week, but at the moment, I doubt it!"

"Good God, girl! That's impossible!"

"Is it? Let's—try. It's simple, really. You put this—hmmmmmmmm —nice! You've wonderful powers of recuperation, darling! Shows you've led a clean life . . ."

"Have *you?*" he said bitterly.

"Absolutely not. I'm the wickedest woman in California, except one. And she's wicked in a different way. Stop making me argue with you, my darling silly sorrel! I've better use for my breath than to waste it talking. Hmmmmmnnnn—it's so nice and big—and pink. Rosy pink. It looks just like a peppermint stick. A *big* peppermint stick, only it hasn't any stripes. I wonder if it *tastes* like one? Mmmmmmmmnnnnnnn—sweet!"

"Mireille!" he cried, utterly aghast.

"Oh well, that can wait. I'll have time to teach you filthy tricks later on. Now, let's play—hide the sausage—with your little brother. Ah, no! Your *so* big brother! Slowly—slowly—Mmmmmmmmmmmmm—*Oooh-la-la!* He is so big—thick—that one cannot— Oh! Big brute! That hurt! Ah! Hmmmmmmmm—softly—soft—hmmmmmm—There! Here we are! Welcome, huge sausage, into my little Turkish steambath. Now be still, An-drew darling. Be—very still—"

"Lord, Mireille!"

"I feel like talking now. While he—your little brother—your little, great big brother!—grows—accustomed to—my warmth—"

"And—your softness," he whispered; "that wonderful way you tremble, tremble on the inside, so that every—quiver—is a caress . . ."

"Ah, so? Then maybe I'd better show you how *wild* I can be this time! No. Wait. Be still. Hmmmmmmmn—Andrew, I've changed my mind.

Take—pull—him out of *mon tout petit trou.* From my boiling springs
beneath *ma colline plein des herbes.* Remove him. You heard me! Go on,
take him—it—*out.* Get up. Put your clothes on. *Leave.* And don't come
back!"

"Good God, Mireille!" he croaked, being at that moment at least
twice as aghast as he had been before.

"*Could* you do that, Andrew? If I asked you to—seriously? Meaning
it?" she whispered.

"I don't know. Maybe. But I'd probably go crazy," he groaned.

"Ah, so? Well, let's take care of that 'maybe.' Change it into a flat
'No!' And alter that 'probably go crazy.' Make it 'surely,' which would
suit me better. More flattering that way, I think. I'm very vain, Andy
dear. My men don't leave me. Not for any reason. Not *ever.*"

She swept her long, slim, beautiful legs up, and locked her calves
diagonally across the small of his back. Put her slender arms around his
neck. Kissed his mouth, murmuring against it the oldest, damnedest lie
in all the world, the one that men, by their very nature, by the idiot force
of male vanity, are forever inclined—or foredoomed!—to believe.

"An-drew, I love you. I fell in love with you the day I met you. In the
cemetery, remember? The first *minute* I saw you. Not even that. The
first thirty seconds. Snap! Like that. Don't ask me why. I don't know. A
low blow of Destiny. One of Fate's dirty tricks, *n'est-ce pas?* I looked into
your blue-green eyes, your dear, sweet, long, worried horse's face—and
there it was. Done. I was lost. And—for always. So, since that cannot
be—"

"You're right. It can't. So now—what?" he said, hell and death and
anguish in his voice.

"This!" she whispered, and tightened that double embrace she had
him locked in, until his breath was cut off, gone, his fair flesh bruised,
and the bones beneath it in serious danger of cracking, letting go. "I'm
going to—kill you, Andy. Kill—me. Murder—and suicide by means of—
love. We'll go down in history, darling. Who needs Romeo's poison,
Juliet's knife? Scalding and flaying are—just as sure. Or simple—exhaustion. Farewell, my love! Here we go!"

That she meant that insane threat of hers is distinctly debatable. Probably not. But what wasn't debatable was how close she came to accom-
plishing it, however little she actually intended to. She was essentially an
actress, and of that intense type who easily convince themselves, come to
wholeheartedly believe, their roles. Enrique Sepúlvera, whose love for her
had the saving grace of distance and was leavened with cool scientific
interest in the extremely *rara avis* she actually was, would have warned

Andy, as he had already warned Willy, against completely disregarding anything that Mireille said, for he was well aware how quickly her lies and her threats could metamorphose themselves into bitter truth.

So now, with grim thoroughness, she went about converting that always unconvincing euphemism "the act of love" into something remarkably resembling a duel to the death—between a naked Amazon and an equally bare retiarius, say. Having elements of the mythic about it: Aphrodite and Ares caught in the net of Hephaestus—for were they not already bound to each other by an invisible web of fate whose skeins were absolutely unbreakable?

It was, and was not, ugly. Those two entwined, savagely twisting young bodies were far too intrinsically beautiful for total repulsiveness to be achieved. But the act was—shocking. Her sharp white teeth locked together in a fold of the flesh of his throat, with bright ribbons of his blood welling up around them as she worried it, jerking her ferociously snarling little face from side to side as she quite seriously tried to tear loose a sizable chunk of him. The gasping, snorting, pounding—furious, animal, all tenderness gone, a hundred million years of evolution canceled out, reversed. The bedsprings creaking, groaning, singing; the wooden slats beneath them clacking audibly. . . .

He, poor dysfunctioning male, hadn't been able to maintain control beyond the first thirty seconds, say; had pulsated, jetted, died, and found, to his vast astonishment, that his ignominious failure made not the slightest difference. Internally, she was astonishingly narrow, small, had been born with—or had learned!—a peristaltic motion, an undulant, flagellant, unceasing, spine-cracking, snap and twist and scald that made castration by flaying a much more likely possibility than mere detumescence was, or ever had been.

He was aware, young as he was, as fine a physical specimen—trained on the playing fields of the better eastern universities, hardened into endurance by the rougher team sports, Rugby, lacrosse, hockey, snowshoe treks through hundreds of miles of the great Canadian forests—that her threat to kill him by love hadn't been, and increasingly wasn't, idle. He was trying to find what consolation he could in the reflection that after all it was the finest possible way to die when, quite suddenly, she opened her mouth, turned his badly lacerated throat loose, stiffened against him, tightened, tightened, shuddered, shuddered, shuddered, every inch of her soaking wet flesh alive and aquiver in pulsating, seismic ripples that went on and on until their epicenter deep in her loins exploded outward in concentric tidal waves that tore through her slight form with devastating force, then very slowly . . . died.

But so, he was horribly certain, had she. Her tiny (in comparison to his great bulk) body didn't so much relax as collapse, go boneless, limp, sprawled out beneath him in a posture so disjointed, unnatural, contrary to any that the human figure normally assumes in sleep or even coma, that a blade of fear whistled into the core of his very being, severing in that awful moment, his very living from his life.

"Mireille!" he screamed, his voice high, shrill, wailing, utter despair given anguished sound. He rolled off her, freeing her of his considerable weight, saw at that moment the first sobbing intake of her renewing, resurrecting breath.

He chafed her wrists, slapped her face stingingly, gathered her total looseness, give, into his great arms. Her eyes fluttered open, unfocused, blank. Then very slowly they cleared.

"Bon Dieu!" she breathed. *"Quelle façon plus belle à mourir!"*

"Oh, Mireille! Mireille! Mireille!" he wept. "You scared hell out of me! I thought—"

"Que j'étais morte. Tu as eu raison, mon amour. Je suis allée au ciel avec des anges, et—"

"Mireille, I don't understand a word you're saying!"

"Ah, so? No matter. An-drew, *dites moi une chose.* Tell me something: *Now* could you walk out that door—and not come back?"

He held her with his eyes. His gaze was deep and sorrowing.

"No," he said humbly; "I couldn't. And I'll never be able to—as long as the two of us shall live. So you'll have to marry me, my dear. As soon as I can possibly arrange it . . ."

She stared at him. And the way she was looking at him became less coolly speculative than troubled. She thought: 'I have won my gamble. But I have also lost it. For he is not to be disregarded, this Andrew. Not at all. And—'

"Andrew," she whispered brokenly, *"tu ne peux pas faire ça. Me marrier, je t'en voulais dire. Suis très mauvaise. Méchante. Menteuse. Malhonnête. En effet—garce. Salope. Poule. Putain."*

"Mireille, I *told* you I don't speak—"

"French. All right. An-drew, you were at—my trial. My hearing before the magistrate. Your lawyer saved me. Mine wasn't worth anything, was he? Well, what I'm trying to say is that the Suttons' attorney told the truth—about me. *Less* than the truth. He didn't know it all. I'm a bad, wicked, good-for-nothing—"

He grinned at her with slow, sly mockery.

"Well, you're good for one thing, anyhow. You've just proved that," he said.

"Oh, Lord!" she wept. "An-drew, tell me something else: D'you *love* me?"

He considered that.

"No," he said honestly; "I don't even know you, so how could I? But I want you, Mireille. I'll go on wanting you until the day I die. And even after that, I'll scream your name from the deepest pit of hell, as the Devil turns me over to roast the other side. So that—feeling, sentiment —emotion, will have to serve. It was what you set out to accomplish, wasn't it? When you chewed my dewlap loose, cracked my spine, and scalded all his poor, pink hide off of 'little brother'?"

"Ohhhhhh dear!" she wailed; "as tired as I am! And now—"

"And—now, what?" he said.

"I've got to start all over again. Lie back down . . ."

"Mireille, for the love of God!"

"No, An-drew. For—*your* love. Because—you're worth it. Because I've got to stop lying, cheating, deceiving people sometime. Start—playing fair. *Now,* for instance. With—you. You heard me: Lie down!"

"But—"

"I don't—propose to break your backbone anymore. Or bite nice big bloody hunks out of you, *quoique je sois très carnivore, même cannibale!* As for your 'little brother'—I mean to take tender loving care of him— and you. An-drew, give me—another chance? To—to make you love me, I mean? Because now I don't want less from you, or a life with you on any other basis. If I were a better person than I am, braver, more honest, I'd simply give you up; but now, I can't do that, either . . ."

"Why not?" he said, a little sardonically; "because you *love* me, Mireille?"

"I don't know," she whispered; "I'm *very* confused—like any other stupid slut—right now. Say—I could, given half a chance. Say—I want to—love, *be* in love with you. *Oh bon Dieu,* how I want to!"

"Why?" he asked her.

"You're—very sweet. Gentle. Good. I *need* somebody like you in my life, An-drew. I'm—your opposite. So either I'll wreck you, or you'll save me. The gamble's—fair, isn't it?"

"Very," he said. "How d'you propose to go about it?"

"Like—this!" she said; "lie down!"

To be caressed with fingertips that seem not even to touch; to be brushed with lips lighter than the breath that swirls and sighs between them, less tactile than moving air; to be bathed in the iridescent shower of never-ceasing tears, kissed in one long, long, unbroken osculation from throat to knee by the million, million tiny mouths of an anguishedly tender body's every pore; to be milked in slow, unending, spurting streams of every sorrow, heartache, hurt thirty-two years of living can inflict upon a man; to be awarded absolute sanity, through having every madness acid-etched along tortured nerves by the daily bitternesses the flesh is ever heir to, woven into the brain's convolutions by disappointment, deception, deceit, treachery, lies, drained out through your loins into that undulant heat, moisture, clasp, grasp, trembling ingurgitation; to have—by means of the murderous sweetness of that incredible warmwetsoftness, the soul's own felt peristalsis, recombining the separate male and female elements, flagellant sperm and waiting ovum, into the major miracle of re-created life—such nonsense words as rapture, ecstasy redefined; to have breached once and forever the demarcations between exquisite pleasure and utterly intolerable pain; to throb, burst, erupt in totally crippling spasms, die, turn stark naked god resurrected into life again, borne up into light, air, sheer glory on wild submarine whirlpools of surfcrashing tidal explosions far greater than one's own—

These were but a few of the prodigies of her mind-shattering carnal black magic that young Andrew MacFarland experienced within the next two hours, until even his sober—if reeling!—reason was convinced that no price whatsoever—wealth, reputation, fame, life itself—was too high to pay for the more or less permanent possession of this—angelwitch, devilchild. This Circe swine-maker. This—woman.

"Mireille—" he said.

"Yes, An-drew," she moaned.

"Don't cry. Please don't cry. There's nothing to cry over. Not—now. Not anymore . . ."

"Oh, yes, there is! I'm going to be crying all the rest of my life, now. I'm never going to be able to ssstop!"

"Why, Mireille? Why, sweetheart?"

"Sweetheart! Don't call me that! An-drew, is there any way I can ggget you to gggo hhhome, and nnnot cccome bbback?"

"To go, no," he said judiciously. "To be carried, yes. You might try shooting me, Mireille. And, even so, whether I came back or not would depend upon how good your aim was. You'd have to kill me outright, y'know . . ."

"Ohhhhhhh Lord!" she wailed.

"D'you *want* me to leave you, Mireille?"

"No! That's the last thing on earth I want now! I want to bring you your breakfast in my wheelchair when I'm ninety-eight years old! Andrew, I—I love you. I just proved that to my own self. But what's more important, I like you. You're—so sound. So—solid. It's—so *restful,* having you around."

"Restful?" he said; "good God!" Then he threw back his head and let his warmly satisfied male laughter boom against the ceiling.

"Well—it is. Or it'll get to be. I don't mean to go on wearing you out. Not to this extent, anyhow . . ."

"That's a relief!" he quipped.

"An-drew, you've got to leave me. Listen! I did all that—to trick you, to trap you, to get you so crazy wild over me that even my awful past wouldn't matter . . ."

"Well, you've succeeded. It doesn't," he said.

"Dear God have pity on me!" she prayed. "An-drew, your life will be wrecked. All doors will be closed to you. People will demand that theater managers put us—me, anyhow—out of boxes, so that the presence of a —harlot—like me will not offend their decent wives—"

"As in the case of General Richardson and the gambler Cora? Nonsense. They'd have to eject three quarters of the married couples of San Francisco then. Commercially unfeasible. Remember that even in that case, the manager refused to comply. You'll have to give me a better reason than that, Mireille."

"*Tes parents* will be heartbroken. *Ton père. Ta mère . . .*"

"That is a better reason. But it's not enough. They've been managing my life long enough. I'm thirty-two. A big boy, honey. Old enough to make my own decisions."

"But—wise enough, An-drew? *Sois sage enfant.* Go back to the frump. She won't cause you any trouble . . ."

"Except a slow death by boredom. Funny. Until you called her that, I'd never realized that she *was.* A frump, I mean . . ."

Mireille laughed then, freely, gaily. Then she sobered.

"An-drew," she said sadly, "let's compromise. I will be—your mistress —for as long as you want me. But not your wife. Agreed?"

"No. What sense does it make for you to be my mistress for the rest of my life? That's how long I'll want you. Besides, you're forgetting something else. You have two children, who will be growing up and who will need a father. D'you realize that they'll be going to school in a few years? You've been to school—and quite a good one, to judge by your speech, your ways, your general culture. So you must know what little beasts schoolchildren are. What do you plan to say to your little boy—and, more especially your little girl—when they come home crying because their schoolmates have taunted them with 'Your mama is a whore!' or 'Your mama is banker Andy MacFarland's fancy woman!'?"

"Ohhhhhhh *bon petit Jésus!*" Mireille wailed. Then she sighed. "Andrew, you—you want to marry me? You—you're sure?"

"I want to marry you. I'm very sure."

"And you—you love me? I won't settle for less, *mon amour.* I am much more than these—" she let her fingertips stray across her extraordinarily beautiful breasts, "and this—" she touched, with wry disdain, the Mohican's scalp lock of her mons veneris, "and *this!*" she concluded, giving one of her buttocks a resounding slap.

"Well," he drawled with that bone-dry sense of humor she hadn't been aware he had, "as long as all such extra little bonuses come included in the bargain, I'll manage to bear up, I suppose . . ."

"You see? Already I'm corrupting you—changing you into a naughty boy!" she said with prim and unconsciously comical severity. "Besides, you haven't answered the main question: An-drew, do you love me?"

He thought about that. Then, very quietly, he said:

"I love you, Mireille. You taught me to—a little while ago, when you showed me—how sweet you can be, how—tender . . ."

"Ohhhhh An-drew!" she cried, and hurled herself into his arms. But a moment later she drew back, her dark eyes filled with doubt.

"An-drew, *think,*" she murmured. "I am—have been—a bad girl. A very bad girl. A—whore. Can you trust me? Will you be able to?"

He stared at her, and his blue-green eyes were very bleak.

"I don't know," he said slowly, evenly, flatly; "I only ask you, very humbly, not to break my heart . . ."

She turned him loose, rolled out of bed, fell to her knees beside it, raised her small face, already awash and glistening with a solid sheet of tears, toward the ceiling.

"I swear by God," she whispered fervently, "and by Thee, dear little Holy Mother, that I will *never* betray this good, kind, just man that you 'ave sent to save me. And if ever I should break this vow that I have made, even in my thoughts, I ask You, God the Father, who punishes sinners, to strike me dead!"

Andrew MacFarland peered at her, worriedly. Then, very slowly, he smiled.

"I'll buy you a nice bronze coffin for a wedding gift, Mireille honey, and we'll keep it in the parlor, just in case," he said.

14

AFTER ANDREW MACFARLAND HAD GONE HOME, MIREILLE WAS reminded of how late it was by the noise and bustle, punctuated by cheery African laughter the Swithers brothers made as they arrived with her new maid, their sister Blossom. Which meant it was practically noon, since Mireille had thoughtfully told them not to come back before then, as the acquisition of a new husband by plain and fancy seduction evidently required a maximum of privacy.

And that in turn made the chaste and demure widow Curtwright recall that she had—or was supposed to have—a *cinq à sept* with Guillermo Kilpatrick at the little cottage she owned out on Fremont Street, almost to its intersection with Harrison. Now a *cinq à sept* was one of the hoariest of French customs, since that eminently logical and practical race had long ago discovered that from five to seven o'clock in the afternoon were the very best hours to indulge in a little occasional monotony-breaking and presumably soul-satisfying adultery, because the number of other, quite innocent, activities that could be undertaken at those hours—going shopping, visiting a sick friend, charitable work among the poor, even an idle spin in one's smart little road cart—provided one with an almost infinite variety of convincing lies with which to answer the classic angry cuckold's or deceived wife's query:

"Where the devil have you been?"

Then, almost immediately, she recalled that only half an hour ago she had taken her most solemn oath to be absolutely faithful to her new darling, An-drew, until death should them part, upon pain of being sizzled to a cinder by the lightning bolts of divine wrath if she broke said vow, and her lovely little face became a picture of complete perplexity and utter woe.

Aided by the fact that his physical health was lately much improved, in the last few months by dint of patient female generalship—a perfect flood of fervently whispered *"attend, attend—doucement, doucement—* slowly, slowly—wait—wait—gently—gently—*comme ça—comme ça—"* and the like, before clapping spurs and applying the whip to her already tormented-past-all-bearing mount with *"Vite! Vite! Encore plus vite! Dur! Gros bête! Animal! Dur! Ah—ça-y-est! Merveilleux!"*—she had finally succeeded in making a first-class lover out of Willy, who had suffered from the classic Latin vice of a too ardent temperament with its consequent and catastrophic accentuation of the already disastrous evolutionary gap between the human female who can, and often honestly wants to, make love all night long, and the poor sad male who practically always collapses like a punctured balloon before three full minutes of nature's best and most pleasant activity are out. That problem solved, their hours together had become nothing short of magical.

Therefore the reason for Mireille's perplexity was her honest recognition that she really didn't want to give Willy up for two whole days, not to mention all the rest of her life. True, they fought like cat and dog every time they met, but their furious roars and shrill screeches always ended up in magnificent bed-wrecking, naked bouts, followed by slow, sweet encores when, rage and lust both burned out, they lay for hours lovingly entwined, and achieved an aching tenderness that was almost reverent, worshipful.

But then she faced the facts. The way she felt about Guillermo Kilpatrick was one thing, and what she necessarily had to do about her life was another. Andy had spelled it out for her. She had two helpless children, so from now on duty and not pleasure was going to have to order her existence. Considering the fact that pointing the finger of scorn was an act few of San Francisco's female pioneers could afford to indulge in, due to the charter membership in the world's oldest profession most of them enjoyed, Mireille was certain that a decade of quiet living at the side of a husband whose social position was as elevated as Andrew MacFarland's would make her place in society as a respectable matron secure, and remove all threats of ostracism from her children's future.

But the immediate problem still remained: what to do about her dearest, darling Willy? Tired as she was, her first impulse was to go back to bed and simply fail to keep their rendezvous. The minute she thought of it she realized that such a course was foolish. Better to make the break now, clearly, and cleanly. Willy was a gentleman. He wouldn't stand in the way of her—and her children's—future. She was very sure of that.

So thinking, she dragged herself out of bed and started to dress. Then she stopped dressing, because her nose told her she needed a bath, badly.

"Ugh!" she sniffed; "I smell like a morning after a busy night at Em's. Oh, dear!"

That exclamation "Oh, dear!" was torn from her, not because her own aroma—*"Essence des sardines en boîte pourris!"* she snorted disgustedly —offended her, which it did, for she was clean to the point of fastidiousness, but by the realization that she was going to have to wait several hours before she could enjoy that necessary and refreshing bath. It simply would take that long for Blossom Lascals, her new, big, buxom, jet-black maid, to prepare her a tubful of hot, perfumed water, what with pumping several large, exceedingly heavy brass vessels full from the cistern in the yard, heating them and their contents on the kitchen range, lugging them upstairs to Mireille's dressing room, and pouring the rapidly cooling water into the bathtub—an ungainly object of zinc-plated sheet iron made for her by C. Nutting's smithy and iron-works on Maiden Lane in San Francisco, after she'd got the astonished Mr. Nutting to understand what the devil it was she wanted and the peculiar shape it had to have, which, in an epoch when practically nobody bathed —at least not with any frequency—had taken some doing.

There being no help for the delay, she called Blossom, *née* Swithers, Lascals, who had recently become a widow by reason of some extremely accurate gunfire on the part of somebody, into her bedroom, and ordered that healthy specimen of Black womanhood to prepare her bath for her. That order given, she lay back and relaxed. While she waited for the water to heat, she reflected on her great good fortune in having been able to obtain a colored maidservant without doing the one thing she was determined never to do again: ask Mary Ellen Pleasant to send her one, and thereby guarantee that everything said or done within her household would be carried back to the distinctly sinister octoroon whom the newspapers were beginning to call "the Woman of Mystery, whose deeds are evil!"

'Which is,' Mireille thought, 'the understatement of the year. Take Blossom, now. Does that mean that Mary Ellen's—slipping? For, according to James and John, she didn't even know they had a sister. Which is proof positive they're beginning to resent her—an item *I'm* going to be able to use. What was it that John said? Oh, yes: "Lawdy, Miz Mireille, her's got enuff on us to hang us both, so we'uns didn't want her gittin' her hooks into Blossom too. So us brung our baby sister out heah our own selfs, wit'out sayin' nothin' to Madame Pleasant, nor axin her fur a dime!"

'I'll have to talk to Blossom soon. About her late husband. Whom somebody killed in an alley in Sydney Town—correction!—on the Barbary Coast as they call it now. Joseph Lascals, alias French Joe—another of those Creole quadroons light enough to pass. Rent collector for Mary Ellen. She gets a thousand, two thousand, three, even five thousand a month in rent from each of those dens she owns. And French Joe tried to cross her up. That's what happened, sure as hell. Held back some of her rents, likely. So now Blossom's a widow. How many people has that evil yellow witch had killed by now? Half a dozen, surely. Only, who can prove it?'

But thinking about Mary Ellen "Mammy" Pleasant wasn't going to help her digestion or her peace of mind, so Mireille again buried her face into her pillows and slept the good sleep of the innocent, the just, the pure of heart until Blossom came to tell her that her bath was ready. Whereupon Mireille popped blissfully into it and a little while later popped out again, smelling, if not like a rose, at least like a lady.

She devoted the next two hours to playing with her babies, whom, never having had to nurse or otherwise feed, or even change their soiled diapers, she treated as though they were living dolls, kissing them end-lessly, tickling them to make them gurgle with infant laughter, rocking them in her arms, and crooning lullabies in Creole patois to them with the greatest possible tenderness until they went to sleep. She had practi-cally forgotten that Stanford was not her child, while little Claire most definitely was. The only reason she remembered it was that her baby daughter occasionally reminded her of the actuality of her physical heri-tage by screaming the roof down in paroxysms of pure, if inexplicable rage, awesome to behold in such a tiny child, exactly like the ones her mother had told her she had indulged in as an infant. In fact the only way to bring little Claire out of her convulsions of almost rabid fury was to sprinkle cold water into her tiny face before it turned altogether blue.

Seeing what time it was after she had had her frugal midday meal—her lovely, sylphlike slenderness being due to what slenderness usually is, the lack of an exuberant appetite for food, plus an actual distaste for sweet, rich, savory, fattening dishes—Mireille freshened up a bit, apply-ing perfume to her strategic areas, then dressing in one of the prettiest dresses she owned, out of a piece of pure female sadism that didn't even have the saving grace of being subconscious.

She meant to break poor Willy's heart, make him cry his eyes out at the thought of losing her forever!

But as James Swithers brought her little road cart around—she had toyed with and rejected the idea of using the landau and thus shoring up her will power, always feeble where dear Willy was concerned, by the restraining presence of her coachman and her footman, because the idea of a lovely, sentimental parting appealed to the essentially theatrical part of her nature—she looked her Black coachman straight in the face and let fly:

"James, Mary Ellen Pleasant *killed* your brother-in-law, didn't she? Or had it done?"

James Swithers stared at her.

"Yes'm," he said grimly, "her sho Lawd did. Only us ain't got no way o' provin' it . . ."

"And you were—well—fond of 'French Joe'?" Mireille asked.

"Fond of—well mebbe not, ma'am. But we'uns got along wit' him real good. One thing, he behaved downright decent 'bout Blossom. You see, he got that po' stupid chile in th' fambly way. And when me 'n' John went after him to git him to do right by her, he acted nice and reasonable. Married up wit' her wit'out no argufyin' atall. Lowed that he loves her for true. And you's from N'Awleens, ma'am. So you's gotta know that high yaller Creole niggers like Joe is mo' down on Blackfolks than even po' white Cajuns 'n' crackers is . . ."

"What happened to the baby?" Mireille said.

"Us got her boarded out. Her's nigh onto three years old now," James sighed, "And tha's mighty hard on po' Blossom—"

"She can bring her here," Mireille said flatly. "She always could have; she only needed to ask me. I love children. You know that. And I don't care what color they are . . ."

"Oh, Lawdy, ma'am!" James Swithers got out, and the sudden tears stood and glittered in his dark eyes; "you's jes' too good to we'uns! 'Deed you is!"

"Only it's going to cost you," Mireille said with a perfect gamine's grin. "Oh, no! Don't worry—I'm not going to cut your wages. All I need from you two spies of Mary Ellen's—"

"Lawd Jesus, ma'am!" James gasped. "We'uns ain't no—"

"Spies. You *are*, and you know it. Good ones, too. Doesn't matter. My past is public knowledge in this burg, so Madame Poisonous can't hold it over my head, as long as I don't do something else—or new—that she could use against me. Besides, you do your work well and that's all I care about. So, as I started to say, all I need from you and John is a little information. For instance, how the devil did she know Lola Montez was going to sell her jewels? And so fast? That burns me up, because *I* was planning to buy 'em. But she got down to Duncan and Company, those auctioneers on Montgomery Street, before their doors were opened the day they knocked down Lola's sparklers. By the time I heard about it and flew down there, Mary Ellen had bought up everything that wasn't pure junk. C'mon, tell me: how did she?"

"Hmmm—you mean that there Spanish dancing woman, doncha ma'am?"

"Lola Montez is *Irish*. Her name is Liza Gilbert. And not only is she an awful dancer, but she can't speak a word of Spanish. I do speak it, and I know. But we're wasting time. How did Mary Ellen Pleasant know that?"

"Well, ma'am, I cain't swear I knows. But I reckons some of them gentlemens what eats in Madame Pleasant's boardinghouses must of run off at th' mouf in front of them nigger waiters of hern. Most whitefolks plumb fergits that Black barbers and waiters and sichlike ain't sticks o' furniture. Madame Pleasant is got hern trained. Them fellas kin tell a real hot stock market tip, fer instance, from one what ain't worth much, better'n yo' fren' banker Kinnan can. Lawdy! Th' times she's done caught them rich gentlemens whut plays th' market by they bal—by whar it purely hurts, 'cause they's done gone and bought on margin, or sold short—"

"I don't understand all that. But I will. I'll get Ross Kinnan to explain it to me, personally. One thing more: Do you know any of the colored waiters in Mary Ellen's supper clubs? The ones who bring her those hot stock market tips?"

"Yes'm. Me'n John know plumb nigh all o' them fellas . . ."

"All right. So here's how you can get even with her for having your brother-in-law shot and leaving poor Blossom a widow. Not to mention making it up to me for all the talebearing you've indulged in at my expense since you've worked for me—"

"Oh, Lawdy, ma'am! Us—"

"Shut up and listen. The next time one of your friends in Mary Ellen's boardinghouses stumbles upon—overhears—something big, tell him to bring it to you. You casually inform him that you've got a little money saved and you'd like to make a killing. Don't mention *my* name to anyone, understand? And if I do pull off a fast one the way she's always doing, I'll cut you and John in on the take. That's fair enough, isn't it?"

"Yes'm," James Swithers said mournfully, "it's real fair, fer a fact. Ain't but one thing wrong with it. Them fellas—they won't let slip a mumblin' word. Not to me, not to nobody. They's too scairt o' her. They jes' doan' wanna end up floatin' in th' Bay. You's gotta understan' that, ma'am. That woman is a killer, her; an' she's got th' cullud folks here in San Francisco bound to her hand and foot. Lawd Gawd, Miz Mireille, us glad to do whut you axes us to, good as you is to we'uns, but—"

Mireille sighed then, long and deeply. 'She's beaten me again, that off-colored witch!' she thought. Then she saw how troubled her coachman was. How—frightened.

"It's all right, James. I understand. And I don't hold it against you," she said.

So it was that when Mireille walked into the cottage on Fremont Street, she was so late that she found Willy both abed and asleep. She wondered if that business of his being asleep wasn't faked. But then she decided that it wasn't. His face wore the characteristic expression of pure, boyish innocence it always relaxed into when he slumbered, and a great wave of truly maternal tenderness washed over her.

"Good God, but I love him so much," she moaned, "that when I think that I must leave him and for always—I die!"

She tiptoed to the bed, bent over him. A teardrop trickled off the point of her pert, turned-up nose and splashed into his face. Instantly he whirled, jackknifed up into a sitting position, and grabbed her.

"Willy!" she shrilled; "Turn me loose! Oh, what a dirty trick! Turn me loose, you hear me! Turn me looo—Mmmmmm—Mmmmmmmmmm-mmm—Oh Willy darling, please! Please! Ple—Mmmmmmmmmmmm—Mmmmmmmmm— Hmmmmmmmmmmmmmnnnnn— Ahhhhhh!— Wait! Stop it! You'll tear my underthings, you'll—Oh. Oh. Ah. Ahhhhhh. *Oh*, God forgive me! I am so weak—so wicked, whorish, bad—such a naughty girl who—Ah. Ahhhhh. Like that, my love! Like that! But dear baby Jesus—it is—so sweet—So sweet. So very sweet—Ahhhhhhhhhh-hhh God! I am lost!"

Willy lay there, listening to her crying.

"Would you mind telling me," he groaned, "what in the name of everything unholy this is all about?"

"You 'ave mmmmmmmmmmmmurdered mmmmmmmmeeeee!" she sobbed. "Assassin! Coward! Pig! Now I'm going to die and you—and you 'ave keeeeeled meeeee! You 'ave, Willy!"

"I've *killed* you?" Willy chuckled then. "How? By poking you up the middle with a very blunt instrument and jiggling you about a little? Nonsense. Not even by half! Why don't you get out of the rest of your things and let me really kill you, Mireille, *bébé?*"

"Ohhhhh *Jésus!* Willy—I swore by the good God and the Sainted Virgin that I would never do this with you again."

"And why did you swear a *pluscumperfecto* rattling, thunderous, absolutely goddamned fool thing like that, may I ask?"

"Because I'm going to get married," she sniffed; "or I was—"

"You were going to get married," he said solemnly, "but now you're
not? And why not, *Mirla?* You mean the poor devil came to his senses?
Bully for him!"

"Willy, I'm going to keeeeeel you! I swear eeet!"

"All right. By—exhaustion, please? Get out of your clothes and get on
with it, will you? Let's see if you can't make me the happiest corpse in
California, dearest!"

"Willy, no. Please, no. This is serious. I—promised to marry An-drew.
Y'know, An-drew MacFarland . . ."

"You can't. You'll never be able to tell him from a horse. And all your
children will *whinny.*"

"Hmmmmm. He is a horse all right. A—stallion . . ."

"*¡Jesús!*" Willy whispered prayerfully. "You don't mean that *already*
you've—"

"Turned An-drew every possible way but loose? But, yes, my darling
Willy! And, for your information he is—great. No. Just won-der-ful!"

"*¡Golfa!*" Willy snarled. "Slut!"

"Exactly that, unhappily. Or else why would I be in bed with a married man? But no more. I took my most solemn oath that I was going to
be faithful to my An-drew. That my horrible past wouldn't make any
difference. And I asked the all-powerful God and the Sainted Virgin to
strike me dead if I broke that vow. Therefore you are an assassin. You
'ave killed me."

"Not yet. You look—very healthy to me, Mireille darling. Hmmmm—
maybe we'd better work at it a little harder. I volunteer to be your
executioner—but I demand the choice of weapons!"

"Willy, I am serious. I am going to marry An-drew. I really am. That
is, if he will have me after I tell him—confess to him—what *we* 'ave
done today . . ."

"I see. All that goddamned money!"

"You are wrong. I do not need money. D'you know what my current
bank balance is? Has not your darling father-in-law told you?"

"Yes. You're worth over a half million dollars. Thanks to that poor
gentle old fool you made a sucker of—"

"Willy, turn me loose. I must arrange myself in order to leave. Talking
to you is a waste of time. Not only do you know nothing about me, but
you despise me."

"You're saying you didn't?" he said.

"I didn't. I told him to leave his money to the Church. An orphan
asylum. His wife's brothers. All I wanted was his name—a chance to be
—respectable—decent—"

"Decency, Mireille—just isn't in you. You're the perfect *zorra*. That's Spanish for 'bitch' in case you don't know. And—by nature."

"There you may be right," she said morosely. "But anyhow, I have to try. Not to be, I mean. I owe that to my children. . . ."

"Oh, God!" he said.

"So—this is goodbye, Willy—unless—"

"Unless—what?" Willy said.

"An-drew throws me over when I tell him I 'ave betrayed him—with you . . ."

He stared at her.

"Mireille," he whispered, "don't tell him."

"And why not? He will not call you out. And if he did, he has no skill with either swords or pistols—so?"

"*¡Mierda!* I'm not a coward and you know it. Don't tell him—for your sake. And for—his. He's a nice old horse's rear end. He'll make you a perfect husband . . ."

"I—have to tell him, Willy. I cannot begin my married life upon a lie—"

"Mireille baby, take it from me: all married lives are based on lies. Lies by the thousands, daily. If all couples started in to tell each other the strict truth, the divorce courts would be full. The jails. The cemeteries. And nobody would be left together . . ."

"You say that only because you are—unhappy—with *her*. And you are unhappy with her because you love me . . ."

"True. So now I propose to get you the hell out of my life, forever. Go —wash yourself. Then put your frilly little drawers back on. Get out. That was what you wanted, wasn't it?"

"*Oh, Dieu Dieu! Bon petit Dieu aië pitié de moi!*" Mireille sobbed. She was still crying bitterly when she went.

Life is not always cruel. But when it isn't, it is complicated, as that very night was to prove. Because, just after San Francisco's new gas lamps had been lit in the streets, Andrew MacFarland called on her again.

The moment she saw his face, her breath stopped, then hissed sibilantly out from between her very nearly perfect teeth. She had all she could do to keep from fainting.

'Somebody has told him!' she wailed inside the echoing vacuum of her heart. '*This* fast. Somebody—followed me out to the cottage and—'

"An-drew," she whispered, murmured—whimpered, really—"*Je te demande pardon. Je suis désolée, mais suis comme ça: Mauvaise fille. Je ne vaux pas absolument rien. Je suis—ordure, tripaille, boue. Pire que ça: merde. Mais je t'aime. Crois moi: je t'aime. Et si tu ne me peux pas pardonner pour une faute si terrible, je—"*

"Huh, Mireille?" he said absently. "Sweetheart, you're speaking French to me, again. Wait. Don't translate. Let me talk. Look, my dear, I don't know how to tell you this. My father—"

Relief washed over her in waves. Of light. Of very nearly—glory.

"What about—your father, An-drew?" she said.

"He swears he'll cut me off without a cent if I persist in what he calls the outrageous folly of marrying you. And kick me out of the office as well. So, since it isn't very likely that any other firm in town would buck the Old Man to the extent of hiring me, I just don't see how—"

"An-drew," she purred like a sublimely contented cat, "kiss me?"

"But Mireille! You haven't heard what I was saying! My father—"

"Has sacked you. Cut you off without a sou. Or he will, if you marry me. Whereupon *I* shall keep you, gladly. Wouldn't you like to be my fancy man? *Ma 'tite maîtresse*—in reverse? *Oh, comme ça será drôle*—a kept mistress in pants! Ohhhhh An-drew! I am so sorry! Do not look at me like that! I am only teasing you, my love! But—seriously, you are an expert in banking, brokerage, real estate and the like, is it not so?"

"Yes," he said dourly; "or at any rate, I'm pretty good at 'em. Even the Old Man admits that . . ."

"Well, I cannot open a bank for you, because I haven't that much money. But how would a combination real estate and stock broker's office suit you? You can manage my properties at first. Later on, I'm sure others will come your—our—way . . ."

He glared at her, his long face as red as a sorrel's.

"That's right," he whispered; "you are—an heiress, aren't you? Y'know, I'd clean forgot that. So now, in one way or another, you propose to keep me, Mireille?"

But she saw the danger. Destroy his pride of manhood, and she'd wreck him. And, thereby, her own chance for escape from the ill fortune that had dogged her tracks so long. When it had to, her brain worked. It worked superbly—as now. 'As long as I don't let my poor little steam-heated tail spoil things!' she thought.

"No, An-drew," she said soberly, "I don't. Forget you love me, if indeed you do—"

"If!" he groaned. "Mireille, I'm mad over you!"

"Oh, darling," she wept, "I'm glad! I'm so glad! But listen to me. I love you. But I also like you. You're my lover and my friend, too. Put it this way: Would you accept a loan from a friend to get your business started? *Tout en regle!* You can even pay me interest, if you want to! But do I have to stand idly by and let an old mossback of a tyrant defeat you? Must I let your father wreck our lives, yours and mine, because of your prickly masculine pride?"

He stared at her.

She came up to him, stood very close. Her perfume rose around his head in an intoxicating cloud.

"An-drew," she whispered, "I will not lie. If I could—buy you, I would. I want you—love you—that much. But I know I can't. And I also know that men who can be bought aren't worth having. I need a man at my side, *cheri*, not a puppet. I don't want to own you. I want you to be mine, as I am yours, only because of the love we bear each other. But for God's sake, and for ours, don't let your father—and the world—*beat* us! I—I've been pushed—beaten down—so far, so very far; and now when my knight in shining armor has come riding to rescue me, lift me up, am I to lose him, lose my life over—dollars and cents? Over the stupid question of which of us has money?"

"No," he said gravely; "but there're questions of honor involved, too, Mireille . . ."

"Yes. The honor I haven't got. That you could grant me, give me back —by making me—your wife. I'll invest in that honor, An-drew. And in your—nobility, and your strength. Or is it that you—consider me not worth the cost—in trouble—the affronts you'll suffer for my sake? In the time, work, love you'll have to put into taking care of me—who am so— so weak, so unprotected? Or am I too great a risk, perhaps? Not ever to be trusted? If that's what you think, say so, and I—"

"No," he said quietly, but with absolute conviction; "you're a great woman, Mireille. A magnificent one."

Then slowly, shyly, pledging thus his faith in her, and—the phrase being, in him at least, anything but meaningless!—his sacred honor, he bent and kissed her mouth.

15

MIREILLE SAT BEFORE THE WASHSTAND IN THE MASTER BEDROOM, bathing little Stanford's bloody face. The boy whimpered quietly, manfully trying to hold back his tears. He was a very good and placid child, so much so that Mireille wondered if the physical resemblance to her husband she sometimes was almost sure she saw in him were not real. Couldn't Andy have had his fling back then, sowed a wild oat or two? But she knew better than that. Stanford Curtwright MacFarland was both fatherless and—motherless, a fact she fervently prayed to all the saints that he'd never find out.

"What did she hit him with this time?" she asked Blossom wearily.

"Th' coal shovel, Miz Mireille," Blossom groaned. "I swear t' Gawd if that theah child ain't th' naughtiest galbaby anybody ever seen! Six years ol'—and meaner than a witch! Ma'am, you sho she yourn? Way that chile act, looks like to me somebody must of switched babies in they cradle, took th' human one away 'n' lef' a li'l she-devil in her place!"

"No, Claire's mine all right," Mireille sighed, "and her behavior's proof of that, Blossom. Maman always swore that I was the single worst little fiend out of hell ever born into this world. If the Devil has left me a changeling, it's Stan, not Claire. Oh, dear! This is bad! I'm going to have to take him to Dr. Sepúlvera and get it stitched. Give me that roll of cotton over there, Blossom. I'll just pack this cut and bandage it up till An-drew comes home, then he can take Stan and me over to Dr. Enrique's. By the way, Blossom—don't put supper on yet. It will have to wait until we come back from the doctor's office . . . ."

"What about hern?" Blossom demanded.

"Put her to bed without it," Mireille said sternly. "I've already warmed her little bottom for her with the back of my hairbrush—for all the good it's going to do . . . ."

"None atall," Blossom sighed; "and making her go wit'out her supper won't neither. That chile eats like a bird anyhow. But spite o' that, she's stronger than a li'l mule. My Periwinkle is bigger 'n' taller than her be, but all th' same Claire whups her li'l high-brown behind ever' time they gits into a scrap wit'out even trying hard."

"I suspect Periwinkle's the one who doesn't try, because you've probably warned her not to beat Claire up for fear of angering me," Mireille said. "Tell her *I* said to defend herself. Next time Claire jumps her, tell Peri to really let her have it. Maybe *that* will cool my little savage down a mite. . . ."

She finished bandaging Stan's head, winding the white cotton cloth around it to make a sort of turban that held the wad of cotton pressed tight against that nasty gash over his right eye.

'An inch lower and she'd have blinded him,' she thought sadly. '*Bon Dieu*, make her change! If she grows up as wild as she is now, I just don't know—'

Then she remembered that she herself had changed. That once past puberty, ravenous fury had no longer been her dominant characteristic.

'Only I changed for the worse,' she thought dismally. 'It's far better to be a virago than a whore . . .'

She bent and kissed the little boy.

"There, Stan! Maman has fixed you up just fine," she said cheerfully; "made a sultan out of you!"

"What's a sultan, Maman?" Stan said.

"Oh, a sort of a king. In the Arabian countries, anyhow. He's very rich, and has lots and lots of wives!"

"Then I don't want to be a sultan," Stanford said. "Girls are awful!"

"I'm a girl," Mireille teased him solemnly.

"No, you're not. You're my Mama, and I love you," Stanford said.

Mireille clawed the sturdy little fellow into her arms, hugged him convulsively, trying all the time to blink back the tears that had filled her eyes.

'Oh, God, if only I were!' she thought. She said:

"And I love you, Stan. Now go lie down till suppertime. You must be real still and—" Then she heard her husband's voice, saying:

"Mireille! Mireille! Are you visible? I've brought company home for supper, my dear!"

Mireille rushed out into the front hall and kissed Andrew MacFarland fervently. She did this every time he came home—not to prove to herself that she loved him, for that was a settled issue no longer needing proof, but to reassure him, who continued, out of his vast humility, very real modesty, to have moments of doubt concerning the sincerity of her affections for him.

He was wrong. Mireille loved him very truly, and without any reservations at all. The only trouble was that she also loved Willy Kilpatrick just as dearly, and with the same lack of reservations. What was more, being a true romantic, she was totally convinced that this schizoid state of affairs was going to go on as long as she did. But since she no longer saw Willy or indulged in cozy *cinq à septs* with him anymore, she was quite comfortable about the whole crazy state of her emotions.

"Lord God, Andy!" a pleasant baritone voice from just behind her husband said. "You sure are one lucky man!"

"I know that," Andrew said solemnly, "which is why I go armed to the teeth, and shoot poachers on sight, Wilbur! So curb your enthusiasm for my better half, will you?"

"Your better three quarters," the visitor groaned. "Ma'am, you're a sight for sore eyes. I just didn't believe they grew 'em that lovely out here!"

"They don't," Andrew said; "Mireille's from New Orleans. Honey, this long, tall, skinny hunk of nothing is Wilbur Phelps. Classmate of mine at Princeton. Geologist. Good one, too. That's why I brought him home for supper, not to give him a chance to ogle you . . ."

"*Enchantée, M'sieur* Phelps," Mireille said.

"French, too, on top of all th' rest. Don't know why, but you French girls have a little something extra that—"

"Only a little, Mr. Phelps? I'd say we have a great deal," Mireille purred. "Over and apart from our horrendous reputation for—well—*sensualité* and general naughtiness, I mean . . ."

"Which is enough hot air to fill up a man-carrying balloon," Andrew said with the transparent complacency of a man whose married life is very satisfactory indeed; "she freezes me to death, most of the time. Well, honey, is supper ready?"

"No, An-drew, it is not. Claire has bashed Stan's poor little head in again—and quite badly this time, so we have to rush him over to Enrique's right *now* . . ."

"Good Lord! Mireille, I swear I just don't understand that child!"

"How could you? She's *my* daughter—and exactly like me. I was always committing mayhem upon the other kids when I was small. But I'm afraid we *must* take him to Enrique, darling. The cut is very deep. It has to be sewn. I've bandaged it as best I could, but—"

"Look, Andy, I'll just mosey along," Wilbur Phelps said. "What you, I, and your missus have to talk over can wait for another night, and—"

"No!" Mireille said sharply; "I'll have James hitch up the landau, and you can come with us, Monsieur Phelps. Dr. Sepúlvera is very skillful. He'll have Stan patched up in no time at all. After that we can come back here, drop Stan off, and go to a restaurant. How does that strike you, An-drew darling?"

"It doesn't. What we've got to talk about oughtn't be discussed in a place as public as a restaurant. Secrecy's the prime essential, it seems to me. Tell Blossom to throw a couple of extra potatoes in th' pot. Did you punish that little wildcat of yours for her outrageous behavior?"

"I most certainly did, for all the good it's going to do," Mireille sighed. "Andy, take Mr. Phelps into the parlor. I'll send John to bring you drinks. I have to order James to get the landau ready, and I have to change. Believe me, this time I won't be long. You'll excuse me, won't you, Mr. Phelps?"

"Of course. But good Lord, you two! What I've got to say really could wait," Wilbur Phelps began.

"No, it can't," Andrew said. "There's an angle to this deal that you don't know, Wilbur. Besides, the Doctor Sepúlvera we're taking the boy to happens to be the very same man you and I were talking about this afternoon, remember? The *legal* owner of the Santa Clara Ranch. So we just might be able to get the major part of the business cleared up tonight. All right, honey—scat! Don't give us too much time to wet our whistles, will you? What we've got to discuss requires clear heads. . . ."

"Look, Mr. MacFarland, and you too, Mireille, I think you'd better leave the little fellow here tonight. And maybe tomorrow as well," Enrique Sepúlvera said.

"Oh, non!" Mireille gasped. *"Es-ce-que c'est sérieux, Docteur? Même grave?"*

"No. It is neither serious nor severe. But the boy's lost a bit too much blood for my liking. I just don't want him hauled all over San Francisco in his weakened state. Not as cool and damp as the nights are now. Catching a cold wouldn't do him any good, y'know. Besides, I want to keep him under observation for a while. He just might have a slight fracture under that messy cut, and, if so I'd rather know it. One of your horses kick him?"

"No. Mireille's daughter did. So say a jenny rather than a gelding or a mare," Andrew said solemnly.

"Funny," Wilbur Phelps chuckled, "how parents tend to give the exclusive possession of a child to each other, when said child is naughty. Of course, you are an even-tempered old soak, Andy, but—"

"You do not understand," Mireille said sadly. "Both Stanford and Claire are my children, not Andy's. I was a widow when we met. My first husband—the father of my twins—was killed in a fire. Accidentally, I believe, though there is some reason to believe he may have been— murdered . . ."

"Arson," Andrew said quickly. "And that's also connected with what we've got to talk about. Doctor, you really think it's best to leave the boy here? Mireille's going to drive me crazy, you know!"

"Bat her one, and shut her up," Enrique Sepúlvera chuckled. "Yes, sir, I do. Rest is definitely indicated. Especially since I had to use chloroform, or else stitching up that gash would have hurt too bad. Don't worry, my wife will take care of him personally . . ."

"And spoil him rotten!" Mireille sighed. "By the way, where is Paci? May I see her a moment, if she's home?"

"At this time of night, where else would she be?" Enrique growled with mock severity. "Don't believe in fertilizing my forehead, y'know! Of course you may see her, but you'll have to go upstairs. We weren't expecting company, so she's not exactly visible at the moment . . ."

"Or rather highly visible!" Mireille laughed. "Paci looks best with nothing on! I'll take Stan up to her—"

"No, don't. Let him come out of it first. Then I'll have my nurse carry him up. Well, gentlemen, there's nothing we can do but wait . . ."

"And while we're waiting, we'd like to have a little chat with you, Doctor. Business. D'you still own the Santa Clara Ranch, down near San José?" Andrew MacFarland said.

"So far as I know, I do," Dr. Sepúlvera said. "As I told Mireille—I mean Mrs. MacFarland—"

"Call her Mireille. You've known her longer than I have. And you probably know her better—what makes her tick, anyhow," Andy said. "You were saying that you told Mireille—?"

"That I wasn't going to waste all of the money I've been able to earn through the practice of medicine fighting a lawsuit to evict squatters from my property . . ."

"Guillermo Kilpatrick says your title's ironclad," Andy said.

Enrique stared at him with a startled expression, but, being very Latino, recovered at once.

"It is," he said dryly. "But what does that mean when you're up against courts whose chief reason for existence is to despoil Hispano-Californians like me of our lands? I'm *Spanish*, Mr. MacFarland! I could never win a suit against the squatters no matter how true and legal my grants are. So I haven't bothered to go to law. Therefore, since no one's tested my land grant titles—awarded to a direct ancestor of mine nearly a hundred years ago by the King of Spain himself—theoretically I still own *Rancho Santa Clara*."

"Some Hispano-Californians have won their cases," Andy pointed out to him dryly.

"A few. And then were run off the land by rifle-toting gringos who defied the rulings of their own courts, and who nearly always had the local sheriffs siding with them. Much ado about nothing. Fighting an already lost cause is foolish, Mr. MacFarland."

"I agree. Tell me one more thing: *Arroyo Cabeza de Vaca* is within the borders of your ranch, isn't it?"

"Yes. But that section's worthless. Pure desert. Unfitted for either agriculture or cattle raising. Which is why the squatters never occupied it."

"Then you wouldn't mind selling it to me and my friend Mr. Phelps, here? And to Mireille, who'll be a third partner?" Andrew MacFarland said quietly.

Enrique stared at him. But *Latinos* are very seldom fools.

"Say—I'll consider it," he said quietly; "after you've told me why the three of you are inclined to lay out money for a desolate stretch of rock, sand, and cactus like Cow Head Gulch, as you Americans call it."

"Of course I'll tell you," Andy said. "You're certainly entitled to know, Doctor. An Eastern mining concern, Robinson, Squires and Kelper, has staked out a claim there. They're only waiting for their heavy equipment to reach them by clipper around the Horn to begin crushing rock. It'll be quartz mining, not placer or hydraulic, you see . . ."

"And the fine print is that as owners of a piece of land that's within a private domain, and to which no staked claim is valid without a deed of purchase from the owners, or a quitclaim deed or other form of renunciation from them, you can get an injunction against that mining company and stop them cold. They'd have to give you your asking price. Hmm. Not bad. But what makes you so sure they've found gold? The forty-niners tore my ranch to shreds and never turned up one speck of color!"

"Didn't know where to look," Wilbur Phelps said; "it's a quartz vein, and far underground. Those old boys with their pans and sluices and rockers simply weren't equipped to find it, Doctor. I'm a college-trained geologist. That's why I found it. I knew the signs . . ."

"*You* found it?" Dr. Sepúlvera said. "Then what's this big Eastern mining company doing staking a claim on my place?"

"I worked for them. I was their geologist. They said that in view of the risks and the heavy outlay of capital involved in quartz mining, they couldn't do any more than grant me a small bonus on top of my salary. I'd asked for a full partnership, or, failing that, a royalty on the gold taken out. They refused me both, which, considering the fact that I discovered the lode, seemed to me unfair. So I quit. Incidentally, I didn't know I was trespassing on private property when I went prospecting down there. That place is so bloody desolate that I thought—"

"No harm done, Mr. Phelps. So now that I know there's gold on my ranch, why should I sell out? Why shouldn't I just get that injunction myself, and make them pay me through the nose?"

"As a matter of fact, you shouldn't sell," Andrew MacFarland said evenly. "You should come in with us as a fourth partner. Wait! You had no way of knowing that *Arroyo Cabeza de Vaca* had become valuable. We told you. Mr. Phelps, here, found the gold that makes it so. Therefore it seems to me that as an ethical man, you should agree that you owe us some compensation. That's one thing. The other is a hard, cruel fact that I don't approve of, that I honestly deplore. Doctor, you're a Mexican. That you're of pure Spanish lineage, a gentleman and a scholar whom I personally admire wholeheartedly, has nothing to do with the bedrock fact that a man named Enrique Sepúlvera hasn't a snowball's chance in hell of making an injunction against a powerful gringo mining company stick in the state of California. While Andrew MacFarland and Company—I'm keeping both Wilbur's and Mireille's names in the background, you'll notice—damned well can. Here's my proposition: We form a holding company and issue, say, one thousand shares of preferred stock. Each of us becomes the owner of one fourth of that stock representing the total value of any minerals taken out of *Arroyo Cabeza de Vaca*, as well as one fourth of the value of the land itself. We don't divide the land up and assign so many acres to each. Too risky. And, as mining works, unfair. You know perfectly well, Doctor, that one man has got rich ten feet from a claim that never produced a speck of gold dust for another. We share and share alike. It's up to you. You can go it alone and take your chances, which will be, I insist, dismal. Or you can come in with us, and greatly improve them. What d'you say?"

Enrique Sepúlvera thought about that.

"I say you're absolutely right on all counts, and I accept your proposal. Here's my hand on it!" he said.

They shook hands, gripping hard.

When Mireille finally came back downstairs after a long and loving chat with Paquita, during which a great many fervent kisses were exchanged, she, her husband, and Wilbur Phelps drove back to the

MacFarlands' modest little dwelling out on Bryant Street almost to Steamboat Point, which was about as far south as you could go in San Francisco in those days without falling into the southern end of the Cove. Their house was as modest as it was because Andrew refused to touch a penny of the money that Mireille's properties earned her. He had, of course, long since paid her back the loan she'd made him to get his business started. Aside from that, his progress had been moderate. Which was to say that in the something over five years he'd been married to Mireille he hadn't got rich; but he hadn't gone bankrupt either. And, in those days, when the gold mining boom had become a colossal bust—except, of course, for the great mining companies that had enough Eastern capital behind them to afford the expensive crushers, high-powered hydraulic hoses, steam shovels and the like that were absolutely necessary after the early primitive placer mining methods had skimmed off all the surface gold, as well as most of the precious metal existing in veins close to ground level—the feat of having been able to stay afloat at all, and turn a steady, if small, profit, was no mean achievement.

"All right," Andrew said, cautiously and cannily summing up the matter as they sat in the parlor sipping their brandies and *café noirs* after that late, late supper, "that vein is on Dr. Sepúlvera's property, but we've treated him fair and square, which is a relief. Especially since, being nobody's fool, he saw and agreed to the point we were trying to make. That mining company, Robinson, Squires and Kelper, staked a claim without even bothering to try to find out whether that arroyo was on private property or not. Then, on top of that, they tried to bilk you, Wilbur, out of anything like your rightful share in a find that you and *only* you made. So I haven't much sympathy for them. Besides, as soon as we get our company organized, they'll have to deal with us. They have no other recourse. And we'll make them pay through the nose for the right to exploit. I'm not worried about them. It's another bunch of pirates who're robbing me of my sleep at night . . ."

"Another mining company?" Wilbur Phelps said.

"No. Another group of stock manipulators who're attempting what looks like a takeover of Robinson, Squires and Kelper. I got wind of it weeks ago. Robinson *et al* are only a medium-sized company, so when, all of a sudden, there started to be an unusual demand for their paper, I investigated. Hit a stone wall. All I could find out was that they were selling stock to finance a big operation—and that somebody with an 'in' was buying up their stock like crazy. Then I stumbled upon you, and you told me what the big operation was that Robinson, Squires and Kelper were selling a flood of H_2O to finance—"

"H-two-oh?" Mireille said.

"Chemical symbols for water, honey. Which is what that stock is. Wonder they haven't washed the ink clean off it. Anyhow, I still didn't know who was buying up their paper until my darling little genius of a wife told me. They're Thomas Bell and Mary Ellen Pleasant. And Ben Holladay—you know: the steamship magnate, and stagecoach king—is backing them. Though Milton S. Latham, president of the San Francisco and London Bank, may be in on it too. If so, he's keeping his connection quiet, and operating through some other brokerage office besides his own . . ."

"Whew! Mighty big fish! Whales, even. Lord God, Mrs. MacFarland, how'd you find a thing like that out? It stands to reason that they'd work with a maximum degree of secrecy and—"

"Spies," Mireille said solemnly; "I've got 'em all over. Trick I learned from Madame Pleasantly Poisonous herself. She puts colored servants in all the important houses, and they bring her back pay dirt she can use for blackmail. I was able to get inside information on this because she disciplined one member of her grapevine too severely, and he wound up dead. That turned two others—the ones she placed here, in our house—against her, and they talked their heads off. I'll tell you the whole story one day, when there's more time. It's long and complicated, and we'd better get on with figuring out how to beat her right now. An-drew, I have a suggestion: May I send for—Willy?"

Andrew glared at her. "Why?" he growled.

"Because he's handled hundreds of stock-raiding takeover cases by now. And he's the city's outstanding expert on Spanish and Mexican land grant titles, which is the first thing they're going to think of as a means to get us out of their way—to test Enrique's title, I mean. He can tell us exactly what to do to fight Mary Ellen and her pirates off—" She paused and loosed a ripple of silvery soprano laughter. "And besides, he's a very, very pretty boy, and I love him very dearly—which is why you're sitting there glaring at me like a mean old ogre! Isn't that what you wanted to hear?"

"*¡En Casa con la pata quebrada!*" Andrew growled.

"*Dieu!* Who taught you that one? Enrique, I'll bet!"

"Right. And I gave him one of our Scottish sayings in return. He liked it so much he wrote it down: 'A woman, a dog, and a willow tree, the more you beat 'em, the better they be!' "

Wilbur Phelps threw back his head and laughed aloud.

"Dear old soak!" he chuckled; "I'll bet she beats you!"

"I do," Mireille said demurely; "every night. Or—wear him to a frazzle otherwise. Seriously, An-drew, I'd like to send for Willy. He really is good at this sort of thing. So, all right, we were sweethearts once. A million years ago. Before I'd ever even heard of you. But along comes Miss Molly Kinnan, an heiress, and *phft!*—a poor little nobody without a sou like me was finished. *Comme ça!*" She snapped her fingers sharply. "So now we're merely friends. She makes him so wonderfully miserable that I haven't the heart to hold a grudge against the poor dear boy. May I, An-drew darling?"

"Jesus!" Wilbur said prayerfully. "We won't even need blasting powder, old soak! We'll just stand her up in front of the mine and let that voice of hers melt the rocks! If anybody ever called me Weeel-burrr darrrleeeng like that, I'd dissolve into a puddle o' grease and flow out under the door!"

"All right." Andrew sighed. "We'll schedule a meeting tomorrow, in my office—"

"We will not!" Mireille said merrily, and pulled the bell cord; "I'm going to send for him right now!"

"But, Mireille!" Andrew said sternly; "you simply cannot get a man up out of his bed, presumably from beside his wife at this hour of the night, no matter how many tender memories he may have of you . . ."

"Don't have to!" Mireille said gleefully. "Right now he's in that groggery on upper Pacific Street trying to get drunk enough to be able to face the dire fate of having to go home to his darling Molly. I'll send John after him in my road cart. But we have to hurry before he gets too drunk to make any sense!"

"Mireille," Andrew said very, very quietly, "mind telling me how you know all that?"

She bounced up out of her chair, flounced over to his, and plumped herself down upon his knees.

"Andy's jealous! Andy's jealous! Andy's a naughty, jealous boy!" she giggled, and kissed him.

"Mireille, behave yourself! This is no way to act before a guest!" Andrew thundered.

"Have to agree with you there, old soak!" Wilbur groaned. "Turning a fellow into a jade-green corpse from pure envy is still murder. On top of which, it's unkind!"

"All right! I'll be little Miss Prim and Prissy, since you both insist!" Mireille said solemnly. "An-drew, when you start being jealous, you insult me. D'you remember Jasmine? No—you couldn't, could you? She left my service to get married before we met—Oh, John. Hope I didn't wake you up!"

"No'm," John Swithers lied. "What can I do for you, ma'am?"

"Take the road cart. Drive over to Mulligan's Grog Shop on Pacific Street and get attorney William Kilpatrick. If he's sober, tell him it's urgent. If he's not, just drag him out of that low den bodily and bring him here. Get going, now!"

"Yes'm," John said calmly. Nothing Mireille told him to do surprised him anymore.

"Where was I?" Mireille said. "Oh, yes! Jasmine, who used to work for me before she got married. Well, she and Julie are friends. And Julie works for Willy and his dear, dear Molly. And Julie visits Jasmine on her days off and tells her things about what's happening *chez les* Kilpatricks. And if those things are sufficiently interesting, such as that poor Willy is turning into a tosspot because he can't stand his wife, Jasmine rushes over here and tells me. *Voilà toute!*"

"Your spy network?" Wilbur asked.

"A part of it," Mireille said seriously. "Mary Ellen Pleasant once told me something I've never forgot, because she was right: 'Information is power.' "

"That's true," Andrew sighed. "Mireille, tell me how you happened to meet that absolutely foul woman?"

"Later. Not in front of Weeeeeel-burrrrrrr. He's a nice boy and I want him to respect me as long as he can . . ."

"That'll be the rest of my life!" Wilbur Phelps swore fervently.

"No. That cannot be," Mireille said with genuine sadness. "Wilbur, we are going to be partners, and, I hope, friends—"

"We are friends, Mrs. MacFarland!"

"Call me Mireille. An-drew really doesn't mind, and if he did, fat lot of good it would do him! Wilbur—the truth: I was a bad girl when Andrew met me. A very bad girl. You're going to find that out, so it's better that you hear it from me . . ."

"Mireille, for God's love!" Andy groaned.

"No, darling—for yours. Who are an angel and a saint, and the noblest, best man alive. I'm going to worship you on my knees until the day I die—"

"But I don't want to be worshipped," Andrew said.

"There's nothing you can do about it. I also promise to love you upside down and swinging from the chandelier and in every other variety of interesting position I can think of, and you must admit I have an inventive mind, haven't I, darleeeng?"

"Oh, Gawd!" Andrew said.

"Bravo!" Wilbur ripped out.

"Where was I, again? *Ah oui!* Wilbur, An-drew saved me, lifted me up, made me his wife. But I am not—or not merely—grateful for that. Gratitude alone will not hold a marriage together. The truth is I love him. And my punishment for—all my many sins is that he will not believe that simple fact . . ."

"Now, Mireille!"

"Now, nothing. Take what he is doing now. He is trying to become a millionaire . . ."

"A laudable ambition!" Wilbur quipped. "So am I!"

"Good for you, only An-drew has no real desire to be feeelthy rich. He is only doing this—to protect me. You see, last year, 1861, when the Yankees and the Johnny Rebs back East started killing each other over whether or not I can keep *mes Negres*—"

"*You* own Blacks? By Jove, that's surprising!" Wilbur said.

"One. Back home in New Orleans. Her name's Lucienne. If I ever go back there I'm going to have her hanged, or burnt alive at the stake, 'cause she's a Witch!"

"More of one than you are?" Andy said with tender mockery.

"Much more! Lucienne's a voodoo mamaloi. But that's not what I'm talking about. Last year, when the transcontinental telegraph got here finally—throwing all those poor boys who rode the pony express out of work!—it dawned on An-drew, that the coast-to-coast railroad couldn't be far behind it—"

"It won't be," Andy said; "if that piece of fratricidal madness back East hadn't stopped the work on it, it probably would be here by now . . ."

"*C'est vrai. Tu as raison, mon chou!*" Mireille said, and kissed him. "The point is, Wilbur, that up till now most of the women in San Francisco have been bad girls, too, because that was the only kind that were brought out here—for obvious reasons!"

"Oh, Gawd!" Andrew said again.

"And this town will never have its share of decent, respectable women until it becomes easier to get to from the East. You know how people come out here now, don't you?"

"Yes," Wilbur said; "Round the whole of South America by clipper. Or steamship down to Panama, cross the Isthmus by train, another steamship up the Pacific Coast of Central America and Mexico to here. Or wagon train across the plains. All three of 'em pure, undiluted hell.

Except that the Panama route doesn't last long enough to kill you out-right."

"Exactly. But what's going to happen when every straw-haired, horse-faced, flat-chested, American female back East has only to board a train and get here in a week? I ask you that, Wilbur?"

"Town's going to fill up with 'em, I guess," Phelps said.

"Very right. And when San Francisco is full of Anglo-Saxon blondes, with their chins down to their knees, and duly equipped with frozen fundaments—"

"Whooopee!" Wilbur roared. "What a phrasemaker you are, Mireille —I mean Mrs. MacFarland!"

"Call her Mireille. I don't mind. Besides, I'm helpless, as you've al-ready seen. She's completely impossible, but I love her," Andrew said wearily.

"Who wouldn't?" Wilbur said fervently.

"They're all going to look down on me, and sweep their skirts aside when I pass, to avoid contamination, and have theater managers evict me from the house as a public disgrace—"

"Long live public disgraces!" Wilbur said.

"But d'you know why they're going to cut me dead, the minute they arrive?"

"More likely they'll put their gentlemen acquaintances and their hub-bies on a leash!" Wilbur laughed. "But no, I don't know why. Tell me, will you?"

"Because they're so horribly afraid that some woman, somewhere, sometime, has actually got some fun out of life. And I look like I might have, don't I?" Mireille said triumphantly.

Wilbur threw back his head and roared.

"But you still haven't explained what my becoming a millionaire has to do with all this," Andrew said.

"Simple. You want to protect me from being insulted, and my—our— children from growing up as outcasts. And what better way of doing it is there, than that? People don't insult millionaires, or even dig up juicy secrets from their pasts. Can't—they're too busy fawning over them, and flattering them, and trying to curry favors out of them!" Mireille said.

"True. And you're right. But I also want to make my old monster of a father eat crow, tailfeathers and all. That after all these years he still won't have us in to dine! Or—oh, hullo, Willy. You got here in a hurry, didn't you?"

"Did my best," Willy said as he put out his hand to Andrew. "John said it was urgent. Dammit, Mireille, what kind of trouble are you in now?"

"I'm accused of double murder," Mireille purred. "Or I will be. When your Molly and my An-drew turn a suspicious shade of green and pop right off to their rewards. And you and I have been dragged back, kicking and screaming, from wherever we will have run off to by then. Hmmm—you're not even drunk! Which means you have been overcome by resignation. Don't I get a kiss?"

"Oh, you!" Willy said; then, "¿Con permiso, Andrew?" And kissed her. Lightly. On the cheek.

"Ohhhhh, merde!" Mireille said.

"Hmmmmm," Willy said after Andy had explained the situation to him. "Bell, eh? He's another canny Scot, Andrew. And Holladay—and even, possibly, Latham? Awfully heavy artillery, old boy! Hmmn—let me think. Tell you what: Don't fight 'em—"

"Whaaat!" Wilbur Phelps said.

"Exactly, Mr. Phelps. Why should you? You've definitely got the whip hand, it seems to me. Enrique Sepúlvera's grant is the most perfect one in California. They call it into question, and I'll murder them for you inside of a week. So what difference does it make to the four of you who owns that mining company? You don't need to own or control it to stop them cold, or make them pay you whatever you ask . . ."

"By Jove! He's right, Andy!" Wilbur said.

"Might even be fun to pull Mary Ellen Pleasant down a peg. God knows that evil yellow witch has got it coming. Anyhow, since I'm here, let me make you a suggestion—a method of saving all of you an awful lot of trouble if things don't pan out the way you hope. In quartz mining, they often don't, y'know."

"That's the miserable truth," Wilbur said.

"What should we do, Willy?" Andrew said.

"Don't sell your holdings or your stock to them. Offer them a ninety-nine-year lease—on a hard cash or a royalty basis. Either way is risky. You take cash, and whatever you agree to will look like lead pennies if the mine turns out to be as rich as Mr. Phelps claims it is . . ."

"I don't claim, I know!" Wilbur said hotly.

"You don't know, Mr. Phelps. I'm not a geologist, but I've drawn up enough deeds, quitclaims, transfers, and bankruptcy petitions to have learned that nobody on God's green earth can determine how a vein of gold in a quartz stratum is going to turn out until the mine has been in operation from at least six months to a year. It may peter out in a week.

Or it may sink in the direction of China—go so deep that even when there're tons of gold down there, the cost of bringing it out exceeds its value. You'll admit that much, won't you, sir?"

"I do—freely. And apologize for letting professional pride get ahead of my brains. You're absolutely right. Nobody can predict even from quite ample random sampling what a deep quartz strata gold mine will do . . ."

"Willy," Mireille said softly, "you've changed. You've got to be smart. And you used to be dumber than a sweet little old burro . . ."

"I can't belt you one, Mirla!" Willy snapped; "only Andy's got the legal right to. A process that can come in handy, old boy! If she can drive you mad, she will . . ."

"Did she, you?" Andrew said mildly.

"Stark raving!" Willy said. "Now, listen! In the contract, there should be an escape hatch clause: Thirty days after they have notified you that they've decided to cease operations, or it has been brought to your attention that they have shut down, or they have declared themselves in bankruptcy, your stock in the original holding company you're going to set up, and the lands themselves revert to you. The lease is automatically canceled. You're the expert, Mr. Phelps. D'you follow my reasoning in this?"

"Perfectly. They exhaust the vein I found—or they find it leads straight down to hell and beyond so that operating expenses become ruinous, so they give up. And two years later some bewhiskered old jackass of a prospector stumbles on the real mother lode, a few hundred yards, or even feet, away. Then back they come, aroaring! Whereas, if they've been legally excluded as per that beaut of a clause you suggest, we can make a new deal with them, or with somebody else, on a far more profitable basis."

"Exactly. But I can't—I even refuse to—advise you on whether to make a cash deal with them for that lease or ask for royalties. If you take cash, you've got that much and can cheerfully watch them go broke. Or, with that same bloody handful of dollars in your fists you can stand by and watch them becoming multimillionaires."

"Royalties?" Andy asked.

"Same odds. That vein peters out in a week, and you're left with nothing, not even the moderate profit a cash deal might have brought you. Or it proves to be the mother lode to end all mother lodes, and you can celebrate drinking champagne out of Mireille's solid-gold slipper. Don't ask me. Any opinion I'd venture to offer now could turn out to be two hundred percent wrong!"

"Willy," Andy said, "will you draw up all the papers for us? Become, officially, our company's lawyer?"

Willy stared at him.

"If you'll make me a partner," he said quietly. "Cut me in on the deal on an equal basis. Divide the shares by five instead of by four. If this mine turns out to be rich at all, the difference will be hardly noticeable. If it's a bust, the difference is nil. What d'you say to that, Andy?"

Andrew thought about that. Long and deeply.

"I agree," he said. "We'll have to ask Enrique, of course, but he'll hardly object. You've been friends practically all your lives. You, Wilbur?"

"Fair enough. Having a keen legal mind aboard could save us a peck of trouble. Agreed."

"Mireille?" Andrew said.

"Opposed! I hereby veto the motion! Damned if *I'm* going to buy Molly Kinnan silks and satins!"

"Oh Lord, women!" Andrew groaned. "Sorry, honey; you're outvoted. It's two to one, y'know."

"That's what *you* think, An-drew! Just wait until I sweet-talk Enrique a little. And bend Paci's dainty little ears into corkscrews!"

Willy studied the perfect della Robbia cameo of her face.

"I withdraw the suggestion," he said flatly. "Get yourselves another lawyer . . ."

He got to his feet. Reached for his hat. Started for the door. In it, he turned. Started to say, "Good night, all," or something like that. Words to that effect. Some exquisite display—or concealment—of bitterness toward this small, slight woman who, he admitted to himself, had wrecked his life. And who was trying to, all over again, now.

But he froze there in that doorway. Became a statue. Unalive. Unbreathing. Only his eyes had something more than static existence in them. They went paler than the pre-sunrise dawns of a thousand tomorrows. Bleaker than the arctic skies above a frozen tundra. Bluer than a wail of utter pain.

"Maman!" that childish voice piped from the stairs. "I'm—hungry. I'm so hungry, Maman! My tummy growls and growls and won't let me sleep!"

"You should have thought of that when you—" Mireille began; but before she could get the rest of it out, Willy had crossed to that stair. Went up it in one long bound to the landing. Clasped that angel sprite— rod-straight, pencil-thin within the voluminous folds of her muslin nightgown, practically buried under, surrounded by, a mane of hair like great

threatening masses of sooty, bituminous thunderclouds, billowing like
the dense, heavy, ground-hugging, inky smoke of an oil well on fire about
her tiny form—in his arms. Those eyes, star sapphires, bluer than a flag-
banner October sky, peered up at him solemnly.

"Who're you?" Claire ('Curtwright?' Mireille wailed from the depths
of the awful desolation echoing hollowly inside her mind; 'Kilpatrick?
Fire Engine Company Number Six? But anyhow—witchchild, Satan's
dark, flowering seed; that's for sure!') said.

"I'm—nobody," Willy said in a slow, grave tone of voice; *"Señor Don
Nadie.* I could have been somebody, but your mama wouldn't let me be.
So I'm not the only somebody I ever wanted to be. D'you know who that
somebody was, little angel, little devil, little witch of my heart?"

"No, who was he?" Claire said.

"Your—papa," Willy said.

"But I've *got* a papa," Claire said in that tone of weary patience that
wise children always use toward stupid grownups.

"I know. The wrong one. *I'm* the right one—or I should have been."

"Willy!" Mireille said angrily. "Will you please stop confusing that
child?"

"I'm not—confused, Maman. *He* is confused. But he is nice, I think.
And—pretty. What's your name, pretty man?"

"Willy," he whispered.

"I love you, Willy," Claire said, and kissed him. "Now make Maman
give me some supper. She wouldn't, 'cause I hit Stan in the head."

"¡Dios!" Willy said, and roared with laughter. "Yes, Mirla, she's *yours,*
all right! Straight as an arrow and right to the point. Andrew, I'll draw up
your papers. Gratis. For—Circe here . . ."

"Lord, Willy, I couldn't accept—" Andrew began.

"Then don't. Make him a partner. I withdraw my objections,"
Mireille said.

16

"WHY DID YOU SEND FOR ME, MARY ELLEN?" MIREILLE SAID.

"As if you didn't know!" Mary Ellen Pleasant said.

She was fairly seething with fury, a sight that ordinarily Mireille would have enjoyed. But on that June day in 1864, she was too depressed to enjoy anything, and she doubted that she ever would again.

"I don't—truly I don't, Mary Ellen," she said.

"Why, to congratulate you, of course!" Madame Pleasant said. "You've beaten me, Mireille. Quite a feat. And with impunity, at that, which is even more of one!"

"Maybe if you'd just calm down a little and explain yourself, I'd be able to make heads or tails of what you're talking about," Mireille said sadly. "I didn't even know that you and I had had a fight, so if I've beaten you, it was quite by accident, I assure you. Not that the news displeases me. So tell me just *how* I've belted you a few. God knows I need something to cheer me up, and that would."

Madame Pleasant stared at her.

"Hmmmm . . ." she said. "You really don't look all that triumphant, d'you? Rather crestfallen, to tell the truth about it. Don't tell me you went and *invested* in that stupid mining company? If so, you were a fool. As big a fool as I was. But, no. You couldn't have. You knew better, didn't you?"

"I knew better than what?" Mireille said.

"Than to invest in Robinson, Squires and Kelper. The now defunct Robinson, Squires and Kelper. In which Tom Bell and I hold a controlling interest. And whose pretty printed pieces of paper I now keep on the top shelf of my commode, just above my chamber pot. To be used for the only purpose they can be now . . ."

"Not even for that. The paper stocks and bonds are printed on is too stiff. It'll scratch. Just burn 'em," Mireille said. "That is, if they'll even burn. As watered as those stocks were, they might not . . ."

"I appreciate your sense of humor, Mireille," Madame Pleasant said. "But what I don't understand is what your motives were. Before this venture, you and I had cooperated very nicely. So why did you set out to ruin me? To revenge yourself for the loss of that ancient, wheezing bag of bones, Alain Curtwright? That makes no sense! Not only don't you have one iota of evidence that I had anything to do with that fire, but it was you who profited from the occasion, not I. We were—simply quits. I thought you had finally learned sense enough to play fair when you paid me the agreed twenty-five thousand for procuring you that baby boy, and I was left with no means of controlling you. That horsefaced jackass Andrew MacFarland married you knowing every, or nearly every, detail of your exceedingly interesting past. So you didn't even need to fear me. So, I repeat: Why did you set out to ruin me, Mireille?"

"The answer to that is that I didn't. And if you'll explain to me just how I'm supposed to have gone about ruining you, I'm sure I can set your mind at ease, Mary Ellen. Not that I give much of a damn whether it's at ease or not; but as a matter of principle, I've found that making enemies unnecessarily is stupid. If I ever need to make an enemy of you, I will, of course. If I ever have good reason to. But until the occasion arises—and I hope it never will—I'd much rather keep what little of your friendship I may. You're much too dangerous an enemy. I'd rather not end up full of bullet holes and lying in an alley, like French Joe. Or floating in the Bay, like Jenny Lou, who ran your house of assignation on Montgomery Street. Just how did I attempt to ruin you, Mary Ellen?"

"Well, first, you sent that long, tall, whipper-snapper of a geologist, Wilbur Phelps, to 'salt' that mine—"

"Oh dear!" Mireille said, and loosed a peal of silvery laughter. "Don't you know *anything* about gold mining, Mary Ellen?"

"Precious little. But you do, don't you? Very well. Prove to me that you and that company the five of you formed—including both your husband and your lover, which called for nerve—"

"Mary Ellen," Mireille said with icy calm, "Guillermo Kilpatrick is not my lover, and hasn't been since before I married An-drew. A fact that you know or else you wouldn't be just sitting here foaming at the mouth like a rabid setter bitch: you'd already be using a mistake, or rather a major tactical error, like that one against me. I'm absolutely faithful to my husband. The reason I am is that I love him, which you won't believe. So I'll give you another, that you will: I damned well don't want you getting your hands on something you can hold over my head, ever again. Clear?"

"Perfectly. And you're right. I know you're not dear Willy's mistress, because I know who is . . ."

"Bon petit Jésus!" Mireille moaned. "Mary Ellen, who—?"

"None of your goddamned business, my sweet! He's half Mexican, y'know. You didn't think he was going to be chastely faithful to that fat Irish sow of a wife of his, while pining away for you, forever?"

"Mary Ellen, that's a low blow. A very low blow. And it hurts. It hurts like hell. But couldn't you have waited to find out whether I've really done something to you before hitting me below the belt like that?"

"Haven't you?" Mary Ellen said.

"No. Take your first accusation: that Wilbur Phelps salted that mine —'salting' being, by definition, deliberately planting traces of gold in a place where there weren't any before, in order to be able to sell a worthless claim to idiots for a big price. It's ridiculous on the face of it. In the first place, if you knew one damned thing about gold mining, you'd know that a quartz claim can't be salted for the very simple reason that it's a visible vein of pure gold embedded in the face of quartz crystal rock. Most of the time it runs along for yards. In one known case for half a mile. So how would you go about salting it? Put two or three hundred miners to carving crevices into the rock with chisels, and then packing pure metallic gold—not dust, mind you!—into it with hammers? An expensive proposition, my dear! On top of which, since veins in quartz are almost never found aboveground, you'd need ten thousand miners, or two or three steam shovels, to move the tens, even hundreds of thousands of tons of earth and rock to get down to the type of quartz that any jackass of a miner can recognize as the right variety to have the long, spiderweb traceries of gold in it. Oh Lord, Mary Ellen, if a quartz claim could be salted, which it can't, it would cost more to do it than you could sell it for! All right, a free-dust placer can be salted, and loose rock with nuggets in it. But a vein in quartz? Just you try it!"

"I see you've studied this subject," Mary Ellen said dryly.

"I have. I study everything that interests me. Including you. What makes you tick, I mean. In the second place, beyond the fact that it can't be done, anyhow: Why should Wilbur have done a thing like that? When he found that vein at Cow Head Gulch, he was working for Robinson, Squires and Kelper. It was only after they refused to cut him in for a fair share of the profits that he quit. You don't salt a mine and then try like hell to get a partnership in, or, failing that, royalties from, the company you yourself have assigned the claim to. That would be moronic, and you know it!"

Mary Ellen Pleasant stared at her.

"Hmmn," she said; "I didn't know that detail. That Phelps tried to get a partnership, or assigned royalties, I mean. But I'll take your word for it. It's an item too easily checked for you to lie about . . ."

"Do check it. I want you to."

"All right, I will. But it will turn out to be so. You're anything but stupid, Mireille."

"Thank you. Coming from you, that's a compliment. Now, let's go on to item three. When the four of us—my husband, Wilbur Phelps, Enrique Sepúlvera and I, formed that company—Willy came in later, when we asked him to draw up the papers—"

"He did a beautiful job. That mine is yours again. Let's see how rich it makes you!"

"Cow Head Gulch is ours. A stretch of sand, cactus, and several hundred thousand tons of broken rock taken out of a hole in the desert. And the hole, itself, of course. Worth absolutely nothing. All that machinery is yours. When are you going to move it?"

"Next week. We've already found a buyer for it, thank God! A small quartz mining company who're working a profitable claim up above Sacramento, near Grass Valley, in fact. We had to take another beating to unload it, of course. But part of the deal is that they'll come after it, and move it—by coasting steamer and barges towed by river steamboat, I suspect—up to Grass Valley. Which is a relief. None of us wants to set foot in *Arroyo Cabeza de Vaca* again as long as we live. Even so, we were lucky. If we hadn't found buyers, even at less than cost, that machinery would have had to sit there and rust away . . ."

"Very well. I'm glad you could get rid of it. God knows we aren't in the market for mining machinery! Now tell me this, Mary Ellen: When you and Tom Bell bought up the majority, controlling share of Robinson, Squires and Kelper stock, did you put a notice in the newspapers telling everybody you'd done so?"

"Of course not! That's not how we operate, and you know it! Oh, Jesus! You mean that you—your company—didn't *know* we were the virtual owners of Robinson *et al?*"

"How could we have?" Mireille said very simply.

"Mireille, I hate apologizing, and it looks like I'm going to have to. Go on. You haven't quite convinced me, yet."

"Mary Ellen, we formed that company to protect the interests of two friends, Wilbur Phelps and Enrique Sepúlvera. And, yes, to make a little money if possible—not to wreck you. We didn't know that vein was going to peter out in a little over three months, so that the mine never had a ghost of a chance of showing a profit. If we had, logically we'd have made a cash deal for that ninety-nine-year lease to your company, and left you all holding the dirty end of the stick. But we didn't do that, Mary Ellen. We—Wilbur, Enrique, Willy, and I—outtalked my poor, cautious, and smart husband on that issue. Royalties would have made us all millionaires, if there had really been a mother lode down there. While the quarter of a million your people offered, split five ways, looked like chicken feed to the bunch of greedy—and stupid!—amateurs we were. So, as I said, we outvoted An-drew, thus putting ourselves in the somewhat less than delightful position of having to depend upon the success of Robinson, Squires and Kelper to make any profit at all. All right, you people lost your shirts; but we didn't make a plugged lead picayune out of the deal either. So, if that's how I got even with you, you've got nothing to worry about: I hereby swear off getting even with people for life!"

Mary Ellen Pleasant stared at Mireille. A long, slow time. Then suddenly, she bent forward and kissed the younger, smaller woman's cheek.

"Now, I do apologize. Humbly. And to prove it, I'm going to do you a favor," she said.

"You're going to tell me her name?" Mireille breathed.

"Whose name, my dear?"

"Le nom de la petite maîtresse de Willy," Mireille said.

"And have you go to jail for mayhem—or even murder? Not on your life, Mireille! Andy needs you. Your children do. You've a first-class brain in that head of yours. Only, so far you've always let your hot little tail broil said brains away. You've got to stop that, child . . ."

"I know. I mean to. Then what favor are you going to do me, Mary Ellen?"

"You've heard of the Comstock Lode, haven't you?"

"Who hasn't? That perfect mountain of silver they found near Virginia City, Nevada, in fifty-nine."

"Yes. Only Virginia City didn't exist then. The lode came first, then the city. All right. When Ophir mining stock comes on the market, buy all you can afford to. Hold it. I'll tell you when to sell. Then, next year, with your profits, invest in the California Steam Navigation Company."

"Sure there'll be profits, Mary Ellen?"

"If you sell when I tell you to, I guarantee it. I'm putting the last fifty thousand I've got to my name in that stock, Mireille," Mary Ellen Pleasant said.

When Mireille got back home that noon, she found Blossom gray-faced and shaking. She had a little blue envelope in her fat, black hand.

"Hit's—a telegram, ma'am!" she moaned. "And hit was sont from San José. Telegraph boy told me that. And Mr. Andrew is down there, him—wit' Mr. Wilbur Phelps. Oh, Lawdy, effen somethin's done happen to that there good kind sweet man o' yourn, us is ruint!"

"Give me that telegram, Blossom!" Mireille said.

She took it, tore it open, read:

GET WILLY, ENRIQUE. COME RANCHO AT ONCE. GREAT NEWS. LOVE, ANDY.

"He's all right, Blossom. In fact, it seems to be good news. Come, you'll have to help me pack a valise. And a carpetbag. I've got to go down there. But first go get James and John. Tell them to come here. I need both of them right now," Mireille said.

"We should have used my landau. It's much more comfortable than this grubby old stagecoach!" Mireille fumed.

"Don't be silly, Mirla!" Willy said. "It's all of fifty miles to San José. The stagecoach changes horses every ten miles. We'd never have been able to make this kind of speed in a private carriage, even if we killed your team. So stop grumbling, will you?"

"Let me see that telegram again, Mireille," Enrique said. "Hmm—seems quite exuberant! And we've all been over that ruddy hole in the ground two dozen times. There isn't any more gold in it. None at all. Wilbur's a first-class geologist. After that vein played out, he explored every inch of that desert country, both on my place and adjacent to it. And nothing. Swears the vein was a pure fluke. Wishes to God he'd never found it, because it's kept him tied to the *rancho* two miserable years, when he might have found a bonanza somewhere else . . ."

"Yet, now they 'ave found gold. I am very sure of it," Mireille said. "Do not look at me, Willy! You are a swine! I *hate* you!"

"*¡Madre mía de mis ojos!*" Willy groaned. "Mind telling me what's got into you *now*, Mirla?"

"As if you didn't know!" Mireille said. Then: "Oh, *merde!* I'm going to ccccry! And I sssswore I-I-I wwwwouldn't!"

Enrique and Willy both stared in perfect astonishment at the flood of tears pouring down her cheeks.

"There, there *pájara negra*," Willy crooned; "don't cry. Tell a fellow what's wrong?"

"Don't call me blackbird! I hate that nickname! I hhhate yyyyyyyou!"

"Mireille," Enrique said gently, "mind telling me what's wrong?"

"*Il est un cochon! Un très sale cochon! Il m'a trompé! Il m'a fair coucu! Il a une petite maîtresse! Je le hais! Je le déteste! Je l'abhorre!*"

Enrique threw back his head and roared with laughter.

"*¿Que pasa con esta idiota,* Enrique?" Willy said. "*¿Que esta diciendo?*"

"That you are a pig," Enrique said in English, the only language that all three of them had in common. "A very dirty pig. That you have deceived her, cuckolded her. That you have a little mistress—another one besides *her,* I gather. That she hates you. That she detests you. That she loathes you. At which point she seems to have run out of vocabulary, even in French . . ."

"Good Lord, Mirla! Who told you that?"

"*Ça ne t'importe pas de toute à toi! C'est vrai? Oui ou non?*"

"Oh, for God's sake speak English, will you? Or Spanish. No—your Spanish is awful. Who told you that?"

"None of your business! Swine! Coward! Cheat!"

"Mirla—*Molly* can call me a swine. And a coward. And a cheat. *¡Con toda la razon!* You can't."

"And why not? You're mine. You belong to me. That I don't go to bed with you anymore hasn't any importance. I can't. An-drew is—too good to me. And I—love h'm. So, I can't."

"Female logic!" Willy groaned. "So I'm supposed to be a saintly little monk with a halo around my head, while you keep old Horse's Hindquarters happy?"

"*Tu te peux couché avec* Molly. You can tumble Molly. I don't mind *that. Elle est ta femme, après toute, et—*"

"Oh, Gawd!" Willy said.

"Willy—who is she? *Ta 'tite maîtresse,* I mean?"

"That's absolutely none of your business, Mirla!"

"I'm going to find out," Mireille said, "and when I do—"

"What?" Willy said.

"I am going to kill her. I will chop her up into *viande hachée* and serve her to you for supper!"

"Hmmmn. You do that. She does taste good, come to think of it . . ."

"No! It is *you* I'm going to keeeeel! And *maintenant!* Right now!"

"Mireille," Enrique said wearily, "please behave yourself. We're in a public conveyance. Besides, if you arm a scandal, it will reach poor Andrew's ears. You don't want that, do you?"

"No. I don't want that. So I will wait until tonight to kill him. But I'm going to. *Dead,*" Mireille said.

"Mireille," Enrique said, even more wearily, "how old are you now?"

Mireille thought about that. Her brown eyes opened very wide. Dismay invaded them.

"*Mon Dieu!*" she breathed. "*J'ai vingt-neuf ans!* I am—twenty-nine! An old hag!"

"At least an adult, responsible woman. The wife of a good, even admirable man. And the mother of two fine children. Act your age, will you? The role of a seventeen-year-old wildcat is no longer becoming. If it ever was, which I doubt . . ."

"And now I hate you, too, Enrique! You 'ave broken my heart. Why did you 'ave to remind me that I belong in a wheelchair? Men! You are all hateful! All!"

"And women are all—impossible," Enrique chuckled. "Without notable exception. I sometimes think that that is nature's cruelest paradox. . . ."

"A—paradox?" Mireille said sullenly.

"That we can live neither with nor without you," Enrique said.

When they drove up to the *casa grande* in the surrey they had rented in San José where the stagecoach had left them, Mireille, Willy, and Enrique found Andrew MacFarland and Wilbur Phelps as drunk as a pair of Scotch lairds, with their clothes absolutely ruined—torn in places, burnt through in others, and covered with soot. Their faces, hands, and even their hair were plastered with it too, so that they looked like a pair of dancing, grimacing pseudo-Negroes in a minstrel show. The only thing they lacked was a banjo to pick.

Whereupon Mireille immediately became a *wife.*

"An-drew!" she shrilled. "Look at you! You—you're feeeeelthy! And what's more—you're *drunk!* Keep away from meeee! Don't touch meeee! Don't—"

To which her darling An-drew paid no attention at all. He clasped her in his arms, effectively ruining her smart traveling dress, kissed her a dozen times, thus adding her to the minstrel troupe by thickly sooting up her face as well, picked her up, whirled her around and around, and yelled:

"We're rich, honey! Rich!"

"Lord, Andy!" Enrique said. "I must say you've surprised me! I thought you were a teetotaler—and just about the least demonstrative man I ever met. Mind telling me what this is all about?"

"Enrique, we're rich!" Andy roared. "Hell, man, we're millionaires! And if that isn't worth getting drunk over for once in my life, damned if I know what is!"

"All right, all right," Willy said; "calm down, you two. Wilbur, you swore there wasn't an ounce of gold to be found anywhere within miles of here—"

"There isn't," Wilbur Phelps said owlishly, and took another pull on the huge bottle of whiskey he had in his hand. "Wanna drink, Willy?"

"Weeeeel-burrrr!" Mireille shrieked. "You give me that bottle!"

"Naw you don't, Meerayee honey," Wilbur gurgled happily, " 'cause you'll bust it sure as old hell. And this here's the only bottle o' panther's pee left this side o' San José!"

"Why, Weeel-burrr," Mireille cried, "haven't you any respect for—a lady?"

" 'Scuse me, honey," Wilbur said contritely. "Meant to say rattle-snake's milk, 'deed I did! How's about it, Willy?"

"Don't mind if I do," Willy grinned, and put out his hand for the bottle.

"Willy! If you drink that vile stuff, I'm going to hit you! So help me I will!" Mireille said.

"Now I see where Claire gets her disposition from," Andrew groaned. "Look, honey, maybe you've got a sort of semi-legal right to henpeck me, but leave the other fellows in peace, will you?"

"I will not! This is *my* company. I'm the *boss*. So all of you stop drinking that coffin varnish before you get too drunk to explain to me what this is all about!" Mireille said.

"C'mon into the kitchen and I'll show you," Wilbur said.

They all trooped into the kitchen of the *casa grande*. It was a mess, too. Hunks of an oily-looking black rock, evidently broken with a sledge-hammer, were scattered all over the table and the floor. The walls and the ceiling were covered with soot. On the big kitchen range stood half a dozen pots and pans filled with a black sludge. One glance at them told Mireille they were ruined forever.

"Men!" she snorted. "Must you always make such a *mess* out of every-thing?"

"Yes'm," Wilbur crowed; "we've plumb got to. Part of our ani-mule natures! Hold out your hand, Mireille! No, not like that. Palm up! Now close your eyes . . ."

Mireille, being Mireille, peeked. So she saw him take down from a shelf a flask that was filled with what looked like dirty silver. But when he poured a little of it into her palm, she found to her astonishment that it was neither dust, nuggets, nor ore, but a liquid. A surprisingly heavy liquid, thick and viscous. When she tilted her hand a little, it formed itself into balls, and rolled.

"What is it?" she whispered.

"Quicksilver!" Wilbur said triumphantly.

"Good Lord!" Enrique gasped. "And I never thought of telling you to look for *that!* Gold on the brain, I suppose. Wilbur, you'll have to forgive me! Rancho Larios, owned by Fossat, has been known to have quicksilver on it since colonial times. And it's the one next to here. It's been found on the Berreyesa place as well, though in smaller quantities. Juan Castillero got a grant from the Mexican Government to work the mine on the Fossat place—and then the lawsuits started. Meantime, Alta California became part of the U.S.A. Knowing that had ended his last chance of winning before the courts, Castillero sold out to a couple of gringos named Laurence and Edgeston. And since the Fossat land grant is almost as good as mine is, and they were Americanos on top of it, the new owners won their case. Sold out three months ago to a New York and Pennsylvania company for one million, seven hundred and fifty thousand dollars . . ."

"They got cheated," Wilbur Phelps said flatly. "This mine, Enrique, is worth God knows how many millions of dollars. But don't make *me* the hero of the piece! It was Andy, here, who found it . . ."

"I did not!" Andrew spluttered. "I merely pointed out to you that the rocks—"

"Taken out of that dead-as-a-doornail gold mine were *black.* And they ought to have been red or brown the way mesa, tableland desert rocks always are. So I picked one of 'em up. And it was too heavy—at least four times as heavy as a normal rock should have been. So I said to myself, 'Shit!'—'Scuse me, honey!—'It's probably lead.' But then the voice of experience whispered in my ear: 'Try it and see!'

"So we broke off some chunks and crushed 'em by hand," Andrew said. "Cooked the sludge on the stove. And quicksilver—mercury—bubbled out. That's the story. Except, even dirty as I am, I want to offer Willy my hand. He's the bloke who really saved our necks!"

"Me? How the hell did I—" Willy began.

"That clause—that lovely, sweet, beautiful reversion to us in case of bankruptcy or withdrawal on the part of Robinson *et al.* So now, thanks entirely to you, Willy Kilpatrick, we're the owners of the richest mine, bar none, in California. Our title's unquestionable. Of course, we'll have to dicker with 'em for that mining machinery that we'll damn well need . . ."

"An-drew," Mireille said; "they've already sold it."

"They have? But it was still there yesterday, honey. Wilbur and I saw—"

"I know," she said; "the new owners will come for it next week."

Her husband stared at her in total perplexity. But living with her had both sharpened his wits and speeded up his thought processes.

"Mireille—" he said sadly, "how on earth did you know that?"

"Mary Ellen Pleasant told me. She sent for me to give me a piece of her evil mind because she thought we—or I, anyhow—had tricked her into investing in a worthless company."

"Mireille—" Andrew said.

"An-drew darling, please don't make me try to explain why she'd think a thing like that. It's too long and complicated, and we haven't the time to waste right now. Let me explain to you at home, alone. Please? Right now I want you—all of you—to promise me one thing: that we'll all keep out of sight and let that new company take the machinery away. Because if we don't, if we offer to buy it from them, Tom Bell, Mary Ellen Pleasant, and Ben Holladay will know at once that we're planning to reopen the mine. And the minute they get an idea of what it's worth, they'll tie us up in lawsuits for years. Maybe with Holladay behind 'em to buy the judge and jury, we might even lose. The best thing we can do is to keep as quiet as a bunch of little mice for about a month or two, and then get our equipment from somebody else. Bring it ashore on the east shore of the Bay, somewhere below Oakland. Have wagon trains there to meet it, and haul it down that side to here. And not through San José, either. We ought to have our mine in operation at least a year, and to have made enough money to fight those pirates when they come screeeeeeaming down upon us claiming that we've cheated them, before anybody finds it out. Once this new company moves the machinery out —they're operating way up around Grass Valley—it isn't going to occur to anybody to come poking around down here. Specially if we don't throw money around in San Francisco, and go on looking worried and downcast and ruined, sort of—for a year. But don't let's attract their attention and get ourselves hooked into a legal battle before we're prepared to fight, and have enough cash on hand to win . . ."

Enrique Sepúlvera stared at her.

"Mireille, I apologize," he said.

"For what, Enrique dear?"

"For accusing you of acting like a seventeen-year-old. You're not. You're at least a thousand. Gentlemen, she's absolutely right. We simply cannot afford to get tied up in a lawsuit at this juncture. That we'd probably win it is immaterial and irrelevant. Win or lose, we haven't the time—or the money—to spare."

"Then it's agreed we follow my devious little genius of a wife's exceedingly devious plan?" Andy growled.

They looked at one another, nodded solemnly.

"Unanimously!" Willy said.

"Willy," Mireille said then, "can you borrow a quarter of a million through—or from—your father-in-law? That's how much we'll need to get started . . ."

"Lord, Mirla—" Willy said.

"I'll put up my properties as security. Including—" she flashed her wicked, gamine's grin, "two or three of the best little whorehouses in San Francisco . . ."

"Mireille, for God's sake!" Andrew thundered.

"I'm only telling the truth, darling!" she purred. "You started your nice, chaste, honorable Scotch-Presbyterian business on the profits of the flesh-peddling trade. Willy, I know you're on the outs with Ross Kinnan, over the miserable way you treat his daughter. So—make up with Molly. Get rid of *ta 'tite maîtresse.* Be a perfect angel—for a year. After that you'll have enough to acquire yourself a harem—and my permission to do so, too . . ."

"Your—permission?" Willy croaked.

"Yes. You see, I've decided not to shoot you tonight, or any other. To let you be. I'm going to be—*une grande dame,* from here on in. A very great lady. So I have to start working at it right now."

Andrew MacFarland stared at his wife, become at that moment all his own. Though he didn't know that then.

"Mireille honey, you don't have to," he said fondly.

"I don't have to—what, An-drew darling?"

"Start working at being a great lady."

"And why not, *mon vieux chou?*"

"Because you were *born* one," Andrew MacFarland said.

17

WHEN THE ANDREW MACFARLANDS CAME BACK FROM EUROPE IN
the spring of 1876, after an extended stay both in England and on the
Continent, every newspaper in San Francisco printed the news on its
front page. "City's Wealthiest Family Back From Abroad!" the headlines
blared. "Stay to Be Permanent, Quicksilver Tycoon Andy MacFarland
Declares!"

After reading that much plain, if not bloody, outrageous nonsense,
Mireille took her lorgnette down from before her eyes. She still refused
to wear the spectacles that she badly needed. Andy didn't blame her for
that. In 1876 it had occurred to nobody to apply the laws of aesthetic
styling to eyeglasses and their frames, so spectacles for men and women
alike were still appallingly hideous. But Mireille's smart, Paris-made lor-
gnettes—of which she had an even dozen, from plain ones for morning
and afternoon use to increasingly ornate ones, some of them with solid-
gold or even jeweled frames to be employed when she and Andy went to
receptions, supper parties, or the theater—served her well enough. For
the theater, of course, she was forced to carry two pairs: a normal one for
reading the programs, and a very special pair of quite high-powered
binoculars, mounted lorgnette-style. Most people assumed these were
ordinary opera glasses, but they weren't. If they had been as low-powered
as opera glasses usually are, Mireille wouldn't have been able to see even
the stage.

"Andy," she said worriedly, "d'you think they'll let us live in peace?"

Andrew MacFarland took off his own pince-nez, and rubbed the
bridge of his nose where that thrice-bedamned style of spectacles with
their spring-loaded clip, pinched, so that he, like all the businessmen who
wore them, had that part of his nose forever red and sore. At fifty-two
years of age he had got stout, but not excessively so, and it became him.

He looked important, imposing, almost a caricature of the general public's concept of a millionaire. Of course he was a millionaire, many times over, but he most certainly was not the richest man in San Francisco. Within walking distance of his imposing—and ugly—Victorian Gothic mansion on Nob Hill were the even more imposing—and far, far uglier —palaces of men like Leland Stanford, Charles Crocker, Collis P. Huntington, Mark Hopkins, James Flood, William S. O'Brien, John W. Mackay, James G. Fair, and William C. Ralston, most of whom could have matched every dollar Andy had to his name with two or three of their own, except the first four on that list, the celebrated "Big Four" of Central Pacific's transcontinental railroad building fame, whose fortunes actually topped Andy's modest wealth by more than a hundred to one.

One advantage, and only that one, did Andrew MacFarland have over his fellow plutocrats: He was going to *stay* rich. His instinct for sound business practice was the closest thing to genius he possessed, and his caution was monumental. The only serious fight that he and Mireille had had in their now close to twenty years of married life took place when he discovered that she had invested her inheritance from Judge Alain Curtwright, plus all she had saved of her considerable earnings from her Barbary Coast properties, in the Ophir Mining Company's stock, and the bonds of the California Steam Navigation Company. He didn't know, of course, that Mireille had an inside tip about both distinctly shady operations from Mary Ellen Pleasant. And he was quite right to be furious, because Mireille came close to losing her frilly lace underwear on that gamble. Madame Pleasant, seething with rage over what she believed had been the foulest of tricks on Mireille's part—the absolutely accidental exclusion of her and her partners Thomas Bell and Ben Holladay from sharing in the millions that MacFarland, Sepúlvera, Phelps, and Kilpatrick made out of the richest quicksilver mine in California's history—deliberately did not tell Mireille when to sell the stocks that she had advised her to buy and that Mireille, following her counsel, actually had bought—at a pittance. The only reason Mireille didn't find herself clad in that barrel with both ends knocked out of it which was so dear to the newspaper cartoonists of the day was that she was far too smart to trust Mary Ellen Pleasant. Therefore she got her double-agent Black spies, James and John Swithers, to pass out some nice-sized greenbacks among the Black waiters at one of Madame Pleasant's supper clubs where most of San Francisco's financial wizards dined. The minute that she found out that Tom Bell—for Mary Ellen, as usual, kept completely out of sight—was selling, she dumped her stocks. She made a clear profit of nine hundred fifty thousand, five hundred seventy-six dollars and twenty-two cents, thus giving rise to the only outright lie Andrew Mac-Farland is known to have told in all his life. He boasted to his friends at the Entrepreneurs' Club—called by the vulgar the Tycoons' Club, and by the more vulgar still the Stay Outa Here If You Ain't Filthy Rich Club—that his little genius of a wife had made herself a cool million behind his back. Which, considering the scale of figures they'd all become accustomed to juggling by then, was a white lie that could be justly labeled tiny.

But he'd roared at Mireille like an angry bull when he found out that she'd engaged in a stock market operation as crooked and as risky as that one had been, and the fact that she'd pulled it off successfully didn't impress him at all. So furious was he that he threatened to spank her bottom if she ever did a thing like that again without consulting him.

Mireille immediately shot back at him, "You wouldn't dare!"

Whereupon dear Andy—moved perhaps by a nineteen years' accumulation of small outrages on his darling wife's part—threw her down across his knees, yanked up her skirt, petticoat, whalebone-and-tape bustle, and vigorously fanned her dainty little fundament, which was, of course, clad in a pair of knee-length embroidered and lace-trimmed drawers. But since that saucy garment was made of an elaborate combination of silk, all but transparent muslin, and sheer nainsook, it provided her no protection at all.

Mireille, of course, tearfully swore she was going to leave him, get a divorce, take the children, move back to Paris to live, and marry herself a French nobleman. But Andy, who knew her very well by then, grunted, "I'll send Otto Eiselberg to draw up the papers. Who d'you want to represent you? Willy?"

Before his utterly infuriating display of calm, Mireille at once changed her mind about getting a divorce. She was, she declared in accents Bernhardt might well have envied, going to cut her throat with his own razor, since he obviously didn't love her anymore.

"It's in the cabinet over my washstand," Andrew drawled. "Lean over the bathtub, will you? Blossom's getting too old and too fat to have to clean up that much of a mess . . ."

Then he calmly put on his top hat and walked out of there.

That night Mireille climbed into his bed and made up with him in absolutely first-class style. And he never had any serious trouble out of her again. What's more, she finally did what he had been urging her to do for years: she sold her Barbary Coast holdings, including not only French Em's, but two other brothels described by the *Morning Call* as "The three best little whorehouses on the entire West Coast," as well as two dozen other more or less disreputable establishments that had paid her magnificently reputable rent. Which, as things turned out after their return from Europe, proved to have been a very smart move indeed.

"An-drew, I asked you a question!" she said angrily. "D'you think they'll leave us in peace?"

Andy polished the glasses of his pince-nez as he thought about that. It was this one trait of his that drove Mireille absolutely wild. He never answered a question without thinking about it first. As a result, he never said a foolish or an impulsive thing, and almost never made even a slight, not to mention a serious, business mistake. Which—though in her calmer moments she appreciated the advantages of this very wise trait of his—most of the time drove her straight up the nearest wall.

"I take it that by 'they' you mean Bell, Holladay, and Mammy Pleasant?" he said finally. "Yes, I'm quite sure they will. In the first place, Ben Holladay and Mary Ellen Pleasant are done for, financially. Holladay dropped all the money he made when he dumped his stagecoach lines off on Wells Fargo just before the transcontinental railroad was finished. Why Wells Fargo let themselves get sucked in like that, only God in His infinite wisdom will ever know. . . ."

"You wouldn't have made a mistake like that, Andrew," Mireille said with genuinely wifely admiration.

"No, I don't think I would have. But as I was saying, he and Mary Ellen Pleasant lost their shirts in the Oregon and California Railroad debacle during the Panic two years ago. Bell, who's a lot smarter, only dropped about twenty thousand or so—"

"But Tom Bell's under her thumb. She's got him hooked, An-drew. She's dangling Teresa Percy in front of him as one dangles a worm in front of a fish . . ."

"But who is Teresa Percy?" Andrew said.

"A whore. An ex-whore now. She used to hustle her little bustle in a Division Street brothel. After that—in French Em's. But Mary Ellen's got her installed in that palace she's built at 1661 Octavia Street. You've heard of it, haven't you?"

"Who hasn't? But listen, honey, I wish that kind of thing didn't interest you so much!"

"It doesn't, An-drew! I'm only trying to protect my children, myself, and you. Mary Ellen Pleasant hates me. She thinks I deliberately cheated her out of sharing in the *Arroyo Cabeza de Vaca* bonanza. And I didn't. Until you and Wilbur explained it to me, I didn't even know what quicksilver was . . ."

"Do you now?" Andy teased her solemnly.

"Yes. It's mercury. And it's used in thermometers, and barometers, and all sorts of scientific instruments, and in medicine, too. I used to take pills made out of it to keep from catching something awful when I was bad. And—"

"Mireille, *will* you forget that, please?"

"I wish I could. Maybe I could sleep nights, then. Anyhow, Teresa's—beautiful. Blond. Violet-blue eyes, with that 'Poor little me, won't you come and save me, you big strong, handsome man, you!' expression in them. So Mary Ellen is using her to hook Tom Bell, and—"

"Well, she hasn't yet. Bell told me personally that he wouldn't trust that high yellow witch as far as he could throw her."

"She'll hook him. A girl as beautiful as Teresa is just too much for male human nature to resist. D'you know, this will make four times that Mary Ellen has taken girls out of whorehouses, brought in music teachers, diction teachers, language teachers—all kinds of damned teachers—to make imitation ladies out of 'em, and then married them off to rich cretins? Blackmail's her specialty. And—murder. She's killed—or had killed—six or eight people to my knowledge. Only, who can prove it? That's why I'm so scared of her, An-drew!"

"Don't be. She'd have to come by me," Andy said grimly.

"I know. But she won't. She'll strike at me through my children—and wild as they are, she'll be able to do that with the greatest of ease. . . . Although I also think that with Holladay tied up in Oregon, she just might put Tom Bell up to doing something to us that—"

"Quit worrying. He won't. He's become a minority partner of ours, y'know—"

"Of ours!" Mireille shrieked. *"Oh, bon Dieu! Sauvez le qui peut!"*

"Thanks to your chum Willy. I told that damned fool not to take a flyer on those Comstock Lode stocks. But he and Enrique, being Mexicans, and with gambling in their blood, lost their shirts."

"Now you're not being fair, An-drew. So did Wilbur Phelps—or dear Weeeel-burrr, as he swears I call him . . ."

"You do. And you're right. That's why he had to take that job with the Titan Copper Mining Corporation down in Bolivia. Had a letter from him the other day. He's doing fine down there. They've made him a vice-president. As he's married a lovely Bolivian señorita, which means he's got over you at last, my sweet!"

"Oh, *merde!* Now I'm jealous! My men aren't supposed to get over me. They're honor-bound to pine quite away of unrequited love. That's what I should do to you—unrequite you a little. Then you wouldn't be so fat and sassy! But, An-drew, tell me: Are Willy and Enrique in serious difficulties?"

"No. I rode to their rescue like the U.S. Cavalry. Loaned them both enough so they wouldn't have to sell all their shares in Cow Head Gulch Mining Corporation. After pinning their ears back for them in fine style on the supreme un-wisdom of going short on margin in an effort to make a killing. But they had to cough up an awful lot. And, as I was saying, Thomas Frederick Bell bought the shares they had to dump. He also bought a controlling interest in the Fossat mine. Now people are calling him 'The Quicksilver King,' and Mary Ellen Pleasant is in debt to him up to her eyebrows. So he's got the whip hand, Mireille dearest. Besides, he's quite aware of her tricks."

"She'll still take him. Mary Ellen's the smartest human being alive. And the wickedest!" Mireille said.

Which, before another three whole months were out, turned out to be the understatement of the year.

Blossom came into Mireille's bedroom just before noon, which was the earliest Mireille ever woke up to have her breakfast, desperately trying to keep her tears from dripping into the coffee pot or the cream pitcher she bore on a tray between her two fat black hands.

"Nom d'un nom!" Mireille said. "What is wrong with you now, Blossom?"

Blossom put the breakfast tray down across Mireille's lap.

"Lemme shet th' do' first, ma'am!" she moaned. "Doan reckon neither you nor me would want somebody t'hear what we'uns is got to talk about now . . ."

"Do it then," Mireille said.

Blossom closed the bedroom door. Came back to the bedside, faced Mireille. Folded her massive arms across her voluminous breasts.

"Lawdy, ma'am, I jes' doan know where'n how t'start tellin' you this—"

"At the beginning," Mireille said.

"Well, ma'am—hit's our chillun. Yours'n mine. My Periwinkle is—bigged—"

"Is whaaaat?" Mireille said.

"Bigged. In th' fambly way. 'N' she say that young mister Stan is her baby's pappy . . ."

"Nom d'un nom d'un sale cochon!" Mireille exploded. She didn't think for a moment that Periwinkle—a lovely, lithe, though markedly Negroid *mulata* of the type that Blacks called a "high brown," with

coppery skin, woolly hair, and the most sensual pair of soft, thick lips Mireille had ever seen on a human face—was lying. She knew her darling Stanford much too well for that.

"Where is he? Blossom, you go get me that young scamp right now!"

"No'm. Jes' you hol' on a minute, ma'am. You kin give him a dressin'-down later on. Reckon right now, you 'n' me as grownup wimmenfolks—'n' frens, 'cause Lawd knows you's always treated me mighty decent, Miz Mireille—better figger out what to do. That fool chile o' mine is talkin' 'bout goin' to Mary Ellen Pleasant. 'N' I doan' want her to. That there yaller nigger woman is th' evilest critter th' Devil ever blew th' breath o' life into, 'cause you 'n' me both know the Good Lawd ain't never had nothin' t' do wit' makin' her—"

"There you're right," Mireille said. "But why on earth does Peri want to go to her, in God's name?"

"You knows. Either Mary Ellen'll decide to let that wicked ol' murderin' quack of a baby snatcher Joe Gammon git rid o' th' po' un-born critter befo' Peri starts showin' for real, or she'll keep my chile over theah in 'Th' House o' Evil'—tha's whut us cullud folks call that place she done built on Octavia Street—till it's born. Then effen hit's real pretty 'n' brightskin, and a gal chile, Mary Ellen will bring it up 'n' use it to hook some real rich man like she's done done two dozen times now. Fer instance, she brung that there swishy-tail white gal Sarah Althea Hill all the way from Missouri, a li'l after they finish building th' railroad, to catch Mr. William Sharon. 'N' she's using that other li'l white ho, Teresa Percy, to tie Mr. Bell up. Everybody know that . . ."

"But if the child is *not* pretty and light enough to pass?" Mireille said grimly. "If it's a boy—and dark, say?"

"They'll smother hit. They's done kilt Lawd knows how many po' li'l single gals' babies already, y'knows. 'N' I doan want that, ma'am. Whichever way hit looks, hit's my grandchile. And—beggin' yo' pardon, ma'am—hit's yourn."

Mireille shuddered a little, involuntarily. 'I am forty-one years old,' she thought. 'People say I look twenty-seven—thirty, at most. They're lying. I look—thirty-five. Maybe even—forty. And now I'm going to become *une grand-mère*. And of *un petit négrillon*. A little nigger. *Bon Dieu*—let it look *pour le moins comme* Jasmine. *Comme* Mary Ellen *même. Ah non! Ça non!* I shouldn't like anyone kin to me to even look like her!'

Then it came to her that since Stanford wasn't really her son, the poor little off-colored bastard wouldn't really have one drop of her blood in its veins. Which was scant comfort. Or none at all.

"What d'you think we ought to do, Blossom?" she said.

"Ain't much we *kin* do, ma'am. Effen our chillun was both cullud, or both white, us could marry 'em up together, 'n' that would be that. But there ain't a state in this heah whole United States where cullud marryin' white ain't ag'in th' law. I axed yo' fren' lawyer Kilpatrick 'bout that, 'n' he tol' me . . ."

'Thank God for that much!' Mireille thought. She said sharply, "Did you tell him why you wanted that information?"

"Yes'm. But not too much. I only tol' him a young white fella done gone 'n' got my Periwinkle in trouble. I didn't tell him th' young white fella's *name* . . ."

"That was clever of you, Blossom. So—the problem is, as I see it, how to persuade Periwinkle not to compound her error by committing a crime, or how to prevent her from doing so. I don't believe in abortion. And much less in murdering babies after they get here. Besides, considering how light-complexioned your late husband was, this child may look very much the way—Jasmine does, for instance . . ."

" 'N' effen she *do*, us gotta make damn sho' Mary Ellen Pleasant don't git her hands on her. Make her happier'n ol' hell to tie up a chile that close to you, ma'am, whether hit be part cullud or no . . ."

"That's the evil truth," Mireille sighed. "Perhaps I'd better call attorney Kilpatrick, or better still, attorney Eiselberg in and ask him—"

"No'm. That ain't rightly necessary, ma'am. I done sort o' felt lawyer Kilpatrick out on that subject 'n' he say we oughta ax th' chile's pappy to settle a little money on hit fer hits support. So much every month. 'N' to guarantee hits education effen hit wanta go t' school . . ."

Mireille thought about that.

"That seems to me only fair, Blossom," she said.

"Lawyer Kilpatrick says ain't no way we kin force th' oh-fen-din party to ak-nowledge th' baby, give hit he name, what wit' him being white, him. But he did say that effen th' pappy is a goodhearted sort o' fella, he might do that on he own, we was to ax him to, mighty kindly. 'N'—'n' put sumpin' by fer hit in he will, mebbe . . ."

'You,' Mireille thought, 'are nobody's fool, are you, Blossom? And Stan would do it, being goodhearted—and softheaded—to a fault. So I've got to prevent that. I'll be damned if I want this little Black bastard going around calling himself either Curtwright or MacFarland!'

She said, "Tell you what, Blossom: Let's compromise on that point. There's no reason why my husband should have to bear the offense of having *his* entirely honorable name worn by an illegitimate child, for whom he is certainly not responsible . . ."

"Well, ma'am, mebbe if he woulda whupped mister Stan's li'l behind or him a sight mo' frequent when he was a boy—"

"And maybe not," Mireille sighed. "Besides, you have to admit that Stan was a relatively good child. It was Claire, who drove us all crazy . . ."

" 'N' still do!" Blossom snorted. "Lawdy! Wild 'n' mean as that child be, I doan know, ma'am—I jes' doan know . . ."

"Nor I," Mireille said sadly. "Blossom—tell you what: I'll agree to the payment of, say, fifty dollars a month—to *you*, not to Periwinkle, who's already proved she's not to be trusted!—for the support of the child. I'll send it to school, through high school or even college, if it has brains enough to take advantage of higher education. And I'll mention it in *my* will to the extent of ten thouand dollars, say. But only if you'll consent to keep the identity of its father quiet. I'm only trying to protect my household from unnecessary scandal. Will you agree to that?"

Blossom thought about that. But she, too, had summered and wintered with San Francisco's financial elite by then.

"I says fair enuff, ma'am—effen you'll give me a copy o' that there las' will 'n' testament to keep my own self. Signed by you 'n' th' witnesses to hit. Oh, no, ma'am! I trusts *you*. But I'se a cullud woman, me. S'posin' sumpin' was to happen to you? Course you's still real young, but anybody kin have a accident, cain't they? 'N' effen I doan have nothin' to *prove* you done gone 'n' done that fer my—*our*—grandchile, who's gonna take a po' ol' grayheaded Black mammy's word fer hit?"

Mireille stared at her. Said, finally: "Unfortunately, you're quite right. I'll have attorney Eiselberg draw up a new codicil to my will tomorrow. Now go find me that young rapscallion!"

"Miz Mireille, ma'am, I doan think he come home yet. 'Cause he ain't been down in th' kitchen talkin' to Duck Soup like he do every morning . . ."

Duck Soup was, of course, the MacFarlands' Chinese cook. Like most of the great San Francisco families by then, they had adopted the custom of hiring Orientals as servants, because since the Central Pacific had been completed in 1869 and their services were no longer required as track-laying coolies, there simply were more Chinese than any other minority ethnic group available to take the ever increasing number of jobs as domestic servants being offered by San Francisco's growing class of authentic plutocrats in their opulent mansions.

Duck Soup's name wasn't Duck Soup, naturally, but something more like Xiaop Siu. The name he was known by in the MacFarland household was very simply a prime example of young Stanford MacFarland's somewhat heavy-handed humor. And he was an excellent cook, preparing tasty Chinese dishes—among which, be it said, was *not* Chop Suey, which wouldn't be invented until 1894, and in New York City at that—and sometimes surprising variations upon European ones, with equal dexterity.

But now the obvious question finally occurred to Mireille, so she asked Blossom, "What on earth does Stan find to talk about with Duck Soup *every* morning?"

"He takin' lessons, ma'am. He payin' Duck Soup five dollars a week to teach him to talk Chinee."

"Bon Dieu! Blossom, is there any conceivable reason that Stan should need or even *want* to speak Chinese?"

"Yes'm. He say hit's fer he scientific reee-search. Him 'n' that crowd o' rich young fellas he hang out wit', not havin' nothing t'do—'A idle brain is th' Devil's workshop,' my momma useta say—is got a bet goin'. Th' first one of 'em who finds a Chinee gal who really *is* built different—you knows, ma'am—wit' her—her *thing* runnin' crosswise twixt her laigs 'stid o' straight up 'n' down like us nachel wimmens' is—wins a thousand dollars. 'N' since he ain't fool enough to try to cundangle *all* th' Chinee slave gal hos they is in San Francisco, he figgered he could cut th' number down to a size he could manage 'n' is got th' strength fer by axin 'em first . . ."

"I weeel keel heeem!" Mireille shrieked; "I really weel, Blossom!"

"Naw you won't, ma'am," Blossom chuckled. "That there boy is purely th' apple of your eye, 'n' you knows it . . ."

Mireille made a disdainful gesture toward her breakfast.

"Take it away, Blossom. I just don't feel like eating, now," she said.

While she waited for the water for her bath to heat (a process slightly improved over the preceding twenty years, but still an unholy nuisance) she heard Stanford's pleasant tenor crooning as he came up the stairs:

> "The boat lies high, the boat lies low;
> She lies high and dry
> On the Oh - hi - O!"

At which Mireille leaped from her bed, ran to her armoire, searched desperately amid the dozens and dozens of negligées she had in it until she found one that wasn't sinfully transparent, and slipped it around the slender form that still caused many a San Franciscan, in that day before the halftone and rotogravure processes had made the faces of the rich and the famous familiar to everybody, to mistake her and her daughter

Claire for sisters. She tied it tightly around her and sallied forth to have it out with Stan.

But before she got to his room at the far end of the hall, she had to pass the door of Claire's boudoir. As she did so, she came to a sudden halt. Stood there with her pert, upturned nose twitching. Then whispering, nasally, sibilantly, *"Nom d'un nom d'un nom!"* she clasped the ornate knob of Claire's bedroom's door, twisted it fiercely, and charged into her daughter's perfumed nest like Custer after a tribe of Sioux.

Clad in a negligée that was, if anything, even more sinfully transparent than the ones her mother delighted in, Claire lay propped up by a small, soft mountain of pillows on her bed. Her hair, which an admiring journalist, who wrote for a yellow journal that wasn't quite the worst of the city's abominable scandal sheets, had already described as "the eighth wonder of the world!", hung loose about her shoulders, extending down below even her hips, spread out over the pale pink satin sheets in a cloud that was not the dictionary definition of black, the absence of light; because its luxuriant sheen and glossy highlights were black's opposite, they were actually brilliant. At her mother's entry, Claire's curiously sullen mouth, which robbed her smooth young face of a little of what would have been almost perfect beauty, and which was but one of the several attributes she possessed that had driven every male San Franciscan who had ever so much as caught a single glimpse of her, up to senior citizens approaching the age when wheelchairs would become their normal means of locomotion, absolutely insane, curled into, of all smiles, the most mocking possible.

As myopic as Mireille was, she didn't see, or couldn't make out, the object whose pungent stink had caused her to cease and desist from going after Stan—on the morally unfair but pragmatically exact Victorian estimation that, within the bonds of any respectable family, male sinfulness was likely to be far less disastrous in its effects than its female counterpart always is—and turn her attention toward her daughter. So, with cool insolence, Claire enlightened her.

From the saucer that served her as an ashtray, she picked up the cigarette she had been smoking, stuck it in one corner of that sullen, sensual mouth of hers, inhaled deeply and, still trailing blue-gray streamers of not exactly fragrant smoke from her exquisitely formed nostrils, drawled:

"Oh, hello, Maman. What's exercising your sweet, lovable disposition this morning?"

Mireille didn't bother to answer her. In two swift strides she crossed to the bed and jerked that cigarette out of Claire's mouth. As it tore free, the end of it stuck to that pouting, maddeningly provocative lower lip and took a sizable strip of skin with it, causing a bright and abundant stream of blood to gush down that shapely chin.

"I will not," Mireille said with terrible quiet, "have you behaving like a whore, Claire!"

Claire picked up the napkin off the breakfast tray that sat, its contents practically untouched as usual, on the night table beside the bed, and pressed it against her torn mouth.

"Then why are you and Daddy always trying to sell me?" she said with wicked calm.

"*Nom d'un nom d'un—*" Mireille began.

"*D'une petite chienne,*" Claire finished for her, mockingly. "You really should try to curb that vile temper of yours, Maman. It's—tiresome. To make a brilliant marriage, to a filthy rich man, has much to recommend it, I suppose. But only if one loves the man in question. If one doesn't, it's still whoring—and rather less honest than being paid by the tumble, it seems to me . . ."

"*Bon petit Jésus!*" Mireille whispered prayerfully.

"Maman, look in my commode and give me a piece of cotton, will you? Or else I'll bleed all over these lovely sheets. And my mirror. I want to see what a mess you've made of my mouth. Good thing Daddy's so calm. Any other man would have beaten you to death by now, the way you're always going off like a string of Chinese firecrackers . . ."

"Claire, I just don't understand you!" Mireille fumed. "Why you should want to make your breath stink, and ruin your health with those vile-smelling, vulgar things I cannot possibly imagine. *No* lady smokes, y'know!"

"Item one," Claire said as she took the mirror and the little tuft of cotton from her mother's hands, "*you* don't have to kiss me, not on the mouth, anyhow. You may save your kisses for Paquita Sepúlvera, Dr. Enrique's wife. That dear, dark, wiggling little creature is in *love* with you, Maman—the *wrong* way. D'you reciprocate? That must be—interesting. Lord, what a mess! Oh well, I can tell the boys some too ardent suitor *bit* me . . ."

"Claire, *pour l'amour du Dieu!*"

"I rather think it's your love—or the desire for it—that makes her wiggle so. Rather—disgusting, what? I'd swear she wets those horribly *démodé* underthings she wears, or at least moistens them a bit, every time she looks at you. Where was I? Oh, yes; item two, I smoke cigarettes—occasionally, when I can persuade Stan or one of his chums to buy them for me—because nobody will take me into a Chinese opium den. *That's* what I'd like to smoke. I'm told it makes you dream the loveliest dreams. . . . Which might make my life endurable, *peut-être.* . . ."

"Claire, if I *ever* hear of you entering one of those dens, I'll keeeel you!" Mireille shrieked. "I'd rather have you dead, anyhow, than a wit-less sot!"

"It's people who *drink*, not people who smoke, who become witless sots," Claire drawled, indulging herself in one of the delights of young, female existence—driving one's mother absolutely wild. "You should be more precise in your choice of words, *chère Maman.* Of course, English is not your native language, but I have to admit you speak it rather well. And, if you really don't want me to become an opium addict, you'd better stop trying to push me off on utterly impossible dullards like Ted Hanson. Incidentally, I've given him back his ring . . ."

Mireille picked up a white and gilt Louis XIV chair and carried it over to her daughter's bedside. Sat down. Stared at Claire.

"Child," she said soberly, "I haven't the faintest desire to make you marry anyone you really don't want to. I thought you liked young Han-son . . ."

"I *do* like him. Very much. Only I don't love him, *ma chère Maman.* And I am rather—fastidious, say. I cannot imagine anything more dis-gusting than having to go to bed—indulge in physical intimacies—with a person one does not love."

'There, you're right,' Mireille thought bleakly. 'You can't even imag-ine how right you are!' She said, "I won't rebuke you for using indelicate language, Claire, because you'd only start talking even more like a *poule* in order to plague me. But—for my guidance in the future, *disons-nous* —what's wrong with Theodore Hanson?"

"Several things," Claire said. "He has no brains. He makes me screeeeam with ennui, *Maman.* And he'll probably end up poor . . ."

"That last is a good reason," Mireille said. "What makes you think that, *ma fille?*"

"He's much too stupid to avoid losing his shirt when his father, old 'Bonanza Pete' Hanson, is no longer around to guide him. That's one thing. Another is that Daddy agrees with me. He says that anyone who depends upon anything as chancy as gold mining is—or any kind of mining, for that matter, even quicksilver, though Cow Head Gulch is showing no signs of running out on us, is it, *Maman?* I should hate being poor, y'know . . ."

"Scant chance of that, Claire. Your stepfather has often made to me that same remark you didn't even finish, that anyone who depends on gold mining, especially quartz vein mining, is a fool. He's never fully trusted even the quicksilver bonanza that gave us our start. So from the very beginning he made sure *Arroyo Cabeza de Vaca* could never leave us penniless—although mercury mines are generally longer-lasting than gold ones are. Those in Mexico have been in operation for centuries, I'm told."

"At the speed that Mexicans work," Claire hooted, "they ought to last forever!"

"There's some truth in that." Mireille sighed. "But, anyhow, An-drew diversified almost from the very moment that the mine at *Arroyo Cabeza de Vaca* gave him the wherewithal to do so: foundaries, steamship lines, all that land between San Francisco's present limits and the ocean that he could get his hands on, and now that's the only direction the city has left to grow. We'll never be poor, daughter mine; you may rest assured of that . . ."

"I know. The fellows say their fathers call Daddy a financial genius. If he only weren't quite so dull! How've you managed to put up with him all these years, *Maman?*"

Mireille flashed her daughter a warm, candid, woman-to-woman smile. "He is not *always* dull, *ma fille,*" she said.

"I've suspected as much," Claire said mockingly, "especially knowing you, *madame ma mère!* You're not exactly the quaint old-fashioned *bonne petite dame* who sits by the chimney and knits, y'know. So tell me: Why haven't there been any more of us, *chère Maman?*"

"That's a question only *le bon Dieu* can answer," Mireille sighed, "and one I've frequently asked Him. I should love to have had three or four more brothers and sisters for you, child—and for that idle, lecherous lout of a brother of yours. It would have been much better for both of you. You wouldn't have been spoiled rotten, then . . . But since we seem to have arrived at a true mother-daughter chat for the first time in years, tell me something, Claire: Are you—behaving yourself? I won't tell your father. I simply should like to point out to you what the— problems, and the—dangers are. You're my daughter. You've inherited my temperament. And I can easily recall—moments—when behaving myself, resisting temptation, maintaining self-control, call it what you will, was—devilishly hard . . ."

Claire smiled.

"For me, it's not, *Maman,*" she said with a little gust of complacent laughter. "Oh, I know you've probably heard that I'm an outrageous flirt, and the worst tease in San Francisco's recent history. But it's all a game to me. It's so much fun to have a host of panting males forever at my beck and call, and to make them suffer the tortures of the damned. I haven't the slightest intention, Mother dear, of throwing away the thrillingly cruel ascendency I have over them for the dubious pleasure of going to bed with one or two of them. All the more so from what I've gathered from the perfectly astonishing number of dear, frail young darlings in our set who've made that colossal error and lived to regret it, bitterly. It appears that the whole curious business is not only dangerous, but painful, messy, and—worst of all, from my point of view!—nearly always disappointing . . ."

Again Mireille smiled. But not at her daughter, this time. Instead, that slow and secret smile was inward-turning, warming itself upon the glow of her memories.

"That would depend—a very great deal—upon one's choice of a—partner, *ma fille*," she murmured slumberously.

Claire stared at her.

"I—quite agree, *chère Maman*," she said in a tone whose soft, purring felinity Mireille, who was anything but malicious, didn't even perceive, much less recognize. "So, to reassure you, *je suis vierge*. You can have Enrique Sepúlvera in to examine me if you don't want to take my word for it. Which would delight his lecherous old Mexican billy goat's heart, wouldn't it? But before you start worrying about a couple of—well—other aspects of the matter that ought to have occurred to you by now: I am neither—twisted, the way your darling Paquita is, nor cold. I have simply decided to follow your example, Mother dear!"

"My example?" Mireille said.

"Yes. Why yes, of course. Tripping—or running—down that well-known primrose path is much safer *after* marriage than before it, *n'est-ce pas, chère Maman?* When one has made one's brilliant nuptials, caught a sweet, amiable old darling like Daddy to blame the fruits of one's sins on —why then, what are the odds? I'll follow your tactics, even—refine them, shall we say? With exquisite consideration, discretion, tact, never for a moment arousing my dearest darling husband's suspicions or wounding, even slightly, his male pride, I'll simply do what you have done to Dad—adorn his forehead for him, as often as the need, the occasion, or even the vagrant whim, arises . . ."

She saw Mireille's eyes flash topaz lightning, and that warned her. Fortunately, she was very quick. Her lithe young arm shot out; her right hand closed over her mother's wrist, halting, inches before it reached her face, the slap that would have surely left her head ringing, her eyes half blind.

"Ma-man!" she laughed merrily. "You really must learn to control that explosive temper of yours! I was only teasing you, *ma vieille . . ."*

Mireille looked at her, studying her smooth young face through narrowed eyes.

"No you weren't," she said quietly, her voice vibrant with an undercurrent of heartbreak, pain; "that's actually what you did—*do*—believe. That I have been unfaithful to your stepfather. Come on, tell the truth. *Tu crois ça de moi, n'est-ce pas, ma fille?"*

"Well—" Claire floundered; then she lifted her chin defiantly. "Yes, *Maman.* As a matter of fact, I do. And I don't hold it against you. Daddy is—sweet, but he's a monument of dullness. Especially when compared with—*ton chevalier servant!* Look, we're both women, so we have—or, at least, should have—few illusions about female virtue. Most of the time, it represents sheer lack of opportunity, that's all. *Maman,* if you're truthful you'll admit that a good woman, a decent woman, *une femme honnête,* is either a female so ugly and so boring that no man wants her, or the woman who has been so tragically unlucky as never to have found herself alone for the scant half hour necessary with the one man alive who could snap his fingers under her nose and lead her off to bed. That's my case, *malheureusement—"*

Mireille went on studying her daughter's face.

"Just what are you trying to say, *ma fille?"* she whispered.

"That there's only one man alive for me, and you've got him, Mother dear. I fell in love with Willy Kilpatrick when I was six years old. The night I bashed Stan's head in for him, remember? D'you know that, even at that age, when he kissed me I got a thrill—*physical* thrill—down *here?"* She indicated the location in question with a wry, disdainful touch of straying fingers.

"Bon petit fils du Dieu!" Mireille said.

"I've kept my hot little hands off him so far, because of you, Mother darling. But I won't promise to, any longer. Raquel Kilpatrick—Willy's youngest, who spends her life swooning over my brother Stan; he pays her not the slightest attention, if the matter interests you!—says her mother's sick. Very sick. Eating like a pig was compensation, I suppose, for what she never had, her husband's love. Anyhow, her heart's gone back on her. All that lard around it, likely. So very soon now, Mother darling, dear Willy will be free. And when he is, I'm very sorry, *chère Maman,* but I'm going to grab him. You've got Dad. So you'll just have to give Willy up, at long, long last. Oh, I'll admit you're formidable competition in that regard; your figure's miraculous for a woman your age. Even so, I'm sure you'll be fair enough to concede that mine is even better, won't you, old dear? So I hope you'll grant me your blessing; but whether you do, or don't—*peu importe!*—Willy's going to be mine!"

Mireille sat there, peering into her daughter's pale blue eyes, comparing them, their shape, their color, with what she remembered of Alain Curtwright's. Then—with Willy's. But she couldn't be sure, not even now, not even yet. And that possibility which she dared not even mention to Claire—explaining the circumstances surrounding it being, of course, unthinkable—remained—a horror. So she descended from the halls of Colonus, away from Oedipus and Jocasta, or, more appropriately in this case, from Electra and Agamemnon, and bent her mind toward less awful arguments.

"Claire, Willy is fifty-three years old. One year older than your stepfather. And you're barely twenty. Remember that . . ."

"Et quoi?" Claire shot back at her. "He has aged—so beautifully, *Maman!* That patina—of old silver . . . Men like him—all whipcord and sinew—never really grow old. Just compare him, if you dare, with the callow young oafs I'm stuck with! That combination's miraculous, too, y'know: the courtly grace of his Spanish ancestors, the smoldering fire of the Aztecs, leavened with the mocking whimsicality of his forebears from the Emerald Isle. I'll wager he's far more attractive to you now than he was twenty odd years ago, when you first met him . . ."

'On Pacific Street, in front of the *Cabeza de Jabalí*, where I was staggering along, with the blood pouring down my thighs from sheer, brutal male abuse,' Mireille thought bitterly. She said:

"He is. But you can't marry him, Claire. It's—quite impossible, child. I won't permit you to . . ."

"Oh, don't be a dog—or rather a *bitch*—in the manger, *Maman!*" Claire said.

"I'm not. Willy is not my lover, Daughter. He hasn't been since before I married your stepfather. To whom, incidentally, I've been absolutely faithful all these years . . ."

"Ha!" Claire said.

Mireille shrugged.

"Whether you believe it or not is irrelevant," she said. "It happens to be true, and that's all that counts. An-drew is one of the best and finest men I've ever known. Though, in that regard, I've been very lucky. I've known three splendid men."

"My—father? Judge Alain Curtwright. My stepfather. And—?" Claire whispered.

"Willy himself," Mireille said softly. "Let's leave this discussion for another day, shall we? It's—futile, anyhow. Besides, I have to go, now . . ."

"Where?" Claire said bitterly.

Mireille laughed. But the sound of it was sad.

"To skin your darling brother alive," she said.

18

MIREILLE FOUND STANFORD EASILY ENOUGH. HE WAS STRETCHED out on his bed while his Chinese valet, Lu Sung—whom, naturally, Stan had renamed "Low Sunk"—applied a huge chunk of ice, wrapped in a towel, to his forehead.

"You get out of here, Low Sunk!" Mireille said.

"Yas, Missly." Low Sunk grinned and disappeared.

" 'Lo, Mama," Stanford groaned. "Tell me—is my head still on my neck? I think it dropped off and rolled under the chest of drawers. Will you take a look and see if you can find it, please?"

"I will *not*," Mireille said. "For all the use you make of it, you can jolly well do without, for all I care. So you've decided to make a grandmother of me? Prematurely, not to mention illegitimately? And to present me with a grandchild with the bar sinister *tarbrushed* across his whole escutcheon?"

"Good Lord, Mama!" Stanford said. "Don't tell me she actually went and did it!"

"*Who* went and did *what*, son of mine?"

"Periwinkle. She's been threatening for the past two weeks to go to you and accuse me of being the father of her brat—"

"*Aren't* you?" Mireille said.

"I doubt it," Stanford said calmly. "The possibility does exist, of course, but it's pretty remote . . ."

"You mean to lie there," Mireille whispered, "and shamelessly admit *que tu t'as couché avec une sale Négresse?* With a filthy, stinking nigger?"

"Periwinkle isn't filthy, Mama. She doesn't stink. She smells as nice as most white girls do—of rice powder and perfume. And that skin of hers —like old gold . . . absolutely lovely . . ."

"Bon petit Jésus!" Mireille moaned.

"Not to mention that she's a great deal more fun than any girl I ever met before. Enjoys what she's doing—really enjoys it. Doesn't fake matters, at all. You can't imagine how—refreshing that is, Mama, why—"

"No, I can't. Nor that my son could grow up to be a lecherous billy goat!"

"Why not?" Stan said cheerfully. "I understand that my real father, Judge Curtwright, was quite a gay old dog in his day. An assiduous patron of all the better parlor houses . . ."

"Stanford, I forbid you to speak about your father that way!" Mireille cried. She wasn't pretending; she was truly outraged.

"Oh, Mama! I *am* sorry!" Stanford said. "I didn't mean that as a reproach. Nobody holds his having had himself a bit of fun against the Judge. Under the circumstances, what else could he have done? They tell me his first wife used to stroll up the walls and across the ceiling almost every night. So a spot of—well, hired relief from time to time seems to me a sight more moral than installing some cute little frail darling in a rose-covered cottage in a back street on a more or less permanent basis would have been. Don't you agree?"

Mireille bowed her head. The tears stung her eyes.

But Stan went plunging on, obliviously and blithely, full steam ahead.

"Nobody holds that against him. The only thing I regret is that he didn't live long enough for me to get to know him. Everybody says he was a marvelous old party . . ."

"He was. And I'm sorry he didn't live, too. For, among other reasons, he was much less easygoing than your stepfather is. He would have surely straightened you out, and possibly even Claire . . ."

"Claire's a witch!" Stanford said bitterly. "Mama, did you know she's thrown poor Ted over?"

"Yes," Mireille said dryly; "she told me."

"After having him jumping through the hoops like a trained seal for a whole year! He even crossed the Pond—and almost died of seasickness on the way!—to propose to her. And when we got back here the first thing he did was to buy her the biggest solitaire in San Francisco's history—the size of a locomotive's headlight. Mama, that sparkler cost a cool twenty-five thousand dollars, but she handed it right back to him as though it were a piece of waterfront bazaar junk, and told him she was still undecided . . ."

"Stan darling, I didn't come in here to discuss Claire's doings with you," Mireille said. "So stop sidetracking me, will you? What makes Periwinkle so sure you're the father of her unborn child?"

"She's not. She can't be. She hasn't the faintest idea who the little off-colored bastard's pappy actually is. I happen to be the youngest, prettiest, and richest among all the *single* candidates for that dubious honor, Mama. The host of married ones, she's given up on completely . . ."

"*Morbleu!*" Mireille swore. "You mean to tell me that a child as strictly brought up as I know Peri has been has managed to play around that much?"

"Well, let's say she had some expert assistance. 'Mammy' Pleasant, of course. Mama, I'm sure you've heard of her Octavia Street establishment—"

"Don't tell me you've been there!" Mireille gasped.

"Of course not! That woman scares me. What I started to say is that I'll bet you haven't heard of her house in the country that she calls Geneva Cottage . . ."

"You'd win. I haven't."

"Well, she's got George Gammon—he's that murdering, baby-snatching quack Joe Gammon's first cousin—out there as manager. But what he actually is, everybody says, is her paramour. And Mama, that woman must be at least fifty-five years old!"

"She's—sixty," Mireille said. "But, for your information, son of mine, human—well, passions—don't die with age. At least not as easily and as quickly as you youngsters seem to think they do. Go on. I am endeavoring, Stan, to discern the faintest connection between all this rigamarole and *your*—well, *contretemps avec ta 'tite Négresse*—"

"*Mulâtresse, disons-nous?*" Stan corrected her. "Believe me, it *has* a connection, Mama—if only by ringing in the law of averages in my defense. Did you know that Madame Pleasant claims to be a voodoo queen?"

"Yes. Or she did, years ago. And her claims were always nonsense. They were her way of controlling the colored people. As well as amusing herself by procuring the—services, as that word is used in stock breeding, I'm sorry to say, of muscular, stalwart Blacks. It seems that her ceremonies always ended in the wildest kinds of Saturnalias, in which all and sundry paired off and disappeared into the underbrush. She with the biggest, burliest buck nigger in the bunch, naturally . . ."

"They still do," Stan grinned; "only the buck niggers have been replaced by rich white gentlemen—*your* good friend attorney Kilpatrick among them . . ."

"*Encore ce cochon d'un* Willy!" Mireille snorted disgustedly. "Will he never change?"

"Apparently not," Stan chuckled. "Anyhow, for the past six months,

Mama, our *soi-disant* mamaloi has been entertaining the cream of San Francisco's society—all male, *bien entendu*—with a rather picturesque exhibition which consists of twelve dancing girls—all colored, but none of them *black*, if you follow the distinction I'm trying to make."

"I do," Mireille said grimly; "go on."

"The costume employed *en scene* consists of a loincloth. A rather scanty loincloth."

"I get the picture. How many times have *you* been out there, young Mister Billy Goat?"

"Never. Word of honor, Mama. You don't believe me? Then tell me this: How many, if not millions, say hundreds of thousands of dollars do I have at my immediate disposal? What markets have I cornered lately? What stocks can I advise anyone to buy, sell, dump, go short on? That is the price of admission to Geneva Cottage, Mother dear . . ."

"Now I do believe you," Mireille said. "But, that being so, how did you find out what goes on out there?"

"I investigated. After the first one or two occasions I was sober enough to be—well, observant. And this sudden onslaught of overwhelming and passionate love that little Periwinkle has suddenly discovered she feels for me just didn't ring true. Besides, I wasn't born yesterday, Mama; I've observed that when a young female—especially if she belongs to the lower orders—suddenly becomes obsessed with the desire to push off a piece of her—excuse me, Mama!—say, rather, to donate a portion of her dainty little anatomy to one, the sad truth of the matter usually is that one is either being made the sacrificial goat for some other chap's sins, or the price ultimately to be paid for said donation is sure to be deuced high. So I checked on dear Periwinkle's comings and goings. It seems she often visits 1661 Octavia Street. Then I had my auditory appendages bent into curlicues by one 'Flowery' George Flowers, an acquaintance though not a friend of mine; he's a trifle too mellifluous of voice and limp of wrist to suit my sturdy tastes."

"Hardly attractive to girls like Periwinkle, I'd think," Mireille said.

"Of course not! It seems that his guv'nor, having become more than a bit concerned about Flowery's mannerisms—he really is an outrageous swish, Mama—decided to take the beggar out and get him bred—Oh, Lord, Mama, I'm sorry again!"

"Forget it. I'm not exactly a hothouse blossom, Stan. Do go on."

"All right. With apologies in advance for what I'm going to say: Old Hiram Flowers, who is the vice-president of nine million banks and chairman of the board of ten million companies dedicated to the proposition that mixing paper with water is an excellent way of becoming rich, decided to remove the lace from his son's drawers by having some ardent little she-creature remove the drawers in question. So—Geneva Cottage, what? It seems from Flowery's glowing report that the treatment worked. Our darling Periwinkle turns out to be *première danseuse*, making up in vigor and enthusiasm what she lacks in art. The first loincloth to be torn off and hurled into the bushes is always hers, Flowery swears. And when the assembled company, with the well-modulated bestial howls proper to their high degree, fall upon the—what's a nice synonym for 'bare-assed,' Mama? Will 'nude' do?"

"Admirably," Mireille said.

"Upon the nude dancers, fistfights have broken out over the possession of the fair—well, maybe, not exactly 'fair'—Periwinkle, the winner bearing her off in triumph to one of the twelve bedrooms on Geneva Cottage's second floor. So I hardly think you should trouble yourself about Peri's accusations, Mama. Tell you what: Just say in Blossom's presence that you've decided to cut me off without tuppence, and see how fast both of them will decide the pea's beneath another shell . . ."

"An excellent suggestion, Stan," Mireille said. "I'll do just that: cut you off without a picayune, I mean. And you may pass the information along to all your dusky and not so dusky lights-o'-love yourself. You're a sturdy lad. A job as a dockworker down on the Embarcadero ought to be just right for you. And—oh, yes; you may sleep in my warehouse at the foot of California Street until you do find work. You see, I'm putting you out of the house, too . . ."

"Ma-ma!" Stan wailed. "You—you wouldn't!"

"I wouldn't? I just *did.* You've an hour's grace to get packed. Shouldn't take you even that long. Not if you make a reasonably wise choice of clothes you'll actually need, in your new surroundings."

"Mama," Stanford whispered, "isn't there anything I can do to make you change your mind?"

"Yes. But you might prefer the dockworker's job. Home every night in the week by nine o'clock. Cold sober. No stink of tobacco on your breath. An immediate appearance in Otto Eiselberg's offices to actually read for the law, instead of talking about it as you've been doing for years. Otto's, not Willy Kilpatrick's. You'd wind Willy around your little finger, soft as he is. Otto will keep you straight. Incidentally, tell Otto I want you to become fluent in German. A man who only speaks one language is an utter ignoramus. And you may come home by ten or eleven o'clock on Sundays, providing it's Raquel Kilpatrick you're calling on."

"Dear God!" Stanford moaned. "And now you're going to pick my female company too?"

"Yes. Or at least get you started in the right direction. So far, your taste has been abominable. The final choice will be up to you, of course. And to the greatly to be pitied poor little creature blind and stupid enough to have you. You'll find me prepared to be the world's best and most understanding mother-in-law your eventual bride could ever hope for—or a she-fiend out of hell itself. Depends on what you bring me home. But you must admit that Raquel is a lovely girl . . ."

"She is," Stan conceded grudgingly. "Only she's so—so—"

"So *what?*" Mireille demanded.

"Sugar and spice and everything nice," Stan said morosely. "And not even much spice when you get right down to it."

"Too bad. It's up to you. The docks, or—"

"Oh, Lord, Mama! All right! All right! You win!" Stanford said.

Thereafter, Mireille went in search of Blossom. She found her in the kitchen indulging in a sweetly loving mother-and-daughter chat with Periwinkle, of an order of intensity fully comparable with the ones she herself often had with Claire, and, measured in decibels according to the volume of the contralto bellows and soprano shrieks emanating therefrom, probably exceeding it; thus proving once again that when it comes to the basic behavior characteristics we flatter ourselves by labeling human nature, race and color make no difference at all.

"I just don't wanna be saddled wit' nobody's damn baby, nohow!" Periwinkle was yelling as Mireille walked in.

"A very exact description of the poor little bastard, Peri," Mireille said coolly. "Blossom, I just came to tell you that the agreement we made is off. I had—and haven't—any objection to contributing toward the education and support of a child my son is actually responsible for, but the ugly fact is that your daughter doesn't even know who the father of her little off-colored bastard is. He could be any one of two dozen or more men. Another thing I'm practically certain of is that my Stan is not numbered among them, for the very simple reason that this little creature only began pushing her—well, call them favors—off on him in search of a sacrificial goat once she'd discovered she was already pregnant."

"Miz Mireille," Periwinkle said sullenly, "that jes' ain't so! Stan is my po' baby's pa, and—"

"You shet yo' trap, Peri!" Blossom growled in her midnight velvet contralto. "Miz Mireille, reckon you better explain me a little o' that there, ma'am . . ."

"All right," Mireille sighed, "but you aren't going to like what I have to say, Blossom. How much are we really responsible for what our children do? You have your troubles with this exceedingly foolish child, and I, mine, with Stan—and with Claire. A pity. In a nutshell, it seems that Periwinkle had been stupid enough to fall into the clutches of Mary Ellen Pleasant; and that entertaining—flat on her dainty little back, of course—certain gentlemen on that old witch's behalf has had its inevitable results. I've been reliably informed that Madame Poisonous owns a place in the country called Geneva Cottage, and out there—"

Blossom listened to her until she had finished, without interrupting her at all.

"That's it, Blossom. That's the whole story. As you can see, this poor little fool has been *used*. But, more to the point, it's evident that she hasn't, and can't have, the faintest idea *who* her baby's father is. So, under the circumstances, I cannot assume responsibility for a little bastard who may be the child of any of two dozen or more men."

"Yes'm," Blossom groaned. "But, Miz Mireille ma'am, how come Mary Ellen wanna go 'n' do a thing like that? Not that she too good to—she wicked enough to cook up any damn thing—but whut I means is: Whut's in it fer her?"

"A lot," Mireille snapped. "After her flock of low-flying dusky soiled doves have softened up these august gentlemen—correction!—this herd of horny swine that men of any race or color seem to be—"

"Tha's th' lowdown, dirty truth," Blossom sighed. "Go on, ma'am . . ."

"After dear Peri here, and—to borrow the pungently exact vocabulary of my son—'bare-assed' company has sufficiently softened up this town's leading lights, it becomes easy for that evil yellow witch to pick their brains for stock market tips or other financial information, and to demand favors of the politicians among them, such as passing or changing zoning ordinances so as to enhance the value of her properties. Or, in some cases, simple blackmail, I suppose. Many a *wife* holds the purse strings in San Francisco nowadays, y'know. A word that friend husband has been tumbling Black whores out at Geneva Cottage reaching the ears of his ever-loving and ever-faithful wife could cause all kinds of marital problems, you realize. In any event, I hope you've noticed how vehemently dear Peri is denying the whole thing, Blossom."

"Hit ain't so! Hit ain't so!" Periwinkle shrieked. "We doan dance nekkid! 'N' we doan do hit wit' nobody! We—"

"The next time you go to seek legal advice from attorney Kilpatrick, Blossom," Mireille said quietly, "ask him what goes on at Geneva Cottage. It seems he has been a witness to *les divertissements* out there. And take dear Peri along. See if he won't—recognize her . . ."

"How come us got to believe *him?*" Periwinkle, quite beside herself, cried. "He yo sweet man! You he ho! You been cheatin' on po' ol' Mr. Andy wit' him fur years!"

That was as far as she got. Blossom's massive black hand sent her crashing full length to the kitchen floor with a slap that would have felled a full-grown ox, not to mention a girl as small and slight as poor Periwinkle.

"That was—unnecessary, Blossom," Mireille sighed. "I don't approve of brutality, y'know. But anyhow, I don't suppose I have to tell you that you'll have to find lodgings for your darling daughter elsewhere from now on? I can't allow her to live in my house anymore. She has displayed too little respect for it, for herself, and for me. And if you object to that, I'm very sorry but you'll have to go too. I should hate to have to discharge you, because you've served me well, and on top of that, just as you said this morning, we've been—friends. The only thing that I'd voluntarily sack you for would be to find out you were a party to Peri's little confidence game. So, Blossom—the truth: Did you know about your child's—activities at Geneva Cottage?"

"No'm," Blossom moaned. "She still 'live, ain't she? I'd of knowed that, she be pushin' up daisies right now, her!"

"Huh," Periwinkle most unwisely snorted, "you ain't got no right t'talk, Momma! Effen Unca John 'n' Jim hadn't of got they shotguns out 'n' gone after my pa, you'd of been in th' same fix I is, right now. Leasewise done had myself some fun, me; them white gentlemens says I'se mighty sweet, 'n'—"

Mireille turned away.

"I leave her in your hands, Blossom," she said quietly; "I have no need to listen to her insolence. Incidentally, punishing her seems to me a waste of time. She's far beyond the place where it would do her any good . . ."

When Mireille had gone, Blossom glared at her erring daughter. Crossed to her and caught her by the shoulder. Propelled her down the hall to the quite comfortable living quarters they shared. Pushed her into their bedroom. Stood there facing her.

"Strip," she said.

"Strip?" Periwinkle quavered.

"Yeah. I'm gonna whup yo' fast 'n' forward li'l ass. Whut you didn't even have sense enough to *sell,* but went 'n' *give* away 'cause that there evil ol' yaller bitch tol' you to. So I wants it bare so I kin stripe it *good.*

So shuck off, Peri! Gonna leave you bloody th' way th' whitefolks useta leave po' slave niggers befo' th' war. You heard me—strip!"

Mary Ellen Pleasant looked at William Willmore, her supposed handyman, but actually her henchman in all the many crimes committed under her roof, both at her former establishment at 920 Washington Street and now here at 1661 Octavia, "The House of Evil." Then she looked at the inert burden in his arms.

"Where'd you find her?" she said.

"Jes' out front," Willmore said.

"Somebody dump her on our doorstep?" Madame Pleasant asked.

"No'm. Her come her own self. There's tracks outside in th' street. Hern. Her slipper fit 'em exact. I took one off and tried it fo' I brung her in. Las' fifty yards or so, her crawled."

"Hmmmn. That was smart, Will. But then you always are. Crawled, you say? How could you tell that?"

"Front o' her skirt, ma'am. Down by th' knees. Mud on it."

"Hmmmn. Excellent reasoning. What's wrong with her, Will? Has she been shot, or stabbed, or merely hit over the head?"

"Her's been whupped, ma'am. By somebody whut knows how to whup. Southerner, whut useta own slaves. Naw. Wors'n that. Po' redneck overseer. Slave driver. Nigger breaker, likely."

"Jesus!" Mary Ellen whispered. "Mireille Duclos!"

"Ma'am?" William Willmore said. Then, "Oh. You means Missus MacFarland, ma'am?"

"Exactly! Who else could it be? This poor, abused child lives in her house. And she hasn't any white Southerners in her employ. That little French Creole witch thinks she can get away with *anything*. And this is her response, her very *Southern* response, to what I told this damned, spraddle-legged idiot—who's always unbuttoning men's flies in her haste to get another length of man-meat shoved up her—to do."

" 'N' whut was that, Miz Mary Ellen?"

"None of your goddamned business, Will! Oh hell, I might as well tell you. I'll probably need you to run an errand or two in connection with this. I told this absolutely moronic little jenny ass to crawl into the MacFarland boy's bed. You remember *him*, don't you? From before he became either—a Curtwright, or a MacFarland?"

" 'Deed I do. Th' li'l fella us tattooed a star behind he left ear. Seen his mama t'other day. In a crib in a Sutter Street cowyard. Em's done put her out. Too ol'—'n' too sloppy. Course she wasn't no mo' than fo'teen years ol' when she birthed him, but she wuz th' kind whut gits ol' fast. 'Sides, reckon thirty-fo' *is* gittin' along for a ho. Tell me sumpin' else, Miz Mary Ellen; how come you tol' this heah po' baby to push a piece o' her sweet li'l high brown tail off on Stanford MacFarland?"

"The usual reason, Will. She got caught. And since I have a super-abundance of things to pay Mireille Duclos MacFarland back for, I thought she'd knuckle under, start shelling out the cash to save the family name and fame. I should have known better. You know that hideous hunk of grease who's bouncer at Em's, don't you? Ray—what's his name? Oh, yes, Coles! Well, she did *that* . . ."

"Did *whut*, ma'am? Notched he snoot for him like a boar hawg's? Or —de-balled him? All th' gals at Em's swear he been cut. 'N' they all jes' loves him. Say he th' bes' cunt lapper in th' business. Huh! He plumb gotta be—cain't do nothin' else! But Missus MacFarland is a mighty *small* woman, her—'n' pretty as a picture, too! I jes' cain't figger how she could of gelded a fella big as Ray."

"Yet she did. Or had it done. Slit his nose open that way, personally, that's for sure. . . . Now tell me: Is this little bitch dead? If she is, take her around back and hide her under some hay in the stable. Then you and Eugene Paillet bury her in the garden sometime after midnight tonight. Tell Eugene to plant a rosebush over her. That way nobody'll notice the ground's been disturbed and—"

"Only her ain't daid, ma'am. Tho effen us doan do sumpin' 'bout her real soon, she jes' might pop off, fur a fact. You wants me t'stick her under that theah straw 'n' come back t'night 'n' see whether her's still 'mongst them present 'n' accounted fur?"

Mary Ellen Pleasant thought about that.

"No, Will," she said finally. "She's a cute little lump of brown sugar, not even too burnt. And since the pappy of her bundle is sure to be white, the child itself might well be a worthwhile investment, if it turns out to be light-complexioned enough—and a girl. I do have to provide for my old age, y'know. Carry her upstairs. Put her into one of the unoccupied bedrooms, face down on the bed. Tell Lucy Mae to undress her. When you've done all that, call me."

Lucy Mae Thomas, Madame Pleasant's maidservant, had to cut poor Periwinkle's clothes off her with scissors, so stuck to that poor damned and doomed girl's flesh were they with great dried and clotted masses of her own blood. After she'd finished that, Lucy Mae called her mistress.

Mary Ellen stood there looking at the unconscious naked girl. Periwinkle's back was a mess. It was striped all over with whiplashes that had cut through her coppery brown skin like a dull knife, leaving puckering purplish welts that still sullenly oozed crimson. Her lamentable aspect would have awakened pity in a wooden image. Only Mary Ellen Pleasant wasn't a wooden image: she had a hide of boiler plate, and a heart of stainless steel.

"Go get the soothing salve, Lucy Mae," she finally said.

Which wasn't kindness. By then Madame Pleasant's iron hold on San Francisco's Black community was slipping fast. At that time, late 1876, she had already, in addition to French Joe—who really didn't count, since the colored people, with the exception of a few friends of the Switherses', hadn't known that Joe Lascals wasn't entirely the white man he seemed to be—caused the total disappearance of Sydney Smith, another of the bill collectors who had cheated her, and murdered at least one of the three Black servants she was to kill out at Geneva Cottage. She hadn't got started on her Octavia Street household yet. But she would. By the time she died—peacefully in her bed at age eighty-eight—seven Blacks and three whites, including her old partner, financier Thomas Frederick Bell, by a partial, imperfect count, would be dead through her agency or by her hand. But now the news was out and spreading:

"That ol' yaller witch, her *kills* folks, her!" the Black people said.

Always shrewd, Mary Ellen realized how badly she needed the people she had used to unobtrusively carry out her subtle, often nefarious missions. How immensely they were aided in the successful pursuit of her devious ends by the whites' complacent failure even to recognize the sheer Machiavellian guile of the Black race, a trait greatly reinforced by the relentless pressures of slavery, was another thing that reincarnation of Lucretia Borgia knew. She was well aware that she hadn't the faintest hope of finding substitutes for her Black minions among any other of the minority groups. And whites were worse than useless; that congenital megalomania which was the cause of their all but irrational concept of themselves and their place in the scheme of things, and out of which sprang their racism, made them automatically the most inept of conspirators. Therefore it had to be the Blacks or nobody. So Madame Pleasant saw, in Periwinkle's arrival in so pitiful a state, a golden opportunity to win back her influence over the race to whom she owed a mere one eighth of her biological heritage, and about whom her feelings were ambivalent to say the least.

"No'm," Periwinkle moaned—some time later, of course—as Mary Ellen personally applied the soothing salve to her lacerated back, "Miz Mireille didn't whup me. 'N' t' tell th' truth 'bout hit, her tol' Momma not to. All she done was to put me outa th' house—cause, smart as she is, she'd done gone 'n' found out I was *already* bigged when I first got around to pushin' a piece off on Stan—"

"And how under heaven could she have found that out, child?" Mary Ellen said.

"Well in a way, reckon that was *yo'* fault, beggin yo' humble pardon, ma'am . . ."

"*My* fault? How so, child?" Mary Ellen said.

"'Twuz *you* whut invited lawyer Kilpatrick out to Geneva Cottage, wasn't it? 'N' you knows damn well, ma'am, that ever' time she lifts up a hoop he jumps right through hit jes' like one o' them trained circus dawgs. 'Sides, there was that there sissy Flowers boy. *Ex*-sissy, now, cause I sho' Lawd done cured him, me. Anyhow him 'n' Stan is frens. 'N' anyhow, Stan, he plenty smart his own self, him. Must o' took after he real pappy, th' Jedge. First time I tol' him he was gonna be a daddy, him, and of my chile, he bust out laffin. 'Peri,' sez he, 'you's done had more sausages in you than a meat grinder has—' "

"Oh, Lord!" Mary Ellen moaned. "And me thinking I *had* her, this time . . ."

"You thinkin' you had who, ma'am?" Periwinkle said.

"Mireille Duclos. Mrs. MacFarland. But she's beat me again. She always beats me. First she went and married the one man in San Francisco softheaded enough to marry her *knowing* she'd hustled her dainty little bustle in Sydney Town before it even became part of the Barbary Coast, so I can't even use the threat of exposing her past to him. Then she goes and makes him so damn rich—partially at my expense, by cleverly cutting me out of a deal I had every right to be in on—that they've become practically untouchable. And in this town I can't even count on the other great ladies rallying around with their tomahawks out to do a hatchet job on her, because too many of them are in the same boat. Back in the early fifties, the miners were marrying whores faster than I could bring 'em in. And now *you* go and fail me . . ."

"Miz Mary Ellen, ma'am, I didn't fail you. You failed *me*. 'N' fucked me up worser'n ol' hell on top o' hit. Here I is, whupped into a piece o' ground beef—o' ground heifer, anyhow—by my own ma. Throwed outa th' house wit' nowheres t'go. Bigged. A li'l bastid in my belly whut Gawd Almighty His own self up theah in glory know who he pappy be— mebbe. An' I doubts even that . . ."

"You have somewhere to go. *Here.* You'll be taken care of until your baby's born. If it's fair enough, I'll adopt it, and—"

"'N' effen hit's black?"

"It will—disappear. Oh, Jesus! Don't tell me you've been going around spreading your legs for niggers, have you?"

"No'm. It pappy white. Tha's fer sho."

"All right. I don't suppose any of this is your fault, though you've ruined my digestion and my appetite for a month of Sundays. I was so looking forward to bringing Mireille Duclos down a peg. And not even to make her cough up a sizable chunk of her ill-gotten gains. I'd do it for free, just to see her grovel, crawl—"

"Ma'am, how come you ain't sent one of them fellas you's got at yo' beck 'n' call to stick a knife down her gizzard? Or punch a nice round hole through her belly wit' a forty-fo' where hit would do her th' most good?"

"Hmmm. Primitive child, aren't you? Tell me, Periwinkle, have you ever been to the cemetery?"

"Yas'm. Momma takes—took me—to put some flowers on my daddy's grave on All Saints' Day. Why, ma'am?"

"It's so peaceful. The dead may even be happy—who knows? And I don't want Mireille Duclos happy. I don't even want her dead. I want her to suffer and suffer and suffer until she goes completely out of her mind!"

"Ma'am, you's done tol' me a million times how damn dumb I is—"

"Well, you do wear your brains between your thighs, Peri; but then I guess most young females your age do. Why?"

"Well, if you cain't figger out how to git next to Miz Mireille, you plain ain't smart worth a shit, you, ma'am. And I don't beg yo' pardon, neither!"

Mary Ellen stared at that saucy brown face, which in that moment had attained its fair share of evil, too.

"If you can tell me how to do that, you don't have to, child. I'll freely admit my stupidity, and reward you for your help. One hundred dollars cash, here and now. How should I go about it, Peri?"

Periwinkle smiled. Those thick, sensual lips curled in the contemplation of a vengeance so blissful that it was practically orgasmic. Then she whispered it, breathed it out—that one short phrase that sufficed to wreck three lives.

"Tell Stan—tell Claire—they mama—was—useta be—a ho," she said. And lay back, peacefully, to contemplate the topography of that map of hell, that expanse of desolation, she had wrought.

19

"WHY ARE YOU SO NERVOUS, CHILD?" MIREILLE SAID.

Raquel Kilpatrick darted a quick glance at this small but absolutely formidable woman at her side. Then she looked away; looked back again. She had been doing that all afternoon long. There was no way to understand Mrs. MacFarland, still less to capture her—quality, say. One instant she looked younger than her daughter, Claire; the next, older than time itself. Her skin was smooth, unwrinkled; her hair, night-black, without a strand of silver in it. And yet—

'It's her eyes that are so—old,' Raquel thought; 'more than old—ancient. Like—the pyramids. Filled with all the wisdom of the ages, all the—pain . . .'

She said softly in her low, sweet, husky voice, "I guess you *know* why, Mrs. MacFarland . . ."

Mireille laughed. 'Bubbles on champagne,' Raquel thought; 'the tinkling of ice in a silver pitcher . . .' ·

"Yes, I'm quite sure I do. How is dear Molly anyhow?" she said.

"Oh, Mother is much improved. In fact, she's doing surprisingly well. It seems that her slight heart attack was a godsend—as a warning. For now she's doing what Dr. Enrique tells her to do, taking his orders seriously. She's lost all of twenty pounds, and the doctor swears that if she continues to follow his instructions to the letter, she'll live to a ripe old age, ma'am . . ."

"I'm glad. I'm so very glad!" Mireille said. She was thinking of Claire's confessed subterranean passion for Willy as she spoke, and that troublesome thought lent her tone immense sincerity. Under the circumstances, she honestly hoped Molly Kilpatrick would reach a hundred.

Raquel stared at her.

"You know, Mrs. MacFarland, you sound as though you mean that," she said.

"I do mean it. Why shouldn't I? Oh, you mean because of your father! Of course, I still love Willy very dearly; but not—at my age!—enough to upset the even tenor of my way over him. I'm very content with my husband, Raquel. Our marriage is a good one—which, when you've dined with us a couple of times, you'll be able to see for yourself. Believe me, I want your mother to live past ninety, for Willy's sake, you children's—and for another reason I'll tell you later on, when you've become—family . . ."

"Family?" Raquel whispered.

"Yes. I mean when you marry my Stan. You *are* in love with him, aren't you?"

Raquel bent her head. The great tears beaded on the rusty gold of her lashes, turned her eyes into star sapphires, light-filled, brimming. She shook her head to clear them.

"Yes—I am," she said a little defiantly. "But what good does that do me, Mrs. MacFarland, when he can't—stand me? When he tells all his friends I bore him stiff?"

"That's exactly why I invited you for this drive," Mireille said. "You see, I'd be delighted to have you for my daughter-in-law . . ."

Raquel gazed at her, long and thoughtfully.

"Have you told Stan that, ma'am? If so, I'm done for!" she said.

"As a matter of fact, I have. And I agree that it *was* a grave tactical error. So now to remedy it. Any boy with blood in his veins immediately becomes convinced that any girl his mother approves of must be, One, insufferable; Two, dull; and Three—and worst of all!—cold. So those are the notions we'll have to rid Stan of."

"Well," Raquel sighed, "I *can* be insufferable upon occasion, and I guess I am dull. But—cold? Well, the answer to that could be—is—rather embarrassing, ma'am . . ."

"Good! Excellent! I want just scads of grandchildren, y'know. So now, from an old campaigner, a lesson in *dirty* fighting. Tell me, d'you have another pretender to your hand?"

"Yes'm. Noel Cunningham. You know the Cunninghams, don't you? They're in shipping. The Cunningham Blue Star Lines—between here and Australia. Hawaii, too. Noel is a very nice boy. I like him. I like him very much. But I—I *love* Stan. Stupid of me, isn't it?"

"Yes. Very. My Stan isn't worth the powder and ball it would take to kill him. But then, all women are stupid that way. So now to remedy matters. Lesson one: Make an appointment with Stan. Then forget to keep it. Ride gaily past the ice cream parlor, soda fountain, or wherever you were supposed to meet him—with Noel. Let him see there are other fish in the sea, my dear. And the next time he calls, don't be so awfully *sweet*. The trouble is, you *are* sweet, so this will come hard to you. But do it anyhow. Roll your eyes heavenward in despair at his stupidity. Repeat half a dozen times in an evening, 'But, Stan dear, must you be so *dense?*' When he asks for another rendezvous, as he will, being intrigued by the change in you and smarting from injured male pride, say, 'I don't know. I'll have to think about it. Ask me again—two weeks from now . . .'"

"Oh, Lord!" Raquel said.

"I know—it calls for nerve. We're always afraid that we're going to drive the objects of our idolatry away from us by being too harsh with them. Stuff and nonsense! Men and dogs are exactly alike—the worse you treat them, the more they fawn. Besides, tell me: Just where has being little Miss Ever Faithful, the Oh So Submissive Maiden at my idiotic son's beck and call, got you so far, child?"

"Nowhere," Raquel sighed. "You're right! I'll follow your advice, Mrs. MacFarland. But before we start back, would you mind telling me one thing, please?"

"And that is?" Mireille said.

"Why didn't you and my father get married? You knew him first, long before Mama did. And you're—so—beautiful. And—interesting, and—"

"That. I was *too* interesting, dear child. I frightened your father to death. No, now I'm not being fair—either to your father or to you. You, I think, can cope with the truth, and hence deserve it. Anyhow, here goes! My own youth was—most unfortunate. There were, of course, reasons for that sad state of affairs, mitigating circumstances, excuses— my father's violent, tragic death among them—but I will not give them. Excuses always beg the issue, don't they? And ultimately the unholy messes we make of our lives are always our own fault, so entering whining pleas in our own defense, failing to shoulder the full responsibility for our own acts, serves for nothing! You've said that the question of your— well, emotional temperature, call it—might prove embarrassing. Unfortunately, in my youth mine was often a great deal more than merely embarrassing to me, my dear! And, in the absence of any kind of adult guidance—my father was dead, my mother entirely unequal to the task of controlling a headstrong, wild, passionate little creature like me—I let matters get out of control, go much too far. In short, at your age I was very naughty indeed. And, as is nearly always the terribly unfair consequence of female sin, I paid for my folly, dreadfully. I've always thought that the cruelest part of that price was the loss of—your father. Oh, he had a fairly accurate idea of my past—except for a couple of items that most emphasized my own guilt in setting into motion the chain of events that sent me slipping and sliding down that well-known road to ruin. Only, quite by accident, after he'd most nobly pardoned me my sins and become engaged to me, he had precisely those two incidents that I'd wisely—or out of cowardice, who knows?—hidden from him not only brought to his attention, but hurled into his teeth, as it were, and presented in the very worst light possible. So, he threw me over. Which was very probably intelligent of him. I doubt that he and I ever could have been really happy together. Oh dear, now I've shocked you, haven't I? Child, I'm sorry! But I hate lying and liars. I'm a very wicked old woman, my dear; but if you do come into my family, you'll have to take me as I am . . ."

"I'm going to!" Raquel breathed. Then, fervently, "I'm going to catch Stan if I have to rope and hog-tie him, as the *vaqueros* on our *rancho* down south say. Because I want you for my mother-in-law, too, now! Oh, why didn't we get together years ago!"

When Mireille got back home from that interesting and instructive drive, her daughter Claire met her on the veranda before she even got inside the house.

"*Maman!*" Claire gasped. "You've a visitor! And *what* a visitor! Oh, *Maman*, may I join the conversation? I've been just *dying* to meet her for years!"

"Meet *whom*, Claire?" Mireille said.

"Why, the wickedest woman in California! The infamous 'Mammy' Pleasant," Claire said.

Mireille looked at her daughter. Her mouth tightened, became grim.

"No, you may *not*, Claire," she said.

"*Ah, Maman, pourquoi pas?*" Claire wheedled.

"Because anything that poisonous old witch has to say, I shouldn't want you to hear," Mireille said.

"What d'*you* want, Claire?" Stanford growled in that tone of sullen ungraciousness that only brothers use habitually toward that bane of their existence they practically always consider a sister to be.

"Sssssshhhh!" Claire hissed, crossing her lips with the forefinger of her right hand to indicate the immediate and overwhelming need for silence. Then she added in a low, melodramatic, exceedingly conspiratorial whisper:

"C'mon, will you?"

"C'mon where?" Stan said suspiciously.

"To Daddy's study! You hear me? Get up from there!"

"And why, in the name of everything unholy, should I have the faintest desire to go to Dad's study?"

"Because it's next to *Maman*'s upstairs sitting room. Because *Maman*'s in said sitting room with—a visitor. Aren't you even going to ask me who she is?"

"No," Stan yawned, "I couldn't care less, sister mine. Say! What did poor old Ted do to make you hate him so? I'm not prying, Claire. I need that information. Mama's trying to saddle me with Raquel Kilpatrick. And the trouble is, I'm growing rather fond of the poor little thing. So, before it's too late, I—"

"Stan, you utter idiot, the woman in *Maman*'s sitting room is 'Mammy' Pleasant! *Now* will you come on?"

"Good God!" Stanford gasped, and fairly exploded up out of his bed.

"As you probably know, I've had quite a bit of bad luck with my investments of late," Mary Ellen Pleasant said.

"And as you *surely* know, luck has not one damned thing to do with investments," Mireille shot back at her. "You simply placed your money stupidly, Mary Ellen. You and Ben Holladay bit off more than you could chew. If you'd asked me, I'd have told you what An-drew said about the Oregon railroad stock. Even though you got Tom Bell to pressure Milton Latham into dumping the company's bonds—so watered you could drink 'em—on his poor innocent English and German investors through his corresponding banks, the Oregon and California still fell through—defaulted, just as An-drew predicted it would. Left you in the costume your colored whores sport out at Geneva Cottage, didn't it? If I were the type who rejoices over other people's misfortunes, I'd be glad, but I'm not. So get to the point: What do you want of me?"

"Say, a small and reasonable percentage of the money you made on the Ophir stocks, and the California Steam Navigation Company, by following my advice. A hundred thousand dollars would come in very handy at this juncture, Mireille dear . . ."

Mireille stared at her.

"You're crazy," she said. "Stark, raving mad. You told me to buy those stocks, all right. And then left me completely in the lurch on the important point, which was when to *sell*. If I hadn't had other sources of information, I'd have been ruined. So I don't owe you anything, Mary Ellen!"

"Not even some tiny part of my share of the Cow Head Gulch quick-

silver bonanza, which you deliberately cheated me out of?" Madame
Pleasant said.

Mireille studied her face, her eyes. Carefully.

"You yourself know better than that. The accusation's so ridiculous I
don't even need to waste breath in refuting it," she said dryly. "But
that's not the point, is it, Mary Ellen? What is it that you think you've
found out that you believe makes such compelling material for blackmail? And to the tune of a hundred thousand dollars, at that?"

"For—starters!" Mary Ellen Pleasant chuckled. "I mean to leave you
without even the skimpy loincloth my dusky little darlings wear when
they're busily engaged in luring suckers out at the Cottage. Actually, the
money is only secondary in your case. Seeing you crawl is worth that
much per minute, my dear!"

"That's one thing you'll *never* see," Mireille said. "Come on, out with
it. Since I've lived an absolutely blameless life ever since I married Andrew, any tales that have been brought to you—any lies about new and
recent misconduct on my part—are, have to be, just that: tales, lies,
misinformation. So I don't see—"

"I know you don't. And you just stuck your finger into the scabbed-
over skin of an old, but imperfectly healed wound. Better hold it there,
my dear! For what a stench of pox and blood and pus will gush out if you
move it! 'New and recent,' I believe you said. Who needs that? The old
and putrid charges will do nicely, thank you!"

"You—intrigue me. An-drew knows the story of my life in complete,
and admittedly unpleasant, detail. So what could you tell him that you
think I'd pay a fortune to prevent his finding out? Old age has addled
your head, Mary Ellen!"

"Not so you'd notice it. Who said anything about your monumental
old bore of a husband? Would you like to gather your *dear children* about
your knees and begin your charming bedtime story? Something like this,
say: 'Look, darlings, my lover Howard Tellefair lost me in a poker game
to Big Jules Tinderman back in 1850. At my new owner's behest I served
as a "pretty waiter girl" at the Dirty Spoon. Clad in a skirt *this* high,
darlings, and quite innocent of underwear the whole time. What need
had I of frilly drawers, when I spent a large part of every night sprawled
out atop the tables with stinking, bearded, louse-infested louts atop me
partaking of my favors—which is a far more genteel way of saying "ram-
ming their enormous red and rusty cocks up me and pumping away,"
isn't it?—right out in the open, while their companions cheered us on?' "

"Bon petit Jésus!" Mireille moaned.

" 'Thereafter, I rose in life, sweet children! I became *belle de la nuit,* every night, *chez Em.* First on the line in that chaste and *soignée* parlor house for three long, sweet, blissfully prosperous years. Oh, what *fun* I had! But then I've always been a lucky girl, y'know, my sugar plums! Then, another climb up the social scale: Judge Alain Curtwright's kept fancy woman. Until I roped him in with *you,* dear Stan! Whom I *bought* from a little dilly who got caught. Would you like to meet your real mother? She's in a crib in a cowyard on Sutter Street right now . . .' "

"Jesus, Jesus, Jesus!" Mireille prayed.

" 'And as for you, my darling Claire, you're mine, all right. But your real name is neither Kilpatrick, Curtwright, nor MacFarland. It's—Six. After Fire Engine Company Number Six, the entire membership of which I entertained singlehanded one night at Em's, almost exactly nine months before you were born. . . .' "

"Mary Ellen," Mireille said, her voice toneless, dead, "you wouldn't—you—won't—"

"No, of course not, darling! I wouldn't think of it! Especially not after you've plastered my mouth tight shut—with a check for a hundred thousand . . ."

She sat there gloating, triumphant. Then she added, softly, "For—starters. As—a down payment, say . . ."

Mireille got up. Walked over to her rolltop desk. Opened it. Pulled open a drawer. Groped in it. When she turned, she had her little silver-mounted, double-barreled, over and under, .41 caliber Remington derringer in her hand.

"You've outsmarted yourself, Mary Ellen," she said quietly. "Oh, no, not that you set your price too high—I'd have paid that, and anything else up to and including my life, to keep my children from being hurt—destroyed—this way. But by letting me see there'd never be an end to it. You'd bleed me white, and after neither I nor An-drew had a red cent left to buy you off, you'd still ring in How-ward, or Ray Coles, or Em herself or Chief Nolan of the fire department who was among the revelers on the night you've mentioned, and ruin me. So if you know any prayers, you'd better say one, right now . . ."

"Don't be a fool, Mireille! You'd hang for killing me, y'know!" Madame Pleasant grated.

"No. I'll never go to trial. This thing holds two shots, in case you haven't noticed. And I won't miss. Not either of us. Start praying, Mary Ellen!"

The door between the sitting room and the study crashed open. Claire stood in it, trembling.

"Maman," she said in the slow, flat, overcontrolled tones of perfect

hysteria, "killing her is—unnecessary. A threat carried out, even accidentally, ceases to be one, doesn't it? Becomes—a *fait accompli, n'est-ce
pas?*"

Mireille stared at her daughter. Sighed.

"Accidentally, Claire?" she said.

"No. Not accidentally. I listened—eavesdropped—on purpose. I had
to find out you were the—cheap, filthy, unspeakably vile whore I always
suspected you had been—*Merde!—are*. And as for you, Mammy Pleasant—"

"*Mammy* Pleasant?" Mary Ellen flared. "Use your eyes, girl! Do I look
like a 'mammy' to you?"

"Yes," Claire said evenly; "you do. A great big fat jet-black nigger
mammy, stinking up the place with your inky sweat. People say you're
part white, but I just don't see it. To me, you're black. Black as night.
Black as sin. Black as your evil heart. And *this* is what I think of you!"

Swiftly she stepped in close. Arched her head foward on the slender,
moving curve of her neck like a cobra striking. When she was near
enough, coolly, carefully, and with perfect aim she spat into Mary Ellen
Pleasant's face.

Mary Ellen didn't even hesitate. She brought her right hand whistling
around in a slap that slammed Claire's small head a full ninety degrees
around on top of a column of vertebrae scarcely meant to pivot so far,
under its almost explosive impact.

"Don't underestimate me, little white bitch," she said, almost
prayerfully. "In one way or another I've sold half a hundred hoity-toity
Miss Annes like you to the flesh peddlers of this town. So I know your
value—and your price. Mireille, let's call this round a draw. But I'll still
win. This one will be on the line in a parlor house before six months are
out."

Then she turned very quietly and walked out of there.

It was then that Mireille became aware of her son. He was kneeling,
bent far over, and vomiting endlessly into the expensive Persian rug that
covered his stepfather's study's floor.

Sometime before dawn of the morning following that same night,
both of Mireille's children left her house. They took with them only the
clothes they had on their backs, and whatever money they had in their
purses or their pockets.

It was to be months before they would be found again.

That is, if they ever were.

20

"HAVEN'T YOU FOUND THEM, AN-DREW? NOT EVEN YET?" Mireille whispered.

"Stan, yes. Claire—no. The earth seems to have opened up and swallowed her," Andrew MacFarland said sadly.

"*Bon Dieu!*" Mireille moaned. "But where is Stan, then? I must see him, talk to him, try to explain—"

"I didn't bring him home. He wouldn't come," Andy said.

"Oh, no! An-drew, you should have forced him to! Got the police, if necessary. He won't be twenty-one until next summer, and you're his legal guardian!"

"That's just the point. I'm not. He seems to have learned quite a lot of law with Otto. He spelled it out to me, honey. It appears I didn't become his legal guardian by marrying you. I could only have done that by adopting him formally before the courts. Even if you had really been his mother, that still would have been the case. And since you're not his mother, either, he tells me, and are additionally guilty of the crime of human slavery, having bought him from Joe Gammon and that evil yellow witch like a side of beef—which he has magnanimously decided to forget, as long as the two of us leave him the hell alone—we have no legal claims on him."

"*Sainte Mère Douloureuse du Dieu!*" Mireille wept.

"Mireille honey—he's fine. Looks wonderful. He's been working on the *docks* all these months, which is the last place on earth I'd have thought of looking for a boy as goddamned lazy as Stan is—no, *was*. Says he got the idea from you. Told me you threatened to put him out of the house for bad behavior once, and suggested to him that he'd make a fine dockworker because of his robust constitution. Well, he has. You should see his muscles! He has jobs on Lombard, Greenwich, and India docks—

and also on Cunningham's and Minturn's Wharves. His foreman speaks highly of him. I tried to take him into a saloon to talk to him over a relaxing snort. He wouldn't take it. Swears he's off the stuff for life. And he's quit smoking, too. Talked seriously about entering a seminary when he's saved enough, and studying to be a Catholic priest. 'You could hardly expect me to ever want to marry, now, Dad,' was what he said."

"Dieu aië pitié de moi!" Mireille sobbed.

"Honey, I suggest we leave him alone for a while longer. He's doing great. Speaks up firmly. Looked me straight in the eye. Treated me with great respect, and even a certain fondness. Said to me—" Andy halted abruptly, bowed his head, looked up with his green-blue eyes humid and misty. "Sorry, honey, I'm a sentimental old cuss, and I guess he got next to me, saying this: 'Dad, I'm glad to have known you. And I only wish I'd paid a little more attention to all the things you've tried to teach me . . .'"

"But me—what did he say about *me*, An-drew?" Mireille whispered.

"Nothing. I tried to bring up the subject of how dreadfully you were suffering, how much you missed him. He said, 'Let's not talk about— Mama, Dad.' But that's going to be all right, too. I'm sure of it. And it is, because of *her*. His real mother. He's found her, Mireille. He told me about it. Seems it was worse than horrible. She's become an opium smoker. Sells herself in a filthy crib in a Sutter Street cowyard to get the wherewithal for that hideous Oriental vice. She's only thirty-four years old, since she had Stanford at fourteen years of age, but she looks sixty. He's not sure that even yet, after dozens of visits on his part, she has understood just what the relationship between them is. Every time he goes to see her he has to convince her all over again that he is not a prospective client for her stinking, unwashed, and hideously diseased— favors . . ."

"Dieu!" Mireille said.

"I took the occasion to point out to him the exact differences between a woman like his mother, who sold him at birth, and you, who, however unfortunate your early experiences, had taken him to your bosom, showered endless love upon him, been a mother to him in the best and truest sense of the word. He looked at me, and said, 'And a *wife* to you, Dad?'"

"Oh, God!" Mireille whimpered.

"I said, '*The* best. Where could I have found a better one? Hell, son, many's the man who's taken a bride straight out of a convent school and then needed a forked stick under his chin to hold his head up under the weight of all his horns! Your mother—by the love she bears you!—has been absolutely faithful to me. I'd stake my life on that—"

"An-drew," Mireille whispered dolefully, "that's not—true. *Je t'ai trompé—une fois.* I cheated on you—*once.*"

"Oh, God!" Andrew groaned.

"Before we were married. *J'avais eu un rendezvous avec* Willy. After you had asked me to marry you. I went to—say goodbye. And to tell him I couldn't see him anymore. He—he grabbed me. I—didn't fight very hard, An-drew. I was still—too fond of him. Too—mixed up. Too *me. Fille mauvaise. Salope. Garce.* An-drew, will you forgive me? Or would it make you feel better to beat me, first?"

"Oh hell, forget it. I should have shot that half-greaser bastard a long time ago. Say! That reminds me. I ran into him on my way home. Willy, I mean. And he tried like hell to avoid seeing me. I had to literally force him to speak to me. I said, 'Hullo, Willy . . .' And he, 'Lo, Andy . . .' And, immediately thereafter, 'Excuse me, old boy; but I'm in a bit of a hurry . . .' God damn! Mireille! You don't mean to tell me—"

"No, An-drew. That's—finished. It has been, ever since you and I were married. All my life I've wanted to be—*bonne, honnête,* decent. And you gave me the chance to be. I wasn't—am not—going to spoil that for ten million Willys. But—I have spoiled it, haven't I? My past caught up with me. Robbed me of—my children. Don't worry about Willy. You don't have to. Oh! *Oh bon Dieu! Lui! Willy! Ce bon salaud! Ce chasseur des jupes! C'est ça! C'est bien ça! Viens!"*

"Mireille, what on earth are you talking about?"

"Willy. *Et* Claire. *Elle était follemente amoureuse de lui! Elle m'a confessée ça! Et—"*

"Mireille, please! English, huh? The only language I kind of, sort of, understand?"

"Willy. Claire's in love with him. She told me so, An-drew. When poor Molly had that *crise cardiaque* and everybody thought she was going to die, Claire was dancing on air. So she would go to him. She is *my* daughter, *après toute.* Which means she has no scruples, and not a moral to her name. And since Willy hasn't any either—"

"By God, if he has debauched Claire, I'll pistol him!"

"No, An-drew. It would be more just to shoot Claire. Willy is not—*méchant.* Just—weak. While Claire *is—méchante.* Very. Come on! I will hold him and you will beat on him until he confesses where he's got her hid!"

"No, Mireille."

"Sacre nom d'un—"

"That's not smart. You stay home. I'll drop in on him, casually. Have a gentlemanly chat—between friends. We *are* friends, Willy and I, in spite of all the excellent reasons you've given me to kill him. As you said, he really isn't a bad sort. I'll make him so damned ashamed that he'll confess—"

"An-drew, don't carry—*ton pistolet* with you. You might get mad. Lose your temper, and—"

"What if *he* gets mad? Loses *his* temper? And has *his* artillery on him?"

"Oh, Lord! An-drew, let *me* go! I can—"

"Shut up, honey," Andrew said, and kissed her. "What problems would you have if I got mine? The richest widow in town? And the prettiest? Hell, when the *Bulletin* publishes my obit, they'll have to call out the Marines!"

"An-drew, that's hateful! That's mean! If anything happened to *you*, my love, I'd die!"

"I know. At ninety-three. Sit tight, honey. I'll have this straightened out by dark . . ."

But he didn't. He couldn't. Not because he didn't get the truth out of Guillermo Kilpatrick, but because part—the main and essential part—of that truth was that Willy really didn't know where Claire was.

"Don't lie to me, Willy!" Andrew MacFarland roared.

"I'm not," Willy snapped. "Oh, for God's sake, Andy, ol' boy, quit playing the heavy father right out of a bad melodrama, will you? The role doesn't suit you. Anyhow, let's remove this session the goddamned hell out of my office, where my secretary, the office boy, and all the clerks in the anteroom are just quivering with delight, waiting for you to shoot me or something. They'd adore that, grubby ink-stained beggars. I happen to be the kind of boss who believes salaries should be earned. What d'you say to a corner table at Dolan's? Where, if you'll keep your temper in check and your voice down, we might be able to arrive at something useful."

"All right," Andy growled. "And I apologize—not for losing my temper, but for losing it in *here*. I shouldn't like for a chap to come into my office roaring like a bull, either . . ."

Willy grinned at him.

"Apology's accepted." He chuckled. "God knows I shouldn't like to be in your shoes, old boy, having to put up with both Mireille and Claire at the same time. One of 'em's enough to send a man crawling up the wall by his fingernails—but two? Andy, I pity you! Now, come on . . ."

"Lord!" Willy whispered. "So *that* was it! Mary Ellen Pleasant gave the kids a *Police Gazette* type report on poor Mireille's past history, and in full detail? Somebody ought to shoot that yellow witch!"

"Mireille almost did. Incidentally, Willy, come off of that 'poor' Mireille business. I resent it. There's nothing poor about my wife—not in the sense of being small-minded, little of soul, mean-spirited, or in any sense I can think of. You can't judge Mireille by the standards that apply to other people. Especially not to other women. To me she's—very simply—magnificent. I'm glad to have known her. Proud."

"I used the word only in the sense that her past was—unfortunate. She's had an awful lot of pure damned bad luck, y'know. On all the other points I agree with you, fully. She *is* magnificent. Which doesn't keep her from being a magnificent pain in the posterior at times, old boy—as you know. But in this case, Destiny knew what it was doing. You're perfect for her, Andy. I shouldn't have been. That God-given calm you're possessed of is exactly what she needed. Although it seems to be running out on you a bit, today. Incidentally, if any of your ire arises from the rumors you may have heard touching Mireille's supposed relations with me, may I say those rumors are lies? She's been absolutely faithful to you, old boy. Or, if she hasn't been, I'm not the guilty party! Take my word for that. And not as the word of a gentleman, both because I'm not much of one, to tell the truth about it, and because a gentleman would be constrained to lie in defense of a woman's reputation. Hell, Andy, if I could have adorned your forehead for you, I'd damn well have done it. But Mireille took her vows, once given, very seriously, believe me. She respects you tremendously, and the institution of marriage even more. So if that's one of the things that's eating at your guts, forget it, will you? Those unfounded rumors have cost me hell enough at home—up to and including my poor Molly's physical health, in fact . . ."

"Thanks, Willy. I appreciate your good will. But I already knew the facts in your case. Mireille told me. And if there's any one human being on God's green earth I believe absolutely, it is she. She simply doesn't lie —not to me, anyhow. She doesn't even conceal too many things from me, which, in a woman, is a miracle, as you know damned well. But let's get back to Claire. You mean to tell me you haven't seen her at all?"

Willy hesitated.

"Andy," he sighed, "you seem to have developed a truly paternal love for Claire. And that's entirely natural, since you brought her up. But may I say I feel exactly the same way about her? To me, she's—or at least ought to have been—as much my daughter as Kate, Molly, and Raquel are—"

"By the way, how is little Raquel?" Andrew interrupted him, with real interest in his voice. "Mireille and I are both terribly fond of her. The other two we never got to know well at all—especially since they both married early and moved away from San Francisco—"

"To escape the utter disaster my married life has been," Willy said bitterly. "Oh, Raquel's fine. Still pining over that runaway lout of yours. I've told her and told her she should accept young Cunningham, who is a much more promising lad than your Stanford ever was. An estimation of their respective characters that you ought to be able to accept, considering the fact that Stan hasn't one drop of your blood in his veins; but she's mule-stubborn on that subject, and—"

"Good. Tell her to stick to her guns. Willy, I've found him. Stanford, I mean. And you wouldn't know him. If there ever was a totally reformed character, it's my Stan. The shock of Mammy Pleasant's revelations seems to have turned him completely around. Too far around. So I'm going to need little Raquel—to stop that fool boy from carrying out his present determination to enter the Catholic priesthood, for one reason. My others—are various. All falling under the heading that I honestly believe our children would be good for each other, my friend . . ."

"Maybe," Willy said sardonically, "though what I've seen of matrimony wouldn't incline me to try to stop a son of mine from becoming a priest, or a monk, either one. I'll tell Raquel you've found him. She'll probably come flying over to your house like a homing pigeon at the news . . ."

"Tell her to. I want to talk to her—take counsel with her—about how to handle the present situation. But Willy, about Claire—?"

"I don't know where she is. I honestly don't. All right, I have seen her. Once. From what you've told me, it must have been the same night she left home. Or the night after. Anyhow, months ago . . ."

Andrew stared at him.

"Willy," he said, very, very quietly, "under what precise circumstances did you see Claire?"

"They were—rough. Which was the reason for that preamble to the constitution I gave you a while back. You know, about my feeling as fatherly as you do toward her, and with almost as good a reason? That feeling saved me from a sin—no, a crime!—that would have unseated my reason, Andy. For if what it prevented—had happened, I'd be dead now. I'd have had no other recourse but to shove the muzzle of my revolver into my mouth, and blow the back of my head off . . ."

"Willy—" Andrew said.

"Look, Andy, Claire is not your daughter. Always remember that. She's not mine. She is, from the evidence brought out by Otto at Mireille's trial—which you attended, remember?—Judge Alain Curtwright's. She and Stanford are twins, however little they look alike; and for twins to have two different fathers would be quite a trick, wouldn't it?"

"It would," Andrew said grimly. "But I don't see the relevance of all this. Why do you bring it up?"

"Andy, I came out of Mulligan's, on upper Pacific Street, that night—or, rather, that morning—as drunk as an Irish peer. And a pretty—no, a gloriously beautiful young thing came up to me and took my arm. It was dark, and my eyes weren't focusing worth a damn by then. I couldn't see —didn't recognize—her face . . ."

"Jesus!" Andrew whispered, prayerfully.

"Wait. Hear me out, old boy! She said, 'Darling—isn't there any place nearby where the two of us could go to be—alone?' "

"Christ!" Andrew said, agony in his voice.

"Even drunk as I was, that surprised me. The girlies who patrol Pacific Street know—or have—places to go. So I blinked at her like a wise old owl and said, 'You're new . . .' "

"And His Mother Mary!" Andrew said.

"She said, 'Yes. You're my first—client—tonight. You aren't going to turn me down, are you, darling?' Her voice would have melted rocks. So I said, 'How much?' "

"Willy," Andrew grated, "as I told Mireille this morning, I should have killed you years ago!"

"For what, may I ask? Oh, for God's sake, Andy, don't be unnecessarily stupid! D'you think I'd have even started in to tell you this if anything had really happened? I could have simply kept my ruddy mouth shut, y'know!"

"True," Andrew whispered; "please go on."

"She said, 'I don't know. What are the going rates these days?' "

"And you?"

"I said, 'Looking like you do, baby, you can name your price!' "

"Then?" Andrew said.

"I took her to Tilly's. It's a fairly decent house of assignation just around the corner on Powell Street. Of course it belongs to Mammy Pleasant, but what the hell, I'm not rich enough for that old witch to bother to blackmail . . ."

"But Claire is. And that she-devil hates Mireille for reasons that you know. She probably hates Claire even worse now, but that's beside the point. Goddammit, Willy, on top of debauching my daughter, did you also have to play into that female monster's hands?"

"Now, just you hold on there, Andy! Apart from the fact that—as I'm trying to tell you—*nothing* happened, consider this postulate, will you? Even if something had, *who* would have been seducing or debauching *whom* would have been distinctly a moot point! *I* didn't station Claire outside of Mulligan's at two goddamned o'clock in the morning, y'know! And she was damned well informed of my nocturnal habits, anyhow. Who told her I hang out at that particular groggery? You?"

"No. And I don't know how she got that information. Go on, will you?"

"We went upstairs. She said to the colored maid who accompanied us, 'Don't put on the gas lights!' Only she said it too sharply—and anyhow, the night air had revived me a bit by then. So I said, 'Why the hell not, baby?' And she, 'I don't want you to see my face.' And I, 'Same question, pet! Why the hell not?' She whispered, 'I'm married. You—might even know me, attorney Kilpatrick. You *do* know my husband. This is the first time I've ever done a thing like this.' So I asked her, 'Why are you doing it now?' She said, 'My husband's—sick. He needs—an operation. His case is—desperate. I have nobody to turn to, so—' "

"And you believed *that?*" Andrew snorted.

"Of course not! It rang falser than old hell. They *all* have sick husbands, or sick babies, or old gray-bearded, crippled granddads to support! But I pretended to go along. So I said, 'All right, sweetheart, get out of your things.' I waited until she was busy with her buttons and suchlike, and struck a match. She whirled, blew it out. But I had seen her face. The second most beautiful face in all San Francisco . . ."

"And the first?" Andrew said quietly.

"As if you didn't know. Mireille's."

"Go on," Andrew said.

"I lit the gas jets, said, 'Let me button you back up again, Claire. We're getting out of here . . .' "

"She didn't make a scene? *Claire?*" Andrew said.

"She could have shown Lotta Crabtree how to do it. Bernhardt herself. I have never received a more passionate and convincing declaration of love from a woman in all my life—"

"And yet—you resisted?" Andrew said in a tone, compared to which the Sahara was a muddy swamp.

"I resisted. Jesus, Andy—she's Mireille's daughter. *Mireille's!*"

"And that makes—made—a difference?"

"That made all the difference in the world. It made the whole proposition too—nauseatingly close to actual incest. My feeling toward Claire
has always been precisely that: that the filthiest trick Fate ever played on
me was to make her someone else's daughter, and not mine, the way she
should have been. I could no more fall into bed with her than you could,
Andy!"

"I'm glad of that. But tell me this: Why didn't you call a hack and
bring her *home*, Willy?"

"I was going to. But when we finally got downstairs—a good bit later,
because unwrapping a young and determined female from around one's
neck takes some doing, old boy—"

"Especially when one really doesn't want to," Andrew said.

"Hell, who, with his male equipment in working order, *does?* But I did
it, finally. Anyhow, outside on the sidewalk she said, very quietly, 'Since
you won't relieve me of the virginity I was saving just for you, whom I
love, I'll get someone else to!' "

"What did you say to that?"

" 'You'll have to, Claire. I don't want you on my conscience. Push a
piece off on one of those pretty boys you go whirling along with in smart
rigs on Sundays. Or, better still—get married. You're old enough to
now . . .' "

"I can imagine what she said to that."

"No you can't, Andy. She shocked even me. She said, 'I'll get somebody loathsome, Willy. Repulsive. A big black buck nigger. A—Chinaman. A greaser.' I said, '*I'm* a greaser, Claire.' 'Only, you're a—beautiful
one,' she whispered; 'I mean a little dark, greasy one. And I'll do it *now*.
I'll go to Addie's . . .' Then she ran off down the street . . ."

"Didn't you go after her?" Andrew asked.

"Of course. But my head was whirling counterclockwise by then. She
was lucky enough to catch a hack at the corner of the next street—
Jackson Street, in fact. And off they went, with the hack driver applying
his whip to his nag with uncommon vigor—probably at her request, or
demand. That's all I know. That was the last time I saw your—*our*—
daughter, Andy. Because damned if I don't have almost as much right to
her as you do, old boy . . ."

Andrew MacFarland stared at Willy Kilpatrick. Like many big, slow-
going, placid-appearing men, Andy was far more shrewd, more subtle
than people gave him credit for being. So he hadn't been able to quite
swallow the elaborate tale Willy had been fabricating. Some of it was
unquestionably true. But—how much of it? The highest pinnacle of the
born liar's art, he'd long since learned, was to tell the strict truth and

distort it a little, twist it away from its natural denouement, its inevitable consequences, into slight tangents that seemed as logical and were as believable to one not in possession of all the facts. As he wasn't. Willy also had the great advantage of knowing both Mireille and her daughter very, very well. So if he wanted to put words in their mouths, he could speak their language, as it were, give what he said their habitual emphasis, tricks of speech, turns of phrase, verbal idiosyncrasies. Except, of course, their lyrical bursts into appoggiaturas, runs, glissandos of silvery French, to which he was as tone-deaf as Andy himself . . .

'The only trouble with this fable,' Andy mused, 'is that it makes this offspring of two very slippery races, Irish and Mexican, look too damned good. Willy's not a bad sort, but his resistance to a well-turned ankle— and a tautly stuffed blouse and skirt—is awfully small. True, he sincerely would have *wanted* to turn Claire down. But, under the circumstances he has described, *could* he have? Let's test the matter and see . . .'

"You may have even more right to Claire than I, Willy," he said quietly.

"Eh? I don't follow you, Andy . . ."

"Know you don't. The evidence at that trial—part of it, anyhow—was faked. Oh, none of it that had any bearing on Judge Curtwright's death. Don't worry about that. It seems that my dear little wife, out of her hunger for respectability—the Judge had already settled a young fortune on her by then, so her motives were definitely *not* pecuniary—in order to induce Alain Curtwright to divorce his mad wife and marry *her*, had that birthmark tattooed behind Stan's left ear. She confessed as much to me. Which may change nothing at all. I didn't know Mireille then. Perhaps she was as faithful to the Judge as she has been to me. A birthmark? Bah! What's a birthmark? It doesn't *have* to be inherited, y'know. Oh, I say, Willy! You look positively sick! What's the matter, my friend?"

"Nothing," Willy groaned.

"Willy," Andrew said sternly, "you still insist that you didn't—touch —Claire that night?"

Willy glared at him like a madman, roared at him like a pride of lions: "On my mother's grave, I swear it!"

"All right," Andy sighed. "But one thing still puzzles me: Who—or what—is Addie's?"

Willy's blue eyes opened very wide.

"I don't know. I truly don't know. I don't recall ever having heard that name before. I'll have to investigate. And you do so, too, Andy. Whichever one of us gets a lead first will call the other. All right?"

"Agreed," Andrew said. "D'you think it might be important?"

"Who can say? But—it's a sore thumb, isn't it? A detail that sticks out, and is incongruous. I vote we start with it, Andy. What else do we have?"

"You're right. So far we have—nothing. Nothing at all," Andrew Mac-Farland said.

21

THE MINUTE STANFORD MACFARLAND SAW THE FIVE YOUTHS WHO
were beating—very likely to death, considering his apparent age and
fragility—the old Chinese, he knew that they were hoodlums. He could
tell that by the way they were dressed, if their membership in one of San
Francisco's numerous gangs of young street rowdies hadn't already been
proclaimed by their actions, for the hoodlums' principal sport consisted
in pounding to a bloody mush with brass knuckles and hickory clubs,
cutting the queues off the heads of, blinding, maiming, otherwise torturing and, quite frequently, murdering any son of the Celestial Empire
who had the misfortune to accidentally pass their way. Their second
principal sport—or perhaps their third, for Stan had to concede that
their first actually was loitering about in front of the low dives on the
Barbary Coast and doing absolutely nothing at all—was breaking into
the cribs and even the parlor houses on the fringes of Chinatown, in
which the Chinese slave-girl prostitutes were confined, robbing the poor
defenseless creatures of their earnings, and forcing them to submit, not
merely to mass rape, but to whatever other types of sexual abuses came
to their fertile—and evil!—minds, among which fellatio and sodomy
predominated.

The hoodlums were strictly a local phenomenon. Even the name itself
had been invented in San Francisco, though Stan wouldn't have ventured to lay money on which of the three theories as to its origin currently being fiercely argued in the pages of as many of the city's newspapers was the correct one.

'I don't care *why* they're called hoodlums,' he thought; 'I hate their
bloody cruel guts, whatever they're called . . .'

He stood there, caught up in another dilemma—like all his problems
nowadays, a moral one. Gazing at the hoodlums as they pounded the

poor old Chinaman with hickory clubs, smashed brass knuckles into his
face, slashed notches in his nose and ears with their knives, ground their
cigarettes out against his pale yellow skin, kicked his ribs in, Stan tried to
maintain the emotional distance not to intervene. There were five of the
hoodlums in that space of muddy ground underneath the wharf, and
there was only one of him. Of course he was taller and stronger than any
one of them; his work on the docks had given him a set of muscles he
was quietly proud of. But five to one just weren't sensible odds when the
five were armed with billy clubs, blackjacks, brass knuckles, and spring-
loaded switchblade knives, and the one had only his dockworker's baling
hook to use against them.

So he turned his mind away from the strong probability that a beating
like that one had already fatally injured the ancient Chinese, and waited,
with the piously Catholic, perhaps even Christian, thought of offering
the old man what succor he could after the hoods got through with him.
To keep his outrage—he was by nature a kindly young man, and his
association with the Chinese servants in his step-parents' house had give
him a keen fondness for that strange and brilliant Oriental race—from
getting the better of his common sense, Stanford focused his attention,
and his contempt, upon the hoodlums' clothes.

Although no single one of them had had a bath in the past year or
two, in spite of the twenty-odd public bathhouses that San Francisco
boasted, so that their collective stench would have floored a herd of
goats, the hoodlums were dandies to the man. Their clothes were extravagantly foppish, wildly exaggerated in their cut: coattails reaching down
to the middle of their calves in the back, shoulders padded pagoda-shape
up to the tips of their filthy ears, enormous lapels stained black at collar
level with the grease that held their rolled, puffed, exquisitely coiffed
hairdos in place, skintight pants, most of them fawn-colored, knee-high
boots, burgundy-colored velvet or black-and-gold embroidered waist-
coats, and various kinds of slouch hats with broad brims, including even
an occasional Mexican sombrero.

Then, quite suddenly, Stan put his hand down to his belt and drew out
his dockworker's baling hook. He always carried that formidable weapon
—an iron claw with a crosswise wooden handle used to dig into packing
cases or bales of shipped goods and haul them either up onto the hand
trucks to be trundled away to the waiting dray wagons, or into the nets
that the steam-operated dockside cranes then lifted and swung out over
the waiting freighters to lower with their contents as gently as possible
into the cargo holds—with him on his way home to his chaste and quiet
rented room on Greenwich Street just back of Telegraph Hill. And the

reason he always wore his hook thrust into his belt when he wasn't working was the hoodlums themselves. They weren't averse to robbing a white dockworker of his weekly pay by sheer force of numbers, though they usually respected his dignity as a fellow member of the superior race by refraining from beating him bloody as they always did Hispano-Americans and Orientals.

'Six!' he thought grimly. 'That's even worse odds, but all the same—'

For by then he had seen the girl. The sixth member of the gang, the one Stanford hadn't seen before, was dragging her out from behind the pillars of the wharf, apparently at a signal from the others, who having—correctly, as it turned out—decided the ancient Chinese was done for, turned their attention to other matters.

"Bring th' slant-eyed bitch over here!" their leader howled. "Tha's it! Now make her bend over on her hands and knees. Tha's th' proper way to mount bitches, ain't it? Dog-fashion!"

"I got seconds!" a gaudily attired hoodlum sang out.

"Hell, Rob, you can hump 'er at th' same time!" the leader laughed. "Ram yourn down 'er yaller throat!"

"Be keerful, Rob! Mebbe she bites! Looks like a *mean* bitch t'me!" the hood beneath the Mexican sombrero chuckled.

Stan moved forward quietly. The hoodlum called Rob caught the Chinese girl by her silken black hair.

"Open up, Cherry Blossom—or whatever th' hell yer moniker is! Gonna swab yer tonsils fer you, baby! Give you a taste o' nice *white* cock! A helluva lot better'n rancid yaller Chink sausage, sugar!"

The leader stretched out his hand and jerked down the ankle-length black silk pajama trousers the girl modestly wore beneath the slit shirt of her cheongsam, exposing a pair of shapely buttocks. Stan was surprised to see how white they were, for he had not yet realized that the definition of skin color is actually a function of racism; that a people capable of calling—when, of course, they were aware of her origins—a blond, blue-eyed woman like his mother's—correction!—his stepmother's friend Mrs. Olaf Svenson a Black, and Mary Ellen Pleasant "Mammy" wouldn't even perceive that many Chinese actually are white, not yellow.

But what surprised him even more was his own reaction to that sight. Ever since he had left home, in his hurt, sick overreaction to Madame Pleasant's hideous revelations about the past life of the good, loving, tender, sweet *mother* he'd adored since babyhood, he had taken a strict, if silent, vow of celibacy, and bent his thoughts toward a profession and a way of life he was absolutely unfitted for—that is, if any normal man ever is fitted for it. So the gut-deep, white-hot burst of purely sexual hunger that gripped his loins at the sight of that lovely, pear-shaped Oriental fundament shocked him to the core, awoke shame in him, and hard upon it, rage. Which, being mostly gentle in all essential ways, was exactly what he needed at the moment.

Then he saw what the leader of the hoodlums was trying—unsuccessfully, so far—to do, which was to sodomize the helpless girl. And that, when combined with the hood named Rod's simultaneous attempt to commit what might best be described as buccal rape upon her, outraged Stanford MacFarland enough to free him completely of the tenuous hold that civilization has on the human male animal anyhow.

With one long bound, he sprang forward and sank the point of that terrible hook as deep as its curve would permit it to go, into the hoodlum leader's back. As he hauled back on the handle, the leader's scream split the very sky.

Stan paid him no further attention. As he knew damned well from the occasional fights between drunken dockworkers he had witnessed, a man who'd had a baling hook sunk into any part of his upper trunk was out of the fight for good, so he yanked the hook free and slung it sidewise at Rob, who still stood there with his genitalia exposed, ludicrously frozen into a posture that would have been excruciatingly embarrassing if that young, perfect example of utter depravity had been capable of either embarrassment or shame.

But he was capable of feeling pain. The gurgling, blood-drenched, choking howl he let out when Stanford's hook tore through the side of his mouth, opening it from jaw hinge to chin point, tearing from it most of his tongue and a shower of yellow, rotting teeth as that awful iron point ripped free, was the ugliest single sound that, up to that moment, Stan had ever heard.

And very nearly the most satisfying. No race has a monopoly upon cruelty. Man, in all his variations of coloring, stature, hair texture, eye formation and the like, remains the most bestial of the beasts. But no tribe among his hosts seems to be more easily autointoxicated by it than the Nordics; it is no accident that "berserker" is a Teutonic word. So now Mireille's darling boy retreated through centuries of evolution back to his filthy, louse-infested, muddleheaded Celtic and Scandinavian ancestors and with roars berserk enough to delight the murderous hearts of the best, or the worst, of them, fell upon his four remaining foes like Sigurd, like Tyr, like Thor.

Fortunately he only reached one more, whom he chopped a couple of convincing holes into, before going after the other three. But a yard away, he halted. Those three valiant defenders of white supremacy against the onslaught of the Yellow Peril were breaking all past, present, and future track records away from the particular, relativistic segment of space and time occupied by Stanford MacFarland.

He turned back to his private butcher shop. Walked over to the girl. To his vast relief, she had pulled her pants up and the slit skirt of her cheongsam down over her hips before he got there. Which gave him the opportunity to concentrate on her face. At once a helpless prey to those mindless little glands that make the survival of the race a certainty by, upon the receipt of the proper stimuli, instantly boiling away or otherwise dissolving the brains, he decided that she was the most beautiful Chinese girl he'd ever seen. Then, as the pink cherry blossoms of her lips curved into a trembling, obviously badly frightened smile, he amended that into, 'No! Of any ruddy race whatsoever!'

He sought for and found a phrase that Duck Soup had taught him.

"What—is—your—name?" he said in slow, careful, atrociously mispronounced Mandarin Chinese.

She stared at him, her dark, lovely, almond-shaped eyes perfectly blank, the incomprehension in them complete.

He tried again.

"What—is your—name?"

She was, as he would soon learn, very intelligent, extremely quick-witted. She guessed that those horrible sounds he was making were supposed to be Chinese. She found this remarkably touching; that a foreign devil had gone to the trouble to try to learn Chinese was outside of all her previous experience.

"Do you not—speak English?" she said.

"Good God! Of course! And so do you! How is it that you speak it, Miss—"

"Wang, Loi Yan," she said.

"Miss Wang Loi Yan—"

"No, no!" she said with a sad little giggle. "Other way around. First name, Loi Yan. Family name Wang. You understand?"

"Perfectly, Miss Wang. Or is it—Mrs.?"

"No, no. Not married, yet—mebbe never. You help me with venerable ancestor?"

"Yes. Sure thing." He walked over to where the old man lay. Bent over him. Straightened up. "I'm—afraid—he—he's gone," he whispered.

"No matter," she said in a matter-of-fact way that he found terribly shocking, since he didn't know then that the Chinese consider the public display of private emotions the worst kind of bad form. "Pick venerable ancestor up. We take him to joss house . . ."

"All right," Stanford said. "But don't you have to notify—your other relatives? Your mother, say? Your—father?"

"Mother, father, both long time dead," she whispered.

"Then your venerable ancestor is—?"

"Father's father," Loi Yan said simply. "Pick him up. He no weigh much."

Stan bent and picked up the dead body of the ancient Chinese. Loi Yan was right. He weighed practically nothing.

"Long time eat very little," she said just as matter-of-factly. "Stomach bad. Understand?"

"Yes," Stanford said. "Tell me, Miss Wang—"

"Loi Yan. Please. I like you," she said.

"Thank you. And I like *you*, Loi Yan. I like you very much. This probably isn't the time to say so, but you're one of the most beautiful girls I've ever met . . ."

"No. Not nice tell lies. China girl ugly. Like monkey."

"Good Lord, Loi Yan, if *you're* a monkey, I'm going to learn to swing from the trees by my tail!"

She laughed at that. In triads. Like Chinese music. Tinkling little silver bells in a pagoda. Then, abruptly, she sobered.

She nodded her head towards the groaning, bleeding hoodlums.

"White devils die, you catch big trouble?" she asked him.

"They won't die," Stan said contemptuously; "and even if they do, they had it coming. Now let's go. You lead me to that joss house of yours . . ."

"All right," Loi Yan said.

"Say that again!" Stan said sharply.

"All right," Loi Yan said.

"Now say—rat. Round. Road. Roll. Rush."

"Rat, round, road, roll, rush," Loi Yan said. Then she got it. "Oh! Lat, lound, load, loll, lush!" she said mischievously.

"You know, you're the first Chinese I've ever met who can pronounce the English 'r,'" Stan told her admiringly.

"Any of us can, who were born here," she said, dropping the pidgin altogether; "as I was . . ."

"When?" he said.

"Eighteen fifty-eight. Old, old woman. See: no teeth. White hair!"

"You're a mischievous little girl, that's for sure," Stan said. "Aren't you sorry your grandfather's dead?"

"Yes. Very. I mean vely."

"Stop it!" Stan said angrily. "Have some respect for him, will you?"

At once her dark eyes hazed over, glittered. Jet. Black diamonds. Her tears made them extraordinarily beautiful, Stan thought.

"I'm—sorry," he said contritely.

"You're—good," she whispered; "didn't know a white man could be good. But you *are*, aren't you?"

"I try to be," Stan said. "But mostly I fail at it. Come on."

In those days Telegraph Hill extended much closer to the waterfront than it would even ten years later when much of it had been cut down and used as fill to bring more of the shallower parts of the Bay above-water to be used as building lots. So to get around its eastern slopes to the Tin How Temple by what they judged to be the most direct route, they walked south on Battery Street. Now Stanford didn't know where *any* Chinese temple was; and as for Loi Yan, the truth of the matter was that she didn't either. The reason for this was very simple: Like any dutiful Chinese maiden, she had seldom ventured out of the nameless alley in Chinatown, somewhere between Pacific and Jackson streets, on which she lived with her now departed grandfather Li Huan Chin, in a rather pretty little house that had been brought from China in numbered pieces and reassembled in San Francisco. More to the point, Li Huan Chin had piously erected twin altars to both the great hero Quan Dai and the Queen of the Heavens, Tin How herself, in one corner of their little house, so that they could worship at home and not have to run the risks involved in walking to the temple. Therefore that Loi Yan didn't know exactly how to get to the joss house was hardly strange. But Stanford had been told by Xiaop Siu, alias Duck Soup, that it was very close to St. Mary's Catholic Cathedral, so they started walking south on Battery Street in the general direction of that well-known landmark, whose towers could be seen from some distance away.

"Why were you so far away from Chinatown, Loi Yan?" Stan asked her. "Cunningham's wharf is miles from Dupont Street."

She seemed to hesitate before answering him. While he waited for her to make up her mind, he reflected with relief on the fact that, except for the smell of blood, the light and fragile body in his arms had a very pleasant odor. Then it came to him why. The dead man was practically smoke-cured by the quantities of incense he had burned daily in that little house before the altars of the gods of his ancestors.

"The venerable ancestor," she said finally, "took me to the wharf to meet my husband."

"Your *husband?*"

"Yes. He was to come from China today on the steamship *Blue Star.*

Only, when the ship arrived he was not on it. We waited until everyone came ashore to make sure. But Djan Ching was not among them. And after that the white devils caught us."

"Maybe he ran off with another girl," Stan teased her solemnly. "Did you love him very much?"

"No. How could I? I have never seen him. Perhaps I should have learned to, later on. His father sent the venerable ancestor a portrait of him when they signed the marriage contract. He seems—nice. Would you like to see it?"

"Sure thing!" Stan said.

She whirled away from him and did some sleight of hand under the front of her cheongsam. A second later she unrolled a rice-paper scroll and spread it out between her two hands so that he could see it. Stanford wondered where the devil she'd had it hidden under that high-necked, close-fitting dress so that no bulge had been visible at all. A man's face had been brushed across the scroll in deft strokes of various colored inks. It was a little masterpiece of Chinese art; but, to his Occidental eyes, it was too stylized to be recognizable as an individual human being. There were Chinese characters running vertically down one side of it.

"What does that say?" Stan asked her.

"Just his name. Djan Ching," she said.

"I'm sorry I'm such a duffer at Chinese," Stan said.

"Oh, no, you're not! You speak beautiful Mandarin!" she said.

"So beautiful that you didn't understand a word I said," he murmured sadly.

She smiled at him. Tenderly, he was almost sure.

"Mandarin is the language of Peiping, which is in the North of China. My family is from the South. Therefore we speak a dialect of Cantonese. I know only a few words of Mandarin. Do you understand—Swedish, say?"

"No," he said.

"It is the same. China is almost as big as Europe. We have just about as many languages. Here in San Francisco we speak English among ourselves when we are from different parts of China, or else we could not understand one another. Are you growing tired? If so, I will carry the venerable ancestor for a while."

"Of course not! I wouldn't think of letting you do that," Stan told her.

"You are very nice—for a foreign devil," she said solemnly.

"I'm not a very successful devil," he teased her; "I'll have to practice snorting fire more often!"

"Oh!" she said. "That is—strange. The translation is a bad one. You see, in all the Chinese languages we have only one word for foreigner and one word for devil. Only, I am sorry to say, it is the *same* word. I suppose that is because our experiences with foreigners have always been—unfortunate . . ."

"And I suppose you're right. We *are* devils, aren't we?"

"I do not think *you* are," Loi Yan said. "I—I'm afraid we're lost. I do not know how to reach the joss house from here . . ."

"Tell you what: Let's keep on till we get to California Street, then turn west on it until we get to St. Mary's Cathedral. It's in Chinatown, and quite close to the Chinese temple, I've been told. One of the Catholic priests will tell us how to get there. Or some of the Chinese people in the street. That is, if they speak the right kind of Chinese . . ."

"Or any kind at all. Many of the younger people don't, nowadays. That used to make the venerable ancestor sad. But your suggestion is a wise one. We will do it that way."

The only problem they had en route to St. Mary's was the number of people who stopped to stare—or glare!—at the sight of a tall, strong, remarkably handsome young white man walking calmly down Battery Street with the unconscious, or dead, body of an ancient Chinese in his arms, and with a diminutive girl of the same despised and downtrodden race trotting along beside him.

That attitude of mind saddened Stanford, who was quite broadminded in his approach to people of races and cultures different from his own. But at the moment it worried him even more. Every time some sturdy citizen dropped open his yellow-fanged mouth with a muttered, "Wal, I'll be gol-durned!" Stan was afraid one of them might recognize him and go rushing off to Andrew MacFarland's office to inform his stepfather. Or, worse still, to the MacFarlands' Nob Hill mansion to inform his —stepmother.

Then, abruptly, he stopped dead. By that time they were walking westward along California Street, and Saint Mary's was in plain sight. So was the slim, striking middle-aged man who was standing on the sidewalk and staring up at the tower of the church—because Saint Mary's was a cathedral only by reason of its recent elevation to that rank by the ecclesiastical authorities, not by its rather modest architectural structure—as though he'd never seen the inscription on the clock before. That inscription read: "Son, Observe the Time and Flee from Evil."

'And he has seen it,' Stanford thought; 'he's had to. He's lived here practically all his life . . .'

"Why do you stop, Stanford?" Loi Yan asked him. "Do you arms ache?"

"A little," Stanford admitted ruefully. "But it's not that. It's that man. I'd just as soon he didn't see us—"

Loi Yan's face fell. And because Orientals aren't any more inscrutable than any other peoples, Stan easily read her thought.

"It's not because of you," he said quietly, "nor because of Grand—of the venerable ancestor. I—ran away from home. And he's—a friend of my stepfather's. And since I won't be twenty-one years old until next May, I'd much prefer that people didn't go back to my house bearing tales . . ."

"He—he's going into the church," Loi Yan said.

"Let's wait till he's inside, then we'll go on," Stanford rasped in an edgy tone of voice.

"He is—a very beautiful man," Loi Yan said softly. "Do you know him well?"

"Jesus!" Stan exploded.

She stared at him, studied his face with those marvelous almond-shaped eyes.

"You—are—angry with me," she said. "What have I done to offend you, Stanford?"

"Made me jealous," Stan said.

"Of—him?" She nodded toward the retreating back of the slim blond man in his early fifties who was disappearing through the cathedral's doors.

"Of him—and of any man you show too much interest in, Loi Yan."

"But why? I am only a little yellow monkey of a China-girl who—"

"Whom I'm in love with. Now shut up and come on," Stanford MacFarland said.

The slim blond man they had seen going into Saint Mary's knelt in one side of the confessional box. In the other, an Irish padre also knelt, listening to his slow, hesitant, confused and confusing words. As the man talked on, the expression of incredulity on the priest's face increased, deepened, began to transform itself into righteous wrath.

"Wait, my son!" the priest said. "What, actually, are you confessing? That you have been guilty of carnal knowledge of a young woman only twenty years of age? By the way, are you married?"

"Yes, Padre," the blond man said.

"Then 'tis adultery ye're confessin' to, my son?"

"I—don't know, Father. It may be that—or it may be something—even worse," the man said morosely.

"Holy Mither of God!" the priest exploded. "Worse than adultery? And just what, son, d'ye consider worse than adultery—amang th' carnal sins, anyhow, may I ask?"

"Incest," the man said.

Immediately the priest calmed down. Got a grip on himself. This confession was far too serious for him to lose his temper over, and he knew it. Conceivably, he was going to have to carry the matter to the bishop, who, in his turn, would very likely take it to His Grace the archbishop himself. ' 'Tis,' he conceded, 'a *very* hot potato, and each hand into which it falls will want to toss it away as fast—and as far—as possible. *Up* the heirarchy, naturally; each little ecclesiastical coward claiming the want of sufficient authority to handle it. It could go to—excommunication. Expulsion from the Mither Church. But before I toss it up, I'd better know just where I stand.'

"Ye're saying that ye've had guilty carnal knowledge of yer own *daughter,* my son?" he said.

"I don't know, Padre. It might be that—"

"By Our Lady!" the priest swore. "Did you, or didn't you? Speak clearly, son!"

"I can't. I'm not sure I did anything to—with—her at all. I'm not even sure she's my daughter . . ."

"Son, you're at the wrong address. The madhouse is out on Mission Street!" the priest snapped. "So, if you haven't anything sensible to say, you may go. I have others waiting to make their confessions."

"Father, hear me out! I'm in torment! In—hell! I was—drunk. I woke up in a roominghouse of—well, shady reputation, with her at my side. She was—naked, Father."

"Jayzus!" the priest said. "And you, son?"

"Likewise, Padre."

"Guilty of carnal knowledge, anyhow. Go on, my son!"

"Padre, I'm not sure I *am.* I don't think so. I don't remember anything at all, and it seems to me I would!"

"Depends upon what brand of coffin varnish ye'd been imbibing. What saloon had ye swilled th' vile stuff in?"

"Mulligan's," the man whispered; "upper Pacific Street . . ."

"Guilty! Th' poison Tim Mulligan sells would dissolve a gun barrel, not t'mention th' wits in yer poor addled head. What did th' pore lass say?"

" '*Encore!*' " the man said bitterly.

"*Encore?*" the priest said.

"That's French. It means 'again.' "

"Hivens save us! A lusty broth of a lassie, eh?"

"Don't know. I think she was plaguing me."

"Did ye—oblige? With an *encore,* I mean?"

"Of course not! By then I'd recognized her."

"Yer—daughter?" the priest breathed.

"I don't know that either. Say, she could be . . ."

"How so, son?"

"Years ago—I had an affair with—was guilty with—her mother. I was —already married, and anyhow, she convinced me that the—children— twins, a boy and a girl—were not, couldn't be mine. But only a week ago I found out, through an absolutely reliable source, that she's been lying all these years. Those twins—could be mine. The boy's my image. The girl, hers. But with—my eyes. Blue like mine. And—"

"Go to th' Mither. Ask th' sinful baggage to confirm th' matter one way or the other!" the priest said.

"Did. She can't. Or won't. Says they could be the children of any of a dozen men."

"Jesus, Mary, *and* Joseph!" the priest said.

"Father, what should I do?"

"Stop drinking. Stop tumbling young wenches. Pray. And, t'relieve yer mind, since I kin see ye're truly sufferin', send th' lass ye're not sure ye've bedded to me. I'll get th' truth out of her!"

"Can't. She's—disappeared. Run away from home. Padre, have you ever heard of a place called Addie's?"

"No. Should I have? Say ten Pater Nosters and twenty Ave Marias and attend Mass every day fer a month! Now git out of here! Ye're wastin' me time!" the old priest said.

22

STANFORD STOOD THERE IN THE TEMPLE TIN HOW, WATCHING LOI
Yan as she burned the paper prayers the priest had written for her, and
the prayer sticks he had bought for her at her request, in the great
fireplace called *yuen bo pon*. That way the prayers for the eternal repose
of Li Huan Chin's soul would rise up to heaven on the fragrant smoke to
reach the attention of the gods. Especially Tin How herself, whose temple this was. She was the Queen of Heaven, and the Goddess of the
Seven Seas, and most of San Francisco's Chinese community professed a
special devotion toward her.

'Doesn't do 'em much good, considering the hell they catch,' he
thought. Then abruptly he wondered how much good the Dear Little
Virgin Mother of Jesus had done *him* lately. And it came to him that the
one sure result of the comparative study of religions was that you inevita-
bly lost your belief in any of them because no other discipline made more
cruelly clear than this one did, what utter nonsense they all were.

Still, he found Loi Yan's devotion intensely moving, especially after he
had become aware of the tears that were pouring down her face. He'd
been more than a little shocked by what had seemed to him her callous
indifference to her grandfather's death. But now he realized that it
hadn't been indifference, but rather a part of a rigid code of behavior
that prohibited the display of private emotions before a stranger. Only,
now he had ceased to be a stranger, become to her—what? Whatever it
was, it had changed the relation between them to the extent that she
could cry.

The venerable ancestor's funeral would be held tomorrow. The priests
in the joss house were taking care of everything, including the preparation of his frail old body. But what with hired mourners, never-ending
strings of popping, crackling firecrackers, eight or ten men to dance

beneath the paper dragon that would writhe and whirl and snort plumes of smoke from its most realistic nostrils at the head of the procession, the baked meats and rice and gin and tea upon which Li Huan Chin's spirit would refresh itself before beginning the long flight up to heaven, the black-robed priests swinging their wooden rattles, and the—to Western ears, anyhow—cacophonic wailing, and the staccato triads of the Chinese band, the whole impressive and moving ceremony was going to cost Stanford MacFarland, good Roman Catholic, three hundred dollars, just about all the money he had.

And, to judge by the look in Loi Yan's eyes, absolutely the most soul-satisfying expenditure he had ever made.

She had been determined to borrow the money from one of the Six Companies: the Sam Yup, Yung Wo, Kong Chow, Wing Yung, Hop Wo, and Yan Wo. These, he had been surprised to learn, were not criminal tongs dealing in drugs and prostitution, but groups of respectable merchants who had banded together to bring order and discipline to Chinatown, where they ruled the commerce and the social life of the decent Chinese with an iron hand. Any one of the Six Companies would have lent her the money to pay for the imposing funeral that it was her filial duty to offer her grandfather—or his departing spirit—upon pain of his and her "losing face." Losing face, Stan soon discovered, was the worst fate the Chinese mentality could conceive of. In comparison to it, death by torture was a mere bagatelle.

But he had seen how worried she was at the prospect of having to borrow the money, largely because, having quietly and fully set aside the barriers of culture and of race and accepted him without reservation as a fellow human being—though beyond that, whether as friend or lover he still didn't know—she no longer kept her face frozen into a mask of Oriental inscrutability before him. It was a marvelous face. It sang hymns of grave grief to her grandfather's memory without uttering a single word. It filled a room with golden butterflies, the fronds of bamboo waving, temple bells ringing far off and faint, across shallow seas of rice paddies, incense rising to her ancient gods, with a kind and degree of sheer beauty he hadn't known existed. And all this with the lift of an eyebrow, a hand sculpturing silent music, a hint of a smile.

He loved her so much he hurt. So much he felt no physical lust for her at all. He knew that he'd be content to sit and contemplate her serene loveliness forever. That he'd be perfectly satisfied with that little and nothing more.

So he'd seen the near terror of her look.

"What's wrong, Loi Yan?" he said.

"I'll have to pay back the money," she whispered. "The interest will be—very high, Stanford. And if I ever fail to meet a payment, they will have the perfect right to—sell me to some rich man as—a concubine. Some fat old rich merchant who has many girls already . . . I shouldn't like *that.*"

"Why not?" he said solemnly, teasing her.

She turned and faced him, there in the temple, her face a lotus blossom floating on a pool of darkness, the long slant of her eyes redefining the word tenderness, pulverizing his heart, stopping his breath.

"Because—I should much rather stay—with you," she said.

He didn't spring up, claw her into his arms, crush her to him in a fervent embrace as he would have done a white girl under those same circumstances without a second thought. The hours he'd spent with her had already awarded him an almost miraculous sense of exactly what to say and do.

"Let *me* pay for the funeral," he said quietly.

She said sharply, bitterly, "At what—interest? At what price?"

He said gravely, slowly, "A half interest in Li Huan Chin—as an ancestor. I haven't any, y'know. The father I've mentioned is my stepfather. I don't know who my father was. My mother, yes. But she sold me —for cash—to a dealer in unwanted babies. So I have no venerable ancestor to light the joss sticks for—burn the prayers. D'you think he'd accept me—a foreign devil, a *white* foreign devil—as a descendant? As a reverent and worshipful descendant—by the love I bear him for his part in—making you?"

She came to him then. But she didn't kiss him. The Chinese do not kiss. She put up her willowy flower stems of fingers and caressed his face.

He had all he could do to keep from screaming. The touch of those soft, clean, perfumed fingers was so unbearably, exquisitely tender, so murderously sweet, that no brand from a furnace could have seared as deep. The tears stood in his eyes and blazed.

She backed away from him. Bowed to him, very deeply, three times.

"The venerable ancestor will be honored to have such a grandson," she said with perfect formality. "I accept for him—and for me."

On the way back to her house, they passed through innumerable alleys. In several of them were the cribs of the slave girls, clad in the ritual costume of their trade, a black silk kimono having a narrow band of turquoise with flowers embroidered upon it running across the front and back. Stanford could hear and finally distinguish the meaning of their plaintive cries:

"China girl nice! You come inside, please? Your father, he just go out!"

"Good Lord!" Stan said. "What's my father got to do with this business, Loi Yan?"

"The Chinese consider it a great honor to possess a girl whom their venerable father has just—enjoyed . . ."

She giggled suddenly; triads of silver. Little chopped-up notes, jewel-bright.

"So maybe you'd better send your stepfather to visit me first, Stanford," she said.

"Huh! I'd *shoot* the old bugger!" Stanford said.

"How—barbaric. It is—a very great honor, you know. Listen to what these poor things are saying. It—one of the three things—may interest you . . ."

Stan listened.

"Two bits lookee, flo bits feelee, six bits doee!" the crib girls sang.

"Well, Stanford, shall I leave you here to—amuse yourself?" Loi Yan said.

He heard, and was pleased by, the edge in her voice. He said:

"I was brought up by a Scotsman. I don't believe in throwing away money."

"You are giving the venerable ancestor—an expensive funeral," she said bleakly.

"That's a good investment. This wouldn't be."

"Why not, Stanford?"

"It's the one thing that can't be bought. Love, I mean. It's only valuable when it's given. Freely. Meant. As I mean it when I say, I love you, Loi Yan. I shall love you till and past the day I die. I'll lean over the parapets of heaven to sniff the smoke of your joss sticks and your prayers. Will you send them up to me? And light some extra-loud firecrackers? I'm kind of deaf, y'know . . ."

"Oh, Stanford!" she said, and touched his face. He shivered like a wet dog.

"What's wrong?" she whispered.

"Your touch *kills* me. Dead. Don't know why, but it does. And when you *don't* touch me, it kills me worse. Wanting you to, so much, I mean. . . ."

"Oh you!" she laughed. "Come on!"

But just before they got to her pretty little house, he halted, petrified with astonishment, staring up into a lighted window above the street. The window was on the second floor of a tall house with a tiled roof, whose eaves tilted upward, pagoda style. A girl stood in the window. A young white girl. She was, he judged, eighteen or nineteen years old. She had lovely blond hair and a splendid body. About neither of the two latter aspects did he have to guess or judge, because she was stark, mother-naked; so he knew her long hair was unbleached, for her pubic bush—though, as is usually the case, a trifle darker than the hair on her head—was also blond. She was smoking a long-stemmed Chinese pipe and lazily scratching her lower belly and her mons veneris with the fingernails of her right hand.

As Stanford stood there a tall, slim Chinese came up behind her and cupped her left breast in a bony yellow hand that looked like the talon of a hawk. He was clad in a Mandarin's skullcap and the traditional long robe of black silk. Indolently he rolled the shell-pink nipple of her breast between his thumb and forefinger until it puckered, stood up. Then he put his other hand down between her thighs and fingered her there too. As she turned to him the lantern light pooled into her eyes, and Stanford saw they were blue glass, glittering vacantly, without any mind behind them at all.

"You like?" Loi Yan said bitterly.

"No," Stanford said.

"Why not? Is not the white she-devil beautiful?"

"No. A corpse is never beautiful—even when it moves. And necrophilia is a vice. More—a perversion," Stanford said.

"Necrophilia?" Loi Yan said.

"Making love to—or rather, in *that* case, indulging in coitus with—a dead body. Her mind is gone. And her spirit—if she ever had one. Opium?"

"And bhang. Other drugs as well. Abuse. Very subtle abuse of which Lew Chan is a past master."

"Lew Chan?"

"The owner of that house. He does not live in it. He only keeps it for the amusement of his friends and of other tong chieftains he wishes to impress. There are no women of my race in it, Stanford. They are all white foreign she-devils. They are enslaved to the smoking of opium. That's why they stay."

"Poor bitches!" Stanford said.

"Yes. Poor white she-devils. They don't last very long. They go mad very quickly under the abuse of Lew Chan and his *boo how doy.*"

"*Boo how doy?*"

"Hachetmen. Tong warriors," Loi Yan said.

"You mean they—torture those women?" Stanford said.

"Yes. But it is a very subtle torture. Very—Chinese. No whips. No hot irons. No instruments at all. They work upon the minds of those poor, sick white foreign she-devils. Teach them to—hate themselves. To grovel before their Oriental masters. To beg like she-dogs for more of the punishment, the degradation, they receive at Lew Chan's and the Sum Yops' hands. It is very complicated, perhaps beyond a Westerner's comprehension. Lew Chan and his friends procure the women of your people for exceedingly rare reasons—bad ones, Stanford."

"Worse reasons than mine would have been if I'd bought myself a little lookee, feelee, doee a while back?" he said.

"Yes. Far worse. No Chinese really likes foreign she-devils or is even slightly attracted to them. They—smell too bad. They don't wash themselves anything like enough. And their bodies are too—furry. Like— animals."

"And yours—isn't? I mean, Chinese girls' bodies—aren't?" he asked with genuine curiosity.

"Much less. Say—a little. A very little. Except on the head, we grow very little hair. And we shave even that little away. How else could one always smell nice?"

"Hmmmn! Interesting! But if Lew Chan doesn't like white women— I mean if they have no attraction for him at all—why does he keep them?"

"I think he enjoys degrading them. And to—revenge himself, and the members of his tong for all they have suffered at the hands of the white male devils. For a Chinese born in China, an authentic son of heaven, to come to this country and discover that a tribe of smelly, noisy, uncouth, hairy barbarians, closely akin to monkeys, actually consider themselves superior to him and, what is even worse, heap upon him contempt and abuse is terribly shocking, Stanford. Our leaders here in Chinatown often have to restrain newly arrived immigrants from running amok with a hatchet."

"Maybe they shouldn't," Stanford said grimly; "maybe a few split skulls would stop the abuse . . ."

"No. We are terribly outnumbered. It would cause a slaughter. Like in Los Angeles in 1871. Nineteen of my people died at the hands of mobs of yours then, you know . . ."

"Not mine," Stanford said; "don't give 'em to me, Loi Yan. Killers are never *my* people, my dear."

"Yes. You proved that, this morning, did you not? You are very—big of spirit, Stanford. But are you, is *any* white foreign devil, capable of understanding the subtlety of Lew Chan's reasoning? To start a war would mean the extermination of all our people in California. So he has chosen this strange—and to me, at least—evil method of restoring face. I don't know if *you* feel that way about it, but for some curious reason, for a man of a darker race to possess the white she-devils seems to drive the white he-devils wild, though they have no objection to taking other people's women—as you have taken me, Stanford!"

"Not yet!" he chuckled. "Just give me time!"

"I hate to pass that house," she said with a little shudder. "It is—a terrible place. Those white she-devils do—disgusting things, especially after they have been smoking bhang or opium. There is a Black man who brings the Sum Yops the she-devils. He brought Lew Chan—his favorite. The most beautiful she-devil I ever saw. Hair like night, but eyes like a morning sky . . ."

"That's an odd combination," Stanford said. "Though not too odd, come to think of it. My stepsister has eyes and hair like that. Is this your house? It looks like it ought to be. Suits you, somehow. Neat. Pretty. Well put together . . ."

"Yes, this is my house, Stanford," she said.

He stopped there before it a little awkwardly, thinking, 'How does a fellow say good night to a girl he's not allowed to kiss?'

She said, "Aren't you coming in, Stanford?" Her voice was doleful, plaintive. It made his heart reverberate like a temple gong.

"No; I don't think I'd better," he said.

"Stanford, please. I—I'm afraid to stay here alone. This is a bad street. It used to be good, but it has changed, become bad, now that it has so many houses of wickedness like Lew Chan's on it. Stay here with me, tonight. Tomorrow we can honor my—*our* venerable ancestor at his funeral—together."

He said solemnly, "I have a *very* furry body. And I stink something awful. I'd better not come in, Loi Yan. I can be a terribly devilish foreign devil at times, my dear . . ."

She stared at him. Said softly, slowly, sweetly, "Stanford, I want you to spend the night here—with me. But I will not come to your bed. Nor allow you to come to mine. That would be—*very* disrespectful to the venerable ancestor with him still aboveground. And displeasing to his spirit. But tomorrow night, after we have asked his permission, and his blessing, at his funeral, you may stay here again. Or I will go to your house. Then I will become your woman, as I have a great longing to be. But tonight, no. Yet—I want you here. It is true that I am afraid to be alone. But it is even truer that it simply hurts too much—to see you go . . ."

He looked at her. Sighed.

"I'll stay, then," he said; "*and* behave myself. You have my word."

She smiled.

"You have already given it to the venerable ancestor when you asked him to accept you as a grandson," she said.

But one thing came out of that first chaste and quiet night they spent together—a very practical thing: Stanford discovered a way they could support themselves, make a living together. After first tasting—rather gingerly, to tell the truth about it, the—to him—exotic Cantonese dishes she cooked for him, then devouring them with great gusto, using his fingers, for the use of the chopsticks escaped him completely, which caused Loi Yan to laugh merrily and accuse him of eating like a monkey —he suddenly burst out:

"A restaurant! We'll open a restaurant! On the edge of Chinatown, Loi Yan—where the white foreign devils won't be afraid to come to it, and—"

She smiled at him tenderly, said:

"But Stanford, we haven't any money. You've spent it all on the venerable ancestor's funeral . . ."

"I have more. I have over three thousand dollars in the Kinnans' bank. Of course, I'd sworn never to touch it, but—"

"Stanford, why had you sworn never to touch it?" Loi Yan said.

"Because . . . because," he floundered; then decided upon a sort of edited truth. "Because my stepmother gave it to me. And we—we're on the outs. But she won't mind my putting it to a good use. And a work that will keep us together all the time, both day and night, *is* a good use, isn't it?"

She stared at him solemnly. Then, at long, long last, she smiled.

"Yes, it is a good use. In fact, it is the very best," she said.

When Andrew MacFarland came into his wife's upstairs sitting room he found both Mireille and Raquel Kilpatrick waiting for him, as he had known they would be, because they had been there when he left.

Seeing that he was alone, the expression on Raquel's face changed. The color drained very slowly out of it, paling it from its natural blonde's shade of lightly boiled shrimp to an excellent approximation of snow. Even her lips went white. Which Andrew saw, and sorrowed over.

"He—wouldn't come with you, An-drew?" Mireille said. "He—refused, again?"

"No," Andrew sighed; "he didn't refuse. The truth, my dears, is that I've lost track of him . . ."

"But you said you knew where he lived!" Mireille cried.

"I did. But he doesn't live there anymore. He's moved. Without leaving his new address . . ."

"But sir," Raquel whispered; "what about—where he works? He has to go *there*, doesn't he?"

"He should, Daughter," Andrew said, "but he hasn't. Not in the last three weeks, anyhow. You see, thinking I didn't have to worry about Stanford, I concentrated all my efforts on trying to find Claire. It never occurred to me he was going to skip again. Our last interview was very friendly. My idea was to give him time. I was absolutely sure he was coming to his senses. But now—"

"But now I'd better go home," Raquel said tonelessly, "or Mama will skin me alive. Sir, if you find out something—have any word—"

"Of course, Daughter!" Andrew MacFarland said.

After she had gone, Mireille faced her husband.

"An-drew—" she said.

"Yes, honey?"

"You are—lying. Or not telling all the truth. You *know* where Stan is, don't you?"

"The—general area, yes. The exact location, no, Mireille."

"And that general area is?"

"Chinatown," Andy said.

"*Nom d'un nom!*" Mireille got out. "And why on earth should he want to live in Chinatown?"

"I suspect he has to," Andy said slowly. "D'you know anywhere else he could live—with a Chinese woman?"

"*Merde!*" Mireille shrieked. "I weel keel heem, An-drew! I weel!"

"You will not. In fact you'll leave him strictly alone, and let me handle the matter. Starting with finding him. And when I do, I intend to talk the matter over with him—and with little Won-Ton, very quietly . . ."

"Is *that* her name?"

"No. I was making a joke. A pretty feeble joke. Incidentally, Stan didn't deliberately move away from his old lodgings. He had to. His landlord refused to let him bring—I quote—'A Chink bitch' into the place. And, in evidence of how serious Stanford's affections are toward this girl, the landlord is nursing a dislocated jaw. Penalty for expressing loudly and profanely his opinion of the yellow race in general, and about little Lotus Blossom in particular."

"A Chinese girl!" Mireille moaned. "A little slant-eyed, yellow, monkey-looking—"

"Stop it!" Andrew said sharply. "She may well be beautiful, some of them are, y'know. But in any case, don't you start in to call Stan down for unconventional behavior. Not *you*, honey—please!"

Mireille bowed her head. When she looked up again, the tears were there on her cheeks, bright and glittering.

"An-drew," she whispered dolefully, "you—you had to remind me, didn't you? To point out to me that I have no right at all to rebuke—"

"I'm trying to point out it isn't—wise, honey," Andrew said gravely. "I had, and still have, hopes of winning Stan over. About Claire, I just don't know. The fact that we've found absolutely no trace of her, even yet—"

"An-drew! I forgot! Willy wants you to come to his office. Right now. He sent his office boy over here. An-drew, Willy's helping you look for Claire, isn't he?"

"Yes. And the fact he's sent for me may be good news. Or anyhow, news. Don't wait supper for me, honey. I'll catch a bite with Willy in some restaurant. This may take some time," Andrew MacFarland said.

It did.

As soon as Andrew walked into his office, Willy got up, picked up his hat.

"Addie's," he said; "I know what it is. And where. C'mon."

"Gent'm'ns, y'all real sho y'all's at th' right place?" the old Black woman said.

"Yes," Willy said grimly. "You're Addie, aren't you? This is your place —1128 Turk Street, a whorehouse. But a goddamned unique one, I have to admit. The first one in San Francisco's history . . ."

"Yassuh. But suh, us doan cater t' gent'm'ns at this heah address. Us is got a annex on Powell Street fur rich white gent'm'ns whut likes prutty boys. This'un in case you ain't heard is fur *ladies* . . ."

"Jesus!" Andrew whispered. "And I didn't believe you!"

"I told you!" Willy grated. "A whorehouse where the whores are *male*. For the benefit of idle, rich, and capricious *women*. The first such establishment in San Francisco. Or anywhere else I ever heard of."

"I still don't believe it!" Andrew said. "Women—just don't react that way. *They* never go off like Roman candles, Willy. And they just aren't stupid enough, and certainly not animalistic enough to try to buy a cheap, badly faked counterfeit of love. *We* are the primitive sex, Willy my friend. The billy goats. The apes. Accepting Darwin's theory as very probably right, they've evolved; we haven't."

"Andy, did you ever get involved with a married woman?" Willy said.

"No, never," Andrew said dryly.

"Well, I have been, several times. And not with *yours*, dammit! You know better than that. Well, put it this way: They're never making love to you—to their partner in adultery. They're making *hate* against their husbands. Vengeance. Women would never think of a man as hired piece of—cock, as we think of them, quite candidly, as rented, useful tail. But —as instruments of revenge, old boy? A means of expressing, implementing the self-hatred so many of them develop after—a string of unfortunate experiences, say? God, Andy, I've known women who had a craving after autodegradation as powerful as people have for opium—or drink. Who *want* to be abused, debased, befouled. Who get a thrill—a very dirty thrill—out of suffering . . ."

"And I've known *men* who do, too," Andrew said.

"Yes. The quirky boys who want to be tied up and beaten. Walked on with high-heeled shoes. Their faces urinated, defecated into. All crude— all physical. I'm not talking about that. A woman would come to a dive like this one to enjoy being humiliated, treated like a quarter-a-tumble cowyard crib slut, have the contempt she's learned to feel for herself made manifest. You've got that photograph with you?"

"Jesus, Willy! You want me to show this old witch—"

"A photo of Claire. Why the hell else did you think I made you stop by your office to get it? She's been badly hurt by what Mammy Pleasant told her—"

He stopped short, glared at Aunt Addie.

"Jesus!" he whispered. "So she owns this dive, too? Is that why you jumped a foot high when I said her name, old woman? She *would*. This would suit her. The perfect setup for blackmail!"

"Suh, I jes' doan know whut you's talkin' 'bout," Aunt Addie said.

"Forget it. Let us in, will you? We've got something to show you. We need more light—"

"Gent'm'ns, y'all doan mean to mek me *trouble*, does y'all?" Aunt Addie whined.

"No," Andrew said sadly; "what you do is your business, Aunt Addie. And the business of your—clients. You must fill a need, or else you couldn't stay open. You have my word that we won't go to the police, or take any steps against you. All we need is information. My daughter has disappeared, and I—we—have reason to believe she may have come— here . . ."

"Wal, suh, effen her did, her ain't heah now. Th' ladies comes heah has they fun 'n' leaves, jes' lak y'all gent'm'ns does when y'all goes to a hohouse . . ."

"I didn't expect to find her here. I only want to know if you've seen her."

"Aw right, c'mon in. Y'all lak to have a snort? Only cost you a dollah a shot."

"Don't mind if I do," Andrew sighed; "I need something to calm my nerves. You, Willy?"

"Oh hell, why not? It'll be a combination of panther piss and rattlesnake milk, but I guess I can stand it."

While Aunt Addie was studying Claire's photo, the maid came in with the bottle and the shot glasses.

"Sho would 'preciate hit if y'all wuz to buy *me* one," Aunt Addie said.

Willy, as usual, was staring at the trim figure of the *mulata* serving maid. But at that moment the expression on her saucy, insolent face caught his attention. As she poured the rotgut, she glanced at the photo in Aunt Addie's wizened black hand and gave a barely perceptible start. At an angle that Andrew couldn't see, Willy opened his left hand with all five fingers spread wide.

The *mulata* maid shook her head negatively, in denial.

Willy closed his hand into a fist. Opened it again—twice.

Again that negative shake of a little, round, woolly head.

He closed his fist again—opened it three times.

The maid shook her head again.

Willy closed his fist once more. Opened his hand, spreading his five fingers, four times in quick succession.

The *mulata* maid smiled—lusciously. Or—lustfully.

Willy nodded toward the door, the street. That little bundle of toothsome sin nodded—affirmatively. Turned. Left the room.

"Nawsuh," Aunt Addie said; "I ain't never seen this heah prutty chile. Galbabies this young most in general doan come heah. We gits—older ladies. Hard up. Gal lak this'n hafta fight th' young fellas off wit' a fence rail or a ridin' crop. She wanta lay down 'n' spread wide, line stretch from heah to th' Embarcadero . . ."

"*Sure* you haven't seen her, Aunt Addie?" Andrew said.

"Wal, suh, sartin sho I ain't. Cain't be. Ladies comes in th' side do'. Stops outside in th' garden in th' dark. 'N' Cindy Lou—th' gal whut jes' served us drinks—give 'em a mask whut kivers up they eyes 'n' nose right down to they moufs. Cain't *nobody* tell whut they reely looks lak thataway. Tha's bein' smart, suh. Some o' th' ladies whut comes heah is from mighty high society, I kin tell yuh that. One of 'em try to buy Leroy off o' me. Wanted to give him a butler job in her house so she could have herself a piece o' mule-sized nigger meat every night!"

"You mean—your—your men are *Negroes?*" Andrew gasped.

"Yas. One or two. 'N' greasers. 'N' Eyetalians. 'N' Greeks. 'N' ordinary white fellas—'ceptin' they's all reel good-lookin'. But a moughty heap o' them ladies wants theyself a nigger, 'cause they done heard that niggers is got hit fo' inches thick, a yard long 'n' draggin' on th' ground . . ."

"And have they?" Andrew asked out of honest curiosity.

"Lawd, no, suh! Menfolks is all 'bout th' same, 'n' color doan have much t' do wit'it. Wal now, I reckon niggers *is* a li'l bigger'n white menfolks, but not all that much. 'Vantage Leroy got, he *cold*-natured. Kin keep hit up all night long wit'out gittin' he rocks off till he want to. That reely drive th' ladies wild. How's about another snort?"

"No thank you," Andrew said firmly. He had the gut-sickening feeling that this old Black witch was probably lying about not having seen Claire, but he had no idea about how to force or induce her to tell the truth. He wanted to consult with Willy about that. 'Tricks—and the dirtier the better—come naturally to this greaser bastard,' Andrew thought. 'Or this Mick bastard. Or both. Lord, what a combination!'

Outside in the street, Willy held up a warning hand. In the silence Andrew heard the staccato click of high heels coming through the darkness.

"All right, brown sugar, out with it!" Willy rasped.

"Tha's gonna cost you twenty dollars, white man. That is, effen *talk* is all you wants. Piece o' my high-brown ass cost you five dollars mo' on top o' it," the *mulata* maid said. "Ten fur th' bof o' you. How's about it, gentlemens? Money always did mek me hot 'n' horny . . ."

"Just talk, tonight, brown sugar," Willy said. "I'll come back for tail some other night. You've seen her, haven't you?"

"Cross my palms wit' silver, honey. I ain't givin' *nothin'* away, not even talk. Ain't no charity gal, me . . ."

Willy took out his wallet, fished up a twenty, held it higher under the gaslight on the edge of the sidewalk for her to see. Gave it to her.

"Yas. She been here, her. Even outside in th' garden them eyes o' hern showed. Bluest damn eyes I ever seen. Jes' like yourn, suh."

"Where is she?" Andrew grated.

"Wal now, suh, I doan know *that.*. All I knows is that Leroy took her home wit' him, th' cheatin' bastid!"

"Leroy?" Andrew whispered.

"Yassuh. Nigger Aunt Addie was talkin' 'bout. Best-lookin' long-tall niggerman in California. Six foot fo', 'n' *built.* Shoulders so wide he hafta turn sidewise to go through a double do'. Li'l ol' tiny hips, real small. No waistline to speak of. But a chest lak a whiskey barrel 'n' muscles all over him like gret big crawlin' snakes—Law Jesus, Leroy is reely sumpin', him! Th' number o' white wimmenfolks he done druv right outa they ever-lovin' minds tek you a month o' Sundays to count . . ."

"Where is he?" Willy got out. His voice was strangling.

"That'll cost you ten dollars mo'," the *mulata* said.

Andrew came out with his billfold. Handed her not a ten, but another twenty.

"The extra's to refresh your memory," he said quietly. "I want to know *all* about my daughter's visit to this house. Everything you can remember, girl . . ."

"*Yo'* daughter, suh? She look mo' lak she oughta be his'n. *This* gentleman's, I means."

"Maybe she is," Andrew said grimly; "in which case I'm going home and put my wife in the hospital for three months. And shoot this so-called gentleman as I should have done years ago!"

"You do that, suh! They bof sho Lawd got it comin'! Anyhow, that theah reel prutty young white gal come heah—'bout fo'-five months ago—"

"Six," Willy said.

"Awright then, six. Aunt Addie showed huh th' pictures. Ain't no men hos on th' place, y'know. Wimmens come one night, mek arrangement fur th' nex'—or even up to two weeks ahead, th' regulars, dependin' on when they husbands gonna be outa town . . ."

"Jesus!" Andrew said.

"Tha's human nature, honey. Us wimmen gits real hard up too, at times, specially when y'all neglects us . . ."

"Go on," Andrew said.

"Anyhow her hemmed 'n' hawed th' longest time, tryin' to mek up her mind which one o' th' ho-fellas to ax fur. Naw. That ain't so. Y'all is Southern gentlemens, ain't you?"

"No. Not either one of us. Her mother is, though," Andrew said.

"Thought so. 'Cause she wanted Leroy th' minute she seen he picture. But he bein' a nigger put her off. Scairt her, too, I reckons. But ain't nothin' worse temptation than sumpin' yo' momma and yo' poppa and th' whole damn world done used up half yo' lifetime tellin' you hit's *awful* wrong. You starts in to wonderin' why 'n' gits curiouser 'n' curiouser till finally you figgers you's gwine to bust effen you doan find out yo' ownself 'n' fer true . . ."

"I can see how that could be," Andrew said quietly.

"Andy—she couldn't! She wouldn't! Not a—"

"Negro? What would hurt *Mireille* worse, Willy?" Andrew said.

"Oh, God!" Willy said.

"Go on, child," Andrew said.

"Anyhow, finally she made up her mind. Leroy doan live far from heah. Round on Ellis Street. So Aunt Addie sont for him—"

"And?" Andrew whispered, his voice retreating out of sound.

"He come over heah. Took his own sweet time about hit. Mos' a hour. That long-tall nigger too damn proud to let any female critter git th' idea he give a shit—"

"And?" Andrew said again.

"They went upstairs. I followed 'em. I'm crazy 'bout Leroy, me; 'n' a white gal prutty as that'un jes' moughta give me mo' trouble than I could handle . . ."

"What happened after that? While you were eavesdropping?" Willy said bitterly.

"They used up damn nigh a whole hour argufying. She 'lowed her'd done made a mistake 'n' she would give him th' money for *nothin'* to get outa theah 'n' leave her alone—'n' stuff lak that theah, doncha know . . . 'N' he jes' laff at her, soft 'n' easy, 'n' sez jes' lak a pappy singin' he babygal chile to sleep, 'What's th' matter, baby? I'se too *black* fo' you?' 'N' her kinda ripped out real fas' 'n' all breathy: 'Yes you are you're too black too ugly too big too burly too brutal too—"

"Then?" Willy all but screamed.

"Her said, 'Oh.' Real softlike. Then, 'Stop it you stop it I won't I can't I hate you I despise you I never could stand niggers anyhow you great big burly black bastard ape. Oh.' "

"Jesus!" Willy said.

"Her said that, too. 'Jesus,' I mean. 'Bout forty times. Then 'Oh,' 'bout fifty. The 'Oh—Ah' 'bout a hundred. Then—you knows th' kind o' things a woman jes' pours into her lovin' sweetman's ears when it's really good 'n' gettin' better ever' minute—all quick 'n' shaky-voice 'n' pantin' 'n' beggin' 'n' prayin' like she was talkin' to Lawd Jesus Heownself. Mos'ly she was moanin' low 'n' axing him not to stop not never to stop but to keep it up keep it up keep it up rip her in half up th' middle bus' her all to pieces kill her daid . . ."

"You're lying! You damned nigger bitch, you're lying!" Willy screamed.

"No. She's not. You know she's not lying, Willy. She's talking about—Mireille's daughter, remember," Andrew said. His voice was grave earth. Tomb mold. Cobwebs across the entrance of a mausoleum. "Go on, girl."

"Ain't much mo'. She wuzn't th' kind whut yells 'n' screams 'n' cusses when they gits theah. She jes' said all soft 'n' shuddery-like, 'Oh Gawd.' Like she wuz chewing th' words twixt her teeth, worryin' 'em t'death like a fyce dawg do a rat, holdin' onto 'em, dragging 'em out, not lettin' 'em go—you knows, lak this: 'Ohhhhhhhh G a a a a a w w w w d d d d—' Then she shet up 'n' didn't say nuthin' mo' fo' 'bout a hour 'n' she sez:

" 'Please.' "

"Jesus! Jesus! Jesus!" Willy moaned.

" 'N' Leroy sez, 'Game li'l bitch ain't you? Aw right Miss Anne from way down South, you cain't break this po' ol' ridin' nigger's sperrit nor his wind 'cause yo' ain't got yo' spurs on right 'n' you's done plumb forgot yo' crop 'n' yo' cinch ring done slipped 'n' this heah ol' Black breedin' studhoss is used to servicin' snow-white broodmares specially th' kind whut knows how t'kick 'n' scratch 'n' bite lak you, so c'mon half-broke filly le's ride!' "

"¡Dios!" Willy got out between locked and grinding teeth. "¡Lo voy a matar, Andy! ¡A ese cerdo Negro no se puede permitir que viva ni una hora más!"

"No," Andrew whispered. "He only took what was offered. Did what he was paid to do . . ."

"¡Eres increíble!" Willy got out. "¡No eres hombre! ¡Ni si quiera eres humano!"

"I suppose that's all," Andrew said to the girl, tiredly.

"Reckon so. 'Cause all th' rest wasn't nuthin' else but mo' of the same over 'n' over agin till mawnin'. 'N' then they come outa theah wit' Leroy lookin' mighty pleased wit' hisself jes' lak a big black cat whut's done et all th' canary birds whut they is in th' whole damn world, 'n' her lookin' lak west hell—death warmed over jes' enuf so hit could move, a walkin' corpse—'n' they left. Tell you one thing though: Whichever one of you gentlemens *is* her pappy kin be proud o' that theah li'l girl 'cause she sho' was a good chile till Leroy got a hold on her. Them sheets looked lak they'd done been used to mop up a slaughterhouse floor . . ."

Andrew looked at Willy.

"So—you weren't lying," he said; "you actually didn't."

"I—actually didn't. That's the *only* bearable thing I've got out of this night: finding *that* out," Willy said. "Now come on! Say, you! Where'd you say that nigger lived?"

"Ten-ten Ellis. Hopes y'all's right wit' th' Lawd. Cause whitefolks what builds up a head o' steam 'n' goes round tryin' to whup 'n' shoot 'n' cut on Leroy mostly winds up daid, them!"

"We'll see about that!" Willy grated.

"Willy," Andrew said, "if you've a revolver in your pocket, give it to me."

"Why? I can shoot a hell of a lot better than you can, Andrew, and that nigger's living on borrowed time right now!"

"I'm going to lend him more. I don't want him dead, and your name and mine and Claire's in the yellow journals. That's what's going to happen if you kill him."

"Hell, Andy! Since when has a white man had to explain why he killed a nigger?"

"Or a gringo, a greaser? It's the same thing, Willy. And you ought to be against it on principle, as I am. Besides which, are you coming back here and pistol the wench? The old woman? Mammy Pleasant? Where will the killings stop, *amigo?* A foolish girl, out of her mind from—pure shock, deception, rage, who knows?—did an idiotic thing. To revenge herself against her mother for the blood she gave her. Or against the Devil—for his seed. Willy, we can't kill this Black. We absolutely can't. Killing him would cost us more than he's worth. Than any man is. All I want to do is to find Claire. Bring her back home. Shower love on her— forgiveness. Till I cure her. Till I heal—her broken heart . . ."

Willy stood there, staring at him. Said, finally:

"You win. You're—a better man than I am, Andy. That kind of courage—*esa clase de nobleza*—I haven't got. Nor that kind of sense, either. Or else I'd be married to Mireille, right now—and not bleeding to death by inches on the inside. Now, come on . . ."

"Yeah, he heah," the other old woman said. She was just as black as Aunt Addie, and maybe a trifle more evil-looking, which took some doing, Andy had to admit to himself, but the old woman managed it. "Only y'all cain't see him right now. He got company—"

"*White?*" Willy demanded.

"Hell, honey, whut other kind do Leroy ever play round wit'?" the old woman cackled. " 'Bout Black gals, he serious. Got one down cross Market Street he plannin' to marry when he gits enuf money saved."

"C'mon, Andy!" Willy said.

"Y'all cain't go up theah!" the old woman shrilled. "I done tol' you 'n' tol' you—"

Willy put out one arm and slammed her back against the wall so hard it shook. Started up the stairs, two at a time. Andrew was one step behind him. On the second floor they paused. But it took them only a minute or two to find the right room. The sounds coming out of it identified it.

Willy bounded to that door. Lifted his foot. Kicked. The door was flimsy. It crashed open. Willy's right hand clawed under the left armpit of his banker's frock coat. Came out with a little snub-nose bulldog revolver. Snarling like a mad dog, he pointed it in the general direction of the bed.

Andrew's big paws shot out, clamped over Willy's wrist, jerked his hand ceilingward. Andy was a head taller, twice as wide, and four times as strong as the slender Irish-Mexican had been on the best day of his life. Only Willy's best day had long since passed. Wine, women, and song had taken their toll, plus a couple of bullets too many through his guts. Illness. Sorrow. Disappointment. Pain. And—perhaps especially of that center of his life named Mireille!—loss. Anyhow, Andy shoved him with the greatest of ease back against the wall. Banged his gun hand with the revolver still in it against the doorframe so hard that Willy gave an involuntary yelp and opened his fingers. That ugly, deadly little weapon clattered to the floor.

Andrew turned Willy loose. Bent and picked up the revolver. Dropped it into his own coat pocket.

"Goddamn you, Andy!" Willy cried.

"Shut up, Willy," Andrew said wearily; "I told you there wasn't to be any gunplay. And being a hot-tempered fool isn't going to help anything, y'know . . ."

He turned back toward the bed.

With a bass chuckle that was like the reverberations of a drum after the beating sticks have been lifted, held above and away from the taut, vibrating head, Leroy rolled the woman in his arms back over from where he'd been holding her between his own body and the muzzle of Willy's revolver.

"Now jes' look at these here two li'l old Southern Lighthoss Raiders," he said mockingly; "bustin' into a man's place o' business whilst he's— negotiating . . . But 'pears t'me one o' you cracker bedsheet boys is got a mite o' sense in he head. So I reckons *you*, anyhow, Big Daddy, has tumbled to th' fact that that there nickel-plated play toy o' yourn would of got this heah po' sorry piece o' white tail kilt *first*, then th' two o' y'all *second* after I'd done took it from y'all 'n' started celebrating Emancipation Day! All right, take a good look. This bitch belong to one o' y'all?"

The woman wasn't Claire. For one thing, she was considerably older. For another, she was blond.

"I'll kill him!" Willy shrieked. "Whoever she is! On general principles, Andrew!"

"Oh, be quiet—and go downstairs, Willy," Andrew said, even more wearily.

"You's smart. You's very smart. That li'l fren o' yourn is gittin' me irritated," Leroy said; "and when I gits irritated, no tellin' whut I might not do. Like breakin' he backbone fur him in fo'teen places. C'mon, you know this heah po' ol' used-up sack o' chitlings? She one o' y'all's old lady? Cain't be yo' momma, 'cause both o' y'all's too ol' . . ."

"No," Andrew said; "we don't know her."

"Then howsabout gittin' outa heah, Mistuh Smart 'n' Sensible white man 'n' takin' that theah li'l sawed-off Kluxer wit' you? Done knowed a sight too many Southern whitefolks—and I done got *tired* of 'em. Mighty tired. Bone-weary, in fact. So now I'm dedicated to th' proposition that they oughta be—ex-term-i-nated. Like rats."

"We're not Southerners," Andy said evenly; "not either of us."

"Leee-roy," the woman said slumberously; "c'mon, you big, sweet Black sonofabitch—You're—not—making me happy anymore. And I want to be—hap-py. Verreee Hap-py!"

She was blind drunk, Andrew saw. Or drugged. Or both. He said:

"Finish—your negotiation, Leroy. Then come downstairs. I want to talk to you. About my daughter, who's disappeared. The only gun between the two of us is the one I just took from my friend, and I have no intention of using it. I don't want to start a war. I just want to find my daughter . . ."

Leroy stared at him.

"You *is* smart," he said; "you's smart fo' real. All right, give me half a hour . . ."

"No!" the woman said. "A whole hour. Two. All night!"

Leroy moved sidewise, ponderously. Thrust powerfully, forward, down.

The woman caught her breath. Gave a little whimpering moan.

"You see, Miss Anne? You couldn't stand a whole goddamn night," Leroy said.

"Yeah," Leroy said as he handed Andrew back Claire's photo; "I remembers *her* all right. She—special. Mighty fine. Yessir, mighty, mighty fine. Had to git rid o' her, tho. She was ruining my business . . ."

They sat in a local barroom that catered mostly to the small enclave of Blacks in that far south district of San Francisco.

"Where is she?" Andrew whispered. He glanced at Willy. Willy was in a state of shock. His rage had caused the gastric ulcer that he had thought was entirely healed to burst loose again. He was bleeding like hell on the inside, and he knew it. Andrew didn't know the reason, but that Willy was out of the fight was evident. He was glad of that. Latin furor didn't help a good goddamn in a case like this.

"Sold her," Leroy said calmly. "To a Chink named Lew Chan. Yaller bastid give me a thousand dollars for her. He cheated me there, now that I come to think on it. She was worth a helluva lot mo' . . ."

"He's in—Chinatown?" Andrew whispered.

"Yeah. Big man 'mongst th' Chinks, Lew Chan. Tong leader. Th' Sum Yops. Controls most o' th' opium dens. 'N' th' ho-houses. 'N' th' cribs . . ."

"Jesus!" Andrew breathed. "You sold my daughter into—"

"Naw. Jes' you hol' on theah, white man. I didn't sell her into th' ass-peddling trade. I sold her to Lew Chan personal. For he concubine. Made him promise to treat her *right*. Tol' him I'd go through fo' dozen hatchet men to git him if he 'bused her, treated her bad . . ."

Andrew stared at him.

"And just why did you tell him a thing like that, Leroy?" he said.

"Tol' you. That li'l girl o' yourn was *special*. Mighty special. She was— gittin' t'me, makin' me come too damn close t' breakin' th' solemn vow I swore on my po' momma's grave . . ."

"And what vow was that?" Andrew whispered.

"To fuck y'all up, any way I could. White man whupped my momma t'death. Befo' th' war. Back home in Gawgia. I wasn't nothin' but a li'l fella, but I cain't never fergit th' way that ol' blacksnake whip bit in 'n' my momma screamin' 'n' th' blood runnin' down. So I swore I was gonna git even wit' ever' livin' white muthafucka on th' face o' th' earth. But wasn't till I got out heah that I figgered out jes' how t'do hit . . ."

"Which was?"

"To tek y'all's wimmen. 'Cause doan *nothin'* else hurt worse'n *that*. Y'all grabs ever' female critter in sight—Mex, Chilean, Malay, Chinee, Black—" He stopped, loosed a midnight-velvet chuckle, went on, " 'N' mostly disappoints th' hell out of 'em wit' yo' half-inch-long dicks 'n' yo' bad habit o' coming in five seconds flat! But let a greaser, a Chink, and wus o' all, a *nigger* look sidewise at one o' yourn 'n' theah you go, right up th' side o' th' nearest buildin'! What make you think yo' pale-ass bitches is so special, white man? They mostly ain't worth a damn in th' hay . . ."

He paused again. Sipped the whiskey Andrew had bought him.

" 'Ceptin' *yourn*. She *was*. And th' bad part about it was that she was gittin' next t'me, makin' me care for her, fur *real*. Lawd Gawd, that li'l gal was sweet! Always after me to run away wit' her t' Mexico or South

America or anywhere else where folks don't give a damn 'bout that race 'n' color shit."

"Why?" Andrew said tonelessly. "Why'd she want you to do a thing like that, Leroy?"

Leroy sighed.

"*Yo'* fault, white man," he rumbled softly in his midnight bass; " 'n' her mama's, too, I 'spects. Reckon y'all done learned her too hard that fuckin' is plain damn wrong les' you loves th' party you's doin' it wit'. So she sold herself a bill o' goods. That she was in love wit' *me*, I mean. She had to believe that or go right outa her po' sweet stupid 'ristocratic white gal's mind."

"And she—wasn't?" Andrew whispered. Looking at Leroy, at the absolutely magnificent maleness of him, at his somber beauty, he couldn't reject that possibility. He wanted to, but he couldn't.

Leroy looked away from him. Looked back again. Loosed another sigh, gusty, deep.

"Naw. Effen she had of been, I'd of gone t' Mexico wit' her. Or to South America. Or—to hell," he said.

There was no sense undertaking a rescue mission into Chinatown at that after-midnight, almost pre-dawn hour. Tomorrow, under the existing and disastrous circumstances, would do just as well. So, after having dropped Guillermo Kilpatrick off, not at his own house, but at Enrique Sepúlvera's, as Willy, realizing how dangerously ill he was, asked him to do, Andrew MacFarland went home.

He quickly and easily decided what to do: He would go to the police and swear out a search warrant against Lew Chan on the charges of kidnapping and white slavery. Even granted the well-known fact that the tongs enjoyed the protection of San Francisco's miserably corrupt officials and its almost equally corrupt police, neither officials nor police could withstand the explosion of public outrage at the news—which any San Francisco newspaper, even the respectable ones, would be happy to print, in view of the increased circulation such a scoop would surely bring them—that a tong leader was maintaining a harem of young *white* female slaves. So they would take action, he knew. All other considerations aside, the bitter racism the Anglo-Saxon has bred into his very bones would compel them to.

So Andy went to bed. And being, after all, fifty-three years old by then and dog-tired physically, slept. In fact, he overslept, because Mireille, seeing how utterly weary he was, took every precaution, including warning the servants to be extra quiet, not to wake him up. She didn't know,

of course, how good the prospects for finding Claire were, for, not wanting to watch her bouncing off the ceilings and the walls like a caroming
billiard ball gone wild, Andrew didn't tell her. And he had no intention
to, until he brought Claire through the front door of their Nob Hill
mansion. Having Mireille driving him out of his ever loving mind while
he was trying to accomplish so serious a task was something he just didn't
need.

What did wake him up at eleven o'clock that next morning was
Willy's voice screaming the house down. Andy slipped on his robe, went
downstairs. Fortunately for him, Mireille was having her hour-long morning bath, so she didn't hear the uproar from the sanctuary of her third-
floor bathroom. Which was just as well.

"What's wrong, Willy?" Andrew said.

"It's Raquel!" Willy groaned. "She's disappeared! Gone to Chinatown!"

"Good Lord!" Andrew said. "Why on earth should she do a thing like
that?"

"As if you didn't know! Seems your niggers told her about Stan and
his Chinese wench before she even left here yesterday afternoon!"

"But my colored help didn't *know* about that, Willy! I'd just found it
out myself, and I didn't even tell Mireille until *after* Raquel left here!"

"Didn't have to, Andy—what with that light horse troop from the
Celestial Empire you've also got on your domestic staff. They knew
about it before you did. Seems it's the scandal of all Chinatown. It
appears they don't like one of us playing around with one of their decent,
respectable girls any more than we'd like one of them tumbling a sweet
little white missy! Your Stan's Chink manservant told Blossom, and Blossom, having damned good reasons to want to be the bearer of evil tid-
ings, told my poor fool daughter! Anyhow, she's gone after him to bring
him home. Andy, she's absolutely hysterical! Swore to Blossom that if he
didn't come back with her, she's going to cut her throat from ear to ear
right before his eyes!"

"Jesus!" Andrew whispered.

"And d'you know where she got *that* idea from? Mireille, no less!
Seems your dear little wife is in the habit of reminiscing at length and in
detail about her spicy past to my innocent daughter! You know that little
hairline scar Mireille's got on her neck? It appears she actually *did* cut
her throat—and quite badly—once when Judge Curtwright was threatening to leave her! And to top it all off, my razor's missing!"

"H. Christ!" Andrew said. "Willy, give me five minutes. I'll get
dressed, and—"

He stopped short, looked at Willy. Said, quietly, firmly:

"Willy, let me handle this. You go home. Or better still, lie down here. I'll send James Swithers after Enrique. You look like a corpse. Except that most corpses probably look a hell of a lot healthier than you do right now. C'mon, Willy; don't be an ass. Go lie down till Enrique gets here."

"It's my ulcer. Getting excited doesn't help it a good goddamn. And that big insolent Black sonofabitch last night—"

Andrew went to the bell cord, pulled it. When the downstairs maid appeared, he said:

"Conduct this gentleman to one of the guest bedrooms, then send James Swithers up to me."

And Willy, all his Latin fury burned out of him by fifty-four years, fatigue, terror, disappointment, defeat, went like a little lamb.

23

THE SLIM, HANDSOME YOUNG CANTONESE STOOD BEFORE LEW Chan. Clasping his two hands together inside the wide sleeves of his rich blue silk pajama suit, he shook hands with himself. Then he bowed three times. Deeply. Reverently.

Lew Chan ignored his visitor. He drew in on his long-stemmed pipe, let the fragrant gray smoke trail through his nostrils as he contemplated the eucalyptus tree at the far end of the vast salon, a full thirty feet from where he sat. The tree was one of his favorite possessions. It was centuries old. The chieftain of another tong, the Sue Yops, who owed Lew Chan a debt of honor, had had it brought from China at great expense, and presented it to Lew Chan as head of the much more powerful Sum Yops, in token of his submission and his loyalty. Lew Chan, to display his magnificence as Seal Holder, or chieftain, of San Francisco's most deadly fighting tong, had had the ancient tree replanted in a huge, highly decorative Ming Dynasty porcelain vessel some five yards in circumference. The vessel was beyond all price; the tree, so tall that a hole had had to be chopped in the roof to accommodate its upper trunk and branches, very nearly so. Lew Chan enjoyed looking at it. Its symmetry reduced the inharmonious and discordant aspects of life to their proper proportions.

And human worms like the rich young Cantonese peasant before him to their evident insignificance.

He took the long-stemmed pipe out of his mouth. Laid it on the beautifully lacquered table before him with its bowl resting in a Tang Dynasty ceramic dish, which, small as it was, had cost him almost as much as the huge Ming vase holding his favorite tree. With an imperious gesture of his hand he waved away the servant girl who had brought the young man into his august presence. And now, at long last, he conceded that his visitor was alive, and possibly even, though remotely so, human.

"Your name?" he said to the young Cantonese.

"Djan Ching," the young man said.

"State your business, Djan Ching," Lew Chan said.

"I have been offended, Honorable Seal Holder," Djan Ching said; "in my person and my honor. I have been caused to lose face. Therefore I ask the aid of the mighty head of the tong Sum Yop in seeking redress."

"I am listening," Lew Chan said.

"A year ago my father, the venerable Chin Poy, signed a marriage contract for me with the equally venerable Li Huan Chin, who now unfortunately has been gathered to his ancestors. The girl in question is the beauteous Loi Yan, granddaughter of the departed Li Huan Chin. Money was exchanged. A great deal of money, Honorable Holder of the Seal of tong Sum Yop. A literary class person like yourself cannot imagine with what difficulty this sum of money was assembled, for my father, though also a literary class person, and a calligrapher of scrolls, was poor. Suffice it to say that, what with this purchase price of Loi Yan as a bride for me, and my passage by snorting dragon smokeship to California, I have been left practically without funds."

"You wish a loan?" Lew Chan said shortly. He was becoming impatient with all this flowery Cantonese oratory. His own style was much more direct. "That can be arranged . . ."

"No, Honorable Literary Class Person," Djan Ching said; "I do not wish a loan. I wish to be enrolled as a salaried soldier in the ranks of the Sum Yop . . ."

"What class of salaried soldier?" Lew Chan said.

"A Highbinder," Djan Ching said.

"You are good with the hatchet?" Lew Chan asked him. The Highbinders were the hatchet men, capable of splitting a foe's skull to the teeth with but a single blow.

"Modesty does not permit this humble person to extol his small accomplishments, but I have practiced with that traditional weapon from my earliest youth," Djan Ching said.

"Good. We will give you the opportunity to demonstrate your skill, and if it is satisfactory we will draw up the contract," Lew Chan said. "Anything else?"

"Yes, Honorable Seal Holder: the terms of that contract. I will voluntarily waive all salary for a year, in return for the life of the man who has offended not only me, but all my venerable ancestors, caused my poor but respectable family to lose face."

"Hmmmnn. Unusual. But still—possible. Who is this man?"

"His name is Stone Ford Kwack Far Land. He is currently running an eating palace of Cantonese dishes on the corner of Dupont and Jackson streets, ably assisted by the beauteous Loi Yan. They have called it The House of the Weeping Willow. It is an excellent eating palace. I have dined there, and can vouch for it."

"And the supposedly beauteous—and demonstrably faithless—Loi Yan was not alarmed by your presence?"

"In my humble but honorable family, Great Seal Holder, we are faithful to the old ways. Loi Yan has never seen me. The bride in a wedding arranged according to the sacred customs of the Celestial Empire never sees her husband before their wedding night. Nor he, her. That is the law. Whether you have departed from it in this strange country, this humble person of course does not know. . . ."

Lew Chan heard the edge in the newcomer's voice. Sensed his steely quality. 'This one is going to be a troublemaker,' he thought grimly; 'I must have him watched.' He said:

"No, we hold most strictly to the ancient ways. What did you say your enemy's name was, again?"

"Stone Ford Kwack Far Land," Djan Ching said.

"Hmmmn. His food may be good, but his name is barbarous. In fact, it doesn't sound Chinese at all."

"It is not Chinese, Honorable Tong Leader. Stone Ford Kwack Far Land is a foreign devil. A white foreign devil. From *this* country."

"I see. And the precise nature of his offense is?"

"To have stolen my bride. He lives with her as if they were husband and wife. He—enjoys her body. And she cannot be his woman. She is *mine*."

"Obviously. He cannot marry her by the laws and the customs of this country, under which such marriages are forbidden. And she cannot marry him by *our* laws and customs, because the mating of a daughter of Celestials with a hairy foreign monkey has also been forbidden from the beginning of time. Therefore, you are right. This union is—irregular. And the loss of face is very serious indeed."

Again Djan Ching shook hands with himself and bowed.

"Then the great literary class person, the honorable holder of the seal of the tong Sum Yop, will permit this humble person to go as a salaried soldier of the ever to be feared and venerated tong, accompanied by a few other salaried Highbinders, to the eating palace of this Kwack Far Land, take back my bride, and facilitate the escape of the demons from the cranium of Stone Ford *et cetera* by splitting it in two halves with my hatchet?" he said.

"No. Of course not," Lew Chan said with perfect calm.

All Djan Ching's celebrated Oriental inscrutability deserted him.

"Whaaaat?" he cried.

"I will not permit one weak and foolish husband to cause all Chinatown to be wrecked by a barbarian horde of the police of the foreign devils, because he has killed a foreign devil who has merely possessed himself of the sluttish wife said weak and foolish husband was neither firm enough nor wise enough to keep at home," Lew Chan said sternly.

Again Djan Ching bowed.

"The honorable seal holder will permit me to say it was not thus?" he said, with a false humility that didn't deceive Lew Chan in the slightest.

"Then how was it?" the tong leader said.

"This humble person was delayed in China by the death of his humble mother. Though she was but a woman, rites and respect were due her—is this not so?"

"It is. Speak on."

"When this unworthy person arrived in San Francisco, he found his bride already in the arms of the foreign devil. As lowly as he is, he cannot accept the blame for either her whorishness, or the failure of the tongs of this city to defend the rights of a fellow countryman and the honor of the Celestial Empire, Honorable Seal Holder!"

"Hmmmn—you have spirit, Djan Ching! I like that. Come, I shall allow you to sit in my presence so that we may discuss this matter . . ." With a languid wave of his long-fingered hand, Lew Chan indicated a low stool on the side of the table opposite him.

Djan Ching bowed three more times. Sat.

"First, Djan Ching, you must understand that we are in the country of the foreign devils," Lew Chan said, "and that they outnumber us, greatly. Even we, the Sum Yop, are able to exist here only by paying ruinous bribes to their officials. So killing one of them is out of the question. It would bring down such a persecution upon our people that generations as yet unborn would make pilgrimages to your tomb to smear filth upon it, and curse your name before the Gods . . ."

"Then—I am to accept the offense? The loss of face, Honorable tong leader?" Djan Ching whispered.

"No. You must accept a lesser penalty. For instance, the destruction of the eating palace of Stanford MacFarland. I happen to know that he invested the last copper of his savings in the business. Of course, his father is a great Taipan among the foreign devils, but the younger Mac-

Farland is in difficulties with his father. Therefore the loss of face would be serious. How would that suit you? Along with, of course, the return of your bride? I will send you, personally, a large bundle of green bamboo rods to beat her with . . ."

Djan Ching thought about that. At once, being as crafty as the Cantonese always were, he saw how he could use the occasion to really restore, or win back, face the way the mere smashing up or even burning of a restaurant would never do.

'For all the airs they give themselves, these overseas Chinese remain mere provincials!' he thought contemptuously. But his smoothly arrogant young face didn't change as he said:

"I accept, Great Leader! How is it to be done?"

"We will stage a comedy. For this once, I shall ask the help of the Sue Yop, with whom we are currently at peace. Tomorrow night, you and five other salaried soldiers of our Sum Yop tong will dine at the eating house of Stanford MacFarland and of Loi Yan. At a nearby table there will be six Sue Yops. We have been fighting them for years—over such questions as control of territory, the extension of protection to merchants, the introduction of slave girls, the profits from gambling, the sale of opium. Though we have lately allied ourselves with them against the Kwong Docks and the Suey Sings, who are a much greater menace nowadays, that a quarrel should break out between Sue Yop warriors and a group of our own Highbinders at adjacent tables will be very believable. Your band and theirs will fight fiercely, smashing everything in sight. And if a lighted lantern or two should fall to the floor and break, the results would be—unfortunate, wouldn't they? In any event, in the resulting confusion, it should be easy enough for you to repossess your erring woman, should it not?"

"The wisdom of the honorable seal holder stirs this humble heart to profound admiration," Djan Ching said smoothly. "But one small objection occurs to me. Am I, with great respect, and in all humility, permitted to express it?"

"Of course, Djan Ching. Say your thought."

"Stone Ford Kwack Far Land is a very large foreign devil, of considerable physical strength. What's more, he has a reputation for courage. It was by defending, alone and unaided, the person of the beauteous Loi Yan against six other foreign devils who were attempting to ravish her that he won her—admiration, say. Three of the foreign devils have not yet emerged from the house for the curing of illnesses and wounds. It is said that none of the three will ever be entirely whole again . . ."

"Are you afraid?" Lew Chan said icily.

Now Djan Ching was actually a Southern barbarian, and as provincial as, in his naïve arrogance, he habitually thought of other people as being. His arrogance was born of his ignorance, which was vast. Both attributes of his personality explain the enormity of what he did next.

Leaping to his feet, he made the tong leader a deep and obviously mocking bow. In one smooth, chain-linked series of motions, so fast they blurred sight, he produced from under his robes a small and wicked-looking ax, whirled and let it fly. The ax soared, cartwheeling end over end through the warm, incense-laden air, bit into the trunk of Lew Chan's beloved and very nearly priceless eucalyptus tree at the exact height of a man's head. As Lew Chan knew, the distance was a full thirty feet. Despite which, he realized, a hypothetical foe standing before that tree would have immediately joined his ancestors.

"I see," he said dryly, prudently concealing his wrath at this impiety; "you have made your point, Djan Ching. I shall order the guards before my door beaten bloody for allowing you to get in here with *that* under your robes. Now listen, you uncouth Southern idiot! You are *not* to kill Stanford MacFarland. If you do so, *I* shall deliver you to their police, and they will *hang* you. A most dishonorable way to die. You are not even to injure him—"

"But Great Literary Class Person, Honorable Seal Holder, what if—in defense of his business, and his possession of Loi Yan, he attacks *me?*"

"You may defend yourself. But inflicting no more serious wounds than an honorable defense makes necessary. Even so, for your information, I shall have the greatest Chinese physician in San Francisco sitting at a nearby table. His mission will be to see that *nobody* bleeds to death. MacFarland will lose his business, his woman, and all the face he ever had before the other foreign devils, by his having been humbled by a little yellow monkey. That's what the foreign devils call *us*, you know. Content yourself with that. It is enough."

Djan Ching bowed deeply. "The word of the most honorable seal holder of the Sum Yop is my law!" he said.

"Good. You will stay here tonight. And, to lend savor to your vengeance, as well as to cool your blood sufficiently so that you will not be tempted into folly, I will send you a white foreign she-devil this night to your bed. Will that please you, Djan Ching?"

The young Cantonese shook hands with himself again. Bowed four times. Which was, perhaps, excessive.

"Enormously, Honorable Leader!" he said.

Loi Yan lay there, running her slim hands all over Stanford's body, touching with never ceasing wonder the downy blond hair it was covered with. Actually, as Westerners go, Stanford really wasn't very hairy: Nordics seldom are. Loi Yan would have been shocked speechless by the thick mats of chest, belly, and pubic hair that the brunette segments of the white race grow. Still, Stanford's moderate coat of natural fur fascinated her. It seemed to her both startling and interesting.

"Big golden monkey-man," she murmured tenderly.

"You want me to shave it off?" Stan asked her. "Of course, you'd have to help with the places I can't reach, but—"

"No! No! It is—beautiful, Stanford! I—love your golden fur. It is like that of the chow chows—"

"The whaaat?" Stan said.

"The chow chows. The little golden puppy dogs we eat in China. One cannot get them here. A pity—they are delicious. One serves them baked and—"

"Good Lord! Baked *dog*—ugh! Hmmmn, so that's what I remind you of! A baked puppy dog. Well, I like that!"

"I think you are probably also delicious!" she giggled happily; "so now I am going to bite you and find out!" She leaned forward and buried her face in the hollow of his neck, caught a fold of his skin between her miraculously even and white teeth, nipped it sharply.

"Ouch!" Stanford cried. He pushed her away from him, held her at arm's length and gazed at her. Her nakedness fascinated him as much as his hairiness did her. For her body was naked to a degree that simply astounded him. She told him she shaved, but he'd be damned if he could see where. There was no shadow of thickening stubble left by her razor on any area of her flesh that he could discern. She was absolutely— except for the mane of thick, ruler-straight, blue-black hair on her small, dainty head, which hung down well below her hips in the back—as naked as a newborn baby.

'But she sure isn't shaped like one, thank God!' Stanford thought contentedly.

"Stanford—" she murmured, "teach me how to—kiss?"

It was their favorite game. Of course he had taught her how to kiss about ten thousand times by then, but she always claimed she'd forgotten how to go about it, and wheedled him into teaching her all over again. But now, looking at the clock on the wall, he decided against another lesson. If they started in on kissing games, they'd never get back to the restaurant on time. Of course, they still had almost an hour before they had to be there to receive their ever growing stream of both Chinese and white clients; but Loi Yan was psychologically incapable of indulging in physical lovemaking without taking an hour-long bath afterward. She was the cleanest human being Stan had ever met, and by precept and example she raised his own standards, already much higher than those of most Occidentals of his times, to a pinnacle more nearly approaching her own; which was to say that he bathed, or rather was bathed by Loi Yan, *every* evening now instead of contenting himself with the Saturday night ablutions that sufficed for most of his fellows. So making love at that hour was out of the question. He told her that.

But she surprised him.

"Stanford," she whispered, "make love to me—please. It is important that you do, tonight. I don't know *why* it's important, but it is . . ."

"Even if we're late?" he said.

"Even if we—never get there. My body—says maybe we shouldn't. It —wants—needs—yours. Twined together. My pale alabaster—milking —your gold. To make a little combination me and you. How funny it will be to see eyes that slant—and are *blue!* Oh, Stanford, please!"

So naturally they were well over an hour late in getting to The House of the Weeping Willow, the charming and immediately popular little Chinese restaurant they had opened on the edge of Chinatown. Which really wouldn't have been important at all on any other night, because their efficient headwaiter Ah Gee, whom Stan had, of course, renamed "Gee Whiz!" had everything under perfect control while their chef, whom Stan had baptized "One Eye" (although he had two perfectly good ones), for the very simple reason that his real name was Won Li, was chanting singsong orders to his three apprentice helpers in the kitchen.

But when Stan walked into the place with Loi Yan on his arm, he stopped dead. Started to tremble.

Loi Yan easily followed the light-locked pointing of his gaze. She stared soberly at the slim blond girl sitting at a nearby table with two Chinese men.

"Yours?" she murmured gently. "Go to her, Stanford. It is—distressing, even to me, to watch her—suffer so . . ."

"No," Stanford said angrily; "she had no business to follow me this way! And to get two of my father's house servants to bring her here was—"

"Intelligent, seeing that they are of my people, able to speak the language and ask the right questions," Loi Yan said. "Dear Goddess of

Mercy, how the poor little thing is crying! She is *very* beautiful, Stanford. You have my permission to marry her. Truly I do not mind at all . . ."

"Jesus Christ!" Stanford exploded.

"Stanford, you *cannot* marry me. Neither the laws of your people nor those of mine will permit you to. So why should you not make her happy? It is very cruel of you not to!"

Stanford stared at her.

"In that case," he growled, "what becomes of *you?*"

"I remain your number one concubine, forever at your side. I will graciously permit you to marry the pale, pretty foreign she-devil with the sapphire and emerald eyes and the sunset hair, because I am sure she cannot win your love away from me. We Celestials have forgot more about love than you big hairy monkey people will ever learn. Tell me, is she also hairy? I have heard from the tong warriors who frequent the white foreign she-devils that the head seal holders keep for their amusement that their bodies are as furry as those of she-monkeys, and that they have a strong and unpleasant odor. Is this true, Stanford?"

Stan grinned at her.

"I wouldn't know. I was a virgin until you took advantage of my boyish innocence, Loi Yan," he said solemnly.

"Oh, you!" Loi Yan giggled. "Come on, let us go over there, so that you may comfort her . . ."

"I doubt that our going over there is going to comfort her a good goddamn; but, anyhow, come on," Stanford said.

But a yard away from the table at which Raquel Kilpatrick sat with Stan's own valet Lu Sung, alias "Low Sunk," and his stepfather's cook Xiaop Siu, better known as "Duck Soup," Loi Yan suddenly halted. Clutched his arm.

"Stanford!" she whispered, urgency and fear in her voice. "You must remove her from our place! At once!"

"And me thinking you were going to be broad-minded and civilized about the whole thing!" Stanford groaned.

"It is not that!" Loi Yan hissed. "There is going to be trouble, Stanford! *Bad* trouble! You see those men?"

"Which men?" Stan said.

"At the tables on her right and on her left. Those on her right are Sue Yops. See the little turquoise ribbons in their lapels? That is the emblem of their tong. And those on her left are Sum Yops—"

"With *red* ribbons in their lapels," Stan said. "So?"

"So she is seated *between* two bands of hungry tigers. Tongs that have been chopping holes in each other's craniums since 1851. Let a Sue Yop say 'Boo!' to a Sum Yop, and the fighting will start. And if they have to kill her and the two servants of your honorable stepfather to get to each other, then kill them they will!"

"Good God! Stay *here*, Loi Yan! Don't move! I'll—"

He took a step forward. Somebody let out a high-pitched, blood-chilling screech. And all hell broke loose in The House of the Weeping Willow.

Lew Chan was amusing himself with his favorite concubine. He admitted to himself, with an internal disquietude approaching actual fear, that he had become as addicted to her as some people were to the smoking of opium. To be so enslaved by the body and the caresses of a woman seemed to him beneath his dignity as the greatest tong seal holder in California. More, such an addiction wasn't even—civilized. And that the concubine in question was a white foreign she-devil with all the animalistic characteristics of her race made the matter even worse.

Yet, he also acknowledged sadly, it was precisely those characteristics that most intrigued him. For instance, why hadn't he forced her to shave her body? He could easily have done so by the same subtle tortures he had inflicted upon her during the past three days in order to bring her to the state of ravenous willingness to do anything to please him in which she whined and moaned and panted, now. That torture was to withhold from her the long-stemmed opium pipe that had become the entire center of her existence, ever since he had first taught her to smoke it. Yet, he hadn't done so. He found the thick mats of inky black hair beneath her armpits and between her thighs utterly repulsive—and totally fascinating. Even her smell—which wasn't due to uncleanness, because the female slave attendants he had provided her with bathed her from once to three times daily, depending upon the warmth of the weather, but rather to the different chemical composition of white devils' flesh, he supposed—seemed to him a powerful aphrodisiac. But what pleased him most was the savage, she-beast wildness she brought to the act, or the art, of making love—especially when she had been deprived of the dream-making pipe and knew that only by leaving him utterly drained and trembling would she be able to regain it.

Lew Chan slipped his rich, loose silk robe down off his shoulders, bundled the lower half up around his slender waist. He was pleased to note that the rod of his manhood stood up proudly. At his age that wasn't always the case. Then he sank to his knees on the straw mat, leaned back until he was sitting on his own heels, supporting himself by placing the palms of his two hands flat on the floor, to each side and slightly behind him, his arms locked and rigid, holding his body at a back-leaning angle of some sixty degrees.

"Come," he said to the beautiful white foreign she-devil with the midnight hair and seawater eyes. She started toward him slowly, walking. He let her take three full steps before he stopped her. Watching what her naked body did, walking, was an unfailing joy.

"No!" he said then sternly. "Get down on your belly, she-dog, and crawl to me, who am your master!"

She got down on her belly, started to crawl. That was a subtle delight to watch, too. But as he reclined there, savoring the sight of the marvelously sensuous motion her slim hips made, crawling, how the deep rose, erected points of her heavy bitch-thing's dugs dragged on the floor, he heard, unbelievably but unmistakably, the knocking on the door.

Which first astonished, then angered, and finally alarmed him. All his servants knew that this hour was always devoted by him to the worship of the goddess of carnal love. Therefore, of the three emotions that gripped him, he conceded that the last was the *only* valid one. His servants would never have dared to interrupt his rituals if there were not cause for alarm.

"What is it?" he cried out, noting at the same time, with wry self-mockery, that the rod of his manhood had collapsed before the onslaught of his fear.

"The police!" his manservant quavered. "The white devil police! They have the house surrounded! They are demanding to see you, Honorable Seal Holder! They wish to arrest you on the charge of keeping white she-devils as slaves!"

Lew Chan got to his feet. Adjusted his robes. Walked to the far end of the salon, behind the eucalyptus tree. Touched a certain spot on the low-relief Chinese frieze near the top of the wall. Noiselessly a narrow section of that wall slid open. Behind it was an even narrower stairway going down. Lew Chan quietly and thoughtfully descended those stairs. The wall slid closed behind him, just as noiselessly. It was as if the tong leader had never been.

The naked white devil slave girl got up. Walked to the wall rack in which Lew Chan kept his pipes. Took one of them down, searched in the cabinet beneath it until she found a ball of opium. She had known it would be there, for although Lew Chan despised the vice of opium smoking, he always kept a supply of the drug in that cabinet, along with his fragrant Chinese tobacco, to offer to those of his guests who favored it.

The slave girl lit the pipe. Stretched herself out, stark naked, on Lew Chan's straw mat, and began to pull on that pipe contentedly.

When the white devil police and the big, heavy-set white devil civilian who accompanied them broke into that room finally, they found her there.

"Oh God, oh Christ, oh Jesus!" the white devil civilian said.

As he rode along in his own closed carriage with his drugged and dozing stepdaughter in his arms, Andrew MacFarland was suddenly jerked forward so that he almost fell out of his seat by the abruptness with which James Swithers pulled up the team of four big Morgans that drew Andy's coach. He clutched Claire's blanket-wrapped form closer to him, leaned toward the window on his side.

At that moment John Swithers' black face appeared beside the window. The footman jerked the coach door open.

"For God's sake, sir—look!" he said.

Andy leaned out as far as he could without turning Claire loose.

"Want—my—pipe," she whined.

Then the quicksilver tycoon, as all San Francisco called him, saw it: the exact amount his fortune, or any man's fortune, is worth in the pitiless balance of the gods.

His two Chinese servants, Lu Sung and Xiaop Siu, walked along the sidewalk of Dupont Street supporting his stepson Stanford between them. Beside them little Raquel Kilpatrick trotted, her mouth wide open, dripping saliva and tears, her whole face distorted into a mask of utter rage, terror, grief. Andy wondered why the two Chinese weren't supporting her instead of Stan, because all her clothes were wet through and plastered to her slender body with—he shuddered under the gut-churning impact of that recognition—blood.

Then Stan stumbled weakly, and he saw why. His stepson's right arm ended at the wrist in a thick white bandage, expertly applied, that dripped huge red drops down upon the sidewalk.

There was, very evidently, no hand below that wrist.

Djan Ching had avenged his loss of face.

24

"MOTHER MACFARLAND," RAQUEL SAID, BUT HALF IN JEST, MIREILLE was sure, "give him back to me; he's mine!"

"*Ah non!*" Mireille laughed. "You are only his mother, while I am *sa grandmère*, which is much more important. Besides, I have to go back to San Francisco as soon as you're up and about, to get things ready for Claire's wedding; and you will have him all the time, Raquel dear . . ."

She rocked the tiny newborn, as red, wrinkled, and ugly as newborns always are, tenderly in her arms.

"How beautiful you are, *petit* Andrew MacFarland the Second!" she beamed. Then, bestowing a smile, whose beatific, madonna-like quality would have shocked speechless any of the legions of men who had passed through her life, upon her bought-and-paid-for son, she added blissfully, "It was good of you children to name him that. An-drew the First is bursting all the buttons off his waistcoat, he is so proud. *Ah non, mon tout 'tit chou! Faut pas pleurer! Suis ta grandmère! Tu ne m'aimes pas?*"

"Mama, you're scaring him," Stanford said, "clucking over him like a mother hen, and bouncing him up and down. It's been so long since Claire and me, you've forgotten how. Give him to me. I've got some rights to the ugly li'l bastard, haven't I? Even if his pappy was a fruit picker, or a plow-hand—"

"Why, Stan-ford MacFarland!" Raquel gasped.

"Can't be *mine*," Stan said solemnly; "he's got *two* paws, hasn't he? Pass him over, Mama . . ."

Mireille glanced at that ugly, rounded stub where Stan's right hand had been.

"Stan-ford, are you sure you won't—" she began fearfully.

"Drop him?" Stanford said cheerfully. "Of course not, Mama. And if I do, he'll only bounce—that is, if this cheating woman's telling the truth when she swears *I'm* the guilty party. Besides, I manage very well. You'd be surprised the chores the old nub serves for—including beating Rachie over the head when she gets out of line . . ."

He took the baby from his mother, cradled him in the crook of his maimed right arm, gazed down at him with an almost owlish expression of gravity.

"Well, son of mine, you're supposed to be human, but damned if you could prove it by me," he said. "Darwin's proof positive, aren't you, you li'l great big monkey man, you?"

"Stanford, you stop it!" Raquel cried. "Don't you *dare* call my baby that! 'Cause I know just *where* you got that expression from!"

"And where did he, dear?" Mireille asked.

"From his Chinese mistress!" Raquel said, and started to cry. "From that aaaaawwful LLLLoi YYYan!"

"If Loi Yan was awful," Stan said solemnly, "please serve me up some horrible, will you? And in double, heaping, soup-bowl portions, at that . . ."

"You see?" Raquel wailed. "He's sssstill in lllove wwwith hhher!"

"I am," Stanford said flatly; "and I probably am going to be for the rest of my life. I told you that from the outset, didn't I?"

"Yes, but—" Raquel whispered.

"You thought you could cure me of that—inclination, call it. You can't. You're only a red-haired foreign she-devil from a tribe of Northern barbarians—from a hairy, ugly race, closely akin to monkeys, while *she* was a daughter of the very sky. The competition's too much for you, Rachie. So forget it, will you?"

"Stan-ford!" Mireille shrilled. *"Est-ce que tu as devenu fou, ou quoi?"*

"No, Mama. I'm not crazy. That's what the Chinese think of us. I find their point of view—refreshing. Since we've been here in California, we've practically exterminated the Indians, robbed the Hispano-Americans of their lands, ruined the landscape looking for absolutely useless yellow dirt, abused and murdered—remember the nineteen Chinese lynched in *one* single riot in Los Angeles in seventy-one?—the Orientals, imported whores from all over the world, invented the concert saloon, the melodeon, and the minstrel show as our contribution to culture— and looked with condescension upon peoples who've forgotten more than we'll ever learn . . ."

Mireille stared at him.

"All—true," she said. "But what's that got to do with your loving Raquel? Your *wife*—and the mother of your son?"

Stanford grinned at her crookedly.

"Nothing. You're right, Mama. It has absolutely nothing at all to do with it, has it?" he said. " 'Cause I'm a big hairy monkey man too, aren't I? And the most devilish foreign devil anybody ever saw."

"You can say that again!" Raquel snapped.

"Mama, you're a big girl now," Stan said with a quiet chuckle, "and even this little red-haired she-devil has to reach adulthood, one day. I promised to honor and cherish her until death us do part. And even to love her, within the limits of my capacity to experience that always irrational emotion. It's neither her fault nor mine that that capacity has —diminished considerably over the past four years. Between 1876 and now, April second, 1880, I've been forced to become a realist. In short, to grow up."

"And you—blame me," Mireille whispered; "blame the life I was—forced to lead for all your misfortunes, don't you, son?"

"No. Of course not. Only one thing can be laid to your charge, Mama, and that was not preparing me—and Claire—for Mary Ellen Pleasant's —disclosures. The truth would have been a shield and buckler 'gainst a host of foes, old dear! You left us defenseless, y'know. Your life—bah! People do what they must, as I have—"

"That you have!" Raquel said severely.

"For which you should be grateful, dear child. Because you, almost alone among married women, can rest assured that your husband's going to be absolutely faithful to you—physically, anyhow—until they put him to bed with a shovel under that old oak tree. But a little mental adultery from time to time, you'll just have to allow me, Rachie dear . . ."

"Well, I like that!" Raquel said.

"You should. The only woman on earth who possibly—and I doubt even that—could take me away from you no longer wants me."

"This Chinese girl?" Mireille said in a tone of purest disdain.

"Oh Mama, don't be such a bloody bigot!" Stanford said. "You've been out of the South all of thirty years now. I won't argue that all men are created equal, because they aren't. Loi Yan's worth ten of any other human being I've ever met . . ."

"Bon Dieu!" Mireille said.

"Here, Rachie, take this little monster and change him. He's sopping wet. Jesus! How can a bladder this tiny hold that much pee? Anyhow, I wish both of you white she-devils would leave Loi Yan in peace. She's out of my life forever. I lost a tong war—my flipper with it—and worst of all, face. I was defeated by a little yellow Cantonese about so high, to whom she was already married by *their* law—"

"And yet—she ran off with you. *Très honnête de sa parte, n'est-ce pas?*"

"Oh, goddamn. Let's change this subject, shall we?"

"Well, didn't she?"

"No. *I* took her away. Agreed, she didn't put up much of a fight. But that day, for once, I was in good form. Let's say I behaved well—was impressive. And anyhow, her grandfather had married her off by trans-Pacific mail to this little bugger she'd never even seen before in all her life. So let's not discuss the morality of the question. Morality is always—disputable, dubious, or hypocritical when it's not all three—as it *is*, most of the time. And afterward, at The House of the Weeping Willow, this little Cantonese was impressive, and I wasn't. So now he's got her. For life. She'll be absolutely faithful to him, give him twenty dozen slant-eyed little yellow buggers, make him a *pluscumperfecto* wife. Maybe she even loves him, by now. Anyhow, being a pragmatic Oriental, she'll accept her lot—with maybe a secret tear or two. I hope she'll dream of me now and again—with calm resignation, leavened with a dash of bitter regret. As I'll dream of her. So don't you two white foreign she-devils and/or hairy female monkeys tell me to forget her. I won't. I have no intention to. She was one of the finest things that ever happened to me in all my life."

"Oh, Jesus!" Raquel wailed.

"You should be grateful to her. After all, she's guaranteed that I'll never treat you the way your old man treated your mother. And, in a way, she's responsible for all this—"

He indicated the limpid, lyrically bucolic landscape outside the bedroom window with a wave of his hand.

"How so, son?" Mireille said.

"That restaurant we started put me in contact with the wholesale dealers in fresh vegetables and fruit. One of 'em, a chap with the unbelievably exotic name of John Smith, also owned four or five farms. Got the produce he sold from them. Didn't work them, himself; his sons did that. But that man turned his rude, ungrammatical English into pure poetry when he talked about the land hereabouts. Swore that the best place in California to settle was near the town of Modesto. D'you know why they call it that?"

"No. Why do they?" Mireille said.

"The Southern Pacific laid it out no more than ten years ago. They were going to name it Ralston, after W. C. Ralston, the San Francisco banker. You know him—he's a friend of Dad's. But he declined the honor. So they named it Modesto in appreciation of his modesty. Anyhow, old Smith was always raving about the sheer beauty of this country-side, and the advantages of having a farm near a railroad shipping center, which Modesto is. So, while I was convalescing, I asked Dad to send me up here. I was going crazy in San Francisco trying to scratch fingers that itched, even though they weren't there anymore . . ."

"I wonder *where* they are," Raquel said; "I guess your poor hand burned up in the fire, Stan—"

"I doubt it. I'll bet Djan Ching's got my paw in a bottle of rice wine on the mantelpiece," Stanford said imperturbably, "just like they keep Joaquin Murieta's head and, more to the point, Three-Fingered Jack's hand in the Museum of Horrors on Halleck Street."

"Ughhh!" Mireille said.

"Or maybe he served up that chunk of me as Sweet and Sour Pork at his victory celebration banquet. Hope it gave him the trots, if he did. Where was I? So I came up here, saw this place, and fell in love with it. It—healed me, Mama. Healed my spirit more than it did my truncated arm. When I realized what this map of paradise had done for me, I wrote Dad to take a few days off, and come see it all. It's a wonder he could read my letter—hadn't learned to write with my left hand worth a damn, way back then . . ."

"Wrote *him*, not me," Raquel said; "and there I was, going crazy, too. Thinking you—you'd gone back to her . . ."

"Fat chance! And, as you know, Dad came up here. Gave me no argument at all. Sat down and wrote me out a check big enough to pay for all this, and a year's operating expenses to boot. Of course he never dreamed I'd actually make a go of it—"

"That's where you're wrong. He was convinced you would, son. He came back and told me, 'That boy's got his growth—in all ways, honey—become a man . . .'"

"Thanks for telling me that, Mama," Stanford said, a little huskily; "my stepdad's the finest male human I *ever* met—"

"Or that *I* ever did," Mireille said. "But speaking of human males, where's your father, child?"

"Out playing cowboy, as usual!" Raquel laughed. "Poor old father! We've got six dairy cows and one fat old sultan of a bull, and Father's always in the saddle riding herd on them. Harmless enough hobby, I guess—"

"As long as he doesn't overdo it," Mireille said severely; "Enrique's told him a million times he's simply not up to ranching, but mule-stubborn as Willy is, he—"

"Mama, he knows that," Stanford said. "But riding about, helping me manage the place—and he *is* a help, speaking seriously about it—is good for him. He looks great. Wait till you see him. Here he is, sixty years old—"

"Fifty-eight," Mireille corrected him.

"Scant difference. He looks like a boy. Slim, straight, good-looking as ever. Got a thing going with a comely widow in Modesto—"

"Well, I never!" Mireille gasped.

"Mama, quit being a dog in the manger about my pappy-in-law, will you please? After all, Rachie's mother has been dead all of three years now. Besides, the widow in question is fiftyish and fat. I doubt that it's serious. But bringing Willy up here was smart. He was sinking deeper into apathy with every passing day, neglecting the business, neglecting himself, starting to drink again—"

"He felt guilty about Mother's death. About all his little playmates. Even about *you* to a certain extent, I suspect," Raquel said, somewhat tartly.

"There, there, child, don't be a daughter-in-law!" Mireille laughed. "Anyhow, I'm glad it turned out so splendidly for everybody."

"Not—everybody. You have to except poor Periwinkle," Stanford sighed.

"Periwinkle?" Raquel bristled. "And just who is Periwinkle, may I ask?"

"Colored girl. Daughter of my maid, Blossom," Mireille said. "She's dead, the poor little thing. She was—rather wild. Married—an Othello, as it were. One of those Black men who consume themselves with jealousy—"

"Cut out the 'Black.' Jealousy's universal," Stanford said.

"You're not jealous of *me*," Raquel said.

"Day I have to be, you'll know it," Stan said; "when you get out of the hospital, anyhow . . ."

"Hmpf! Take care I don't put *you* in one!" Raquel sniffed. "There, there, Andy darling! You want your dinner, don't you? Notice what a pair of lungs he's got, Mother MacFarland?" She put the red, wrinkled mite to her breast. He tugged at it greedily. "What happened to this—Periwinkle, you called her, didn't you?" she said.

"Three bullets in her back. Another three in the man her husband caught her with. He had to reload to kill himself," Mireille said.

"And her baby? The one she was expecting when you put her out of the house?" Stanford asked.

"Don't know. I suspect Mary Ellen Pleasant's got it. If so, it's doomed to a life of shame," Mireille said. "I never see Mary Ellen anymore. Age and the lack of money have clipped her wings more than a little. For which *le bon Dieu* be thanked!"

"Amen!" Stanford said quietly. "Mama—about Claire . . . Is she all right, finally? Really all right?"

"I don't know," Mireille said sadly. "I truly don't know. Your stepfather bailed the Hansons out of the financial disaster they'd fallen into, gambling on those Comstock Lode silver stocks, on the basis of a gentleman's agreement that young Ted would forget the awful things the yellow journals wrote about her—"

"Awful *truths*," Stan said grimly.

"I know. Which makes matters even worse, doesn't it? As I was saying, An-drew bailed the Hansons out of the well-deserved punishment for their own stupidity and folly, upon young Ted's pledged word to marry Claire. Which shouldn't be any hardship, considering the fact that he's been in love with her for as long as I can remember . . ."

"It *is* a hardship!" Stanford snapped. "Claire has the temper of a fiend and the disposition of a viper. On top of which, she's enslaved to the vice of smoking opium. Or drinking laudanum. Or ingesting the vile stuff in any form she can procure it. If it were left to me, I'd shoot her—just as one shoots an incurably suffering animal. A perfect description of my sister Claire, incidentally!"

"*I* shall cure her—that is, if I haven't already," Mireille said.

Stanford looked at his adoptive mother. Shook his head slowly, sadly.

"*Your* vice is optimism, Mama," he said.

They sat around the supper table, with the exception of Raquel, of course, who had had a rough time bringing her firstborn into this world and was, on the advice of her doctor, keeping to her bed for the first ten days thereafter.

Willy, his blue eyes alight, leaned across the table and took Mireille's hand.

"You grow ever more beautiful with the years." He sighed theatrically. "How's about leaving old Horse's Ass, and running away with me, *Mirla, queridísima?*"

"To do that, I should have to be the posterior of a she-donkey, or some other animal equally as stupid, Willy," Mireille told him serenely. "Andrew's worth ten of you, and you know it."

"*De accuerdo.* But I am much prettier than he is, and a far better lover!" Willy chuckled.

"Listen to the old goat!" Stanford hooted. "Don't you ever give up, Willy?"

"Never. The day I give up as far as a beautiful woman is concerned, you have my leave to bury me, *Hijo-político!* For then you will know I am dead. Besides, your mother is *the* most beautiful woman I have ever known and—"

He stopped short and stared at the Mexican cook, a niece of the Sepúlveras' Josefina, and just as fat, who came waddling into the dining room.

"*¿Que pasa,* Catalina?" he said.

"*Es una telegrama—para la Señora,*" Catalina said.

"*¡Damelo,* Catalina!" Mireille said.

Catalina handed her the telegram. She tore it open, read it swiftly. Sat there, frozen.

"For God's sake, Mama! What's happened? Don't tell me that Dad—?"

"No. Your stepfather's all right. It's—Claire. She's—disappeared. Again," Mireille said.

25

OBVIOUSLY THE FIRST AND MOST IMPERATIVE ITEM ON MIREILLE'S program upon her abrupt and unplanned return to San Francisco was to find Claire. The method she chose was flawless: She sent Xiaop Siu and Lu Sung, her Chinese menservants, searching through all the opium dens in Chinatown. Even so, it took them more than two weeks before they finally encountered their mistress' willful—or will-less?—daughter, in a state of appallingly sluttish dishevelment, stretched out on a couch and sucking on the long pipe, deep sunk in mindless apathy, among a stinking mob of other human derelicts in a den that had the reputation of being the Oriental quarter's vilest. Which wasn't important. Once Claire was safely home again, the only important question to Mireille was what to do with, or about, her maddening offspring. That is, if anything could be done at all, which everyone in the MacFarland household was beginning to doubt.

In her despair, Mireille consulted the wisest man she knew, the old Spanish-American doctor whom all his patients, including the surprisingly large number he had gained even among the gringo population, considered a magician and a sage.

Enrique Sepúlvera listened to her piteous tale of woe without interrupting her even once. Then he sighed, long and deeply.

"You want me to tell you what to do, Mireille? Really tell you? I warn you, it will be—rough . . ."

"Yes," Mireille said.

"All right. I wouldn't suggest this procedure to anyone else . . . but you're the strongest, meanest, toughest little she-cat of a woman I ever met. Sssh! Don't open your trap, damn you! To have gone through what you have, and survived it, practically undamaged, is—most admirable. And it inclines me to bow before you in purest reverence. That I—like everything in pants even ten percent male who's ever spent five minutes in your company—have been in love with you from the first hour I laid eyes on you is, of course, immaterial and irrelevant. Men fall in love with the most miserable bitches alive when said bitches are possessed of your —damn! I don't know the English for it, or the English I do know isn't right—*de tu arrolladora sexualidad, ta écrasante sexualité*—"

"All you're saying is—I'm a slut. *Suis salope. Garce. Soy golfa.* In any damn language. I know that, Enrique darling—"

"You're not. You're—if not a great lady, a great woman. The proof of which is not that men fall in love with you, but that they *stay* in that lamentable state, hopelessly enslaved to your goddamned female witchcraft until the hour they die. Judge Curtwright. Willy. Andrew. *Me.* Who ever fell *out* of love with you, Mireille?"

"How-ward Tellefair," Mireille said.

"I said *men*, not *sin cojónes*, ball-less wonders. All right. Here's what you do: Send one of your slant-eyed yellow perils down to Chinatown to buy a pipe and a supply of opium—"

"What?" Mireille cried.

"You heard me. *Keep* Claire under the influence until you get her to a place I own: a little fisherman's hut down by Big Sur. Bought it to avoid being hanged for murder, which is what I'm driven to when Paqui, my daughters, and all their little *golfillos* start yapping at one and the same time. You've never heard a *Spanish* family in full cry, have you? I go down there three weeks out of every summer. Alone. I say it's to fish, but actually I escape to Big Sur to be able to hear myself think, enjoy the blessed silence. Anyhow, the hut's got stout barred windows, a thick oaken door, and two rooms, one of which I use for storage. No sanitary conveniences whatsoever—you'll have to use a lonely stretch of beach for nature's necessities, my sweet!"

"And after I get her there?" Mireille said.

"You take the little furniture I've got—the bed, chair, table—out of the big room. Strip it as bare as a baby's behind. Strip her equally as naked. Any clothes you leave on her she'll tear into strips and use to strangle herself. It goes without saying that you must leave *nothing* she could possibly use as a weapon in that room with her. They *always* try to kill themselves when they realize that they really can't get the stuff."

"You mean I'm to take the opium away from her completely?"

"And throw it into the ocean, weighted down with *rocks*. Smash that damned pipe to bits. When you feed her, push some bread and cheese and fruit through the bars—not in a plate. She'll smash the plate and use the edges to cut her throat, if you do . . ."

He stopped. Stared at her bleakly.

"Mireille, it will be—horrible. She'll lose all control of herself. She'll urinate and defecate with no consciousness of what she's doing, like a baby. She may even menstruate out of season. And you've got to let her alone, beyond feeding her, giving her water. You mustn't show her the slightest sign of pity, or else she'll trick you. Addicts are not only totally amoral, they're as clever as old hell. You'll know when she's coming out of it, when she starts to eat again. She'll try to starve herself to death, too, failing any other method. But she's a tall, strong, healthy girl or she'd already be dead by now, so suicide by starvation *should* be beyond her willpower . . ."

"And if I do all that, she'll be cured?" Mireille whispered.

"*Maybe.* The probability is rather high. And her being *your* daughter makes it higher still. Of course, I don't know who her father was, unless you want to insist he was Judge Curtwright. I'd bet on Willy, of course . . ."

"Don't," Mireille said morosely.

"Then who was he? It would help my prognostication to know . . ."

"Then we're lost. I haven't the faintest idea, dammit! I went through a period of sheer irrationality—or pure bitchery!—back then, old dear!"

"Oh God!" Enrique groaned. "Are you going to try it?"

"Yes. Or rather I'm going to *do* it. And—bless you, Enrique darling!" Mireille said.

They went down to Big Sur, not by land, but by sea, in a steam yacht that Andrew rented, crew and all, from one of his fellow millionaires on Nob Hill, since he had never felt the slightest desire to own one of the ostentatious, expensive toys himself. Despite its hellish cost, this choice of their means of transportation was a wise one. In 1880, there were still no direct rail connections to such outlying, unimportant places, therefore the only alternative would have been a murderously fatiguing combination of trains and stagecoaches, and the latter over some pretty abominable roads. Besides which, public conveyances of any sort would have denied the MacFarlands the prime essential of privacy; while to have attempted a journey of that length in one of their own vehicles, involving the reservation of lodgings and changes of horses along the way, was a logistic nightmare not to be countenanced. Besides which, it would have alerted the yellow journalists as effectively as employing public transportation, and perhaps even more so.

So they steamed out of Yerba Buena Cove into the Pacific, and down the coast to Big Sur. Andrew almost spoiled things by insisting upon staying with them when he saw that lonely, fog-drenched spot with the gulls mewing and crying above the beach and the winds whipping the sawgrass endlessly. But Mireille overruled him by appealing to his profound respect for feminine modesty, which she did by revealing to him some of the unavoidable, and most unlovely, physical aspects of that Draconian cure of opium de-intoxication that Enrique had predicted would—had to—occur.

So he went back aboard the yacht, after giving Mireille his revolver and a box of bullets to defend herself and Claire against prowlers, and steamed away northward, with something very like death in his heart.

And everything Enrique had predicted would happen, did. Tripled. Quadrupled. Raised to the tenth power. Plus a few he hadn't predicted, because they lay at a depth of sheer degradation within female human nature that he, out of the instinctive chivalry of a normal human male, wasn't prepared to admit, even to himself, that a few rare women are capable of plumbing.

Mireille came within a hair's breadth of losing her mind under the impact of the obscene spectacle and verbal assault her daughter subjected her to day in day out, round the clock, until pure exhaustion ended it. And then only temporarily. An hour's sleep and Claire returned to the attack with a ferocity a tigress would have envied.

Her vocabulary was unbelievable. She knew every absolutely filthy epithet in the English language, all *les saletés crapuleuses et écoeurantes* in French, and a good many of Spanish's rich barnyard compost of *tacos y palabrotas.*

She displayed—proudly!—a detailed knowledge of every deviate sexual practice extant in the Western world. And topped even that—granted both her mother's native Southern tendency toward bedrock bigotry as far as the members of all the "lesser breeds without the law" were concerned, and the Orientals' native gift for subtle and exquisite refinements —by demonstrating an equally thorough command of every Chinese variation upon the basic theme. She discoursed at sickening length— gleefully watching, from between the bars, her mother's utterly stricken face—upon the subject of comparative male anatomy, from the anthropological standpoint, with special emphasis upon the dimensions of the African's equipment—which she wildly exaggerated, though poor Mireille, Southern to the bitter bone, had no way of knowing that.

"Take my big buck nigger fancy man Leroy," Claire purred on one such occasion; "I used to keep him on the spending money Daddy gave me. His was as thick as my arm, and almost as long—and, oh, Maman; it used to *hurt* so good! You mean to say you never tried a burly black fieldhand when you lived down South? Why—"

Whereupon Mireille screamed, "You shut up, Claire!" And stuffing her fingers in both ears to shut out that hateful, raving voice, fled wildly down the beach.

That chaste and delicate subject exhausted—for the moment, anyhow!—sweet Claire started in on the precise dossier that, following the leads accidentally provided her by Mary Ellen "Mammy" Pleasant, she —with the insane cunning of the addict—had compiled on the subject of her mother's every sinful act from childhood on. She had somehow met Howard Tellefair, grown old, bald, fat, and living in homosexual bliss with a pretty youth, admitting thus his basic nature to himself at last, and got out of him a highly distorted picture of Mireille's early years in New Orleans. She had obtained opium money for months from that obscenely hideous mountain of grease, the ex-Maniac, ex-man, Ray Coles, by allowing him to paw and slobber over her slender body to his heart's content, on the sound theory that he was incapable of doing her any serious damage, such as getting her pregnant, for instance. From that unsavory pair of no longer, or not quite males, from the surviving members of Fire Engine Company Number Six, from Madame Pleasant whom she assiduously visited in secret, she had acquired a crushing—if inaccurate, inflated, and maliciously twisted—store of information that was more than enough to break Mireille's heart, and came very close to cracking her lucid mind.

That stage passed. Then came the suicide attempts. By starvation. By a method not even Enrique had ever encountered in all his years of practice, for it required such absolute ferocity of sheer destructive will as to be beyond what nearly all human beings are capable of. One night, Claire gnawed both her wrists almost to the bone with her own sharp white teeth, and came close to bleeding to death.

Which proved to be the catalysis.

Mireille bound her unconscious daughter's wrists, and bathed her outrageously stinking body with great tenderness. Claire woke up while she was doing it.

"Maman—" she whispered.

"Yes, child?" Mireille got out through the choked-back sobs that were almost strangling her, trying to focus her blindscalded eyes upon the moving blur that was Claire's face.

"Don't—cry. Oh, Maman—please don't cry!"

"You—tell me that? *You?*" Mireille said.

"Yes. I can't—*bear*—seeing you cry. It—it *kills* me, Maman!"

Mireille dashed the tears from her eyes. Which took some doing. They were as many, and as briny, as the waves rolling up the beach. But she managed it, finally. Stared at Claire. Saw that, strangely enough—or, rather, now at long, long last!—her daughter meant it. So she said, softly:

"All right. *D'accord.* Subject's closed. *Dors, ma fille.* Sleep, Daughter —sleep."

And Claire went to sleep, quietly, peacefully, in her mother's arms.

The next morning, she asked for food. Ate it with good appetite. Said:

"Maman, let's go for a walk on the beach. I need—air, and sun. I want to listen to the sea, the gulls—to know I'm alive again . . ."

"Claire, if I let you—give you a dress to put on, you won't—"

"Tear it in strips, and use them to strangle myself? No, Maman. I promise. I'm going to be good, from now on. For the rest of my life. As long as it lasts, anyhow—"

That odd phrasing should have warned Mireille. But it didn't, somehow. She had no idea how deep madness entwines its twisted roots into the human psyche. Almost as soon as they were on the beach, Claire fell a step behind her, stooped swiftly, picked up a heavy stone, and hit Mireille on the head.

Then she whirled and dashed into the ocean.

Mireille lay there until her senses cleared. Fortunately for her, Claire had been too weak from starvation and the loss of blood to crush her skull in. All Mireille suffered was a nasty cut, high above the hairline, that bled sullenly, dyeing half her face with scarlet.

She got up, swayed dizzily. Hung there a moment until sky and sea and rock and surf thunder steadied, snapped back into their accustomed and relative places in the scheme of things. Then she ran out into the Pacific after her daughter.

Claire was floundering over the wet sand, slippery rocks, falling, getting up again, going on. The cove slid shallowly into the ocean. To reach a depth beyond her standing height, Claire needed to wade out at least a half a mile. That was one thing. Another was that due to the different kinds of lives they had led over the past few years, even at forty-five years of age Mireille was in much better physical health, and considerably more agile, than her daughter. She caught up with Claire within minutes. Put out her hand to her. Said, quietly:

"Come, Claire . . ."

"Oh, Maman—you—you're bleeding!" Claire got out; "You're bleeding something awful! I—I didn't mean to hurt you! I only wanted to—to stun you a little so that I could get away—"

"For what?" Mireille whispered.

"To die," Claire said.

Mireille looked at her, through a pinkish haze of tears, sea, salt, blood. "Why?" she said.

"What good is my life?" Claire said. "What reason is there for me to go on living? I *hate* myself. I'm—horrible. Disgusting. I've always spoiled everything for everybody. I always will—"

"That makes two of us, doesn't it?" Mireille said.

"Oh, no! Maman—you—you're *good!* Sweet! You've always been. All right, you—you've made mistakes, done bad things, but *you* are good. On the inside. I'm *not.* Only, Maman, don't you know, can't you *realize,* that even as *awful* as I am—I love you?"

"Prove it. Come back with me."

"Ah, non, Maman! Ça non! Je me vais tuée," Claire said firmly.

"All right, then. Come on. Both of us. Together," Mireille said.

"Maman!" Claire cried.

"You're mine. Everything that's wrong with you is—*my* fault. Born of the blood, the madness, *I* gave you. The seed of the very Devil himself, maybe, taken into my loins during some witches' sabbath of drunkenness and riot I don't even remember now—to shape you. So if the punishment for that is—death, I accept it. Come on."

"Maman!" Claire wailed. "That's not fair!"

"What is, ever in this life, *ma fille?* Why do you hesitate? It will be over quickly enough. Then we'll be at peace. Both of us, maybe."

"What about—Daddy? Stan? Your grandson—little Andy?"

"What about them? Come on, will you!"

Claire stood there.

"Maman," she whispered, "give me—a *reason.* Any reason at all—just *one*—to go on living . . ."

Mireille stood there. Thought about that. About what her response to that ought to be. And about what the truth was. And about how far apart the two things were. But then, being very lucid, very clear, she realized that a response that wasn't the truth wasn't going to work. And that the truth in those shoal waters between life and death, between now and eternity, just might. And that anyhow she had to try.

"I can't," she said slowly, flatly, bleakly, "because there isn't any. Not really. So we have to make up our reasons as we go along. Give meaning to meaninglessness. Invoke sanity—out of madness. We weren't put here to be happy, y'know. I confess I haven't the faintest idea *why* we were, or where we're going, or if anything we do, good or bad, matters even slightly in the stone-blind eyes of God. Probably not. Likely the whole of Creation was a cosmic accident—or a mistake. So we have to pretend we know why we exist, and that heaven's our destination, and that happiness is possible. I have to convince myself that my poor, dull, backward—oh, so good and sweet! An-drew is a prince—"

"Oh, he is! Maman, he is! He is! Don't say he isn't! Don't you dare!"

"And you that that nice, moronic Ted Hanson is your *chevalier* come riding. We can't live without the lies we tell ourselves hourly, *ma fille;* the truth's—too dreadful. But it's the only life we have, and when it's over we have to invent God—and heaven—and the angels, because the grave mold and the slime and damp and rot and those greedy, monstrous little worms are beyond contemplation, too . . ."

"Maman, you're saying that I ought to—*invent* a reason for living? Dream up some motives—opium-pipe style!—for going on?"

"I'm saying we'd better *both*—make up—imagine—a little courage, patience, grace, even hope *peut-être*—and believe in them like blazes! Now *do* come on, Claire darling!"

"Come on—where, Maman?"

"Back to shore. To suffering. To life. Because it's worth it, Daughter mine," Mireille said.

On September ninth, 1880, Claire Antoinette MacFarland married Theodore Washburn Hanson. The bride, naturally, was clad in clouds of billowing white, as befitted her maiden state. Young Hanson, son of "Bonanza Pete" Hanson and heir to one of San Francisco's greatest fortunes, was described jovially in the society pages of all the newspapers as appearing appropriately overawed, even stunned, at his astounding luck.

The young couple sailed away through the Golden Gate toward the Orient on the first stage of a round-the-world honeymoon voyage.

Three years later, they returned to "Baghdad on the Bay," and settled down in the MacFarlands' imposing Nob Hill mansion.

And, of course, they lived happily ever after.

As in the fairy tales.